Above: South lawn of Oneida Community Mansion House, 1870. Below: John Humphrey Noyes in front of the Summer House with members, ca. 1870.

Silken Strands

A Novel of the Oneida Community

Rebecca May Hope

Gabriel's Horn Press
2019

Contact editors@gabrielshornpress.com

Published in Minneapolis, Minnesota by Gabriel's Horn Press

Publisher's Note: This novel is a work of fiction. Names, characters, places,
and incidents are either products of the author's imagination or used fictitiously.
Apart from historical figures, all characters are fictional, and any similarity to people
living or dead is purely coincidental.

First printing: August 25, 2019
Printed in the United States.

For sales, please visit www.gabrielshornpress.com

ISBN-13: 978-1-938990-44-1

To Connie:
My friend and cheerleader on this and so many other journeys.

Table of Contents

Dear Reader,

Perhaps you've only heard of Oneida as a brand of silverware. That was true for me seven years ago. While preparing to teach utopian literature to my high school students, I discovered the widespread utopian movement that swept the United States during the nineteenth century. As an idealist myself, I was fascinated by that heart for Eden that drove people to build a perfect society. The experiment at Oneida, New York, intrigued me the most.

The Oneida Bible Communists were a hundred years ahead of their time, practicing birth control, communal childrearing, eugenics, socialism, and "complex marriage," that is, multiple sexual partners for men and women. In their sociological microcosm, they experimented with cultural patterns that would characterize the late twentieth and early twenty-first centuries. How did things work out for them? Not well—especially their sexual system. As I read memoirs and accounts of the "Old Community," I learned that girls as young as twelve years of age became communal wives, yet few written works condemned this abusive practice.

That's because, as Ellen Wayland-Smith explains in *Oneida: From Free Love Utopia to the Well-Set Table,* the Oneida Ltd. silverware executives whitewashed the less savory aspects of the commune in order to protect the corporation's reputation. Former members with a vested interest in the company's success wrote memoirs that described the commune as a true utopia. Only when I read the now-published private diaries of Tirzah Miller (*Desire and Duty at Oneida: Tirzah Miller's Intimate Memoir*) and Victor Hawley (*Special Love/Special Sex: An Oneida Community Diary*), painstakingly edited and annotated by Robert S. Fogarty, did the true nature of life at Oneida Community take shape. Tirzah declared that her life could be a novel, and I agreed. Victor and Mary's poignant story also deserved to be told. Since significant parts of Tirzah's and Victor's stories overlapped in 1877, I set my fictional tale in that year. To my knowledge, *Silken Strands* is the first novel to accurately depict life in the Oneida Community Mansion House.

As a survivor of childhood sexual abuse, I felt outrage for the generations of girls at Oneida who were "married" before they could understand what the word entailed. In a small way, this novel seeks to right the wrongs perpetrated over four decades on scores of young women. I wondered what would have happened if a girl had been passed over until she was old enough to comprehend. Unfortunately, based on my research of Oneida Community, I doubt any young girls were left behind. Also unfortunately, Millie's conflict is relevant today, as many modern women learn when they go off to college and face pressure to participate in casual sex. I hope Millie's victorious journey will be inspiring and therapeutic for anyone who has endured any kind of sexual abuse.

As an Evangelical Christian, I'm disturbed that those young girls suffered abuse at a Christian commune, founded by some of the first converts of the Second Great Awakening. The first step Christians can take to atone for those wrongs is to expose them. Many contemporary works about Oneida Community glorify its "free love" without considering the widespread abuse it represented. Particularly in light of the #MeToo movement, the girls whose rights were violated via complex marriage deserve to be heard—even though they died years ago—and they deserve an apology, especially from Christianity. I offer this novel to serve both purposes.

While weaving a meaningful tale for contemporary women, I have made every effort to accurately portray a unique historical setting. The term "Negroes" is used for accuracy only, not to show disrespect. Please refer to the Author's Notes for definitions of unusual terms and for clarification of historical details.

Thank you for reading *Silken Strands*. I hope it will inform, entertain, and bless you.

Sincerely,
Rebecca May Hope

Acknowledgments

Many scholars, researchers, and former Oneida Community members have published books on Oneida Community. I am indebted to their work, which I devoured and relied upon to faithfully recreate the world of the commune. Besides those mentioned in my introductory letter, I found *A Lasting Spring* by Jessie Catherine Kinsley and *Without Sin: The Life and Death of the Oneida Community* by Spencer Klaw to be especially helpful.

This book would not have been possible without the support and encouragement of a wide range of people. Anthony Wonderley, then curator of Oneida Community Mansion House Museum, patiently answered my questions and gave me a private behind-the-scenes tour during my 2016 visit, allowing me to step inside many of the rooms featured in *Silken Strands*. The Syracuse University Library archive also assisted me with my research. The owners of the building formerly called The Villa went out of their way to provide me with architectural drawings of the original home.

The cover photo features model Kylie Nybakken; Ian Bauer was the photographer, and Lucas Brist was the art director. The costume was provided courtesy of Historic Eidem Farm.

I extend special thanks to the following: Kristine Klein, my very first reader, who slogged through what I now realize was an amateur manuscript; Connie Swan, the best research assistant and cheerleader anyone could ask for; Dee Griffon and Patti Stockdale, my ACFW pals, who provided endless encouragement; Night Writers, my writers' group, who provided the impetus for me to keep polishing my drafts; and my kids, who have never quite grasped my fascination with "that creepy cult."

Finally, Laura Vosika, my publisher, believed in my book when others in the industry didn't. Thanks to her, it has become a reality.

Floorplan of the Mansion House

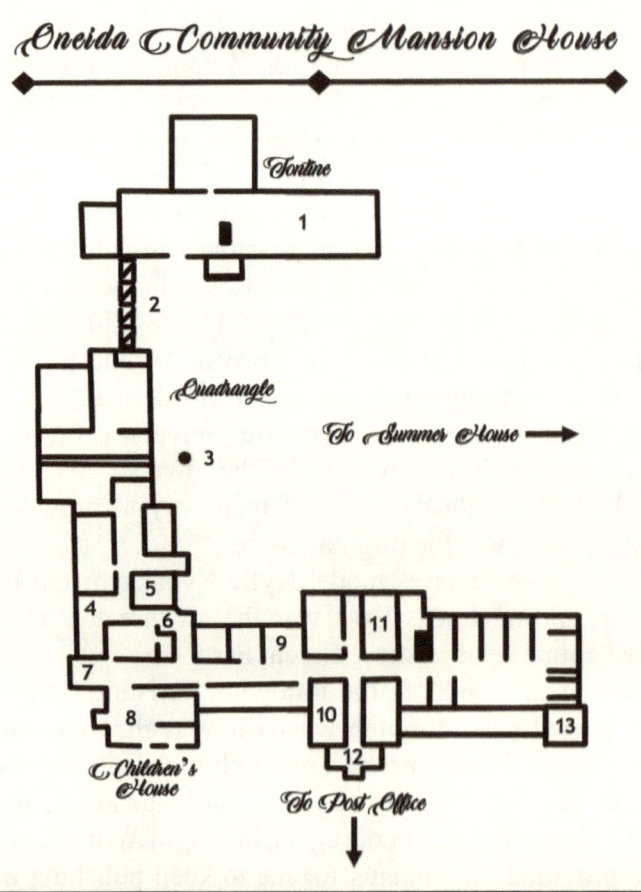

Oneida Community Mansion House

Tontine

1

2

Quadrangle

3

To Summer House →

5

4

6

9

11

7

8

10

13

12

Children's House

To Post Office

1st Floor				Cellar
		9. Little Court		**Cellar**
1. Dining	5. Lavatory	10. Business Office		(not pictured)
2. Tunnel	6. Nursery Kitchen	11. Library		Chain Room
3. Tulip Tree	7. South Tower	12. Portico		directly below
4. Veranda	8. East Room	13. North Tower		East Room

2nd Floor

1. Tirzah's Room
2. Hamilton Avenue
3. Father Noyes's Apartment
4. Sewing Room
5. Millie's Room #2
6. Henry's Room #2
7. Virginia's Room #2
8. Big Hall
9. Stage
10. North Stairway
11. Upper Sitting Room

3rd Floor

1. Constance's Room
2. Millie's Room #1
3. Virginia's Room #1
4. Balcony
5. Henry's Room #1

Area open to floor below

Mansard roof

Chapter 1: Virginia

When Meeting ended, Millie smiled at the young people sitting near her, hoping to be included in their chatter. But they looked right through her. She scanned the Big Hall, which was quickly emptying. Like every night, some members hurried toward a sitting room for games and conversation, some headed toward the Nursery Kitchen to watch the bedtime rituals as children said good-night to their mothers, and some wended toward their sleeping rooms with this evening's partner.

Alone as usual, Millie trekked to her room in the farthest reaches of the Mansion House to retrieve *Lady Audley's Secret.* Its murderous intrigues had set her mind reeling. For her next escape, she'd choose something lighter.

Book in hand, she again passed the south sitting room, known as Hamilton Avenue. A boisterous company of young men and women thronged the couches and game tables. A cheer rang out over a play in a squails match. No one noticed her. She made her way past the Big Hall and down the wide front stairway to the library.

By now she'd gotten used to living on the outskirts. She didn't mind socializing. It was an important part of communal living, after all. But being alone with a book felt better than being alone in a crowd. A few nights ago she'd stopped by Hamilton Avenue to watch the squails matches, but she hadn't wormed her way to a table to slide the discs herself. Once all the excitement wore off, she'd give it a try.

Unlike people, books always welcomed her warmly. Lately Mark Twain's stories and sketches had lifted her spirits. His new book, *The Adventures of Tom Sawyer*, hadn't come in yet, but perhaps she'd try his travelogue, *The Innocents Abroad, or The New Pilgrim's Progress.*

When she entered the library, the calming scent of words on musty paper greeted her, but the only occupants—a couple of elderly men reading newspapers—didn't look up. Even before the buzz over the Community's new pastime, the library had been sparsely populated.

She knew just where to find Twain's book among the thousands of volumes on the shelves. But when she reached the farthest recessed alcove, she drew back in surprise. A feminine shape huddled on the step that extended from the bottom shelf. The girl's face, buried in her arms, rested on her drawn-up knees. Every few seconds a silent spasm rippled through her body, jiggling the wild curls on her head.

"Virginia?" whispered Millie. "Is that you?"

Virginia tilted her head, barely peeking up. Shrinking back even farther into the alcove, she looked at Millie through one puffy eye.

Millie sank onto the step and put a hand on the girl's back. "Virginia, what's wrong? Are you ill?"

The girl straightened, showing her swollen, tear-streaked face. She threw both arms around Millie and held her tight. Warm, wet tears brushed Millie's cheek.

Millie blinked in surprise.

Virginia pulled away, pressing her finger to her lips. "Shhh!"

Millie gaped. She'd never seen anyone radiate such fear. Oneida Community was a very safe place. "Are you hiding from someone?"

Virginia glanced out into the room. "Please be quiet!"

Both white-haired gentlemen sat with their backs to the alcove, oblivious. No doubt their hearing wasn't what it used to be.

"I will!" Millie whispered back. "Now, please tell me what's the matter."

Virginia bit her lip and studied Millie's face, then dropped her eyes. "You'll think I'm silly."

"Of course I won't."

The girl succumbed to a paroxysm of stifled sobs that tore at Millie's heart. She pulled her close and stroked her back.

Although she was five years younger than Millie, Virginia was at least six inches taller, more buxom, more flouncy. Her bobbed hair, plain knee-length dress, and baggy pantalettes detracted not one iota from her feminine charm. In fact, her transitioning womanhood lent a previously unknown beauty to the dowdy Oneida uniform. When she had turned twelve last May, she'd moved into the room next to Millie's in Ultima Thule, the south wing. Her exuberance at graduating from the Children's House hadn't diminished. More than once as Millie ascended the stairs, the bouncing downward force of Virginia Hinds had nearly bowled her over.

Virginia squirmed out of Millie's embrace and wiped her cheeks with both hands. She dropped her eyes. "I had my first interview last night."

Millie flinched at the word *interview*, the term the Community used for the relations of complex marriage. Her face grew hot.

Millie had never had an interview. Despite the scores of romantic stories she'd read, she didn't live in a fairy tale kingdom, on the English moors, or even in *The Wide, Wide World* of Elizabeth Wetherell. Nor would she ever walk down the aisle in a white wedding gown to marry her handsome prince like Queen Victoria. She lived among the Perfectionists of Oneida, who had improved upon old-fashioned marriage. Father Noyes taught them that communism, the calling of true Christians, required shared ownership of all property, including human property.

She'd grown up as the Community's child—not just her father's. When she married, she would marry all the men here. The thrill of falling in love and spending her life with just one man was a delight she'd experience only vicariously, through the printed page. Until now, her own marriage had seemed years away. No need to think about it. Could it already have happened to Virginia, who wasn't yet thirteen?

With her own lack of experience, she couldn't advise Virginia. But the dear girl needed help. Maybe she just needed to talk. Millie placed her hands gently on Virginia's arms to steady her trembling shoulders. "With whom?"

Virginia raised her eyes slowly. "Theodore Noyes."

It could have been worse. In order to impart proper spiritual training, the older, central members of the Community initiated the younger members. Dr. Noyes was only three times Virginia's age. She could have been introduced to marriage by Father Noyes himself, who was now sixty-five.

"Did Mrs. Skinner arrange it?" A man never asked for an interview directly, but chose a respected woman to bear his request. Women weren't required to receive the attentions of men they weren't attracted to, but Virginia would have found it difficult to refuse the intimidating older woman.

"No. Tirzah did."

Millie's heart sank. Tirzah Miller, the woman she admired more than any other of the second generation, had acted as go-between. How could she have put this burden on such a young girl? "What did she say?"

"She said—" Virginia wrinkled her forehead. "She said Dr. Noyes is our leader now, so it's his duty to teach us the ways of heavenly love. She said he wanted to help me." Virginia twirled her hair around her finger, the same childish habit she'd indulged when Millie tutored her in spelling just a year ago. "Oh—she told me I was one of the most magnetic young women she knew, and that many men could benefit from my magnetism."

Such compliments would certainly be persuasive—especially coming from Tirzah. "But did you say you wanted to wait until you were older?"

"I tried. But she said I already have everything necessary to please a man, and that waiting would be selfish." Virginia began to sob quietly again. "I didn't want to be selfish."

Her heart aching, Millie waited for the sobs to subside. "Was that on Monday?"

Virginia nodded.

Millie pictured Virginia playing squails on Sunday night. After making a good play, she had pirouetted, causing the skirt of her dress to flare out. All eyes were on her. She had looked beautiful.

Had Theodore been in the room? Millie didn't think so, but Father Noyes had observed the frolic from his favorite chair in his chamber. Through his open door, he could view the entire Hamilton Avenue Sitting Room. His approving looks had cast his blessing over the whole party. Perhaps he determined at that moment that Virginia was ready to become a wife and had commanded Theodore to do his duty.

"Was Dr. Noyes ... unkind?" Millie winced at her own words.

"Unkind?" Virginia bit her fingernail and slowly shook her head. "No. He was kind. He told me he was being kind. But—but—"

"But you weren't ready, were you?" Millie finished the thought in the most delicate way she could.

"N-n-no!" Virginia sniffed.

What help could Millie give? The damage had already been done.

As she gave Virginia's hand a half-hearted squeeze, a flash of panic seized her chest. This very situation awaited her. Soon—very soon—Tirzah or another respected woman would inform her that some older man, as old as or older than her father, wanted to have relations with her. And unlike Virginia, she wasn't too young. She was seventeen, and it was time for her to take her place as a Community wife. Would she find the faith and courage to do her duty?

Millie sat in the alcove with Virginia until the girl felt ready to leave. With her arm around Virginia's waist, she walked her from the room. Rather than return to her room by passing Hamilton Avenue, Millie led her through the Nursery Kitchen to the first floor stairway at the end of the Children's House. From there they climbed the two flights to Ultima Thule. Millie lit Virginia's lamp, keeping the wick low, and helped her into her nightdress. As the girl snuggled into her narrow bed, Millie folded the quilt beneath her chin. She placed a chair next to Virginia's pillow and sat stroking her forehead. Virginia closed her eyes.

"Three little kittens lost their mittens..." Millie's lilting tones filled the little space. By the time the kittens found their mittens, Virginia was asleep.

* * *

"My fin-ders are sticky!"

Millie took three-year-old Haydn's gummy hand in hers and led him down the hall to the lavatory. Saturday afternoon had stretched out peacefully after story time as the children snipped illustrations from old magazines and glued them to discarded paper from the print shop. Teaching in the Children's House was one of Millie's favorite job assignments.

She ran water from the two faucets to get the right mix of hot and cold. She couldn't resist giving Haydn's silky, nearly white hair a tousle before dipping his hands in the sink and drying them on the towel. Holding his rosy hand in hers, she led him back to the East Room, where he dropped onto the smooth plank floor among the blocks.

She shouldn't have favorites. But if she had one, it would be little Haydn with his dark eyelashes, rosy complexion, and round cheeks. Every time he used a grown-up word or recited a nursery rhyme, he wiggled deeper into her heart. She lowered herself to his side and passed him a square red block.

He installed it atop his structure. "Dis is da Souf Tower." He pointed across the room toward the window. "It's right dere. See?" Rising onto his stocky legs, he pulled on Millie's hand. "Tum see!"

She followed him to the bay window, where he climbed onto the window seat. He jabbed his finger against the glass toward the brick wall that jutted out to their right. "Dat's da Souf Tower!"

"You're absolutely right!"

Millie tousled his hair again. With those pronounced cheekbones and the curls brushing his forehead, there was no mistaking him for Tirzah's son.

Tugging Millie's arm, Haydn pulled her back to the block version of the tower. He pointed to the floor. "Now build da bv'anda."

She seated herself and obeyed, laying out blocks to represent the veranda.

Haydn put his hand on hers. "No! No!" he scolded. "Da door! Make a door dere!"

Smiling at his bossiness, Millie separated some blocks to make a doorway.

Solemnly he nodded his approval. He placed his right hand outside the row of blocks and walked his index and middle fingers toward the opening.

"Dis is my twooly papa." He watched his hand. "Papa's tumming to see me." He scooted around the other side of the block wall and with his left hand walked his fingers to the opening. "Dis is me." He smiled up at Millie. "I'm tumming to see my papa."

Then, without warning, he swept all the blocks into a big pile with both arms, razing the veranda and the South Tower. "My papa is a bad, naughty man," he said matter-of-factly as he began building again.

What an odd little play. And such an odd thing to say. "Oh?"

Haydn continued stacking blocks. "Mmm-hmm."

"Why is that?"

"Tuz Mistuh Townuh said so."

Why would Judge Towner describe Haydn's *truly papa* that way? Millie kept her voice casual. "What did he do?"

"He went 'way," Haydn said with more narration than emotion.

"But he came back, didn't he?"

It could be hard for children this age to understand the comings and goings of their parents, who usually only visited once a day for only an hour at a time.

"No. But Mama sez I tan pway, and dat will help Papa tum back."

How heart-rending that conversation must have been. "Have you prayed?"

"No. Not yet." He knocked down the new tower. "Mistuh Townuh won't help me."

Judge Towner must have assumed temporary fathering duties for Haydn. Perhaps the boy's own father had become too philoprogenitive.

"He doesn't want you to pray for your papa?"

"My twooly papa is a bad, naughty man." Haydn had recreated the veranda wall with its open doorway and put his fingers down next to it again. "Here he tumz!"

Millie's chest constricted at the boy's steadfast love for his papa. At the age of five, she had sat in this very spot, eyeing the doorway to the ground corridor for her father's face. As soon as she spied him, she ran to him, and he whooshed her high into the air, then hugged her tight. By definition, a father always came back.

After she finished working, she headed to the third floor and toward her father's room. He could answer her questions about Haydn's papa better than the boy had. Glancing over the partial wall into the Upper Sitting Room on the floor below, she saw William Langston, domino champion, engaged in a match. No matter. He always made time for his daughter.

She descended the stairs and navigated past clusters of tables and chairs. When William saw her, he turned his back on the game and pulled an empty seat closer. He motioned her into it. "How are the children?"

"I was playing with Haydn, Tirzah's boy." She lowered her voice. "Do you know who his father is?"

William cocked his head. "You don't remember?"

"Should I?" She felt silly. By the look on her father's face, this was common knowledge. "I've never paid much attention to who was paired with whom. It didn't affect me."

"No, you were never a chinwag." William gave her jaw a playful tap. "And living in Ultima Thule like you do," he winked, "you miss out on some things."

She patted his knee. "That's why I have you."

"Edward Inslee was the father."

"I don't know him." Millie furrowed her brow. "Is he at Wallingford?"

"No—he was. But he left there, oh, about a year and a half ago."

"Left? For where?"

William dropped his voice even lower. "He seceded. But he's visited the boy a few times, I understand."

"Oh!" Now Haydn's little play made sense. "But how could he secede when his son is here? And why did he go?" She studied her father's face for clues. "Maybe I shouldn't be asking."

"It was openly discussed at the time." William leaned back in his chair and crossed his legs, settling into his storytelling posture. "Tirzah and Edward had a special love relationship. It didn't start until they paired them for stirpiculture—otherwise they wouldn't have put them together."

Intrigued, Millie scooted her chair closer. Such passionate relationships were forbidden, even between a man and woman who were assigned to have a baby together. "Go on."

"While Tirzah was carrying the child," William continued, "Father Noyes tried to stop their exclusiveness. He made Inslee drop out of the quintet—Tirzah was their accompanist. Too bad, too. Inslee was the best musician we've ever had. He played 'most any instrument: clarinet, cornet, viola, alto horn. Sure you don't remember him? Thick black beard, plenty of black hair on top? Distinguished-looking, I'd say."

The image of a black-haired, black-bearded man playing a black clarinet surfaced. "Oh, him! I remember now. Is that why they named him Haydn? After the composer?"

"So you *do* know something about music," her father teased.

Millie slapped his arm with mock offense.

"Actually, Father Noyes had Tirzah change the boy's name to Paul. But that was later. First he weaned Inslee from the baby."

"Father Noyes weaned *Mr. Inslee* from the *baby*?"

William chuckled. "That's what Father Noyes called it. Until he was five months old, Haydn slept with Inslee every night. I've never seen a more devoted father here. He spent almost as much time with the baby as Tirzah did. So they sent him to Wallingford."

Wallingford, their branch commune, was a day's train ride away. "That must have been hard for him."

"Hard on them both. Tirzah glowed when Inslee was with her, and she loved that baby. He was her second, you know."

Millie nodded. "After Georgy. He just turned six."

"When Inslee was at Wallingford, he kept sneaking back to see the boy." William glanced around the room. "Many here thought he intended to kidnap Paul and run away."

"Oh, my!"

Stealing a child from his home? That would be outrageous.

"Well, I think that was just talk." William waved his hand. "But you see, Haydn—Paul—was the youngest child they ever put into the Children's House. Tirzah only kept him till he was six months old."

"Six months?" Millie drew in her chin. "Mothers keep their babies at least until they walk."

"Now they do." William nodded. "But Father Noyes wanted to find out the earliest age for communal child-raising. Paul was the test."

"Is that why people thought Mr. Inslee would take the baby?"

"Could be. Myself, I thought it was sort of unnatural." William stroked his pointed beard. "At any rate, we soon heard Inslee had seceded. Tirzah was beside herself. That's when Father Noyes had her change the boy's name to Paul—to help her forget Inslee. After that they put Judge Towner in charge of the child and sent Tirzah to Wallingford."

"Did she ever get over Edward?"

William shrugged. "I hear she's trying for a child with Homer Barron now. But Towner thinks she's still pining for Inslee."

It was like a tragic novel—right here at the Mansion House. "Haydn—we still call him that—said his mama told him to pray for his papa to come back, but that Judge Towner says his papa is a bad, naughty man."

William rolled his eyes. "Out of the mouths of babes."

Whether his sarcasm was meant for Edward Inslee or Judge Towner, Millie couldn't tell.

With Tirzah's tragedy weighing on her heart, Millie set out for her room. After leaving the Upper Sitting Room, she crossed the Big

Hall and passed the sewing room that overlooked the Quadrangle. Continuing on past Father Noyes's corner suite and Hamilton Avenue, she followed the jagged corridor past multiple sleeping rooms to its very end. There was the stairway to Ultima Thule, the outer reaches.

In her room, she stared out her window at the bare tulip tree that guarded the snowy, vacant Quadrangle. Yes, living in the distant regions of the Mansion House and spending her time in the library rather than in Hamilton Avenue or the Nursery Kitchen had sequestered her from Community gossip. But if her isolation had spared her some of the anguish of this place, it had been worth it.

She flopped onto her bed and with her fingers traced the stitching on her quilt. Poor Tirzah and Haydn, yearning for a man who had deserted them. He had loved them so much once. If he had controlled his passions and followed the Community rules, he would still be here, sharing his child and Tirzah with others, instead of selfishly wanting them all for himself—and ending up with nothing.

He was a seceder, like Virginia and the other states that caused the War of Rebellion. Though Mr. Inslee's departure hadn't provoked war, it had left devastation in its wake. No good could come from severing the bonds of allegiance—that much was obvious.

Soon Tirzah would approach Millie with news that Dr. Noyes or Father Noyes wanted to schedule an interview. Now that Millie understood Tirzah's personal sacrifice for the Community, how could she ever refuse? All the girls here, even twelve-year-old Virginia, had unflinchingly complied. Millie, too, would have to do her duty.

Chapter 2: Constance

Stepping on the hem of her skirt, Millie stumbled up two steps of the railroad car before regaining her balance. Thankfully, no one was behind her. Since she'd never worn a long dress before, she hadn't anticipated its hazards. She pinched the folds of fabric more tightly in her hands that already held a travel bag and a picnic basket.

In the car a few sleepy passengers slouched in their seats. They must have boarded before dawn at a previous stop. Aunt Constance, whom she was here to assist, carried her bag in her right hand while her injured left arm hung limply at her side.

Following the older woman down the center aisle, Millie summoned all her poise. She mustn't stumble again. She stared straight ahead, trying to ignore the eyes that bore into her. A couple of men studied her dispassionately, as if observing a new species at the zoo, but two women put their heads together and whispered to each other behind their hands.

When Outsiders came to visit the Community, *they* were the odd ones. Now she was the outsider.

Constance chose a row at the back of the car and nodded to Millie to sit near the window. With her back turned to the other passengers as she stowed their bags in the overhead rack, Millie's face cooled. She composed herself, then presented Constance with a copy of the *Circular*, the Community newspaper. Primly, she selected her own books from the bag.

Just as she contacted the seat, the train lurched forward with a loud hiss of steam. She gripped Constance's arm—too firmly—as her books slid from her lap and thumped onto the floor. Chagrined, she relaxed her grip into a more nurturing touch and smiled at the older woman. As the cars gradually gained speed, the metal wheels comforted themselves from angry complaint to contented hum.

"Don't worry, dear." Constance used her right arm to position her unresponsive left arm on her lap. "I was just as skittish on my first train ride."

Laughing at herself, Millie bent to retrieve her books. "I wasn't afraid. Just surprised. It's wonderful!"

Instead of opening her novel or her diary, she unfolded her senses to the rhythmic clatter of the wheels on the track and the bumpy sway of the passenger car. At last she was going somewhere. Fast.

Why her? That was the enigma. Surely one of the other young women would have been a more qualified helper for Aunt Constance. But Millie, the girl who was never chosen for anything, had received the assignment. Perhaps Constance had requested her, even though she didn't know Millie that well. Constance wasn't her aunt in the way Outsiders named relatives. At the Community, most older women bore that title.

Whatever the reason, Millie reveled in her good fortune. "What time will we arrive in New York City?"

"We'll reach Jersey City by six o'clock." Constance stifled a yawn. "Then we'll take the ferry across the Hudson. So possibly seven."

Millie raised her shoulders in delight. She'd never ridden a ferry, either. From New York City they'd take another train to Meriden, Connecticut, and then travel by carriage to the branch commune at Wallingford.

Outside the window, snow-covered fields sped past, dotted occasionally with a barn as red as the first ripe strawberry on a bed of pale blossoms. Leafless trees glistened, decorated with a delicate coating of frost. So far Millie's existence had been just as bare, but every clack of the wheels and jerk of the car told her that was about to change.

She was the last of the girls her age to journey away from Oneida Community. Two years ago Theodora, who was a year younger than Millie, had traveled to Wallingford. And Ellen was forever bringing up her two trips to Cozicot.

Millie pulled her cape more tightly around her arms. If only it were summer and she were heading to Oneida's seaside resort. Still, this was an adventure. Like Catherine Morland from Jane Austen's *Northanger Abbey,* she was leaving home for the first time as a helper to an older woman. Of course, Wallingford wouldn't compare to the glamor of Bath, England. But at least she'd have a chance to see New York City—if only for a few hours.

Hearing Constance chuckle at something in the *Circular,* Millie remembered her plan. She tucked her novel behind her, opened her diary, and pulled the stubby pencil from its sheath. As far as she knew, the *Circular* had never featured an account of traveling to Oneida's Connecticut branch, although members went there often. She'd write such an article and submit it to Tirzah, the newspaper's editress.

She discreetly studied the other passengers—half a dozen commercial travelers, two pairs of middle-aged women, and a young man who was seated two rows up and across the aisle. He was by far the most interesting. The attractive determination of his jaw reminded her of a valiant knight pursuing a daring deed of chivalry. She pressed her pencil against her lip. Could she work such an anachronistic reference into her report?

If—no, when—her article was published, members young and old would read it and smile, just as Constance was smiling now. Subscribers around the country might appreciate it, too, but their reactions didn't matter. If her own people recognized her talent, she would no longer feel invisible. She wasn't a performer. She couldn't sing, act, or play an instrument like other young women. But she could entertain people with words—if given the chance.

The train hissed into a larger station. As several women stepped into their car, Millie sucked in her breath. "Oh, Aunt Constance!" she whispered. "How elegant!"

Two women flowed into the seat behind the young man. The younger one had coiffed black hair and wore a deep green dress with four rows of pleated ruffles along the bottom. A modest train extended from beneath her cape. Her companion, probably her mother, was dressed less strikingly in a dignified dark blue dress of similar cut.

Millie closed up her diary. She'd take notes later.

As she examined the couples and groups who boarded the car, she breathed in a thousand competing smells. Perfumes. Damp capes. Cigars. Packed lunches with pickles and fresh-baked bread.

A steady hum of conversations played under occasional shouted commands that faded away when everyone had found a spot.

When the train pulled away from the station, Millie dropped her eyes to her own ample dress. "Our clothes must be years behind the time," she muttered.

Constance stole a glance at the women to their left. "They're dressed for a parlor car," she whispered, "not for this little train."

That was no consolation. "Our skirts are much too full, and our bodices are too high." Millie cheeks grew warmer as she eyed the women's fitted cuirasses. "Those stripes make them look so thin and straight."

Constance grimaced. "Don't forget, they're wearing corsets."

Millie had never worn one, but to look like that, she'd consider it. She sighed. "At least we're not in our short dresses and pantalettes."

"The first time our women traveled to Brooklyn after they cut their dresses short, they made quite a scene." Constance raised her eyebrows. "The police had to be called to break it up."

"Oh, my! I never heard that. Was it written up in the *Circular?*"

Constance laughed. "Hardly."

Millie laughed, too, to make her question seem like a joke. Of course something so unflattering would never be recorded in the paper that aimed to attract Outsiders to Bible Communism.

"So that's why we keep a closet full of long dresses for traveling."

"The world already thinks we're radicals." Constance winked. "No need to confirm it."

Millie smoothed her billowing skirt. "If only there was a dress my size. Two of me could fit in this one. And yellow is *not* my color." With irritation she tucked her bobbed hair—another sign of her peculiarity—behind her ear. She slouched in her seat. "It makes me look ill!"

"It's more gold than yellow." Constance patted her hand. "It's a shame there wasn't time to take it in. You're petite, like your m—" Constance cleared her throat. "Like you're meant to be. And you look as sweet as always."

Millie looked straight ahead, barely taking in her words. The large plumes on the hats of the women ahead of them performed an exotic dance, dipping and swaying with the motion and clacking of the car. She'd seen those hats before—in *Godey's Lady's Book.*

The train jolted, and Constance let out a muffled moan.

For the first time Millie noticed the dark circles under her companion's eyes and the creases around her lips. "Oh, you're in pain!" Millie bit her lip apologetically. She'd been ignoring her duty. "Let me get my pillow—to support your arm."

Constance braved a halfhearted smile. She must have been struggling to hide her discomfort all this time.

Steadying herself, Millie stood on tiptoes, reached into the travel bag, and found the pillow. "Dr. Cragin will surely have a cure for you —and you'll feel much better on our trip back." She tucked the pillow under Constance's left arm. "Would you like some water?"

Constance exhaled deeply and her eyelids drooped. Before Millie could pour the water, the older woman's chin had dropped onto her chest and a breathy snore escaped her lips.

Good. A nap might ease her pain.

Millie jotted down a few more notes in her diary about the passing scenery and her fellow passengers. Her eyes kept returning to the handsome young man. Though he wasn't much older than she, he seemed comfortable traveling alone, as if he'd made this trip before. Earlier he'd offered the window seat to a man who was boarding, and the two had carried on a brief, friendly conversation. Now the young man seemed engrossed in the thick volume on his lap. At times he furrowed his brow and flipped back a few pages. Clearly he was studying, not reading fiction.

Millie, for her part, was ready to rejoin Dorothea Brooke's adventures. She sheathed her pencil, pulled out *Middlemarch* by George Eliot, and found her place.

Before Millie finished a chapter, Constance jerked awake. She lifted her head and blinked a few times. Millie pulled out their water bottle in its knit jacket, filled a tin mug with water, and placed it in Constance's hand. "Feeling better?"

Constance took a sip. "I am," she murmured groggily.

The train ride settled into a routine of short stops, passengers embarking and disembarking, steam hissing, and the train speeding up to a rhythmic rocking. As noon approached, Millie's stomach started to rumble, but she dreaded opening their rustic picnic basket in the presence of the elegant women.

At the next stop, Constance folded the *Circular* on her lap. "Let's stretch our legs." She stood and adjusted her cape. "Bring our food."

Millie rose and spread two copies of the *Circular* across their double seat, covering *Middlemarch*.

Constance moved into the aisle and waited.

Millie dreaded the walk past the women, but she straightened herself to her full five feet. At least now her back would be to the passengers. With the wicker basket in hand, she stepped into the aisle and took a few bold steps toward the front of the car. She heard a voice behind her.

"This way, Millie dear."

Glancing over her shoulder, she saw Constance walking the other direction, away from the engine. Of course. The nearest exit was behind them.

As Millie whirled about, she tripped. She'd stepped on her hem again. The basket careened into the chest of the young man. Wrapped potatoes and nutcakes spilled into the aisle.

He rose in an instant, placing his hands on her arms to steady her. Mortified, she met his laughing brown eyes. If only she could disappear into the ground like Rumpelstiltskin.

"I'm so sorry!" She inched backward, freeing her dress, and bent to retrieve the wayward food.

He was already crouching and holding two potatoes toward her, chuckling.

The blood pulsed in her cheeks. "Thank you."

She quickly repacked the basket and scurried after Constance, avoiding the stares of the well-dressed women. How could she have enacted such a scene right under their noses?

She stepped onto the station platform, happy for the frigid air that cooled her burning face.

Constance ignored Millie's *faux pas*. She gestured to hurry her onward. "Follow me."

Weaving around people on the platform, Millie tried to keep up. She couldn't shake the young man's amused expression from her mind.

Constance mounted the steps of the second car behind the engine, which had the words EMIGRANT CAR emblazoned on its side. Confused, Millie trailed her. The older woman opened the door, and they both stepped in.

Millie's hand instinctively flew to her face, in surprise and in an attempt to block the powerful odor. Instead of mahogany paneling, padded seats, and decorative ceiling lamps, this dim, grimy car had scuffed slats of pine on the walls and bare wooden benches. Sconces held flickering candles. In the front of the coach a man, woman, and three children huddled around the stove, cooking griddle cakes. The thick, sour smell of animal fat hung in the air, mixing with the stench of damp wool and unwashed bodies.

Not wanting to cause offense, Millie quickly dropped her hand. Why had Constance come here?

On a nearby bench sat the only other people in the car. A man in a threadbare black jacket and dirty trousers slouched with his hands in his pockets, his chin covered with black stubble. Next to him was a woman about Millie's size wearing a drooping black hat, an oversized black cape, and a rough skirt and blouse. The nursing baby in her arms must be getting more comfort than nourishment from her gaunt mother. A boy with matted hair, dirty cheeks, and runny nose pulled on the woman's sleeve, then buried his face in her waist.

Millie's heart went out to them.

Constance stepped toward the ragged little family. "Excuse me." She used the same tone she would have used to address the dignified women in their own coach. "May I offer you some luncheon?"

The woman looked confused. The man looked over his shoulder to see if Constance was talking to someone else, then said in a thick accent, "I-I sorry. No money." He turned his trouser pockets inside out and shrugged. "No money to buy."

At Constance's signal, Millie held out the picnic basket.

Constance smiled. "It's free. It's not much—we don't have any meat." She eyed the nursing mother apologetically. "Please take it."

For a moment Millie's stomach pinched, but compassion chased her hunger away. She'd never gone a day without eating, but these people certainly had. The Community storerooms were stocked with abundance, and at least a hundred baskets like this one lined the shelves. It would never be missed. She moved toward the man and folded down the napkin, revealing the nutcakes, potatoes, and little crocks of applesauce nestled inside.

His eyes brightened as he grasped the basket with both hands. His wife looked between him and Millie, questioning. She probably didn't speak English.

"I thank you!" He stood, making excited bows. "Very much I thank you! We think we no eat today." He motioned with his head toward the front of the car. "They have only for them. No more."

Millie followed Constance out of the car. This time as she

encountered the stares from people on the platform, a comfortable warmth filled her chest, kindled by the grateful faces of the immigrants. She barely noticed the chill wind.

As they neared their passenger car to reboard, the train boy came down the forward steps, his basket hanging from his neck.

Constance stopped him on the platform, holding out two coins. "Two oranges, please."

Surprised, Millie quickly accepted the two plump oranges from the boy. Her mouth watered as she closed her fingers around the cool, dimpled balls.

Constance smiled, her eyes twinkling, and climbed the steps first.

As they entered the car, Millie instantly regretted having come in the forward door. The car was nearly full, and those who hadn't noticed them earlier assessed them now. Millie steeled herself, suddenly thankful for her long dress. If she'd been wearing pantalettes, the women would have fainted. She proceeded down the aisle, holding the oranges in front of her as she lightly gripped the top of her skirt.

The young man she'd hit with their basket sat reading his heavy book. She hoped he wouldn't look up.

But he did. His eyes met hers, then dropped to the oranges. Quickly he raised his book like a shield and ducked his face behind it. In a second he lowered it, revealing first his laughing eyes and then an enormous grin.

Millie laughed and shook her head as she passed him, her chest warming as she slid into her seat. He acted as if he'd known her all his life. The sting of the critical stares melted away, replaced by the camaraderie of his gentle tease.

Millie peeled the fruit. "Thank you for the orange." She broke apart the sections, laying them on Constance's lap on a napkin she'd retrieved from their bag. "Did Father Noyes give you traveling money?"

Constance turned away for a second, then turned back, arching her eyebrows. "He gave us everything we need for our journey."

Millie tilted her head at the coy response, but Constance popped an orange segment into her mouth. If not from the Community, where would she have gotten the coins? They didn't need money at the Mansion House because all property was held in common.

"I'm glad we gave our lunch to those folks." Millie tasted the fruit herself, relishing the tangy sweetness. "It's not right for anyone to go hungry."

"No, it's not." Constance's eyes softened. "But when we return, going west, that car will be packed full—like a tin of sardines."

"Oh!" Millie's heart twisted.

"That's why our Community is so important." Constance took Millie's hand. "Father Noyes is showing the world a better way. A way that *is* right."

As the afternoon ride dragged on and on, Millie read, then dozed, then read some more. At four o'clock, when she could ignore her stomach's growling no longer, she retrieved their supper from the special compartment of her traveling bag. Unfortunately, the jam sandwiches made barely a dent in her hunger. Still, she was happy they'd given their dinner away.

When they changed trains at Middletown, New Jersey, the young man she'd assaulted with the picnic basket boarded their car. He must be bound for New York City as well. Between genial conversations with people near him, he pored over his book.

From where he sat, he couldn't see Millie eyeing him as she drafted a story into her diary. He was heading to Long Island to investigate the mysterious death of his fair cousin, Priscilla. Along the way he rescued a woman he found wandering in the woods who turned out to be his destined soul-mate.

When they reached the Jersey City terminal, pandemonium erupted. Passengers crowded the aisle, pushing to get out. By the time Millie and Constance stepped onto the platform, it was teeming with people rushing this way and that. Millie gripped her bag in one hand and Constance's in the other, jostling and being jostled. Constance studied their tickets in the dim lamplight.

Suddenly Millie felt a tug on her bag. "Oh!"

She gasped as it was yanked from her hand.

"Allow me."

Millie laughed. "Thank you."

It was the young man from their car. He took the bag from her other hand. His own satchel was strapped over his shoulder. "Are you taking the ferry to New York City?" He addressed Constance. "We need to board at Pennsylvania Station."

"That's right." Constance scanned their surroundings. "It's changed since I was here last."

He nodded. "It's all new. This way." They walked toward the low building where a crowd was entering. "I'm Noah Martinson, by the way."

"From Oneida?" Recognition lit Constance's face. "Any relation to Reverend Martinson?"

"I'm his son."

Surprised, Millie stopped in her tracks, then hustled after Noah's receding figure. Reverend Martinson was Oneida Community's most vociferous critic.

As they found their way onto the ferry, Constance and Millie introduced themselves. In the dim light, Millie couldn't gauge his reaction to hearing they were from the Community, but surely he'd already guessed. If nothing else, their hair gave them away.

Stuck in the middle of the crowd, Millie could barely see the lights on the opposite shore. Noah helped them disembark at the Cortlandt Street landing. Millie held her breath at the unsavory characters who lurked in the shadows, revealed by glowing ends of cigars. Noah hurried them away from the docks.

When they reached a streetlamp on a safer corner, he set down their bags. "Do you need a hansom cab?"

"We have several hours before our train leaves for Connecticut." Constance looked about as if getting her bearings. "I know a pleasant place nearby where we could dine. Will you join us?"

Millie's heart leapt, then quickly sank. Surely his chivalry didn't extend to eating with communists.

Noah's face brightened. "That sounds wonderful. I'm famished." He picked up the bags. "How far?"

Constance nodded toward the right. "Less than a mile."

Millie's feet hardly felt the pavement. The magnificent buildings and the hustle and bustle of horses and carriages seemed only a painted backdrop against the prospect of spending time with Noah. Real, not imaginary, time.

Soon they stood on Broadway before a five-story granite building with Doric columns at its entrance.

Noah's eyes grew round as he peered up the wide steps. "This is the Astor House."

Women wearing fur capes and flowing dresses emerged from elegant carriages, taking the arms of men in shiny top hats and knee-length overcoats.

Millie eyed Constance. "You want to eat here?"

Constance started up the steps. "This way."

Noah gazed at the entablature above the pillars. "Abraham Lincoln spoke from that balcony." He glanced at Millie. "Can you afford this place?"

She saw her own awe and confusion reflected on his face. She shrugged and followed Constance.

They entered a grand foyer where an enormous chandelier reflected its light from hundreds of dangling glass teardrops. Mammoth marble pillars and lush, patterned rugs decorated the mirrored lobby. A classical melody wafted through the air from a grand piano positioned at the other end of the large hall.

Grinning, Constance led them confidently up the wide marble stairway. At the top, they checked their bags and wraps at a cloak room. Then they approached a small, luxurious dining room. The attendant viewed them suspiciously, running his eyes up and down the women's traveling dresses.

Millie's face grew unbearably warm. They weren't properly dressed. She dropped her eyes. A placard on the table before her read *Unescorted Women Will Not Be Seated.* She glanced at Constance. Was that why she invited Noah?

Undaunted, Constance stepped forward. "A table for three, please." She extended a calling card. "Please advise Mr. Streed that I'm here."

The man's expression changed immediately. He bowed deferentially, then ushered them into the room.

The opulence took Millie's breath away. Positioned around the room were a dozen small dining tables covered with the crispest, whitest tablecloths she'd ever seen. Ornate carvings decorated the mahogany paneled walls and ceiling. A warm glow from the crystal chandeliers fell upon gleaming silverware rolled in linen napkins secured with silver rings. Sparkling mirrors reflected the setting, making the room seem three times larger than it was.

As they followed the attendant to a table, their feet sank into plush maroon-and-gold carpet. The attendant pulled out Constance's round-backed chair, and Noah, attempting to match his decorum, pulled out Millie's.

Imagining herself in a fitted gown, Millie seated herself stiffly on the cushioned seat. Before she could shower Constance with questions, a middle-aged man in a black dinner jacket approached.

Constance stood to meet him. "Robert!"

The two conversed with their backs to Millie and Noah. Millie responded to Noah's curious expression with a half-shrug. She was as bewildered as he. Soon the attendant beckoned, and the man rushed away after touching Constance's shoulder.

Millie and Noah stared at Constance as she took her seat. She smiled coyly, then picked up her menu and nodded to them to do the same. "Order whatever you like. With Mr. Streed's compliments."

Millie studied Constance's face, trying to guess her relationship to Mr. Streed. She saw no family resemblance. The self-satisfied curl of Constance's sealed lips signaled that she didn't care to divulge her secrets.

Millie pored over the mysterious offerings on the menu. Sirloin steak smothered in mushroom sauce struck her fancy. The dignified black waiter in his short white jacket took their orders with great formality.

Sighing contentedly, Constance leaned back in her chair. "What brings you to New York City, Mr. Martinson?"

Millie was glad for Constance's question, which gave her an excuse to study Noah's face. She'd memorized his attractive profile on the train, and she knew his teasing brown eyes only too well. But sitting so near him at the small table afforded her a better angle to drink in his good looks at close range. She took note of the tiny cleft in his chin, his well-shaped eyebrows that gave him a scholarly appearance, and his neatly trimmed brown hair.

"Please, call me Noah." He fingered the napkin ring. "I'm visiting a law school here. Trying to decide whether to read law at home or attend the university."

Constance eyed him piercingly. "Then you won't follow your father's footsteps?"

Noah shifted. "Probably not."

"And would your father approve of your dining with communists?" Constance peered down her nose. "He doesn't care for our ways."

Millie held her breath. Why was Constance taunting this young man who'd been so kind to them?

Noah flashed his huge grin. "His reputation precedes me."

Constance laughed, and Millie joined in. The tension dissipated like steam from a cup of tea.

Constance explained that her arm had been injured by the rollers of a wringer washing machine and that they were seeking the help of their Community's doctor at the Wallingford branch.

"I'm sorry about your injury." Noah cocked his head. "John Humphrey Noyes couldn't heal you?"

Millie looked for mockery on Noah's face, but saw only concern. Father Noyes was considered a powerful medium of healing in the Community, but she doubted Outsiders—especially Noah's father—accepted that.

"He knows modern medicine has its place." Constance lifted her chin. "Two of our men trained at Yale Medical School."

"So I've heard." Noah nodded. "And yet he claims mutual criticism can heal disease."

Everything about him put Millie at ease. Noah's tone was curious, not confrontational. But the topic of mutual criticism made her tense. She fingered the folds of her dress under the table as she remembered Constance's ordeal.

When Father Noyes had learned of Constance's injury, he ended that evening's Meeting by commanding all spirits of disease and infirmity to leave Constance's arm. But she appeared at breakfast the next morning with it hanging useless at her side. That evening at Meeting he announced that his words hadn't healed her because she needed criticism. He invited members to tell Constance of her faults. One woman, who gripped Constance's injured hand so hard that she winced, accused her of displaying too much ownership of the canning business over which she was foreman. Other members piled on, pointing out Constance's pride, until eventually she broke down. She cried for ten minutes straight in front of the entire assembly.

When she was able to speak, she stated the final words of every mutual criticism. *I confess Christ in me a spirit of subordination to Mr. Noyes.*

Constance's arm still hadn't improved. She'd been performing duties one-handed for three months.

If remembering that experience bothered Constance, her expression didn't show it. "Some have been healed by mutual criticism." She calmly sipped her tea. "But I'm seeking medical attention."

The waiter arrived and presented their meals, attractively arranged on heavy china plates. He took the linen napkin in front of Millie, ceremoniously unrolled it, and positioned the silverware at the sides of her plate. He then laid the napkin across Millie's lap. She felt like Queen Victoria.

Before tasting her own food, Millie discreetly reached for Constance's plate and sliced her veal cutlet.

At a table beyond Constance sat an older man with a pointed beard and military bearing. A dainty woman, probably his wife, sat across from him. The empty left sleeve of his dinner jacket was pinned to his side. Millie's heart went out to the couple. Had she cut his steak for him? It had been almost a dozen years since the War of the Rebellion had ended, so he'd lived without his arm for more than a decade. She hoped Constance's disability wasn't permanent.

Millie turned to Noah. "You said President Lincoln spoke from the balcony here?"

"Mmm-hmm." Noah nodded and swallowed. "On his way to his first inauguration."

"The war was so sad." Millie sighed, glancing toward the veteran again. The black waiter was pouring him coffee. "Do you think it was worth it?"

Noah followed Millie's gaze. "Absolutely. Ending slavery was essential." He slathered a roll with butter. "As was keeping the Union intact."

Constance tilted her head as she finished chewing. "Both sides fought for control." She laid her fork across her plate. "The Southern states didn't want to be forced to remain in a Union that no longer served their needs. But the Northern states tried to force the Southern states to be loyal."

Noah set aside his half-eaten roll. "Loyalty to one's country is a virtue."

Constance nodded. "Certainly. But forced loyalty is no loyalty at all." She leaned forward with her forearm on the tabletop. "Father

Noyes understands that. If one of our members wants to leave the Community, he may leave. Unlike President Lincoln, Father Noyes doesn't force anyone to stay."

Including Edward Inslee, Millie thought. Constance sounded as if she would have been a conscientious objector to the war, as Millie's father had been. But Millie had never heard anyone contrast Father Noyes with President Lincoln in that way. She dabbed her mouth with her napkin. "That's a good point."

Ignoring Millie's comment, Noah leaned across the table toward Constance. "The South didn't like being controlled? Such hypocrisy!" Passion edged his voice. "They tried to control an entire race of men."

"Men are ever blind to their own faults." Constance's voice was gentle. "That's why we practice mutual criticism."

Noah's tense posture eased.

Millie had feared an unpleasant debate, but Noah's tinge of anger quickly cooled as he considered Constance's point of view. Millie relaxed her clenched fists.

Constance lowered her voice. "There's a woman just behind you who's facing us. Can you get a good look at her without staring?"

Millie dropped her napkin, and she and Noah leaned into the space between their chairs. With their faces side by side below the level of the table, Noah grinned like a conspirator at Millie. A surge of excitement tickled her shoulders as Noah's breath warmed her cheek. Tearing her eyes away from his, she took a long look at the woman.

The chestnut-haired lady wore an olive dress trimmed with cream lace. When she lowered her fork, a crimson ribbon choker adorned with a pink-and-ivory cameo came into view.

After rising back up, Millie whispered to Constance, "She's simply stunning!"

Constance raised an eyebrow. "Did you see her necklace?"

"It's beautiful!" Millie gushed.

Raising her index finger, Constance looked first at Noah, then at Millie. "Tell me, how is her necklace different from a dog's collar?"

Millie grimaced, finding such a comparison distasteful. "Both are worn around the neck, but otherwise, they're different in every way."

Noah jutted out his chin. "A dog has no choice in the matter, but she does."

"Ah!" Constance gestured toward Noah. "And she chooses to

wear it because it pleases her and those who see it. So how does that relate to our discussion?"

Millie tried to remember what they'd been talking about before her pretense with her napkin. She still felt Noah's exhilarating breath on her cheek. "About the war?"

"And our Community."

Millie lifted her shoulders. She placed her right hand to her cheek as if to preserve the remnants of Noah's closeness forever.

Noah gestured to Constance to continue.

"Loyalty is like that silken choker. We *choose* to bind ourselves to our Community—for our own pleasure and for others."

Noah gave a slow nod. "It's not a real choice unless you can choose to unbind yourselves."

* * *

Settling into her seat aboard the New York, New Haven, and Hartford train at Grand Central Depot, contentment enveloped Millie —outdated dress, short hair, and all. Although she would probably never see Noah again, she suspected he would occupy her daydreams for weeks to come.

The delicious food and lush surroundings of the hotel dining room satisfied an emptiness she hadn't known she had. Where was the part of the body that craved and thrived on symmetry, color, and texture? In the heart? In the head? In the eyes? Wherever it was, it was now filled to the brim and overflowing. She revisited the pattern of each carved cornice and the feel of each luxurious fabric at the Astor House.

And then, without warning, another picture, like a dull daguerreotype, flashed in her memory: the ragged little family to whom they'd given their picnic basket. She had seen two poles of American life in one day. What an intriguing article this was going to make.

She turned toward Constance and met her eyes. "Do all the girls who travel to Wallingford see such extremes of poverty and wealth?"

Constance's mouth fell open, and she closed it quickly. She pursed her lips, but her eyes sparkled. "I'd rather you didn't mention our visit to the Emigrant Car or our meal at the Astor House." She patted Millie's hand. "Women can be allowed some harmless secrets, don't you think?"

Millie tried to hide her disappointment. She couldn't record this journey for the *Circular* after all. She shook her head at Constance, who was already nodding off. How could she be so loyal to the Community while harboring so many secrets?

Chapter 3: Silk and Sorts

When Millie woke, the winter sun was high in the sky, flooding the room with its pale rays. For a moment she looked around, confused by her strange surroundings. Then she bolted up in bed. The clock atop the bureau showed it was after ten o'clock. She couldn't remember the last time she'd slept so late. She had neglected Constance. Glancing toward the other bed, she let out a relieved breath. The older woman lay peacefully under the heavy quilts.

Considering they'd arrived at two in the morning, maybe it wasn't too late. Millie rose quietly and washed at the washstand, then donned her comfortable short dress with pantalettes.

Constance stirred.

Millie crossed the room and knelt beside her. "How are you feeling?"

"Not well." Constance raised herself a few inches against her pillow. "My arm throbbed so much I barely slept." She dropped her head back. "Could you bring me my breakfast? I'd rather eat in bed."

Following the aroma of malt coffee, Millie found the kitchen. She signaled to a plump matron who seemed to be directing the other bustling women, already at work on the midday meal.

"Awake now, are you?" she beamed. "Welcome to Wallingford. I'm Margaret. We always let the folks who come from O.C. sleep in the first day. They're always tuckered out. But I've saved some breakfast for you."

Margaret greeted the request for in-room service as the best news she could have heard. In a twinkling she loaded two plates with baked potatoes and steaming graham mush and plopped them onto trays. She lifted one tray and nodded at Millie to carry the other.

Millie followed the chatty woman up the stairs.

"Hope you enjoyed your room. Our guests from O.C. always sleep here." Balancing her tray on one arm, Margaret swung the door open and stepped in, nodding a greeting to Constance. "It was Mary Cragin's, you know—when she lived here."

She set her tray on the table. "She slept in this very room just two days before she drowned in the sloop accident."

Margaret lifted her chin toward the portrait that hung over the bureau.

Following Margaret's gaze, Millie set her tray down. She had already noticed the familiar countenance of one of the Community's founders, but she shivered as she studied the face anew. She might have slept in the revered woman's former bed. The legendary figure seemed suddenly real.

After Margaret left them alone and Millie had cut Constance's potato into bite-sized portions, she regarded her own plate with skepticism. When she tasted the gritty graham mush, something she hadn't eaten since her days in the Children's House, her appetite vanished. If this represented their typical fare at Wallingford, no wonder so many were ill here.

Margaret frowned at the uneaten mush on the returned trays, but when Millie asked for Dr. Cragin, the woman wiped her hands on her apron and scuttled out of the kitchen, delighted to be of service again.

Dr. Cragin sat reading in a parlor. Atop a cherrywood writing desk, an assortment of mechanical pencils, fountain pens, and wooden pencils topped with rubber erasers stood in a ceramic mug. Next to the mug lay several small brass pencil sharpeners of various designs.

Millie caught her breath. Never had she seen such a wonderful array of writing materials all in one place. She had accumulated a few pencils in various lengths, all without erasers, which she sharpened with a pen knife. She'd often wished for a pencil sharpener.

Dr. Cragin, dressed professionally in a tailored gray suit, white shirt, and black ribbon bow tie, rose from his arm chair. "You must be Miss Langston. Welcome to Wallingford." He smiled and gave a courteous bow.

She liked him immediately.

As his deep brown eyes assessed her, he seemed to be looking beyond her exterior shell into her soul. "You're a writer, I see."

"Yes. I mean, yes, I'm Millie Langston." Warmth spread up her neck but soon cooled under the doctor's friendly gaze. "I do like to write. And I teach the children spelling and handwriting, but we use slates and slate pencils." She nodded toward the desk. "We don't have fountain pens or mechanical pencils."

"More's the pity." He nodded gravely. "Every time I get a new pen or pencil, my writing improves. I consider them wise investments." He winked.

She would love to keep talking about writing, but Constance was suffering. "Mrs. Arnotte's awake and has eaten breakfast, but the pain in her arm is worse. She managed the journey so well yesterday, but now it seems to have caught up with her."

"I'm not surprised, no, not surprised." His brows pressed together as he shook his head. "I myself am always worn out by the long journey from Oneida, and in her condition it would be doubly exhausting."

He scooped up a black doctor's bag in one hand and brushed Millie's arm with his other, directing her across the parlor. "I only wish I could have come to her instead of making her come to me. What kind of a physician behaves so selfishly? But my other patients here demand my attention—two in particular have been giving me quite a scare."

They went up the stairs side by side.

After asking Constance a few questions to update what he'd learned from correspondence, Dr. Cragin palpated her arm, causing her to cringe and suck in her breath. As if deep in thought, he brought his long fingers to his face and drew them down his bearded cheek to his chin. He tapped his lower lip with his index finger.

Finally he sat back in his chair, looking grim. "The bones in your hand have been crowded out of place, and the ligaments have been stretched, injuring the nerves here—and here." He traced his finger along her forearm and hand. "It's no wonder the hand is as good as paralyzed."

Constance nodded, her lips pursed.

"I wish I could give you better news, but based on my experience, I expect you won't be able to use your hand for the next twelve months or so, if even then."

Constance's lips parted, but no sound emerged. Her shoulders dropped.

Millie's hopes dashed to the ground like a damaged kite. She blinked hard a few times. She couldn't imagine Constance having to live another year this way. "But is there no medicine to help or any treatment at all?"

Dr. Cragin pushed his chair back, keeping his eyes on Constance. "Any amount of massage you can apply yourself, since you know your level of tolerance, can do no harm. I wouldn't advise painkilling drugs, since they'll only result in further distress in the long run. Laudanum addiction has destroyed many lives. I cannot prescribe it except for a very short course. We can only let time and rest do its work."

Seeing Constance's disappointment, he patted her arm. "Despite what I've told you, I wouldn't discount the work of God. We know the power of faith can extend far beyond what they teach us at medical school. I would cast your care upon Him. I would cast it with all your might."

At this, Constance broke down. Tears trickled down her cheeks, and silent sobs jerked her shoulders. Soon she buried her head in her good arm that rested on the table top and cried outright, just as she had during her criticism.

Millie swallowed past the lump in her throat and brushed at the tears that fell onto her own cheeks.

Dr. Cragin looked helplessly from one miserable woman to the other. He offered his handkerchief to Millie, then approached Constance. Kneeling, he wrapped her in his arms and let her cry on his shoulder.

She did so for another minute. After two breathy, broken sobs, she pulled away from the doctor's embrace and wiped her eyes with her handkerchief. "Thank you, Doctor." She squared her shoulders and set her jaw. "I'll bear up under this burden. If it's only for a year, then I'm blessed, for many veterans are living out their whole lives with no arm. I haven't sacrificed as much as they."

Perhaps Constance had noticed the one-armed man in the Astor House dining room after all. *Dear, strong Aunt Constance. How good you are.*

After Dr. Cragin left, Constance curled up in her bed and napped.

Millie tucked the bedspread under the sleeping woman's chin. She pulled out her pencil case and diary. In her best script she recorded the heart-wrenching scene in great detail and with so much sentiment that she nearly cried all over again.

Closing up her journal, she considered her companion in the next bed. Aunt Constance was a kindred soul with Dorothea Brooke, the

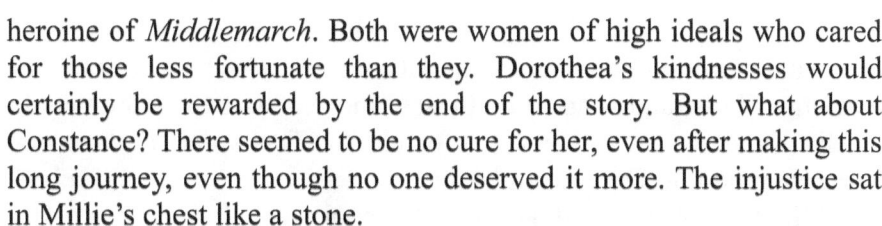

heroine of *Middlemarch*. Both were women of high ideals who cared for those less fortunate than they. Dorothea's kindnesses would certainly be rewarded by the end of the story. But what about Constance? There seemed to be no cure for her, even after making this long journey, even though no one deserved it more. The injustice sat in Millie's chest like a stone.

After dinner, with Constance still sleeping soundly in their room, Millie accepted an invitation from a young woman named Jessie to tour the Wallingford buildings. Although she was a bright and enthusiastic guide, the tour began unimpressively. Wallingford was simply a smaller, poorer version of Oneida Community. Instead of the spacious Italianate Mansion House, with its three stories and three connected buildings, Wallingford had a square brick house with only about twenty rooms.

Next to the house stood a three-story wooden factory building. They hurried through the first floor's noisy, smelly trap manufacturing operation. It was just like the one in Oneida's cluster of factory buildings known as Willow Place.

They ascended a stairway to the third floor.

"Our silk works is up here." Jessie grasped Millie's hand and pulled her along. "We patterned it after Willow Place. We just built this building last year. Before that, it was a ten-minute walk to our factory."

Although Millie had never seen the Willow Place silk works, she had often seen the elderly women skeining silk by hand inside the Mansion House. They chatted with each other for hours as they twisted and knotted the strands into embroidery hanks that were then sold to Outsiders all over the country. Silk was the second most important industry for the Community now.

Millie gaped in awe at the cavernous room filled with rows and rows of humming machines.

Jessie explained the process. At one end, workers fed the shiny white silk onto rollers, and the machines combined two, three, or up to six strands into one thread, twisted it, and rolled it onto large bobbins. At the other end, workers removed the full bobbins and replaced them with empty ones.

The silk as it came from Italy was called *reeled silk*. "Not *real* silk, but *reeled* silk," Jessie emphasized, her eyes sparkling.

According to Jessie, the raw silk, which came in single strands from the unwound cocoons of the silk worms, was too delicate for weaving. The strands had to be twisted into thread before they could be dyed and woven into ribbons or cloth. "That's called *throwing*. Then we send it to O.C. for finishing."

Millie nodded. "And *we* dye it, spool it, and pack the pretty spools in cases."

Occasionally she worked in the room above the dining hall, putting spools of multiple colors of thread into display cases for their commercial travelers.

Jessie frowned in exaggerated self-pity. "No pretty colors here. Ours is only white."

As Millie watched the continuous turning of the huge machines, the monotonous whirring sound seemed to penetrate her entire body. Queasiness rose in her stomach.

"So many women own Singer sewing machines now, and they all need thread." Pride edged Jessie's voice. "We had to add more machines and hire more girls to keep up with the orders for machine twist."

Millie stopped looking at the flying silk and focused on the workers instead—nearly fifty girls and women who stood at the incessantly spinning bobbins. So that's why most wore long dresses. They were hirelings from the town. "Some of them are so little."

"They can start as young as ten."

Millie's heart went out to the girls who shifted from one foot to another in their work boots with blank expressions and glazed eyes. Their dour faces contrasted starkly with the genial, contented faces of the elderly women who skeined silk by hand at the Mansion House. Millie shook her head. If this was progress, Heaven help the world.

Jessie sensed Millie's distaste. "Let's go! I'm getting dizzy!" She wobbled her head around and rolled her eyes, making Millie chuckle. "I'll show you the raw silk."

At the far end of the room, rows of square cotton bags stood against the back wall. Each open bag revealed skeins of shiny white silk that had come reeled from Italy.

"Go ahead," encouraged Jessie. "Touch it."

Millie stroked one of the floppy skeins and instantly pictured Haydn's silky hair—the softest thing she'd ever felt, until now.

Jessie grabbed two skeins from the bales and dangled them from the top of her head so they hung down on either side of her face. "How do I look as a blonde?" She tilted her head coquettishly and batted her eyelashes.

Millie snorted with surprise, and before she could answer, Jessie suddenly called, "Catch!" and threw both skeins to Millie.

Millie caught one, but the other landed in the top of the bale behind her. She giggled as she put two skeins up to her own head and pinched her face into a scowl. "And this is me when I'm eighty," she said in a crackly voice. She hunched over and shuffled a few steps toward Jessie.

"Oh, oh! My turn! Toss them!" Jessie squealed.

Millie tossed the skeins, one at a time, and Jessie caught them.

"Good throw!"

"Good catch!" Millie laughed.

Jessie held one skein at her throat and the other on top of her head, pinching them in the middle to make them look like fashionable bows. Then she paraded around like an aristocrat, tossing her chin from side to side. In a falsetto voice she warbled, "Only the best ribbons for me. Straight from It-a-ly! Straight from the co-coo-oons!"

Millie broke into uncontrollable giggles, and Jessie joined her. They doubled over and leaned against each other in spasms.

Millie couldn't remember when she had laughed so hard.

The two young women, still smiling, trudged their way arm in arm past the main brick house toward a wooden frame house down the road. They left footprints in the few inches of snow that had fallen overnight.

"That's where our children play during the day." Jessie nodded toward the house ahead. "Our printing office is there, too. Unfortunately, it's not very exciting now that we don't print the *Circular* anymore."

Millie sensed disappointment in Jessie's voice for losing the prestige the paper had given the poorer branch commune. "I heard Father Noyes moved it to Oneida for Tirzah—so she could be there with him but continue as editress."

Jessie kicked up the fluffy snow playfully as she walked. "I think he was trying to make peace with her." She lowered her voice, even though no one was within earshot. "For sending her here, to this penal colony. She hated it here."

Millie nodded. Living off the beaten track would not have suited the vibrant Tirzah.

"I loved putting the mailing labels on the *Circular.*" Jessie regained her cheery attitude. "We sent them to every state in the country. Two thousand copies a week."

"I've done that, too."

Millie scanned the distant pines on the horizon. Putting spools in cases, putting labels on newspapers—the Community had no end of mindless jobs to be done.

"What I want to do most is write for the *Circular* some day." The words slipped out before she knew it. She scanned Jessie's face for signs of scorn, but she didn't see any. Still, she quickly added, "But, of course, that won't be for many years—if at all."

Jessie puckered her lips in thought. "It'll be hard to get that job. Father Noyes treats the paper like a favored son. You have to be one of his protégés—like Tirzah—to write the articles."

As they stepped across the threshold into the house, a child's ear-splitting scream greeted them. Jessie put her hands over her ears and wrinkled her features in mock pain. "The pressroom is quieter."

In the pressroom, a low-pitched rhythmic slapping sound filled the air as a brawny man in a full leather apron tended three cylinder presses. Two girls stood by, ready to replenish the paper supply. Millie inhaled the delicious, satisfying aroma of ink and paper.

She followed Jessie to the composing room where Jessie showed her the sorts, the letters in different fonts that were arranged by typesetters onto composing sticks to create each line of type in an article. The tiny metal squares, each with a backwards letter, were all arranged by letter in the compartments of large wooden trays, and each font had its own tray.

Millie picked up square after square, examining the reversed letters. She wished she could sit and play with them for hours as she'd played with the wooden ABC blocks as a child. Relishing the feel of the sorts, she regretted that she'd never learned to set type. But Mr. Warne's typesetting class had always conflicted with her Latin class at Seminary—and Latin was much more important, after all.

Just then a tall, lanky man in rolled-up shirt sleeves, suspenders, and a heavy chest-to-knees apron came into the room. He halted when he saw them, his eyebrows knit together in surprise.

"Ho-ho! Visitors!" He chuckled, rubbing his hands together.

Jessie introduced him as Mr. Jocelyn.

Assuming they'd come to be educated, he explained the type-setting process.

"Want to give it a try?" He handed each woman a composing stick. "Write whatever you want. You have fifty characters. Remember, spaces count."

Millie stared at the stick and immediately broke into a grin. *Happy are the hands that throw the silken strands.* The words popped effortlessly into her mind. Visualizing the letters and spaces, she counted them. Exactly fifty!

She couldn't wait for Jessie to see the joke in print. The girls at the machines who were *throwing* the silk weren't happy. But Jessie and Millie had been quite happy with their method of throwing the silk.

Millie easily found the letters, even though they were backwards, and lined them up inside the narrow stick with the beginning of the sentence at the right, remembering to put blank sorts between the words. She even found the period.

From time to time Mr. Jocelyn glanced at them to check their progress.

When Millie finished first, Jessie stamped her foot and shook her curls. "This is hard," she whined, exaggerating her frustration. "I can't read what I've written because it's all inside out."

Millie pushed back a rising feeling of superiority. It wasn't a race, after all, and Jessie had talents of her own. When she finally finished, she reticently slid her stick toward Mr. Jocelyn as if presenting uneven stitches to a sewing teacher.

After taking their compositor's sticks, he worked some magic with the hand press. With a flourish, he produced a printed sheet and spread it on the counter.

Jessie's read, "I amJesssieHayes I llive atWalingford." She cupped her palms over her eyes and shook her head.

Mr. Jocelyn read Millie's aloud. "Happy are the hands that throw the silken strands." He looked at her as if trying to peer inside her brain. "Where does that come from?"

"From me." She grinned at Jessie. "I made it up just now."

Jessie giggled.

"Well, now, I like that." Mr. Jocelyn stroked his beard. "Makes a good motto for the factory. I thought it might've come from Father Noyes himself. Sounds worthy of him."

Millie flushed at the undeserved compliment. The couplet was an intimate joke for Jessie—and an irreverent one at that.

As Mr. Jocelyn busied himself cutting their sentences from the paper, he kept repeating under his breath, "Happy are the hands that throw the silken strands." He offered Millie her keepsake. "You might have told me you'd learned typesetting from Mr. Warne."

Millie shook her head. "I've never had any instruction."

"Indeed?" He squinted. "You're faster than some of my assistants who've been at it for years. You have no trouble reading backwards, then?"

Her cheeks grew hot under his gaze. "I suppose it's like reading to the children. They sit on the floor in front of me and I read the books upside down—so they can see the pictures."

Jessie stared at Millie as if she'd announced she could lift an elephant, but Mr. Jocelyn only nodded.

With the tour of Wallingford over, Millie returned to her room to find Constance in a chair by the window looking much improved. A dose of laudanum from Dr. Cragin had taken the edge off her pain. Millie told her about Jessie, their game at the silk factory, and their chance to set type. When Millie quoted her little rhyme and described Mr. Jocelyn's reaction, Constance threw back her head and laughed.

Despite Constance's high spirits, Millie's conscience pricked. She should have spent less time playing with Jessie and more time keeping Constance company.

At Meeting that night as Dr. Cragin presented Constance's case, everyone eyed the visitor with sympathy.

"Although we bring science to bear on every possible issue, that doesn't mean we put our faith on the shelf." Dr. Cragin's words sounded like one of Father Noyes's Home Talks. "Who here has experienced a faith cure?"

Several people stood and spoke at length about being cured from various maladies, from warts to fevers. At last an elderly woman, perhaps the oldest person there, rose to her feet, leaning on a cane.

"That's all well and good." She glared at those who had already

told their stories. "But I was cured of consumption—*overnight*."

She looked around to make sure everyone grasped her words. Several members nodded politely while a couple stifled yawns. They seemed to have heard the tale before.

"And do you know how? All I did was have a talk with Father Noyes and your mother." She pointed at Dr. Cragin with a bony finger. "Your mother, Mary Cragin—and the next day, my chest was clear, and I never coughed again. Your mother was a saint, Dr. Cragin, and if she were still among us, she could cure this woman just as she cured me. If not for that blessed lady, I'd have died thirty years ago."

She dropped into her chair and dabbed at her eyes with her handkerchief.

"Thank you for that, Mrs. Hall." Without looking at her, Dr. Cragin scanned the room. "Anyone else?"

After a few people related how they'd been cured of illnesses by mutual criticism sessions, Dr. Cragin adjourned the Meeting. Constance stayed in the reception room talking.

Jessie invited Millie to her room. Before long, Millie found herself sharing secrets she'd never shared before. Not just her dreams of writing for the *Circular,* but feelings about her long-dead mother that she'd never before put into words.

After listening sympathetically, Jessie vouchsafed her own confidences, including her fascination with a young man who had recently arrived at Wallingford.

Jessie drummed her fingers on the mattress where they sat. "Tell me, is there someone *you* have your eye on?"

Instantly, Noah's face next to hers as they huddled behind the Astor House dining table flashed into Millie's mind. She blinked the picture away.

Jessie moved to her mirror and wash basin. She began wetting her hair and fixing pins into twisted strands as she watched Millie's reflection expectantly.

Millie called up the image of the dashing black-haired violinist whom she had admired since he came to Oneida Community four years ago. His good looks had inspired many daydreams, and now every novel's leading man—whether Mr. Darcy, Mr. Rochester, or Will Ladislaw—was simply a variation on a theme.

"Henry Hunter." She raised her shoulders with a little shiver.

"He's the nicest young man at O.C. And so handsome."

It felt strange to talk about boys. She'd never done so with the girls she'd grown up with. The Community rule against horizontal fellowship discouraged close friendships between girls of the same age, and Millie had always followed rules. Assiduously. Now, sitting on Jessie's bed, pouring out her heart to a relative stranger, she relished an unfamiliar glow, a warm ember somewhere deep inside.

"Do tell!" Jessie's eyes twinkled into the mirror. "How old is he?"

"Eighteen."

"Oh." Jessie's shoulders sagged. "Then you have a long time to wait before he's *teleoi*." Turning to face Millie, she raised her chin and her eyebrows. "George is twenty-three. I think he's planning to request an interview."

Millie looked away. She hadn't been thinking about interviews, but she knew what Jessie meant. According to the rules of ascending fellowship, young men had to prove their mastery of the birth control method Father Noyes required before they could request interviews with young women. Until then, their complex marriage partners had to be women past childbearing age. That meant only older men could partner with young women.

Remembering her encounter with Virginia in the library, Millie frowned.

Jessie noticed her change of expression. "Is something wrong?"

Millie shared Virginia's story. Jessie seemed unmoved, and Millie squirmed. Perhaps she shouldn't have brought it up. She traced the grooves of the rag rug with her toe. "How old were you when you had your first interview?"

Jessie wrinkled her forehead in thought. "Probably thirteen—same as most girls. I can't quite remember it. They all blur together after a while, don't they?"

Millie tucked her hair behind her ears and looked at Jessie through her lashes. "I haven't had my first interview yet."

Jessie's eyes widened, and she drew back. She assessed Millie for a moment, no doubt taking in her small stature and flat chest. She shrugged. "Good for you. You haven't missed anything."

Later, lying in her bed, Millie couldn't sleep. A heavy weight nagged at her stomach for indulging in horizontal fellowship. "The penal colony." That's what Jessie had called Wallingford. Often members who broke rules and didn't respond to mutual criticism were sent from Oneida Community to Wallingford, or vice versa. Luckily Jessie lived at Wallingford already, so they couldn't be sent away from each other for their friendship.

Long into the night Millie mulled over their conversation about interviews. Somehow she'd been passed over. All the other Community girls had become wives at thirteen, but she hadn't. If she'd had friends to talk with about private matters, she would surely have realized the truth long before now. At thirteen, such things had been far from her mind. Only recently, in fact, had she begun to wonder why girls her age and younger were pairing up after Meeting while she wasn't. But she'd pushed those thoughts from her mind as she immersed herself in yet another novel.

Perhaps she should feel slighted, left out, or inferior. But she felt only relief. There was no older man she looked forward to having relations with. If she didn't feel ready now, she certainly wouldn't have felt ready four years ago.

* * *

As weak morning light suffused the room, Millie heard movement and opened her eyes. Something sounded different. When she sat up, she blinked in disbelief. Constance was making her bed— with both hands!

Millie sprang from her bed. "Aunt Constance! Look at you! What happened?"

Constance tapped the bed with her left hand, and Millie sat next to her, her eyes wide. Constance grasped her hands with both of hers. "After Meeting, I came back here and prayed to God to take the pain out of my hand. I told Him if He did, I'd glorify Him with it. I had a warm feeling right here." She patted above her heart. "Like God was truly here. The pain left, and I stretched my arm out farther than I've been able to since I hurt it. I wanted to tell you last night, but I fell asleep before you came back."

"Then you're truly healed?" Millie gently squeezed Constance's hands, and she squeezed back with a surprising amount of strength. "You can move your arm normally?"

"Watch!" Constance raised her left hand over her head and traced a circle in the air, then returned it to her lap. "I slept soundly until four o'clock. When I woke, I felt no pain at all." Her eyes glistened as the words bubbled out. "I could still stretch out my arm and move my fingers, so I knew I was healed."

Last night Millie had rolled her eyes inwardly, doubting Mrs. Hall's testimony. Now the placid portrait of Mary Cragin chided her for her unbelief. Millie couldn't deny what she saw with her own eyes. Miracles could happen after all.

She bounced up off the bed. "I can't wait till everyone hears!" She yanked her nightdress over her head. "Let me dress. Don't go down without me. I have to see the looks on their faces. Especially Dr. Cragin's."

Breakfast was joyous.

When Dr. Cragin came by afterward to examine the arm, he declared that everything had moved back into place and the ligaments had relaxed. "Wonderful, just wonderful," he kept murmuring as he tapped his lower lip. Finally he put his long fingers up and stroked his right cheek. "I give you a clean bill of health. I see no reason why you can't return to Oneida on tomorrow's train."

Millie's heart soared—then dipped. That meant she'd be leaving Jessie soon.

She found her friend in the sewing room and helped her with her work for the day. In the afternoon when their mending was done, they sat in the parlor looking at stereographic photographs of Cozicot in the summer and of Connecticut in all four seasons.

After Meeting, since telling and retelling her story was keeping Constance busy, Millie went to Jessie's room again. Sitting with her on the narrow bed, Millie demonstrated how to solve the riddles and puzzles in the current *Godey's Lady's Book*. Before long, Jessie insisted they look at the women's fashion. She obviously kept up with style trends, even though they had no effect on Community women. She pointed out how the trains were shorter this year, the waists longer, and the bows on the bustles larger.

Without giving away any harmless secrets, Millie described the woman in the dining room who wore the cameo choker. Paging through the fashion plates once more, Jessie found an illustration of a woman modeling a crimson choker.

"That's it!" Millie clapped her hands. "I believe it's the very one."

Jessie sighed. "It's so elegant. I should like to have one."

"But you know we never can."

Jessie curled her hand daintily under her chin and stared at the far wall. "Ah, but one can dream, can one not?" Then, spreading both arms out in a royal flourish, she crooned in falsetto, "Nothing is too fine for the Queens of the Co-coo-oons!"

Once in her own bed, Millie grew sober. She would miss Jessie dreadfully.

Although Millie couldn't see the watchful portrait of Mary Cragin in the dark, she felt her presence keenly. Father Noyes had fallen into special love with Mary Cragin when he took her as his first wife under complex marriage, after his legal wife, Harriet. But in 1851 Mrs. Cragin had died in Brooklyn when the sloop she was sailing in capsized. To Father Noyes, the accident was a judgment from God on "special love."

Since then, Father Noyes had instructed the members clearly. Men must love all their wives equally, and women must love all their husbands equally. Even beyond the matter of complex marriage, all members must value each other without favoritism—or Providence might intervene.

Millie rolled over in bed, turning her back on the dead founder's invisible image. For the first time in her memory, Millie had formed a deep connection—special love—with someone other than her father. Jessie. Now that she'd experienced it herself—not just through a story about an ancient, drowned woman—she couldn't understand why God would frown upon such bonds. Her heart felt alive, larger somehow. She felt like a better person. She'd made a friend.

Early the next morning Dr. Cragin drove Millie and Constance to the train station. As he helped them onto the train, he slipped Millie a flat package wrapped in brown paper and tied with a string.

"To remember us by," he whispered in her ear.

At the train's first jerk forward, Millie took out her pen knife, cut the string, and folded down the brown paper. She gasped with delight. On top of twenty or so sheets of white vellum stationery lay a mechanical pencil with a wooden stem and mother-of-pearl inlay. Dr. Cragin had thoughtfully included a container of replacement lead.

He'd also passed on one of his eraser-topped wooden pencils and a brass pencil sharpener imprinted with a strutting peacock.

"Oh! Oh, my!" Millie picked up the mechanical pencil, rotating it between her fingers. She showed it to Constance. "Have you ever seen anything so lovely?"

Constance's amused expression implied that in fact she might have, but Millie didn't mind. She fitted the wooden pencil into the sharpener and gave it a trial turn.

Other than some trinkets at Christmastime, she'd never received a personal gift. Her heart was overflowing. "I must write to Dr. Cragin right away."

She spent most of the return trip writing rather than reading. After effusively expressing her appreciation to Dr. Cragin, she dashed off a thank-you note to Mr. Jocelyn and a quick letter to Jessie, promising to correspond regularly. The mother-of-pearl mechanical pencil felt like heaven in her hand and produced an admirable script.

She quickly updated her diary, then positioned the vellum sheets on her lap and composed the story of Constance's faith cure. Her heart fluttered with excitement. The miracle made an even better story than the Astor House experience. She told the tale with great pathos, putting the rubber eraser to use as she perfected the narrative.

As they neared the Oneida Community station, she hid her gifts away in a separate compartment of the travel bag. In her room, she'd tuck them into her small personal bureau where she kept her pencil stubs and sewing utensils. She'd use these instruments only in private. Since the yearly inventory had just been completed, she wouldn't have to declare ownership of them until next December. So for now, for almost a year, they were her very own.

Was she being seduced by a selfish spirit of exclusive possession? And what about Jessie? Had she made Jessie her exclusive possession as well? A friend she cherished more than all others? She tucked those troublesome questions away in her travel bag with her gifts to sort out later. She wanted only to savor the silkiness of the mother-of-pearl pencil in her hand and the sound of her own well-formed phrases in her ear.

Chapter 4: Fathers and Mothers

The Tontine was buzzing. No doubt word of Constance's faith cure was spreading among the members eating breakfast. No one seemed to know that Millie had been Constance's companion, nor would she call attention to the fact. She'd had nothing to do with Constance's cure, after all. She had selfishly preferred Jessie to Constance.

Now that she was back at the Mansion House, Millie could view her actions on the trip more clearly. Her biggest regret was that she hadn't seen Constance's cure in person. If she'd been taking care of the older woman as she should have been, she'd have been in the room to witness the miracle firsthand. Surely that was a sign from God that she must mend her ways. Perhaps the letter she'd written to Tirzah would be a start.

The large dining hall no longer seemed the comfortable place it was five days ago. Just as the lush surroundings of the Astor House had satisfied some internal need, so the hours she and Jessie had spent laughing and sharing confidences filled an emptiness she hadn't known she had. How strange that she should feel closer to someone she'd known for only two days than she felt to these people she'd lived with for most of her life.

"No, no!" Ellen Stoner, sitting to Millie's left, tossed her head from side to side, and her voice rose emphatically. "Dr. Cragin could do nothing for her. He only wanted to prescribe laudanum for her."

"Actually, he didn't want her to—"

Millie tried to correct the record, but as usual, Ellen didn't hear her and kept talking to the others. Millie toyed with her fried apples. She'd learned long ago that she was invisible to Ellen, the only girl just her age.

Ellen had always longed to be included in the group of seven girls who were a few years older—who continually got into trouble for too much horizontal fellowship. Ellen hadn't changed. Today, as usual, she was enveloped in conversation with the young musicians and actors—

a cadre that didn't include Millie.

Millie had always shrugged off Ellen's snubs and the older girls' disregard, but today her stomach burned at being excluded. Until now, she'd never felt the need for a friend of her own. She had filled her time with classes at the Seminary or reading in the library, where every book opened a secret passage to a different world. But she couldn't hide in books all her life. And now that she'd tasted true friendship, she didn't want to.

The conversation at Millie's table had shifted from Constance to the basket-making bee.

Millie looked around the table. "Wait! It's today?"

"Of course!" Henry Hunter, on her right, wagged his head. "Where have *you* been?"

Now the charged atmosphere in the Tontine made sense, and Millie absorbed the excitement herself. The basket-making bee was her favorite of all the Community-wide project days—travel bag bees, hoeing bees, pea-husking bees, apple-picking bees, raking bees.

People were already exiting the Tontine to head across the snowy Quadrangle toward the Big Hall.

"You'd better finish up, Millie." Henry pushed his chair back as several others at their table stood. "Shall I wait for you?"

"No, no. I'm fine. Please go ahead."

Henry gave a quick nod and hurried off, catching up to another young man and clapping him on the shoulder.

Millie bit her lower lip. She should have accepted his offer to wait. He must think her awfully stand-offish.

When Millie entered the Big Hall, a towheaded bundle of excitement bounded up and grabbed her hand.

"Teacher, will you help me make my baskets? I don't know how!"

She let the six-year-old pull her to the back of the room. "Of course, Ford. I'd love to."

As soon as Millie joined the other children, one of the guardians who had dressed them and brought them over from the Children's House found her way to another table. The remaining guardians would move to adult tables if others like Millie volunteered to work with the little ones. The children's mothers would be unlikely to volunteer because they wouldn't want to be suspected of philoprogenitiveness, or excessive attachment to their children. A few hours of togetherness wouldn't be worth the risk of being sent to Wallingford.

When Mary Jones and Victor Hawley arrived, the remaining two guardians left. Victor, in his late twenties, crouched down face to face with Ford. "You look bright-eyed today." He flashed a grin, then made a wide-eyed show of looking around the little boy's back. "And bushy tailed!"

Ford looked behind himself to see his tail, and Victor, chuckling, moved on to greet the next child. Mary, whose middle was beginning to bulge with pregnancy, winked at Victor and escorted Ford to his place at the table.

As Victor strode off for their supply of willow shoots, Mary had a kind word for each boy and girl, often squeezing a hand or patting a shoulder as she pushed in a chair. A twinge of sympathy shot through Millie's chest as she watched her. If the previous baby Mary had carried hadn't been stillborn, the child would have been almost Ford's age by now.

Grinning, Victor came back carrying a huge armful of rehydrated willow sticks. He set them down on the table with mock triumph. He sidled close to Mary and tickled the back of her neck with his wet fingers. She shivered and giggled, turning her eyes up to meet his. Then he touched several children on the backs of their necks, producing giggles and shrieks around the table.

Millie braced for her turn, but Victor rested his eyes on Mary again. Clearly she was the one he wanted to touch.

After assigning each child a partner, Millie, Mary, and Victor helped each pair start the bottom of their basket by weaving a pliable willow shoot in and out of the willow spokes.

At the other tables, adults wove while someone read from one of the library's short story collections. Millie had noticed volumes of Edgar Allan Poe, Washington Irving, and Nathaniel Hawthorne, or the English magazine *All the Year Round* at the other tables. She'd already read them all.

Thanks to Victor, their end of the room had its own gripping tales. As he told of Hansel and Grethel getting lost in the forest, finding the house made of gingerbread, and being captured by the old hag, some of the children covered their faces with their hands and peeked out through their fingers. Mary lifted one little girl onto her lap and swayed from side to side in a vaguely familiar motion. Millie couldn't place the memory.

Next Victor told "Three Billy Goats Gruff." The children grinned with delight at Victor's "trip, trap, trip, trap" and his squeaky, "Don't take me! I'm too little, that I am!" While telling his stories, Victor darted playful looks at Mary, who watched him as if he were some magical gnome who'd enchanted her. They seemed able to read each other's mind, Millie thought, just as she and Jessie had begun to do. She missed her friend.

Suddenly, Millie's stomach cramped, and her cheeks grew warm. Mary and Victor were displaying the exclusive and idolatrous attachment to each other that Father Noyes had forbidden. Millie glanced up at the portrait of Father Noyes on the wall behind her, with the portraits of Harriet Noyes on one side and Mary Cragin on the other. They had been the first people to practice Father Noyes's revelation about complex marriage—that living in communism meant sharing human property like all their other possessions. Since then, all adult men and all adult women were married to each other, and exclusivity was grounds for mutual criticism. Here as at Wallingford, Mary Cragin's portrait was a constant reminder that *special love* could have disastrous consequences.

Had any of the ascendant members observed Mary and Victor's inappropriate behavior? Probably not. No one paid much attention to the children's side of the room. Millie's face cooled, but her nerves remained on edge.

At midmorning, trays of raised nutcakes and pitchers of apple cider and milk appeared across the room. Millie went with Victor to get the refreshments for their table. When they returned, the children poked their thumbs in their ears and wiggled their fingers at Victor as Mary led them in a game of Simon Says. Victor feigned offense, then set down his load and returned their gesture, producing a ripple of giggles from the little girls.

Millie laughed at their antics. Victor was so entertaining.

Late in the morning, Millie felt the mood in the room shift. Father Noyes had entered the Big Hall. Now that their loved and respected founder had appeared, members took renewed interest in their tasks.

Dressed in his dark blue suit, white shirt, and black ribbon bow tie, he exuded confidence and authority, creating a large presence despite his average stature. His trimmed gray beard covered his square jaw, and his large, deep-set eyes under his wide forehead seemed to take in everything at a glance. He was looking for someone —probably his son, Theodore, who was at the table nearest the stage.

Father Noyes meandered that direction, stopping at every table along the way to inspect baskets and deliver a few pleasant words to each group. After he left a table, the members' faces fairly glowed with happiness and contentment, as if he sprinkled pixie dust in his wake. Theodore rose as his father approached, and they stood talking for a few minutes. But when Father Noyes turned away, Theodore didn't glow. He alone seemed immune to the prophet's magnetism.

Father Noyes moved toward the refreshments, still stopping at each table along the way, leaving smiling people behind him. As he helped himself to a nutcake, Tirzah Miller wove her way toward him from where she'd been sitting with Theodore. When she reached him, he put an arm around her shoulder, drew her close to him, and bent his head toward her as she spoke.

Tirzah backed smoothly out of Father Noyes's arm and produced a folded paper, which she handed to him.

Father Noyes and Tirzah both turned to look directly at Millie. She froze. Her eyes met Tirzah's.

Embarrassed, Millie dropped her eyes, and when she looked back, Father Noyes was studying Mary and Victor. Seated side by side, they were sharing a private joke that lit Mary up like a lamp. Father Noyes's mouth, which often wore a pleasantly perplexed expression, plunged into a frown.

Millie's heart sank.

The prophet turned his gaze on Millie for a moment with the same disapproving expression. He gruffly slipped the paper Tirzah had given him into his jacket's inside pocket, then sat down at a nearby table with a group of youth, among them Henry Hunter.

From what Millie could see, his normal expression had returned. But that didn't unwind the unpleasant knot in her stomach.

Had she been tainted in their prophet's eyes by Victor and Mary's special love? Or had Father Noyes also heard about her special relationship with Jessie? The Community had spent money to send her to Wallingford to assist Constance, and she had repaid that generosity by violating one of its core principles. Perhaps Constance had reported Millie's selfish behavior to their leader. Her stomach churned. Her error had caught up with her.

When the bee ended in the middle of the afternoon, Millie scanned the room to see if her father had left yet. She would need his help. She spotted him among a group of men and made her way toward him. Like most men at Oneida Community, he wore a full beard and mustache, but his beard was short and pointed over his narrow chin. His brown hair had no hint of gray yet. To her eyes, he was one of the handsomest men in the Community.

Together, Millie and her father climbed the stairs and entered his room. Millie sat on one of the wooden chairs at the side of a low square table. The room looked much like her own—indeed, like all other sleeping rooms in the Mansion House—with its narrow bed against one wall, a bureau on another, a trunk next to that, a washstand, the stark wooden table, and three spindle-backed chairs with woven cane seats. Millie had slept in many different rooms growing up, sharing rooms with various women, but this one, with its faint fragrance of lemon-scented hand salve, always felt safe and warm, like a heavy quilt.

William sat across from her. "Did you enjoy your trip to Wallingford?"

Millie shivered with delight. "It was wonderful! Dr. Cragin was so hospitable. I saw their brand new factory, and the printing office, and I met a woman named Jessie—" She stopped and knitted her brows together. "That's what I need to talk to you about."

"Go on."

"Oh, Father!" She put her fists on the table and leaned toward him. "I was selfish on the trip. I preferred Jessie over Constance. And Father Noyes just scowled at me today. Constance must have given him a bad report about me. Will you help me put together a committee for mutual criticism?"

William's lips curled as he shook his head, his eyes twinkling. "Constance told me you were all she expected you to be. *Sweet, helpful, and trustworthy.* Those were her words, I think."

Relief washed over Millie, and she relaxed against the back of the chair. "So do you think Father Noyes's scowl was only for Mary and Victor? I was working with them."

He raised his eyebrows, the hint of a smile still tugging at his lips. "No doubt."

"Because of their special love?"

He nodded. "They've been under scrutiny ever since Mary was chosen for stirpiculture last fall. Don't you remember all the hubbub?"

"No." Millie shrugged. "That only involves the older women. It doesn't affect me."

"Older women." William winked. "Those old twenty-five-year-olds."

"You know what I mean."

"I know. You don't go in for gossip. So you wouldn't want to know."

"But I do—" He was teasing. "What happened last fall?"

William stroked his beard. "Mary had a stillbirth a few years ago, you know."

Millie nodded. That much she had heard.

"So when she petitioned to be part of the scientific breeding program, she wasn't considered a good candidate—unless the father was strong enough to make up for her weaknesses. So of course it had to be Father Noyes's son."

"The baby is Theodore's?"

"Yes. She wanted to have a child with Victor but wasn't allowed to. Now they're acting like two lovebirds feathering their nest. Despite several criticisms."

"Which explains Father Noyes's scowl."

Millie sat in silence for a minute, then stood and took a few steps to the bureau. Absently she arranged William's comb, coat brush, and nail file so they were evenly spaced and parallel. She recalled the warm ember she'd felt in her chest during her late-night talks with Jessie. Now her chest ached with guilt and confusion.

She looked back at William. "I'm not much better than Victor and Mary. I pursued horizontal fellowship instead of helping Constance."

"Nonsense! I'm glad you made a friend." William rose and joined her. He patted her hand where it sat on top of the bureau. "If it's not an exclusive relationship, it's fine."

"I keep thinking about Edith and Lily—those harsh criticisms they had month after month. They never seemed to learn their lesson about being too close."

William's eyes softened as he studied Millie's face. "But *you* learned their lesson, didn't you?"

Understanding burst through. "Maybe that's why I've never made friends here. I feared those condemning words too much."

William's eyes brimmed with sympathy.

She sighed. "Do people find me cold and aloof?"

"Cold and aloof?" Smiling, William shifted the toiletry items back into disarray. "Let's just say you could try to be less stiff. Friendlier."

Millie returned to her chair and sat—her elbow on the table and her cheek on her fist. If her own father saw her stand-offishness, it must be glaring indeed.

"I will." She straightened. "I'll be more sociable. Then my friendship with Jessie won't be exclusive."

"Exactly." William joined her at the table. "Love is what we stand for, after all. And you have so much to give. Don't be afraid to share your heart."

Share your heart. Good advice, but would he follow his own suggestion? Perhaps he'd be more open now than he'd been in the past.

"Father?"

When William tilted his head to listen, she folded her hands together on the table top and looked up from under her lashes in the sweetest pose she knew how to make. "Can you tell me a little about Mother? What she was like?"

Instantly his posture stiffened as a shadow crossed his face. He seemed to fold into himself, like a closed morning glory blossom. "What brought this on?"

Millie sat back, defeated. Her charm hadn't worked. She should have used more tact. "Watching Mary today, I suppose. Some of her mannerisms."

William stood and walked to the window with his hands crossed behind his back. "Since you were only four when we came here, I guess you don't remember much." With his back to Millie, he scanned the scene below. "We'd just lost her. You needed a mother, and here you had many. And many fathers. Plenty of playmates and a good education. And I've kept busy repairing the buildings." He turned to face her. "You like it here, don't you?"

He was avoiding the question. Grief formed wrinkles on his normally genial face.

Despite his discomfort, she had to proceed. "I remember sitting on her lap. She was reading me a picture book. But I can't see her face."

He swallowed, then a wistful smile formed. "Yes, you loved books even as a toddler. What a bright little thing you were. And are!" He stepped to the bureau. "Speaking of that—" He opened the top drawer and drew out a book. "The library finally got that copy of *Little Dorrit* you've been asking for. It came while you were away, so I snatched it up for you."

He placed the book next to Millie on the table. It was one of the most powerful levers he could have chosen to pry her mind away from her topic. She picked it up, but she wouldn't look at it. Not yet.

"Do you have a photograph of her?"

Without a word he returned to the bureau, opened the top drawer, and reached beneath the clothing. He pulled out a rectangular frame and brought it to her.

She dropped the book onto the table and, trembling, took the frame in both hands.

It held a photograph of her father, beardless and much younger, posing with a small woman—*Mother*—who wore a dark dress with a dome-shaped skirt under a black shawl. William stood to her left, gripping the back of a chair where an inverted top hat rested on the seat as an elegant prop. Her mother's hair was dark, parted in the middle, and done up in a bun, with smooth bangs sloping across her forehead and tucked behind her ears. Her lips were set in a thin, dignified line, but her large-lidded eyes made her look sad. Her father, evidently, couldn't keep his lips from edging upward.

"Taken on our wedding day. You may keep it."

He paced back to the window and resumed his previous posture.

So much more lay locked in his mind, maddeningly close, yet out of Millie's reach. Speaking about Mother caused him pain, but his silence caused Millie just as much distress. Why couldn't he share his painful memories? Then the sorrow might be halved for both of them. Wouldn't that be consistent with communism?

A twinge of pique gripped her chest. Like father, like daughter.

No wonder she had such a hard time getting close to people. But she wouldn't follow her father's example. She wouldn't shut people out like her father was doing to her.

"Thank you." She rose, pressing the picture to her chest. "I'll treasure it."

She took the copy of *Little Dorrit* from the table and left the room without looking back.

In her own room, she couldn't tear her eyes from the photograph. Her mother had been tiny, despite the voluminous skirt that gave her breadth. Her slender fingers that rested on William's forearm seemed no larger than a child's. Millie ran her finger down the pictured gown's bodice, counting the large black buttons. Ten. She squinted at the brooch that fastened her mother's shawl. What had become of that? Though she studied her mother's face until her head ached, the image awakened no memory.

Three quick knocks on her door made her jump. Had her father reconsidered? Still holding the photograph, she opened the door. To her surprise, Tirzah stood in the hall.

"May I come in?"

Flustered, Millie stared blankly. "Oh! Of course!" She motioned Tirzah into the room. "I was expecting someone else. Please, take a seat."

"Thank you." Tirzah remained standing. "I won't stay a minute."

Tirzah's confidence spread energy and vibrations through the room. She wasn't very tall or even beautiful—Ann Hobart and Leonora Hatch had lovelier features. Yet with her engaging hazel eyes, her round cheek bones that pulled her lips up in a perpetual smile, her perfect teeth, and the tiny auburn curls that bobbed on her forehead, she exuded more charm than any Community woman.

"May I help you?"

"Oh, my dear, you already have."

Tirzah took a step closer to Millie and reached for her hand. Millie set the portrait on the table, face down, and presented both hands to Tirzah, who took them in hers.

"What a lovely account you've written of Mrs. Arnotte's faith cure. You're right—it must be printed in the *Circular*. But you're wrong to think it needs my touch. It shall go in word for word as you've penned it."

Millie couldn't hold Tirzah's intense gaze. Flushing with joy, she lowered her eyes.

Tirzah dropped her hands and stepped back. "You've described it so well. You're an excellent writer." She flashed her hand dismissively. "Better than I, I freely admit."

Millie's tongue seemed glued to the roof of her mouth, but she managed to whisper, "Thank you."

Surely she was dreaming. She hadn't expected the account she'd written on the train to garner Tirzah's praise. To avoid seeming too forward, and to ease the stab of rejection she feared, she'd attached a note inviting Tirzah to edit the story.

Tirzah smiled graciously. "I told Father Noyes all about it at the basket-making bee. He read it and approved it. A week from now, you shall see it in print. Now, I mustn't keep you. You're expecting someone. Good-bye, my dear."

As Millie looked on, still awestruck, Tirzah floated toward the door and let herself out.

Millie dropped onto her bed, her head in a whirl. She picked up *Little Dorrit* and tried to read, but even Charles Dickens had no power to direct the crowded thoughts that wandered about in her brain, bumping into each other like passengers on the railway platform. Far from being annoyed with her, Father Noyes had approved her words. Her article would be published. And Tirzah had praised her writing.

That night during most of Meeting, Millie's mind continued to wander. Eventually Theodore Noyes turned the lectern over to Father Noyes. The prophet cleared his throat two or three times and attempted to speak, but no words came out. Millie felt her cheeks warm with embarrassment for him, but that was silly. His confident stance showed he wasn't diminished in the least by the throat ailment he'd suffered from for years that routinely stole his voice. He barked out a cough, and his voice issued forth, scratchy but strong.

"By now you have heard the good news about Mrs. Arnotte. I am happy to report that her faith has cured her arm and hand. I have here a full account of the case, and I believe it would be edifying for you all to hear the entire truth of it. What the human knowledge of Yale Medical School could not accomplish—"

He turned to glare at Theodore, seated behind him on the stage. His son responded to the dig by uncrossing and re-crossing his legs.

"—one devout believer, walking by faith, not by sight, achieved overnight."

He reached inside his coat and pulled out the folded sheets of vellum writing paper—the ones Millie had delivered to Tirzah. Heat rushed up her neck and into her face. Would Father Noyes announce her name from the platform? Would he praise her writing skills before the entire Community as Tirzah had done in person that afternoon? Such words from Father Noyes could transform her from being an obscure, nearly invisible part of the Community to someone the Community recognized as especially talented.

No—such thoughts were haughty and selfish. Each member of the Community was as important as every other member. No person's talents were superior to another's—except for Father Noyes's, of course.

Father Noyes began reading her account, but his voice stuck, and he handed the paper to Theodore, who stood and read the rest. When he finished, Father Noyes took back the papers, coughed several times, and said, "I would be remiss if I did not credit Tirzah, editress of the *Circular*, for providing this thorough and well-written account."

A weight like a brick settled in Millie's stomach. He had credited Tirzah with her work.

Would Tirzah object? Of course not. From where she was seated, and with Father Noyes's diminishing hearing, it would be impossible for her to correct him, even if she felt it necessary. Besides, he had spoken accurately. Tirzah had *provided* the report to him. Millie could fault neither the prophet nor Tirzah. Exhaling slowly, Millie released her offense. She needed this lesson to squelch her rising pride.

After Meeting, Millie watched as men and women paired up for interviews. Theodora left with Ellen's father, and Ellen walked away with Mr. Warne. Millie returned alone to her own sleeping room, reminding herself she wasn't missing much.

After donning her nightdress, she hopped into bed with *Little Dorrit* and pulled the quilt up to her neck. Before long she set the book aside and pulled her mother's photograph into bed. She studied it until her eyes grew bleary. Then she extinguished her lamp.

In her dream she was a little girl sitting on a wood floor playing with a doll. Gentle feminine arms scooped her up and onto the lap of a

crinoline-lined skirt. Slender fingers held a book with pictures of tabby kittens dressed in aprons. Little girl Millie melted into a rocking motion as a melodic voice soothed her ears.

"Three little kittens, they lost their mittens, And they began to cry..."

She turned to see the face of the woman but found herself back on the floor. A panicked craving rose to her throat as she scanned the room. A woman sat by the window next to a chair that held an inverted top hat. Little Millie dashed to the woman and scrambled onto her lap, climbing over the flowing folds of the skirt. She faced the woman.

It was her mother's face, exactly as it appeared in the photograph.

Taking the face between her two pudgy hands, she drew herself forward. She kissed the closed lips. The woman didn't respond. Her large-lidded eyes stared, unblinking, as if they didn't see.

"Mama!" screamed the little girl, tapping the woman's soft white cheeks with her open hands. "Mama!"

The expression didn't change. It remained as lifeless as the photograph.

Millie woke with a start, her heart racing. She whispered into the darkness.

"Mama."

Chapter 5: Observer

Millie rose before dawn at the sound of the early bell. Although an icy wind blew outside, her room with its heat register was snug and warm. In the dim lamplight she washed at her washstand, then slipped into her short dress with its attached pantalettes, trying to shake off her dreams. She'd had the same dream multiple times—sometimes with a warm feeling of contentment, but sometimes with an overwhelming terror.

Although she was already a bit late, she decided to take the tunnel, which took a few minutes longer, rather than face the wintry wind. She made her way down two flights of stairs to the main floor, then followed the separate stairway in the Little Court into the cellar, where lamps were already burning. She hurried through the Chain Room and the arched underground passage to the communal kitchen.

Last night when she'd seen her name listed under *Tontine* on the work assignment board, she'd released an exasperated sigh. It was her least favorite job, but thankfully she didn't have to work in the kitchen very often. To prevent boredom, the Committee changed each member's work assignments frequently. No doubt she'd soon be back working with the children again.

In the spacious cellar of the Tontine, half a dozen other women and one man were already getting started on the hot breakfast. At the far side of the room at the yeast bread table, Mrs. Charles—one of a handful of Negroes from the Outside whom the Community employed—was kneading bread dough, her pink palms flashing rhythmically.

"Good morning, Millie."

Millie turned to see Constance's friendly face—a welcome sight.

Before she could return the greeting, Harriet Skinner, Father Noyes's sister, began barking out orders. "Millie, wash the potatoes. Constance, go ahead and mix up the hasty pudding. Eliza!"

A wiry, energetic woman of about sixty, Mrs. Skinner managed the kitchen with factory-like precision. She'd given Millie, the youngest woman there, a job that was impossible to get wrong.

That was fine. Millie opened the door of the potato washing machine and removed the two peeling bricks. Years ago one of the men had invented this labor-saving contraption, which looked like a white wooden barrel lying on its side. Through the door in the top, Millie poured several pitchers of water. After dropping three dozen potatoes inside, she secured the door, grasped the rotary handle, and cranked it. The potatoes splashed and thumped.

When two hundred potatoes were baking, she presented herself to Mrs. Skinner. Starting today, she intended to be friendlier—even toward this intimidating woman—so she flashed her a cheery grin. "It's nice to be eating your breakfasts again after being at Wallingford."

Mrs. Skinner peered over her wire-rimmed glasses. "We eat our bread with gladness and singleness of heart—whether here or at Wallingford. Help with the breakfast cakes."

Millie turned quickly toward the table, hiding the flush she felt rising in her cheeks. She took a spot next to Constance and grabbed a mixing bowl. The wooden spoon trembled in her hand. She must stop being so sensitive.

She cracked two eggs into the bowl and beat them, then scooped up an amount of butter about the size of a hen's egg and dropped it in the bowl with a small cup of sugar. Creaming the eggs, butter, and sugar into a smooth, lemon-colored paste calmed her enough to speak.

"How are you feeling today, Aunt Constance?"

"Fine." Constance responded brightly, as if nothing were different. "And you?"

"Your arm doesn't hurt?"

"It ached a bit when I woke up." Constance passed Millie the flour, baking powder, and salt. "But I told God I wanted to glorify Him with both hands today, and it started feeling better."

Her mood was as sunny as the golden egg yolks—and it was contagious. Millie poured a pint of milk into her bowl and let Constance's good cheer spread over her.

"Too bad Father Noyes didn't name you as the author of what he read last night." The older woman spooned batter into a muffin tin. "He made it sound as if Tirzah had written it."

"It's better this way." Millie looked behind them to assure no one else had heard. "It shouldn't be about me, but about you."

Constance tucked in her chin. "I couldn't disagree more." She raised her eyebrows and pointed her index finger heavenward. "It's not about *me*—but about *God.*"

Millie directed her embarrassment into the batter, mixing with large, strong strokes. Evidently she couldn't say anything right today. First she'd offended Mrs. Skinner, and now Constance.

With horror she stopped stirring and stared at the over-mixed batter in her bowl. The breakfast cakes would come out of the oven as mountains instead of hills, and diners would suspect a novice had been in the kitchen.

With the hot breakfast nearly done, Mrs. Skinner directed the workers to start on the rest of the day's meals. They'd prepare food for the entire day and store it in the pantry in covered crocks. The Negroes would come in to set the food out, picnic style, at noon for dinner and at five-thirty for supper. Since she'd finish her work as early as ten o'clock, Millie could devote the rest of the day to the pastimes of her choice. That was the best part of kitchen duty.

Without approaching Mrs. Skinner again, Millie started washing potatoes for the next two meals. As she turned the crank, she tried to shake off the rebukes she'd received from the two older women, but Constance's words especially nagged at her. So much for trying to be friendlier. She'd rather stay in the shadows than be called out for her mistakes. Being invisible had its advantages.

According to Jessie, Millie's invisibility had kept her from years of unwanted interviews. Did she want that to change? After her initial surprise, Jessie had implied Millie was better off than other girls. Millie agreed. She was in no hurry to be a wife. In novels romance was sweet, noble, and life-changing. But being married to multiple older men wouldn't be like that. And as Jessie had pointed out, Henry, the only man Millie felt attracted to, was years away from being *teleoi.*

At Mrs. Skinner's command, Millie helped set trays of baked potatoes, breakfast cakes, and fried corn mush in the dumbwaiter. She interspersed the peaked cakes among the round ones, hoping to make them less obvious.

Mrs. Skinner gave a nod of approval at the load and called the table attendants above through the speaking tube. "Pull it up, girls!"

* * *

Monday morning Millie grinned at the big fluffy snowflakes that tickled her face as she crossed the Quadrangle. Her heart fluttered with joy. Today she was taking one step closer to her goal of becoming a writer. For the first time ever, she'd found her name posted under *Circular* on the job assignment board.

She entered the Little Court and rounded the corner of the library, pausing to gaze with satisfaction at the Best Quilt hanging on the wall. Of all the women's jobs depicted by the squares—phonographer, factory supervisor, bookkeeper, lathe operator, silk skeiner—the only one that had sent shivers up her spine when the quilt was first displayed was the Journal Editor block. Often over the last four years she'd admired the embroidered image of Tirzah's desk and pictured herself sitting there.

She skipped down the front steps of the Mansion house. As she followed the driveway, the snowflakes tickled her face, and she swallowed a giggle. She studied the patterns of the intricate white crystals as they landed on her black cape. If she were still a little girl, she'd stick out her tongue to catch the falling flakes. But since she was a young woman going to work at the *Circular,* she only imagined herself savoring the icy crystals.

She crossed the road at the end of the driveway as a group of students scurried into the Seminary, just to the south. Directly in front of her stood the building that housed the printing office. Previously the horse barn, the two-story building with a walkout basement now contained the store that sold goods to Outsiders, the post office, a tailor shop, and a shoe shop on the main floor above the office of the *Circular* and the print shop.

As she entered the front door, the pungent scent of shoe leather greeted her. Trembling with excitement, she descended the stairs and stepped through the door marked *the Circular*.

A tingle of delight ran down her spine at the sight of Tirzah's desk. Two women sat at other desks nearby. Across the large room above a long counter, trays of sorts like those at Wallingford covered the wall. Between the desks and the counter, separating the two spaces, stood a large rolling chalkboard with headlines scribbled on it.

Tirzah sprang up and advanced gracefully. "Miss Langston!

You've come to us!" She touched the back of Millie's arm and pointed to some hooks against the wall that held several capes identical to hers. "You know Mrs. Thayer and Mrs. Burt."

Millie hung her cape and greeted the other women, who nodded and continued proofreading.

"Come have a seat!" Tirzah motioned Millie to a chair and settled into her own. "Now, Millie, let me explain why you're here." She studied Millie with penetrating hazel eyes. "Our Mr. Pitt, who runs our press, received a letter from Mr. Jocelyn at Wallingford. He told Mr. Pitt in no uncertain terms that if he didn't snatch you up as a typesetter, he'd request you move to Wallingford to set type for him."

A flood of emotions assaulted Millie. Had she truly received such a glowing reference from a man she'd met only briefly? If she did move to Wallingford, she could spend more time with Jessie. What fun they could have! But Wallingford had so little to offer compared to Oneida, and their food was disgusting.

Tirzah eyed her expectantly.

"That was certainly kind of him."

"So you already know how to set type?"

For a moment Millie felt like the miller's daughter whose father told the king she could spin straw into gold. "No, not at all." She shook her head. "Mr. Jocelyn let me set one line as a demonstration. That's the extent of my knowledge."

"Oh! Well, don't care for it." Tirzah patted her hand. "You'll be fully trained. But we have it on Mr. Jocelyn's authority that you're what's called a natural, so I know you'll learn quickly." She motioned to one of the women. "Mrs. Thayer will explain everything. But if I can be of assistance, don't hesitate to call on me at any time."

How different Tirzah's spirit was from Mrs. Skinner's. In fact, Millie had never worked under anyone who made her feel so welcome and so valued.

Mrs. Thayer spent the next three hours at the compositor's counter with Millie, patiently explaining and demonstrating. She double-checked Millie's initial attempts and praised her accuracy. At last she gave her a short article to compose onto a form independently, and Millie set to work.

When Mrs. Thayer and Mrs. Burt asked if they could leave for dinner, Tirzah looked up from her work absently, her pencil

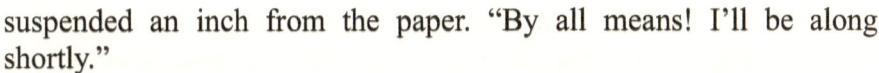

suspended an inch from the paper. "By all means! I'll be along shortly."

She continued writing as the women donned their capes and left the room.

Though Millie was hungry, too, she wanted to complete her task. To stop now would be like leaving a puzzle unfinished. As a comfortable silence settled over the room, Tirzah seemed oblivious to her surroundings. Millie placed the sorts as quietly as she could so she wouldn't disturb her supervisor's concentration.

Suddenly the door flew open with a bang, and a man strode powerfully into the room. Theodore Noyes. "Tirzah! Good! You're here. Can we talk?"

Even from across the room, tucked away in her corner, Millie sensed his agitation.

Tirzah looked up at Theodore's eyes glaring out from under his stern eyebrows. His fists were clenched, and his jaw was set.

"Theodore!" She dropped her pencil and motioned gracefully with her right hand for him to sit at the next desk. "Whatever is the matter?"

He strode to the chair, grabbed it with both hands, and pulled it within a foot of Tirzah. After turning its back toward her, he sat facing her, straddling the chair with his long legs. He clasped his hands together with his elbows on the chair back and rested his bearded chin on his knuckles. "It's this wretched Victor Hawley business again."

With Theodore's back to her and Tirzah possibly having forgotten she was there, Millie observed them without being observed. Now that Theodore had mentioned a name, if she made her presence known, she'd embarrass him. She turned away from the pair and soundlessly shifted over until the chalkboard hid them from view. Still, she could hear every word.

"What's happened now?" Tirzah asked.

"Father told me Victor and Mary were trumpeting their special love like a beacon for all to see at the basket-making bee."

"Uh-oh! That is upsetting. He used such a mixed metaphor as that?"

"It's not funny, Tirzah," Theodore chided, exasperation edging his voice. "I've been away for a week, and when I come back, the first thing he wants to discuss is Victor Hawley. Not the accounts. Not my plans for the new wing. But Victor Hawley and Mary Jones."

"I know what your father saw," said Tirzah, calmly yet sympathetically. "I hoped he wouldn't trouble you with it."

"Trouble me is all he does these days." Hearing Theodore stand, Millie feared he'd look her way, but she didn't turn around. She heard him pace toward the door he'd left open, close it gently, and return.

"What can Victor be thinking? After they pestered us incessantly about having a child, and after we sent Mary to Wallingford. She's carrying my child, after all, not his. And not by my choice. I was in favor of their having a baby together. You know that."

"I know. I remember it well." Tirzah's voice was soothing. "But you did what was required of you, and you showed great love and holiness toward Mary. With her history, and in her emotional state, you were the best choice—the only choice—if she were to bear a child. Only your strength could make up for her weakness. You've acted admirably, and the whole family knows it."

"But does my father know it?"

"He does, Theodore. He's invested all his confidence in you."

It seemed odd to hear Tirzah encouraging Theodore and assuring him of his father's support. But that just confirmed Tirzah's power. As one of the Community's first members and their prophet's niece, she was the most influential woman of the second generation.

"Then why does he brush me off?" Theodore's tone became more measured. "I've spent months researching the most advanced ventilation systems for the new wing. I've gone to Philadelphia to meet with Dr. Leeds himself. My plans will make our new building as hygienic as any building in the country. But he'd rather I spend my time handling these petty squabbles. He jerks me around as if I were on a chain—giving me authority one day, taking it back the next."

"That's how it seems to you because so much depends on you, and you suffer under the weight of it. But I see what your father sees. A strong leader. A brilliant thinker. A father to our next generation." They sat in silence for a minute, and then Tirzah asked gently, "What will you do about Victor?"

Theodore let out a loud breath. "I'll send him to Wallingford for a few months. I'll let him come back when Mary's time gets close."

His words stabbed Millie's heart. Victor would be exiled—to the penal colony.

"Your father will be pleased."

"Thank you for bearing my burdens, Tirzah. You always have."

As Theodore left the room, Millie's cheeks burned. Now Tirzah would notice her and realize she'd heard everything.

But she apparently didn't. Tirzah's footsteps moved toward the capes, and the door opened and shut with a click, leaving Millie alone in the room. Relieved, she puffed out her cheeks with a long exhale.

As she headed for her own cloak, she eyed the spot where Theodore and Tirzah had sat. Theodore's back had faced Millie's side of the room except when he approached Tirzah. He could easily have missed seeing Millie in her corner. But from Tirzah's desk, Millie's legs and feet would have been visible despite the chalkboard. And surely Tirzah had seen Millie's cape hanging next to her own. Perhaps Tirzah wanted to spare Theodore the embarrassment of knowing his first remark about Victor had been overheard. Still, it was odd Tirzah wouldn't have admonished Millie to ignore the conversation once Theodore had left.

That afternoon, Millie continued setting type, and Tirzah gave no indication she was aware of Millie's eavesdropping. But at the end of the day when Millie donned her cape to leave, Tirzah motioned for her to take a seat again. Millie's heart fluttered. Would Tirzah scold her for having overheard Theodore's words?

But Tirzah only flattered her for being such a quick study. In fact, Tirzah almost seemed to be buttering her up. But she had no reason to curry Millie's favor. Perhaps she treated all new workers this way.

At last Tirzah dropped her eyes and rearranged some papers on her desk. "Now, Millie, I wonder if I may impose upon you."

Millie blinked in surprise. She'd read her supervisor correctly after all.

Appearing reticent, Tirzah lifted her eyes and bit her lip. "You see, Father Noyes wants me to create a play about Mrs. Arnotte's faith cure—to be performed for Outsiders during the spring tourist season. To portray the glory of our experiment to the world. Since you observed the miracle and wrote such a lovely article about it—who better than you to write the play?"

Millie's heart skipped. This could be the opportunity she'd been dreaming of—to use her writing talents in an even bigger way than writing for the *Circular*. Immediately doubt seized her. "But I've never written a play before. Are you sure—"

"Oh, you'll have no trouble." Tirzah rose and ushered Millie to the door. "You're such a good writer. Let me know if you need a day off. I promised Father Noyes he'd have the script by the end of the week."

Walking back to the Mansion House, Millie reviewed the day's events. The morning's giddy enthusiasm had given way to a hot uneasiness that the winter air couldn't quell. If only she could un-hear Dr. Noyes's complaints about his father and his decision about Victor. It was so unfair. Victor shouldn't be sent away. He and Mary had done nothing wrong—their relationship was sweet. And Mary's baby should have been Victor's.

But such things were beyond Millie's control. There was no use dwelling on them. She summoned the delight she should be feeling. She was working on the *Circular,* and now Tirzah had asked her to write a play. Her dreams were coming true.

* * *

Millie sat in the library, her pencil flying across the page. Tirzah had granted her two days away from typesetting to write the play. She wrote non-stop. Often she took out the little brass pencil sharpener to expose more graphite. By now the rubber eraser atop the pencil had shrunk to a pathetic nub. At last she wrote the final line of the final scene, smiling to herself at its double meaning.

After dinner, still brimming with a sense of accomplishment, she joined a procession of members rushing over the freshly shoveled path that connected the Tontine to the Little Court. Inside, she stopped with the rest, and, like them, rubbed her hands together to warm them. They crowded together with their backs to the Fire Department, the thirty green papier-mache buckets filled with sand that lined the four shelves on the north wall of the vestibule. Several people made a show of examining the gigantic century plant, a favorite ritual. It would bloom only once every hundred years, they'd heard, so their chances of ever seeing a nascent blossom were slim.

Millie examined the plant herself. Only a new leaf was unfurling today: a fitting symbol of her role as a budding author. She extended a finger to touch the sliver of greenery, wishing it and her own leaves, newly written, Godspeed.

Glancing at the cellar stairs to her left, Millie pictured her childhood teacher, Aunt Sarah, who'd be working in the Chain Room with the children now, helping them make the chains for the animal traps that supported the Community financially. When Millie was only eight or nine, Aunt Sarah had encouraged her to write poems and stories and had fawned over her first silly attempts. She'd love to hear about the play. Millie skipped down the stairs, strode past the Turkish bath, and entered the Chain Room.

Inside the large musty room, children from six to twelve years old stood around low tables. Instantly she felt like a little girl again. The smell of iron mingled with sweat and the constant clicking of metal on metal brought back a flood of memories. She'd spent an hour here almost every day for six years. Shaking off the heavy sensation of the past, she joined Aunt Sarah where she stood at one of the tables.

"Millie! What brings you here?"

Her teacher's delighted expression warmed Millie's heart. It had been too long since she'd connected with her, but nowadays Millie had no reason to come here. The room never lacked for women helpers because it offered mothers a chance to work side by side with their children for an hour without being accused of philoprogenitiveness. Today, as usual, many women were here, each relishing this special time with her own child.

The image of the unmovable face in the rectangular frame on her bureau flashed in Millie's mind. She'd never had a mother of her own to join her in the Chain Room.

Millie sidled in between Aunt Sarah and a little girl. "I'm writing a play about Mrs. Arnotte's faith cure." She helped the girl push a stubborn link through an opening. "It was Father Noyes's idea. He wants us to perform it for Outsiders this spring."

Aunt Sarah's eyes shone with pride. "And he chose you to write it?"

Millie lifted her shoulders. "Well, he wanted Tirzah to, and she asked me to do it." Seeing Aunt Sarah's expression fall a bit, Millie added, "I wrote the account Father Noyes read at Meeting last week."

Aunt Sarah gave a knowing nod. "I thought I recognized your style. Of course, I knew only you had accompanied Mrs. Arnotte."

"Did you?"

"I keep track of my former pupils." She gave Millie's hand an encouraging squeeze. "You have talent, Millie. It's only right for you to use it to make a difference in the world."

That echoed Constance's words on the train: *We're showing the world a better way. A way that is right.* The same fervor she'd felt after they'd given away their basket throbbed in Millie's chest now.

"That's what I want. If I'm to be a woman and not a child, I want to do something important." Immediately she recognized the spirit of diotrephiasis, or love of preeminence, that hung in her words. "Not that what we all do isn't important."

"Of course." Aunt Sarah's kind eyes showed no offense. "Just by following Bible Communism, we're helping to bring this earthly kingdom nearer the Kingdom of Heaven. Every duty we perform for our brothers and sisters here is an act of worship, a living sacrifice." She squeezed Millie's hand. "But I understand what you mean. You're young, and you have a fire inside. That's good. Many young people seem to have fire, but not for things of God. Not like my generation."

Millie nodded politely. She'd never considered whether her fellow young people had fire inside, and if they did, for what. No doubt every generation from the beginning of time had made a similar complaint about its successors. "Would you do me a favor?"

"Certainly."

"Would you read over the script before I give it to Tirzah? Just to tell me if it's good or not?"

Aunt Sarah smiled. "Of course. But I already know it will be."

Aunt Sarah had always made Millie feel she could achieve things. She'd insisted Millie take Latin, and she'd introduced her to novels. She was the closest thing Millie had to a mother—just as encouraging as the women in the room were to their children. She felt her confidence about the play growing already.

Her eyes came to rest on the brick arch on the south wall of the room where the now filled-in tunnel to the previous Children's House had been. She suppressed a shiver. "Do you remember when you read us *A Christmas Carol* for the first time?"

Aunt Sarah shook her head and rolled her eyes good-naturedly. "How scared you all were of Marley's ghost!"

"I always pictured him coming right through that arch." Millie hugged her upper arms. "For a long time whenever we worked in here, I kept hearing him moan, 'I wear the chain I forged in life!' I thought the more chains I made in here, the more tormented I'd be when I became a ghost."

Aunt Sarah chuckled as if Millie had made her day.

* * *

The next morning as Millie headed down the drive, the brave January sun matched the hope in her heart. Would Tirzah praise the script? Millie couldn't wait to give it to her.

The first to arrive in the newspaper office, Millie set to work right away. She commanded her fingers to steady themselves enough to pick out each tiny sort and place it in the compositor's stick. Meanwhile, jittery moths flitted inside her stomach.

Within a few minutes, she heard the door creak open. Tirzah entered, but it was a Tirzah Millie hadn't seen before. Instead of gliding into the room, she shuffled to the coat hooks, hung her cape, and drifted to her desk. Her eyes were swollen, her cheeks were pale, and her usually upturned mouth was drooping. Even the auburn curls on her forehead seemed limp and listless.

Millie's first impulse was to rush to her side and comfort her like a child who'd skinned a knee. Her father's words sounded in her mind —she had so much to give. But she and Tirzah weren't on those terms. That would be presumptuous.

When the other women came in, they went right to work, but a tangible pall hung over the entire office. Tirzah's magnetism controlled the ambiance wherever she went, whether for good or ill. She could bring sunshine to a cloudy day, as she had three days ago to Millie and to Theodore, or she could cast a shadow upon a sunny scene, as she was doing today. She barely forced a smile when Millie handed her the script.

Millie felt nervous all evening, knowing Tirzah could be reading her play at that very moment. She finished *Little Dorrit*, which she'd neglected while writing her play, and went to the library in search of something new. Nothing looked interesting, so she picked out *Northanger Abbey* to reread. Jane Austen's humor and facility with words might be able to distract her. The stuffy glamour and ridiculous propriety of the Pump Room at Bath were a universe away from life at Oneida.

Returning to Ultima Thule with the book, she decided to check on Virginia. She tapped lightly on her door, hoping to hear Virginia's typical happy step. Instead, slower footsteps sounded, and when the door opened, Millie stared into the sullen face of Ellen Stoner.

"Oh! Ellen! Is Virginia here?"

"No, she's not."

Millie wrinkled her forehead. "Do you know where she is?"

Why would Ellen be visiting Virginia if Virginia wasn't there?

"She may be in her room."

Millie willed her eyes not to roll. Ellen obviously didn't intend to offer more information than necessary. She'd have to pull it out of her. "But this is her room."

"No. She switched places with me today."

"Oh. So where is she now?"

"201. Right outside the Big Hall."

"I guess I'll visit her there, then." As Ellen shifted and started to close the door, Millie spoke quickly. "Welcome to Ultima Thule."

"Thank you, I'm sure," Ellen sneered, clicking the door shut.

Millie returned to her room with a heavy feeling in her stomach. Virginia had been moved to the most visible place in the whole Mansion House. Everyone would be aware of her comings and goings, especially the many older men who would request interviews with her now. And sweet Virginia would no doubt accept every invitation.

Chapter 6: Practice

The next morning was clear and sunny again, and the mounds of snow that covered the ground were beginning to shrink. Millie had worked at the *Circular* for two days so far, and the weather there had been first tropical, then arctic. Perhaps today would be temperate.

When she entered, the room was already bustling. Fridays, she learned, were the days when the paper was *put to bed*. Tirzah had to finish any remaining articles and get Father Noyes's approval, everything had to be proofread, and all the forms had to be laid out in their final version. Extra workers had come in to set type, so Millie stood with several women at the compositor's counter all day. Tirzah's mood was cheery and businesslike. A spirit of camaraderie, like the spirit at a working bee, reigned over the office.

At the end of the day, Tirzah pulled out a gallon jug of apple cider, and they all drank together, reviewing the highlights and close calls of the day. Millie wasn't sure which tasted sweeter: the cider or the feeling of a job well done.

As each woman went for her own cape, Millie approached Tirzah and asked if she'd read the script.

Tirzah shook her head as if trying to recall a long-ago event. Then a smile crept across her face. "Oh, the play! Yes, you've done it again! Such a way with words you have—and such a lovely hand! It's heavenly to read."

Embarrassed but pleased, Millie dropped her eyes.

"Father Noyes agrees wholeheartedly. He said it will be an auspicious beginning to the tourist season, and he wants it performed early in May."

For the first time Millie realized that Father Noyes would assume Tirzah had written the play. Unless Tirzah had told him otherwise. She couldn't ask the question without sounding as if she desired acclaim—or worse, as if she were accusing Tirzah of stealing her work.

Trying to hide her thoughts, Millie nodded. "I'm glad."

She started toward the wall to claim her cape.

"Now, we must decide how to proceed." Tirzah raised her index finger. "Do you intend to be the director as well as the author, like the great Bard himself?"

Millie stopped in her tracks, snickering at the effusive comparison. "I've never directed a play before."

"Oh, well, I've been in many plays." Tirzah touched Millie's arm and led her to a chair. She pulled out the script and laid it on the desk between them. "If we get you some experienced actors, you'll do fine. In my opinion, no one can know the play as well as the author, who sees it all in his mind's eye. So you shall be our director."

Tirzah hadn't given her the chance to say no. She'd taken ownership of the process while still keeping Millie involved.

Millie cleared her throat. "The actors. I don't really know...."

"Fear not!" Tirzah interrupted in the most pleasant way. "I've chosen the three main characters already. In fact, I spoke to them at breakfast, and they've agreed to do your bidding."

She spread out her arms and bowed with a dramatic flourish.

Millie giggled. While she'd been eating her breakfast in the Tontine, Tirzah had been recruiting actors in the very same room. "Whom have you chosen?"

"You'll like this." Tirzah leaned forward conspiratorially. "Do you know Henry Hunter? Of course, you do. Everyone knows our dear Henry. *He* will be your Dr. Cragin. And none other than Leonora Hatch will be Constance—or Eunice, as you've called her. A nice touch. Do you remember when Leonora played Antigone? Now *that* was a performance!"

Millie grinned, caught up in Tirzah's enthusiasm.

"Oh! And little Martha Whitsong shall play *you*. I know she's young, but she has a strong voice, and that's one of the most important qualities for the stage, don't you agree?"

Millie's heart sank. She would be played by a twelve-year-old. But, after all, the age of Eunice's attendant would make little difference to the story. She nodded her assent.

Tirzah continued. "Do you have enough energy to stay and set the script?"

Millie looked at her quizzically.

"Yes! You and each actor shall have a printed script. I'll let Mr. Pitt know, and he'll help you set up the form for it." Tirzah patted the script as if it were a toddler's head. "You'll see Father Noyes has made some improvements." Tirzah's voice became reverent and tender. "He showed me much kindness last night in reading it on the spot and making revisions by his own hand."

Millie's eyes rested on the script. What had he changed? She raised her eyes to Tirzah. "What about the other actors?"

"There we must put our heads together. Give me a list of anyone you think should play any particular role. For the Criticism and Meeting scenes, we can bring in Mr. Underwood's rhetoric students."

Exhilaration washed over Millie—just like when the train had first pulled away from Oneida Community station. Unexpectedly, she was part of this production that had jerked into motion and was flying along the tracks under a full head of steam.

After Tirzah brought Mr. Pitt in and explained the project, Millie handed him the script.

Although he seemed perturbed at the interruption, he succumbed to Tirzah's request. Within minutes he'd laid out the form and returned to tend his press, leaving Millie alone to examine Father Noyes's revisions.

Several large Xs deleted certain passages. Everything pertaining to Father Noyes had been redacted. Millie flushed hot. Naturally Father Noyes wouldn't allow any actor to depict him, and he wouldn't stoop to act in a play himself. How naïve she'd been to include him. Drops of sweat formed on her forehead, and her stomach cramped with embarrassment.

Paging through the script, she saw that, other than the deletions, only a few words had been changed here or there, crossed out and written over with fountain pen. Many of the changes were helpful, but several made the dialogue sound stilted. But who was she to question Father Noyes, who'd been writing and publishing since before she was born?

* * *

The next day, Millie met several other women for sewing duty in the second floor Community workspace overlooking the Quadrangle. She'd much rather work with the sorts than with a needle and thread, but the *Circular* office was closed on Saturdays. She selected a torn apron to mend from the stack of projects at the window.

A slow, sad tune from the orchestra practicing in the Big Hall next door wafted into the room. Looking into the Quadrangle at the tulip tree staunchly anchored in the snow, leafless and barren, she longed for its fragrant blossoms. Summer seemed a lifetime away.

Apron in hand, Millie moved toward the chairs lining the wall. Mary Jones, looking lost in thought, sat by herself, her belly even rounder than it had been at the basket-making bee. Millie's heart brimmed with sympathy. If Victor had been sent to Wallingford, Mary might need a friend.

She took the seat next to her. "How are you feeling?"

Contentedly, Mary rubbed her abdomen. "Bursting with energy now that the birth is only three months away. But the little fellow kicks and kicks." Her complaint sounded proud, not annoyed. "He wants my attention, I presume."

Millie smiled to hide her concern. If Mary was this upbeat, she must not have heard that Theodore was sending Victor to Wallingford, and she had a bitter pill coming. But Theodore had calmed down after speaking to Tirzah. Perhaps he'd decided to let Victor and Mary enjoy each other's company after all. What possible harm could it do? And the joy it would bring Mary could only benefit the child she carried— Theodore's child.

Mary chatted happily as they sewed side by side. "I can't wait to put the little fellow into Victor's arms. I'll send for him as soon as the baby's born. When he's by my side, holding Baby, we'll feel as if he's our very own."

Millie scanned the room. Had anyone else heard Mary's words? With the music filling the air, Millie couldn't discern the other conversations, so probably not. Still, Mary was unwise to voice such thoughts in public.

"You know, it should have been Victor's." Mary leaned a little closer to Millie and lowered her voice. "Last January they promised us we could try for a child. But as soon as we started trying, they announced that everyone had to stop for a while. When some received permission to try again, Victor and I assumed we could, too. But then they told us we couldn't. Why would they go back on what they'd promised?"

The discordant note lingered in the air, making Millie's stomach turn. She had no answer. She raised her shoulders in a barely

perceptible shrug.

"So they sent me to Wallingford, and I got started by Theodore there."

Mary's forlorn look and plaintive tone pricked Millie's heart. Tears sprang to her eyes, and she blinked them back. She concentrated on her needle, hoping Mary had finished.

Mary shook herself a bit and brightened. "But then they let me come back, and Victor has been a dear. He's so concerned about me. He brings me strawberry leaf tea in the afternoon and cocoa every night. He even sings to Baby and tells him nursery rhymes." She giggled. "He'll be the best father. He's so good with children."

Millie relaxed. This subject was safe. "The kids loved his stories at the basket-making bee. And he was so good at teaching them to weave."

"I know. He's very patient, and so kind."

One of Victor's specialties, besides being a dental assistant, was catching and mounting insects. Both his vocation and his avocation required the same gentle touch Millie had seen him use with the children. She nodded. "He's a good man."

Mary let out a long contented sigh. "I know." She gave a little jump and dropped her mending as her left hand flew to rest on her midriff. "Baby agrees!"

They sewed in silence for a while. Surely Theodore had changed his mind about sending Victor away. Anyone could see that the stress of separating them wouldn't be good for Mary.

The orchestra had stopped practicing, and lively violin music lilted in from the Big Hall. Millie couldn't tell for sure, but she suspected Henry Hunter was playing. Although only eighteen, he was the Community's most accomplished violinist—even better than Frank Wayland-Smith, who'd been playing violin for a decade longer.

The cheery tune lifted Millie's mood as she contemplated Henry in the role of Dr. Cragin. He was a good actor—but more importantly, she'd get to spend time with him. She told Mary about her chance to direct the play.

"It's about Mrs. Arnotte's faith cure. I wrote it myself." She hoped she wasn't boasting. "Tirzah chose Henry Hunter to play Dr. Cragin and Leonora Hatch to play Constance. Father Noyes himself approved the script. Well, he changed a few things, but he approved it in the end."

Mary continued to sew. "Yes, they're very good at choosing actors and changing scripts." She spoke to the mending on her lap. "They have much practice in that department."

Millie stopped in mid-stitch at the double meaning of Mary's remark. Like a snapping violin string, it resonated to the core of her being.

She recalled how Tirzah had chosen her to write and direct the play, and she visualized the large Xs Father Noyes had drawn through her words. But Tirzah and Father Noyes had been nothing but helpful to her, and she should only be grateful to be involved in their project.

Her internal argument sounded off-key as she watched the gentle rise and fall of Mary's belly—where resided a child who'd been robbed of his or her rightful father before birth. Millie shifted uncomfortably. She shouldn't have sat next to Mary after all. There was nothing she could do for her, and her rebellious spirit was infectious. She made an excuse to take a break, and when she returned to the room, she sat with someone else.

* * *

When Millie arrived for the first play rehearsal the next Saturday afternoon, Henry Hunter was already in the Big Hall finishing a dramatic violin number to Tirzah's accompaniment. Millie wasn't a music aficionado, but the song made her want to throw her shoulders back and embrace the world.

With Henry's help, Millie arranged chairs in a circle on the stage. Soon Leonora, Martha, and the five other actors who had speaking parts arrived and took their places. As she handed a script and practice schedule to each one, they stared at her, awaiting further instructions.

Her mouth went dry.

Henry rubbed his hands together. "So, fellow thespians," he intoned, casting his gaze around the circle, "who's ready to thesp?"

Instantly Leonora mimed ripping the hem from her dress and looping it around her neck. "I'm dying to thesp!"

She dropped her head, letting her body slide limp to the floor in a reenactment of her Antigone finale. Everyone laughed and clapped as she rose to her feet and took several quick bows.

"Unfortunately," Millie giggled, "you have a happy ending in this play."

Henry had broken the ice resoundingly. Millie launched into her prepared instructions, then directed the actors to read through the script, scene by scene. When Henry read the lines for Dr. Cragin, he stroked his clean-shaven right cheek with his hand, the way Dr. Cragin stroked his beard, and tapped his lower lip with his index finger just as the real doctor often did. Millie and the others burst out laughing at his flawless imitation, making Henry lose his composure.

Millie's pleasure grew as the practice went on. Henry, Leonora, and Martha already sounded convincing, and the dialogue was even more powerful than it had sounded in her head. It would be a great performance.

As the actors went their separate ways, Henry stayed behind, helping Millie return the chairs to their places. "That was a good practice, Millie. Outstanding job with the script."

Millie's heart leapt. His compliments were balm to her soul. "Your imitation of Dr. Cragin was perfect. I loved it! Do you know him well?"

"He treated my mother for influenza last winter." The briefest of shadows crossed Henry's brown eyes. He shook off the memory, sending a tremor through his mound of thick black hair that brushed across the tops of his ears. His full lower lip transformed from an attractive pout to a smile that revealed perfect teeth. "He's a fine doctor."

As she studied him, Millie could barely withhold a shiver. With that classic nose and the slightest cleft in his chin, he was by far the most attractive young man in the Community.

"I remember how ill she was. I'm so glad she recovered."

He pursed his lips and nodded. "Anyway, that's when I learned to mimic him."

Millie returned his direct gaze. "What was that lovely piece you and Tirzah were playing when I came in?"

Henry snickered and rolled his eyes. "Oh, that was 'A Nice Dilemma We Have Here.' From *Trial by Jury.*"

Millie laughed. "No wonder it sounded so dramatic!"

Thank goodness she hadn't said any more. She'd been taken in by a silly melodrama.

Henry's eyes drifted to the piano. "Tirzah ordered it just for the two of us." He seemed to be imagining her on the bench. "When I play with anyone else, I'm not half as good. But Tirzah's magnificent. Playing with her, everything resonates." Holding an invisible violin in his left hand, he moved his right hand as if drawing an invisible bow. "The timbre of my violin improves, and my fingers find the perfect position."

Even Millie could imagine the notes he'd been playing.

He dropped his arms and faced her again. "Have you heard of *synergism*?"

"I have." Enjoying the vocabulary challenge and spurred by the passion in Henry's eyes, Millie recalled her language lessons. "It's when you get more from combining two things than you'd get from those things separately."

With a slow, playful nod, Henry studied her face, pursing his lips in exaggerated approval. "Exactly correct."

"I've worked some on my Greek, but more on my Latin."

"Good girl!" Speaking in a professorial tone, he punctuated each word with the wave of an imaginary director's baton. He looked back to the piano. "Well, when I play with Tirzah, it's synergism. I can't take the credit."

"Tirzah's wonderful. I work for her on the *Circular*, and it's remarkable how she pulls it all together."

"You work with her all day? Then you're fortunate, indeed." Henry's eyes glazed over. "What we could accomplish if we could spend six hours together."

Was he still talking about music? It didn't sound like it.

The chime of the supper bell roused him from his imaginations. "Supper! And not a moment too soon. I'm famished!" After a pronounced bow, he offered his arm. "May I escort you, milady?"

Millie slipped her hand around the inside of his elbow. His arm felt warm and strong.

She enjoyed her supper of hash, coleslaw, custard, and grapes more than she'd enjoyed any supper for a long time. Henry was right: It had been a good practice.

As others entered the hall, the word *synergism* echoed in her brain. Her father, Aunt Sarah, and even Aunt Constance had all mentored her. Tirzah had inspired her more than anyone with her vibrant, encouraging words, and she'd given her a chance to play a bigger role in the Community.

And Henry—wolfing down bites of food as he bantered cheerfully with others at the table. He'd spread his enthusiasm to Millie's entire cast. Without the help of Tirzah and Henry's magnetic personalities, her script would be mere words on a page. But with them, it would be even more than she'd envisioned. That was synergism.

But wasn't that just another word for *communism*? With everyone here working together, they'd produced something greater than the sum of its parts. Millie had never understood Father Noyes's vision as well as she did at that moment. And she'd never felt so satisfied to be a part of it.

Chapter 7: Mentor

When Millie arrived at the *Circular* office, she hung up her cape, and with her usual cheerful nod to Tirzah, started for the compositor's counter.

Tirzah rose and took three fluid steps toward her. "Millie! Come! You'll be working here today!" She motioned toward the little desk adjacent to her own. Seeing Millie's surprise and confusion, Tirzah laughed. "I want you to help me write today!"

Millie took the chair Tirzah pointed toward. "You want me to recopy something?"

"Oh, you *are* modest! I appreciate that so much." Tirzah's voice bubbled, as if she were presenting someone with a surprise gift. "From time to time, we need short articles for the *Circular* to fill in extra space." She pulled out a copy of the paper and pointed to an article of about ten lines at the bottom of a column. "You've probably noticed them."

Millie nodded enthusiastically. "Those are some of my favorite parts." She bit her lip, hoping she hadn't caused offense. "Not that I don't love your long articles—and Father Noyes's columns."

Unfazed, Tirzah returned a dazzling smile. "I agree completely. They're lighthearted and humorous, and one can read them in a mere minute. But for me, they're some of the hardest things to compose. I find myself having to dash them off on Fridays when everything here is all a-flutter. So I thought, why not have you write many of them up in advance, so we'll have them at hand? You're such an excellent writer. We're wasting your talents having you set type and proofread."

Was this actually happening? For the last three weeks as Millie had stood at the compositor's counter setting type or sat at one of the desks proofreading, she'd imagined the day she'd write articles herself. But that day was at least a year away. Or so she'd thought. Her heart swelled with delight.

After giving her a few tips, Tirzah let her get to work. Millie's hand trembled with excitement, but her mind was clear. She

immediately wrote down an idea that had popped into her mind while reading *Northanger Abbey*. By noon she'd amassed a small treasury of items for Tirzah's review. When the other women slipped out to dinner, she passed the papers to Tirzah.

As Tirzah read, her lips curled up more and more, and the little auburn curls on her forehead began to dance merrily. "Oh, Millie, you *are* clever! This one is my favorite:

'Water-Cure Establishment. –I will sprinkle clean water upon you, and ye shall be clean: from all your filthiness, and from all your idols, will I cleanse you. A new heart also will I give you, and a new spirit will I put within you: and I will take away the stony heart out of your flesh, and I will give you a heart of flesh.—Ezekiel xxxvi.25, 26.'

Of course, it's mostly Scripture, but you've set it up so cleverly that people will look on it in a whole new light."

Millie tingled all over at the praise. Tirzah read another: "To Jewelers.—A single pearl of great price! This inestimable Jewel may be obtained by application to Jesus Christ, at the extremely low price of 'all that a man hath!'"

Millie warmed. Had she gone too far afield on that one?

Tirzah waved the paper before her. "It's exactly what we need. The more of these you can concoct, the better. We shall never want for fillers with you writing for us."

Millie relaxed her hands. She'd been clenching them so tightly that fingernail marks studded her palms.

Suddenly all business, Tirzah rose to her feet. "Now, Millie, I have one more favor to ask. Eat your dinner first, but do this directly afterward." She rustled through some papers on the top of her desk and extracted a folded letter. "I might as well let you know," she said, her voice taking on a confidential tone, "that I have another reason for wanting to train you as a writer. This note," she waved it in the air, "informs Mr. Homer Barron that we have successfully started our child. So, you see, I'll need some assistance in the months ahead with my duties here. I'm depending on your aid in that department. But for now, would you be so good as to deliver him this announcement? You should find him at Willow Place at the trap factory."

At the factory, as Millie waited for Homer Barron to be called, noisy clatter filled the air, and a strong odor of sweat and steel stung her nose. She surveyed the hired workers at the rows of tables—mostly rumpled, stubble-faced men who slouched and scowled.

Suddenly her eyes widened. Standing a few tables away was Noah Martinson.

He noticed her at the same time, and his face lit with a wide grin.

At that moment Homer appeared, and she placed the note in his hand. She glanced toward Noah and nodded. She didn't dare speak to him here. Others would question how she knew him, and she couldn't give away Constance's secret.

As she returned to the newspaper office, her mind buzzed with questions. Why was Noah working at the trap factory? His father must have warmed toward the Community—otherwise Noah wouldn't seek employment here. Would she have a chance to see him again? She seldom went to Willow Place.

The afternoon was quiet. Several typesetters finished their work and left. Millie had several more ideas for little articles, and she filled two more pages before she began doodling, waiting for more inspiration.

Suddenly Tirzah jumped up from her desk and left the room. When she returned, she wore an odd look on her face. Perhaps she was experiencing morning sickness, even though it was midday.

At around three o'clock, after Mrs. Thayer left, Tirzah placed a letter in Mrs. Burt's hands, and Mrs. Burt exited, leaving only Tirzah and Millie in the office.

When the door clicked shut, Tirzah sat with a sigh and looked squarely at Millie with the same inscrutable expression she'd worn earlier. "It seems I've acted too soon and made a fool of us both."

Millie's heart plunged into her stomach. Had Tirzah already come to regret her decision to bring her on as a writer?

Tirzah studied her hands in her lap. "There is no baby after all. I sent you to Willow Place to relay a falsehood."

Millie cocked her head.

"That is, I didn't know then that it was a falsehood, but I know now. I was simply past my time. I've sent Mrs. Burt to Mr. Barron with the news."

Millie set down her pencil. An awkward situation, to be sure. "Oh, I'm sorry."

Tirzah lifted her chin, but her eyes drooped. "I'm not, to be honest." Her lower lip twitched. The cloud that had obscured the real Tirzah drifted away, and her true persona appeared. She looked vulnerable and tired. Her vibrant confidence had vanished, revealing a woman filled with doubts and insecurities—not so different from Millie herself.

"I'm relieved. There! The truth is out, standing before us, and we cannot ignore it." She motioned dramatically with both arms toward the center of the room, palms up, as if pointing to a disgusting ogre that had appeared out of thin air. "I didn't want a child—not by Homer. There was a time when I dreamed of being his, but now my only thought when we come together is—that he's not Edward."

Tears began to course down her cheeks. Tirzah cried silently at first, but soon great heaving sobs wracked her body as she buried her face in her arms atop her desk.

Millie went to her side and rubbed her shoulders.

Soon the spasms grew weaker. Tirzah lifted her head and turned into Millie's waist. Millie crouched so she was staring into the red eyes of her supervisor. Tirzah threw her arms around her neck and began sobbing again.

Millie felt Tirzah's hot tears brushing her cheek. Patting her, she whispered, "There, there. It's all right," again and again.

After a few minutes, Tirzah pulled herself away and dried her eyes with a handkerchief. "I think I'm better now. Please, sit down. The tears have stopped."

She stared absently at the far wall, beyond Millie's face. "Do you remember Edward Inslee at all? Many here don't think of him anymore, but I do."

Keeping her voice soft, Millie tried to match Tirzah's reflective mood. "I remember him playing the clarinet."

"Ah, the clarinet! He could make it sing more sweetly than a mourning dove." A single tear trailed down Tirzah's cheek, and she brushed it away with a limp hand. "The spring after he left, whenever I heard a mourning dove, I thought my Edward had returned."

"Sometimes I dream I'm walking in a meadow." Tirzah rose and strolled around the room, reenacting her dream. "I hear a mourning dove coo, and I turn to find Edward by my side. We walk together through the grass, hand in hand, the fresh wind blowing on our faces. I feel a deep, bubbling joy in my heart as I look into the peace of his beautiful eyes."

Tirzah placed her hand to her chest—dramatically, as if on stage. "Once I put my hand on my heart and said, 'I know in here that the child will be yours.' I clasped his neck, soaking in the depths of his dark, tender eyes, full of soul-love." She dropped her hands to her side, bowing her head. "Then I awoke—and he was gone."

She returned to stand before Millie. "Don't you think that if I were going to stop loving him, I would have done so by now?"

Enraptured with the heartrending performance she'd just seen, Millie couldn't reply.

But Tirzah didn't expect an answer. She lifted her chin wistfully. "I'm destined to love him the rest of my days, though I doubt I shall ever see his face again. Unless he makes peace with Father Noyes and rejoins the Community."

A lump formed in Millie's throat as she recalled the prayers that Haydn didn't know how to say. "Do you think that could ever happen?"

Tirzah dropped back into her seat. "If he showed Father Noyes a heart of flesh, instead of a stony heart, as you wrote. Perhaps. Perhaps."

They sat in silence for a few minutes. Finally, Tirzah straightened, and her eyes focused. "You've been good to hear me out, Millie. I can trust you. Though we haven't been friends long, I have a great affinity for you. Your spirit is sound. I know I can depend on you in my darkest hour. Of course, I hardly need say it, but I trust you'll keep our conversation in strictest confidence. The Community wants to believe I'm well over Edward by now, and there's no reason for them to know otherwise."

Millie nodded. "Of course." Constance's words seemed perfect. "Women can be allowed some harmless secrets."

"Yes, we can." Tirzah reached both arms across the corner of her desk, her delicate hands palms up. Millie placed her hands into Tirzah's, and Tirzah squeezed gently. "We certainly can."

Just then the door opened forcefully and Father Noyes strode into the room. With an astute glance he took in the intimate posture of the two women. Tirzah jerked her hands back and stood.

He closed the door. "Tirzah, I need to speak with you."

With a glance at Millie and nod toward the compositor's counter,

Tirzah signaled her to leave them. Millie skirted beyond the chalkboard, hidden from their view.

"How pleasant to see you!" No one would be able to tell Tirzah had been crying just moments before. "Please, sit down."

Glancing over her shoulder, Millie saw Father Noyes sit on top of the desk she'd been working at and peer down at Tirzah. His form, topped by his nearly white hair, towered over her like a great craggy mountain.

He surveyed the papers on Tirzah's desk. "I see you've finished the article we discussed last night." His voice was raspy but fully audible across the room. "Inslee made you think you had no writing talent, so you lost your confidence. But you've been blossoming. As I told you, when you're stuck, I'll get down in the mud with you and extract you."

"Without your kindness, I could never get along," Tirzah said. "Is there something else you're thinking of?"

"There's something we have neglected," Father Noyes rasped, "and it's time we make our foray into this fallow field. I want you and Harriet Skinner to go into the study of literature. Dig into it and show it up, just as I am doing with the American Socialisms."

Millie peeked out again from behind the chalkboard. He was speaking passionately about one of Millie's favorite topics.

"Theodore and I will attend to the sciences; you and Harriet attend to the literature. Study the *science* of literature. Get at the *causes* of literature." His eyebrows rose and fell erratically, and he dropped his right fist into his open left hand for emphasis. "Find out how this infernal German atheism got sifted into so much of our literature."

He got up from the desk and paced, causing the little sorts to vibrate in their trays. "I want literary criticism included in each issue of the *Circular*. You must criticize all the authors. Shakespeare and the English authors wrote with honest intentions, to entertain, but the Boston and German writers seek only to spread their atheism and hatred of revivals. That kind of writing is dishonest—needs to be kicked out!"

He moved his right leg spryly as if to boot the offending authors.

"But do not stop there." He waved both arms. "Criticize the critics. You can make a better critic than Margaret Fuller, or Miss

Peabody—or Miss Q-Body!"

Pleased with his pun, he sat down on the desk again with his arms crossed.

Tirzah seemed unable to grasp his enthusiasm. "It's something we haven't turned the Perfectionist lens on, you mean?"

"Ah! Quite!"

"I'll give it as much attention as I can." Tirzah's voice contained more doubt than passion. "Until the baby is started."

"Homer has not succeeded yet?" The prophet relaxed his posture and softened his tone.

As Tirzah shared her most private details, including the two notes she'd sent to Homer, Millie's stomach soured. She couldn't imagine sharing such intimate facts with the prophet.

"Well, if Homer cannot make a go of it, it may fall to me." He stroked his white beard along his square jaw. "Which might, in fact, be propitious. It's my duty to pursue stirpiculture in the consanguineous line. Breeding in and in is the way to gain the most excellent stock, and combining with you as my niece would be the best way to intensify the Noyes blood. I'm curious to see what kind of a child we could produce. Perhaps I shall have more than one child by you."

"I should like that very much."

Tirzah's tone was as light and airy as if someone had just invited her for a carriage ride.

Millie didn't like the pictures that sprang to her mind from Father Noyes's words. Tirzah's oldest child had been fathered by her other uncle, Father Noyes's brother, and such relationships weren't forbidden under complex marriage. But this conversation was much too frank for Millie's ears. She shook her head to banish the unwanted images.

"And now—would you like some criticism?" Despite his raspy voice, his tone became rich and fatherly.

Tirzah lifted her face. "Yes, of course."

Father Noyes cupped her chin in his hand and tipped it up toward him. "You've become a man-killer, and it's bad for you. I've observed that many men here worship you. And I perceive you like it."

She nodded. "That's true of my natural character, I'm afraid."

"Do not fear it. It doesn't frighten me." He stood and took her right hand in both of his. "I will make a league with you. I will take all your sins on me, as though they were mine. I will have charity for them but be as sincere about getting rid of them as if they were mine. I will make a better woman of you and bring you nearer to God." He placed his left hand on her head. "I don't quarrel with your power, but I want you to have a conversion in that part of your life, so you will use it for God."

"I'm at your disposal."

Tears trickled down Tirzah's cheeks, and Father Noyes wiped them away with his thick thumbs.

"You will emerge from this all as a mother of the Community." He drew her to her feet and dropped her hand. "Tirzah, your spirit is sound." He placed a hand on each of her shoulders as he faced her. "You and I have a great affinity for each other. Of anyone here, I know I can depend on you, even in my darkest hour."

"Of course you can." She nodded. "You always can."

Millie shivered as the prophet left the room. His parting words, so eerily similar to those Tirzah had spoken just minutes before, layered more discomfort upon her already unsettled heart.

She made a few loud clinks with the sorts to remind Tirzah of her presence.

"Oh, Millie!" she said. "Thank you for being so patient."

Millie returned to her desk, eyeing Tirzah's face for any sign of embarrassment.

Instead, Tirzah's countenance glowed. "Such a kind, goodhearted man, isn't he?"

Thank goodness she didn't expect a reply. Millie's skin was still crawling.

Tirzah shook herself and straightened her posture. "Now, Millie, you must help me with these literary criticisms. Do you read novels?"

The odd feelings dissipated as she guessed Tirzah's request. She nodded enthusiastically. "All the time."

Tirzah clapped her hands. "Oh, you'll be my salvation! With my music, I don't have time to read all he wants me to read. And I daren't disappoint him. You must tell me all about your favorite novels. Together we'll fulfill his request."

Exhilaration rose in Millie's chest. That she had something to offer this important and powerful woman was too good to be true. Of course she would help her in any way possible.

Chapter 8: Desire

Millie was in literary heaven. Every weekday she ate dinner with Tirzah and Mrs. Skinner as they discussed the literature Father Noyes wanted them to criticize. Millie volunteered to read stories and literary criticism in the *Atlantic Monthly* while Tirzah compared the Fireside Poets to Walt Whitman. Mrs. Skinner tackled the Transcendentalists.

Granted, Millie wouldn't have chosen Mrs. Skinner as a reading partner. Years of testing puddings for doneness and sending back soups for better seasoning had made her more interested in finding fault than in experiencing joy. The woman's dour expression as she peered through her wire-rimmed glasses threatened to poison some worthy materials.

Still, as she helped Tirzah with her vital mission, Millie felt a satisfaction she'd never known before. Associating with Tirzah in public caused her own reputation to grow. Even Ellen Stoner paid attention when she spoke—sometimes. Between this assignment and the play, she was starting to fit in.

And she was advancing a cause Father Noyes cared about—although he probably didn't even know her name. He evidently hadn't minded her listening the day he assigned Tirzah the literature project. Millie had previously heard some of the things he had said to Tirzah—that he would bear others' sins for them. But speaking so frankly about wanting to have a child with his niece—that was a surprisingly intimate conversation, one she wished she could erase from her mind. Still, if she wanted to fit in, she had to ignore the things that bothered her—the things she couldn't change.

Millie stood on stage in the Big Hall waiting for play practice to begin. She'd been on her feet at the compositor's counter all day, and she was exhausted.

As the first actor to arrive, Henry hoisted himself onto the stage without using the stairs, doing a forward roll and leaping to his feet, then taking a low bow. "Henry Hunter, at your service, Madame Director!"

"You're chipper."

"Chipper as a clipper shipper."

Like a sailing vessel at sea, he weaved in and out around Millie.

Millie laughed at his antics. "Well, I'm sinking fast, so I hope you'll bear me up."

Henry glided from his sailing imitation to Millie's side, pulled her to him, and began waltzing her around the stage. Warmth flowed from Henry's hands into hers, and she felt energy spreading up her spine, down her legs, and from her hand down to her chest. All her fatigue vanished. She'd never felt so alive. The other actors arrived and joined the levity. Leonora caught Martha in her arms and took her on a few revolutions around the stage.

After that, they all threw themselves into their roles with gusto, producing their best scenes yet. And just in the nick of time. Tirzah wanted Millie to make an announcement at Saturday's Meeting—naming a date for the dress rehearsal when the Community could view the play before Outsiders saw it.

As usual, Henry stayed to help Millie straighten up after practice before they went to supper together. Was their time alone together as meaningful for him as it was for her? She hoped more than simple kindness made him linger.

Giving the stage a final inspection, she felt Henry's light grasp on her upper arm. He pulled her a little closer, leaning his face down toward hers. "Millie, can we talk?"

Her heart leapt at the intimacy of his tone. "Of course."

He led her by the hand beyond the grand piano to sit on the low ledge of one of the tall windows that looked out over the portico. Grinning boyishly, he faced her. "You may have noticed, I'm in high spirits today."

Millie's pulse raced, and she giggled. "It would be hard not to notice."

His dark eyes sparkled. "The most glorious thing happened last night. I've simply got to tell someone, and I know you can keep a secret."

She arched her eyebrows, encouraging him to go on. Pleasure warmed her chest as she sat by his side, his arm nearly touching hers. He'd chosen her to confide in.

Henry rubbed his palms against his thighs. "Last night, I was in the Nursery Kitchen getting some tea, and Tirzah walked in. My word, she looked wrung out! She was looking for something to help her headache. I told her I knew a great neck massage—my mother gets horrible headaches. So she said I could come to her room and give it a try."

Millie felt her blood stop. She didn't want to hear the rest.

"She lay down on her bed, and I began to massage her neck." Henry kneaded the air with his hands. "I could feel all her muscles unwind. She looked up at me with those lovely hazel eyes and said it felt heavenly. She was so beautiful lying there, right in my hands. So I kissed her. And she kissed me back. A real kiss!" He let out a long sigh. "So she must feel for me as I feel for her. For weeks I've wanted to kiss her." He motioned to the floor behind the piano. "To pull her off the piano bench and bring her backstage. But I didn't think she'd want me to." His pouting lower lip spread into a grin. "She sent me away after we kissed, but she said I'd done an excellent job. She probably meant the massage, but I hoped she meant the kiss."

Millie felt queasy. She'd let herself imagine Henry cared for her, even though he'd hinted before that he was sweet on Tirzah. Alarm bells clanged in Millie's head. Henry's face telegraphed the same fervent desire that Mary and Victor had for each other, the same longing Tirzah had for Edward. Victor had already been sent to Wallingford so he and Mary couldn't continue their love affair. And Edward had seceded from the Community because he couldn't follow the rules regarding equal love.

Thinking of Henry and Tirzah together stabbed her heart, but that didn't matter. She didn't want his passion for Tirzah to end in punishment and suffering.

"But Henry, are you falling into special love with Tirzah?" She rested her hand on his. "That can only end in heartache. I think you should try to control those urges."

Even as the words left her mouth, she cringed inwardly. She sounded like Theodora Campbell, Oneida's version of Goody Two-Shoes.

"Control it!" scoffed Henry. "Have you ever been in love, Millie?"

Millie felt her cheeks redden. Was she in love with Henry? Sitting so close to him, feasting her eyes on his handsome face, her heart fluttered and her pulse raced. If she was, she certainly couldn't tell him now. She shook her head.

"There's nothing I can do to stop the way I feel." Henry placed both hands on his heart. "I've tried to forget about her. I've even thought about skipping our music practices, but when it's time to be with her, a giant magnet draws me here." He clenched his fists. "And when I'm with her, it takes all my strength to not pull her into my arms. Whenever we play, I search her eyes for a glimmer that she loves me, too, but last night was the first time she's given me any hope."

Millie's chest tightened. Poor Henry. Tirzah was still in love with Edward, and by her own admission always would be. But seeing the longing on Henry's face, Millie couldn't bear to dash his fantasies. Besides, she was sworn to secrecy in the matter of Edward.

"Will you request an interview with her?"

Fear leapt into Henry's eyes. "Oh, no! They'd never approve. I'd have to ask either Harriet Skinner or Ann Hobart. I'm petrified of Mrs. Skinner." He shuddered. "And Ann has eyes for me herself—and it's no secret she and Tirzah don't get along." He hung his head. "Neither of them would ever allow it."

He was right. For a young man like Henry to request an interview with a woman like Tirzah, one of the most desirable and important women in the Community, was unacceptable. In all cases, men had to go through a mediator. Older men chose their own mediators, but young men who were not yet *teleoi* had to go through one of the women who controlled such relationships.

"What will you do, then?"

"What can I do, but keep loving her with all my heart?" Henry stared forlornly out the window. Suddenly his eyes widened as an idea seemed to strike him. "But you work with her every day. You bask in her presence hour by hour. If it ever comes up, if you can ever put in a good word for me, let her know how much I love her—"

He finished his sentence with an imploring look.

Was he asking her to act as a mediator? Or just to relay his love to Tirzah? Either way, she could never broach this subject with Tirzah. Henry continued to beseech her with big, doleful eyes, as if he were a lapdog and she held a tasty morsel.

"If it ever comes up, I'll speak highly of you."

That was the most she could promise.

Henry took that as a *yes* to whatever question he'd meant to ask. He jumped up and offered his hand. "You're a pal, Millie. Best director ever! If you ever need anything from me, I'll be there for you."

Millie smiled. She'd have to be satisfied with that. For now at least.

As they exited the Big Hall, Millie almost bumped into Virginia coming out of her new sleeping room, the first room next to the auditorium.

Millie skirted out of her way. "Virginia! We miss you in Ultima Thule."

Virginia walked with them down the corridor. "And I miss living there. It's so different here. I like all the excitement—sometimes. But sometimes I long to just sit and stare at our bare old tulip tree."

Millie ached at the homesickness in Virginia's voice. "When it starts to bloom in May, you must come to my room to see it."

Henry gestured, palm up. "But now you look out over the front portico and get to see all the comings and goings."

She started to agree, then scowled. "But everyone sees all *my* comings and goings, too." She had lowered her voice as she looked ahead toward Hamilton Avenue, the busy sitting room that offered a clear line of sight down the corridor to the Big Hall. "It's rather like living in an aquarium."

Indeed, as they neared the stairway, several middle-aged men looked up from their games or conversations to watch Virginia. She dropped her eyes to her feet, holding her body stiff.

Obviously sensing her discomfort, Henry maneuvered his body between Virginia and Hamilton Avenue. "Well, *I've* got a great location."

Millie placed a light hand on Virginia's back as they began descending the stairs. She gave Henry an appreciative nod for changing the subject. "Where *is* your room?"

"Third floor, right outside the Big Hall." Henry pointed with his thumb over his left shoulder. "Whenever I can't sleep, I can slip up the stairs to the garret."

"The attic?" Virginia stopped in her tracks, horrified. "You go up *there*?"

Henry arched his brows. "Of course. Especially when there's a full moon."

Virginia shuddered, but Millie smirked at the teasing glint in his eyes.

"Have you ever been up there?"

Before the words were out of Henry's mouth, Virginia exclaimed, "No!"

Millie laughed with Henry. Virginia must still harbor the prevailing belief among the children that the upper realms of the Mansion House were haunted.

Millie shook her head and raised her shoulders, resisting the temptation to tease. "There's nothing up there."

Henry patted Virginia's shoulder. "Millie's right, Virginia."

The girl squinted, unconvinced.

"Should we show her, Millie?"

Virginia opened her mouth to protest, but Millie nodded sagely. "You must see it for yourself. That way you'll know there's nothing to be afraid of."

The three retraced their steps and crossed the Big Hall, then mounted the north staircase.

When they reached the third floor, Henry pointed to the left. "My room's the first door there. The night watchman passes it at exactly half past the hour, then goes down these stairs to the first floor and dozes for half an hour. That's when I know it's safe to go up to the garret. Come on!"

Henry tiptoed as if on one of his midnight excursions, and the girls followed his example. After turning right, at the end of the hallway they found a closed door on their right.

"This is it," Henry whispered.

When he opened the door, a tube of blackness greeted them. He felt on a shelf for a lantern and lit it with the safety matches that sat near it. A narrow wooden staircase appeared in front of them with a closed door at the top. Henry led the way, lighting their path, and Millie gently prodded Virginia to follow him.

At the top of the stairs, Henry opened the door, and they all stepped into the dim expanse of the garret. When he clicked the door shut behind them, Virginia jumped. With his left hand he held the lantern high, and it cast eerie shadows onto the floor from the wooden beams that angled from the ceiling. Scattered among stacks of crates and boxes, a few broken chairs and tables gathered dust, consigned to lonely disuse.

Virginia shuddered again. "It's awful up here," she whispered. "How can you like this?"

"Mostly because of its rich and storied past," Henry declaimed melodramatically. "Of course, you know that *there*—" he motioned abruptly toward the north windows with his right hand as if on stage — "was where the séances were held, and Ann Hobart called up the ghost of Mary Cragin." He paused for eerie emphasis. "And her exhumed skull is in that crate—over *there!*"

He gestured forcefully again. Virginia's eyes grew wide, and she began backing toward the door.

Millie swallowed a giggle. "Oh, stop it, Henry."

Henry cranked his arm. "Now, come this way."

He moved away from the north wall, where a faint tint of light shone through the windows, and toward a windowless area before them. Millie motioned to Virginia to go ahead of her, and she reluctantly followed their guide. Henry and Virginia had to duck to avoid bumping their heads on the support beams, but Millie could stand erect. Virginia gasped and flailed her arms, brushing cobwebs away from her face. As they came into a higher-ceilinged part of the attic, they saw the dim outlines of the east windows above the portico.

"On your left you may observe," said Henry in a schoolmaster's voice, "the very spot where crazy Lady Haas spent her final days, living in a tent."

"Her bed is still here!" Millie eyed the narrow bed, which was just like hers, neatly made up with a faded white quilt. Beside it lay heavy canvas curtains, crumpled in a heap. "And her tent."

Virginia backed away from the scene. "H-how long did she live here?"

"Nobody quite knows." Millie stepped back, placed her arm behind Virginia, and guided her closer to the bed. "Some say she returned to her duties after a few weeks. But some say it was years."

Virginia cowered at the long shadows cast by the flickering lamp. "I don't like it here."

Henry sidled up to her, dragging one leg. "Is it because you don't like *phantoms*?" He widened his eyes and leaned toward her, holding the lantern next to his face, leering like a madman.

A stifled scream escaped Virginia's lips, and Millie slapped Henry's arm. "Henry, you're a monster! Stop scaring the poor girl."

"Sorry, Virginia." He backed off, relaxing his face. "No, there's nothing terrifying up here. I do my best thinking here—especially now that I have to share a room. And especially when there's a full moon. You almost don't need a lantern then. Anyone like to join me sometime?"

He posed the question as if he were inviting two chums to play baseball.

"Sure. Next time I can't sleep, wake me up, and I'll meet you here."

Millie waited to see how long it would take them to get the joke.

Henry snorted, and a moment later Virginia said, "But if you can't sleep—" and then burst out laughing.

That sweet peal of laughter warmed Millie's heart. Even if she couldn't assuage Virginia's concerns about real men, she could at least put to rest her irrational fears.

* * *

A couple of evenings after their trip to the garret, as Millie left Meeting to go to the library, Tirzah caught up to her in the vestibule.

"Oh, Millie! Just the one I've been looking for."

Millie stopped at the top of the wide stairway and leaned against the museum case that housed such treasures as a mastodon tooth, arrowheads from the Oneida Indians, relics from Pompeii, and shells from South Sea islands.

"Could I have a moment with you?" Tirzah's voice sounded unusually strained.

Millie cocked her head. "Of course. I was just on my way to the library for another copy of the *Atlantic Monthly*."

Tirzah gave a single businesslike nod. "Let's go to my room for a few minutes first."

Before Millie could reply, Tirzah guided her by her elbow around the corner of the Big Hall and into the second floor hallway. They passed Hamilton Avenue, where people were gathered around for squails, not quite as excitedly as a month ago. Father Noyes, from his chair against the wall, first made eye contact with Millie, then nodded to Tirzah. Tirzah gave him a knowing look, as if to continue some previous discussion.

Millie's pulse quickened. What was going on? Had Father Noyes learned that Millie was feeding Tirzah information for the literary project, and was he upset about that?

Inside Tirzah's room, which was a duplicate of Millie's, the two women sat on either side of the square table. Tirzah's formal posture and expression made Millie squirm.

Tirzah cleared her throat. "Millie, dear, I first must extend you a sincere apology on behalf of the Community."

"An apology?" Millie slid her feet under her chair. "For what?"

"I understand that you've not yet had your first interview."

The statement struck Millie like a shot. Of course. She should have guessed. Her face burned, and she looked at the floor. "Oh, that's all right—"

"No, no!" Tirzah paused until Millie raised her eyes. "It's not at all!" The little curls danced indignantly on her forehead. "Here you are, seventeen, and not enjoying the love of the Community that you're due. Why, you must have felt you were unattractive or undesirable, but I assure you, that's not the case. You're a very pretty young woman, and this has been a terrible oversight."

Millie's tongue stuck to the roof of her mouth, and her stomach cramped with dread for what would come next. She tensed every muscle and eyed the door. Though she imagined herself rushing out, she anchored her toes to the floor.

"Dr. Noyes—Theodore—has asked me to request that you meet him in his room after Meeting tomorrow evening."

Tirzah made the declaration as if she were a herald angel, but the words fell on Millie's ears like thunder. She'd known this was coming. She should have prepared an answer so she could eloquently state her case. But now the only words she could think of were, *No! I don't want to!*

Tirzah smiled sweetly. "Shall I tell him to expect you?"

"No, Tirzah," Millie managed to say, "no, I, I—"

Tirzah studied her. "Oh, is it your time? Would next week be better?"

Finally, she remembered what she'd said to Virginia. "No, it's not that. It's just that I'm not ready yet."

"Not ready?" Tirzah drew in her chin and looked down her nose, as if she'd never heard those words before. "At seventeen? Why, of course you are. You needn't be modest, for it's obvious you're quite ready."

She smiled approvingly at Millie's chest, a compliment her skinny figure didn't deserve.

Millie folded her arms in front of her. "But I don't *feel* ready."

"I suppose no woman does." Tirzah lifted her shoulders innocently. "That's Theodore's job—to help you feel ready."

Millie bit her lower lip. This approach wasn't working. She'd have to invoke the law. "Isn't it true that I don't have to receive the attentions of anyone I'm not attracted to?"

Tirzah was visibly taken aback. She thought a moment, with knitted brows. "But the man who has invited you is the leader of our entire Community. As ascending fellowship goes, you could do no better unless you were to meet with Father Noyes himself." She leaned toward Millie. "Theodore is the best man to teach you the physical, emotional, and spiritual aspects of love."

Millie licked her lips. "But Dr. Noyes doesn't even believe in God, they say."

Anger sparked in Tirzah's eyes. "Those are the rumors Ann Hobart spreads about him, and you'd do well to ignore them. If Father Noyes is satisfied with Theodore's spirituality, so am I, and so should we all be."

She wouldn't apologize. She'd managed to change the subject.

Tirzah rose and paced about the little room. Finally, she shook off her anger. "Why are you objecting? Surely you know the requirements of Bible Communism. It's our duty to love one another. That's how we show we're Christians."

Millie's throat ached. It was agony to be at odds with her mentor. But the image of the somber, stiff-shouldered, balding Theodore contracted her very pores, and her ears buzzed with Virginia's heart-wrenching sobs. She could not submit. "I was under the impression that I'd have some choice in the matter."

"Choice," repeated Tirzah, as if looking for the exact angle that would convince Millie. "Well, yes, we have choice." She sat down again. "Now, as you know—" She lowered her voice in a confidential

tone. "I don't want to have a child by Homer Barron, and today I was told that I need not try any longer with him. James Herrick is assigned to me now." She sat back in her chair, as if confident in the wisdom of her reply. "So, of course, women have choice, and I'm your proof."

Was Tirzah even listening to herself? Obviously she didn't have the choice she truly wanted, namely Edward. The Community had removed her first choice from her. Yet there Tirzah sat as if her logic were indisputable.

They were at loggerheads. Millie clenched her jaw and refused to speak.

Tirzah shook her head coquettishly, then rose, smiling. "I'm afraid I've taken you by surprise," she said airily, "and you're one who likes fair warning. So here's what I want you to do. Come back here after Meeting tomorrow night. I'll tell Theodore I was unable to get an answer but that I'll attempt tomorrow." She shooed her away with three regal back-handed waves. "Now run to the library, and we'll talk again tomorrow."

Millie stood up, murmured, "Goodnight," and left the room as quickly as she could without a backward glance. Instead of heading to the library, which would have taken her past Hamilton Avenue and Father Noyes again, she hurried to the end of the corridor and climbed the stairs two steps at a time. She ran to her room, threw open the door, and slammed it behind her as if hellhounds bounded at her heels. Standing with her back against the door, she looked straight ahead to her bureau, on top of which stood her parents' wedding photograph. She walked to it and picked it up in both hands.

"Did you choose each other?" she asked the stony gray faces. "Were you enough for each other? One husband, one wife? Did you marry for duty—or for desire?"

Chapter 9: Scapegoat

Saturday was a Community-wide cleaning day. After claiming her bucket and cloth, Millie roamed from room to room washing doorknobs, accompanied only by the caged wild animals that crashed around inside her head. What arguments could she present to Tirzah that would buy her more time? And why was she balking at being instructed in love by Dr. Noyes, someone she should revere as the Community's leader?

She envisioned the gentle touches and loving glances that passed between Mary and Victor. She brought into focus her parents' wedding photograph, of which she knew each minute detail. And she relived Tirzah's dream about Edward. Now even Henry was surviving on the memory of one delightful kiss from a woman he was magnetically drawn to.

Besides those real-life love stories, all the inspiring romantic novels she'd ever read came back to her. How satisfying at the end of *Northanger Abbey* that both Eleanor Tilney and Catherine Morland were released "to the home of her choice and the man of her choice." The delight Elizabeth Bennet felt in being called *Mrs. Darcy* was enough to sail on for the rest of her days. After being released from her dispassionate marriage to Casaubon by his death, Dorothea Brooke married her soul-mate, Will Ladislaw. Each of those heroines held out for true love and ultimately found it.

Was that all foolish romanticism? They didn't live under Bible Communism, and they weren't dedicated to showing the world a better way.

But was this a better way?

Instead of approving the gleaming brass orb she'd just finished shining, she scrutinized the distorted visage it reflected back at her. Her features were petite, even delicate, but beyond that, she had no distinguishing characteristics. Her brown hair was parted in the middle like almost every other woman's, and she tried to keep it pulled behind her ears, which were almost pretty, but because it was so straight, it always flopped back against her cheeks, making her face look too thin and her skin look too pale.

When no one was watching, she smiled her prettiest smile into the knob. Perhaps she could be magnetic if she tried. No—even with her most gracious expression, she'd never attract attention. No matter how inviting she tried to make her thin lips, they still looked austere, and her front teeth were slightly rounded at the bottom and turned in on each other, creating an embarrassing tiny cleft. Her eyes, blue like her father's, added to her mild appearance. If she'd been blessed with deep brown eyes, they might tie her hair and features together. But no. She was a conglomeration of parts that made up less than a whole. The opposite of synergism.

Given her plain appearance and lack of magnetism, complex marriage was the best she could hope for. She'd be cared for by many men, not passionately desired, but treated with love and tenderness in the holy bonds of Bible Communism.

She sighed and moved on to the next knob.

If only there were a noble, modern-day knight who would value her quick mind, her talent with words—even her ability to bond with children. She pictured Noah's laughing eyes and teasing grin and remembered the story she'd written about his rescuing the lost woman. It was a fairy tale. Women who left the Community had tarnished reputations among Outsiders. The son of the Community's biggest critic could never fall in love with a Community girl.

Besides, whether inside or outside the Community, beauty and liveliness aroused passion in men. That's why Henry pined for Tirzah and considered Millie only a friend. A thoughtful woman who lived more in the realm of ideas than in the corporeal world could look forward to many long days and nights alone.

As she stepped outside to clean the exterior doorknob of the Children's House entrance, she warmed at the sight of her father repairing a spindle on the veranda. She stepped toward him, her breath making frosty clouds in front of her.

"Good morning, Father."

William turned away from the railing but didn't rise from his crouch. He held a baluster in place, no doubt waiting for the glue to set. "You're a sight for sore eyes!"

She responded with a harrumph.

William reproved her with a tilt of his head. "No face in the whole world I'd rather see."

She managed a halfhearted smile. "Only because beauty's in the eye of the beholder."

William rose and put a hand on her arm. "And any beholder who didn't see your beauty better see Dr. Anselm in a hurry."

His reference to the eye doctor was meant to make her smile, but she couldn't even attempt it. The corners of her mouth quivered, and she blinked back tears.

William gave her a quick hug. "Stuck in the doldrums?"

"I'm feeling a little down." She swallowed against the lump in her throat. "How about a game of dominoes when we're done today?"

Her father rarely turned down such an offer.

"Sounds good." After pausing a moment, he frowned. "But I've got a Bible class at four. After supper?" Seeing her disappointment, he offered, "You could come to the class with me."

"Bible class? Is that new?"

"Somewhat." He shrugged. "Remember those lectures George Miller gave when he came from Wallingford last November?"

"Tirzah's brother." Millie nodded. "I remember."

"It started after that. I've been going for about a month."

"Does anyone my age go?"

She enjoyed attending classes, but not when she was the only young person in a room of older adults.

"Theodora Campbell comes."

Millie closed her eyes and slowly reopened them. She wouldn't be catty. But Dora, who had always avoided horizontal fellowship even more than Millie had, didn't count as a potential companion. For years the older girls had teased Dora without mercy for her good behavior, claiming she put the *perfect* in Perfectionist.

"I'll just meet you for supper. Five-thirty?"

Millie polished the knob and went back inside. She must stop thinking about the answer she'd give Tirzah tonight. It must be affirmative. Instead she needed to rehearse her announcement of the play.

At supper, William and Constance filled Millie in on the Bible lesson, explaining how Jesus promised that the Spirit of Truth would guide his disciples into all truth. Imagining her talk with Tirzah, she barely maintained a polite level of interest.

While playing dominoes with her father, she admitted she was nervous about announcing the play at the upcoming Meeting, but she didn't tell him she'd be arranging her first interview afterward. Like every member, he'd pledged his loyalty to Father Noyes when they joined the Community, so he was fully aware of the social requirements she would face when she grew up.

During Meeting, when Mr. Woolworth turned from one item of routine business to the next, Tirzah mounted the stairs to the stage. Pausing mid-sentence, he eyed her with surprise. Millie's heart leapt to her throat, and she prepared to come forward when Tirzah called her. She'd chosen a seat near the front so she could get to the stage more quickly, but she hadn't expected to be summoned until the end.

Slowly whispers spread throughout the Big Hall as Tirzah spoke privately to Mr. Woolworth. All eyes watched him go backstage.

Standing erect behind the lectern, Tirzah took a breath. In a strong, steady voice, she announced, "I am here to present myself for complete criticism."

Millie sat back in her seat. She wasn't going to be called upon after all—not yet. Mr. Woolworth returned with a chair and placed it on the apron of the stage.

Tirzah sat straight and tall without touching the back rest. "I know there have been rumors here that I still long for Edward Inslee."

With an air of humility, she lowered her eyes. She had never looked more charming. How brave she was. Millie couldn't imagine opening herself up like this.

"Those rumors are true. I've been unwilling to give him up or to listen to those who spoke against him. I've tried to be Edward's salvation by saying that his wicked behavior was because of me— because he loved me. But today Judge Towner showed me documents that prove Edward was a wicked man before I ever met him."

Approving whispers rose in the auditorium. Sitting in the first row, Father Noyes nodded slowly, his eyes fixed on her. Had he required this?

Tirzah went on. "Judge Towner suggested we lay all the facts out for public consumption, but I objected. I objected strenuously, insisting that it has been spoken of too much already." Her dainty dabs to each eye with her handkerchief could have aroused sympathy from a stone. "But the fact is, I'm morbidly sensitive about being mentioned in public."

She took a deep breath. "If anyone has anything to say against Edward, let's have it laid bare right now." Lifting her chin, she cast her gaze across the auditorium. "I'd like you all to help me forget him. And I'm open to criticism for any fault that should be brought to my attention."

No one stirred. Millie had never seen the Big Hall so filled with people, yet so silent. She could see the muscles tense in Tirzah's neck as she clenched her fingers into fists on her lap. Millie's heart ached for her.

Judge Towner was the first to rise to his feet, turning his stern face with its menacing eye patch toward the crowd. In his early fifties, he had delicate, aristocratic features and an almost regal bearing. "Many here know the fears we had that Edward would come to steal our little Paul away from us. Although he required Tirzah to sign a release that freed him from financially supporting his own offspring, we found him lurking around the Children's House on more than one occasion. Paul has been known to sit on the window seat for hours watching for him. To torment the boy is cruel. I propose we obtain a court order to assure he never sets foot on the premises again."

Murmurs of agreement spread through the hall.

Mr. Kinsley rose next, clearing his throat and adjusting his tie. "According to my New York City acquaintances in the legal field, Inslee is looking into gaining custody on the grounds that our social system is an unfit environment for children. When he was chosen for stirpiculture, he pledged his submission to the Community and Father Noyes." Mr. Kinsley slapped his fist into his palm. "For him to go back on that pledge makes him a liar!"

A few assenting shouts arose from the crowd.

Ann Hobart stood, tossing her black curls and assuming a warrior stance. Of course Ann would pounce on the opportunity to publicly condemn Tirzah.

"Tirzah, your insights are years past due. There's a stubborn streak in you, and a desire to put your fingers into more than you need to. When you see an area is well managed, you don't need to put your hand to it. There are many talented and intelligent women here besides you. Your haughty spirit sets a bad example. I call on you to

show a meek and quiet spirit, even as Sarah of old."

As Ann spoke, Father Noyes's shoulders stiffened. Millie had heard rumors that Father Noyes disliked Ann for many reasons, not the least of which was her hold over Theodore.

When Ann sat, Father Noyes made eye contact with Theodore.

Theodore stood and looked up at the stage. "Tirzah, although at times you show great wisdom, you tend to display a general indiscretion." Loud and firm, his voice was kinder than Ann's had been. "You become familiar with people too easily. You often share a confidence with someone, but not a confidence they need to know— putting that person in your debt. It's as if you were making friends for yourself of unrighteous Mammon, so that when you fail, they will receive you into everlasting habitations. This isn't worthy of you. People here will love you whether you've taken them into your confidence or not."

A surprised murmur of approbation spread among the members as Theodore sat again, probably due to his use of scripture. Father Noyes looked toward Theodore with a thin smile, but the prophet's son only leaned toward Ann and spoke in her ear.

Millie's stomach turned as she considered Theodore's comments. Hadn't Tirzah done exactly that to Millie twice? Once on her first day at the *Circular* when she allowed Millie to overhear Theodore's entire conversation, and again when she shared her feelings about Edward. Millie didn't want to believe Theodore's words, but they resonated. Tirzah tended to psychologize people, as it was called. But had she suffered by her relationship with Tirzah? She'd only benefitted—so far.

But what about the way Tirzah had encouraged Henry, lighting a fire in him that she could have—should have—extinguished? Millie looked for Henry in the audience but couldn't see him. Had he taken Theodore's words to heart?

Many others stood to criticize Tirzah. People who normally vied to bask in her magnetism were making her pay dearly for being so highly esteemed. Tirzah bore the fierce rebukes like Mary Queen of Scots. She sat stiffly enthroned, facing the audience, and listened dispassionately as members flung accusation after accusation at her or Edward.

Eventually Harriet Worden stood up. "I've received information about Edward from Mary Leonard of Newark." At this many people leaned forward in their seats. "She told me it was generally expected there that Edward would shortly marry a certain Miss Ricker." For the first time, Tirzah flinched. "I made some inquiries. It seems that she's a girl of good reputation—a pianist."

Tirzah twitched again at the word *pianist*, and Millie felt the pang herself.

Finally Father Noyes joined Tirzah on stage, standing with his hand on her back. "Tirzah," he said, looking at the crowd, his voice unusually clear, "you have accepted my judgment of Edward Inslee, and it feels like it has cost you something. But Edward is a devil, and you are right to flee from him with all your strength. You may feel like you're in a tight place right now, with nowhere to turn. God has often treated me like that—put me someplace where the only way out was to trust God. I can feel the great and mighty power of God reaching out after you, determined to save you. And you will be saved as you continue to seek for righteousness."

Tirzah looked up at him and nodded. "I confess Christ in me a spirit of subordination to Mr. Noyes."

"Our time here is finished. Go and sin no more."

There would be no announcement about the play tonight. Millie's stomach cramped as she watched Tirzah leave the Big Hall. As far as she knew, their appointment was still on. Her thoughts wheeled as she made her way to Tirzah's room.

Was this the New Testament era's way of placing all the Israelites' sins on the scapegoat and sending it outside the camp? But Tirzah remained inside the camp—she hadn't been driven away. And what of her sins? They'd been exposed, but they remained, despite Father Noyes's previous promise to take them on himself. Now Tirzah had a list a mile long of things she needed to improve.

In the meantime, others had displayed jealousy, mean-spiritedness, and vindictiveness to one of the Community's kindest members. That wasn't bearing one another's burdens. If they were Perfectionists, why did they have to have these brutal criticisms—if they had ceased from sin? Maybe she should have attended the Bible class after all. She could use a Spirit of truth to guide her.

When Millie reached Tirzah's room, she lifted her hand to knock, but paused at the sound of sobs wafting through the open transom above the door. She dropped her hand and waited. Soon she heard what sounded like a fist slammed on the table. The crying intensified to a sort of wail. She heard softer things, perhaps pillows and clothing, being thrown to the floor, and then a chair shoved forcefully against the table.

Millie slipped away.

Chapter 10: Accused

On Monday Tirzah appeared to be in a stable, even sunny temper as Millie arrived and settled herself at her desk.

After they had both written in silence for several minutes, Tirzah spoke again, barely looking up. "Oh, by the way, Millie, Dr. Noyes is leaving for Wallingford today. From there he'll be going to New York City to meet with the architects. He may be gone several weeks, so we'll have to arrange your meeting when he returns."

Embarrassed, Millie glanced toward the other women. But Tirzah's tone was so matter-of-fact, they would think her comment related to an article for the *Circular,* not Millie's first interview. Tirzah had assumed Millie would answer yes. After all, no other answer would have been allowed. So now the matter was settled, but at least she had a few weeks to get used to the idea.

At three o'clock, Tirzah cleared her desk and nodded toward Millie. "I'm starting work earlier in the mornings now so I can leave at three. There's a young man I've agreed to read the Bible with." She stood. "But of course, you know him! It's Henry Hunter."

Millie gaped.

Tirzah dropped her eyes. "I'm sure you can manage on your own for the last hour."

Millie did manage, though it was hard to concentrate on her work. It seemed unlikely that Tirzah would have suddenly taken on Bible tutoring. What was going on?

When Millie got back to the Mansion House, she followed the classical violin music to the Big Hall. A dozen people sat reading books or newspapers at sundry small tables scattered around the room —its typical daytime arrangement. As she'd expected, Henry stood playing his violin behind Tirzah, who accompanied him on the grand piano. Millie joined Mrs. Campbell, Dora's mother, who watched the musicians with a serene expression, her head bobbing rhythmically. Though she didn't play herself, Mrs. Campbell was a great connoisseur of music.

Millie whispered, "Do you know this piece?"

Mrs. Campbell nodded. "That's a Beethoven Romance for Violin —I think in F Major."

Tirzah and Henry were obviously enjoying themselves, often exchanging meaningful glances. When they chose another piece from the book before them, Henry leaned his face very near Tirzah's. Tirzah rested her hand for a long moment on his forearm. They began to play again, and this tune was even more passionate.

Mrs. Campbell whispered, "No—*this* is Romance in F Major. The last one was in G."

Millie rolled her eyes. Romance, indeed. They were acting like Victor and Mary. What could Tirzah be thinking?

Later that week, Millie hurried to catch Tirzah and Henry as they exited the Big Hall after Meeting—probably headed for Hamilton Avenue. Before she reached them, they walked straight past the sitting room and entered Tirzah's room in view of everyone. Perhaps Henry had found the courage to talk to Mrs. Skinner after all. The next night, the same thing happened. This time Mr. Herrick, who was now assigned to have a baby with Tirzah, walked over to George Hamilton, who headed the Social Committee. The two men huddled solemnly, and both kept looking toward Tirzah's room, obviously displeased.

Millie didn't like the situation either. If Henry wasn't romantically interested in her, that was fine. In truth, she'd never expected it. But just a few days ago Tirzah had professed to Millie her undying love for Edward. Her heart-wrenching wails after the mutual criticism confirmed she hadn't given him up. Besides, Henry was half Tirzah's age. Why was she leading him on?

At the next play practice, Henry trudged up the stairs with drooping shoulders and shuffled toward the other actors. He missed cues and stumbled over lines he'd delivered perfectly last week. It took every ounce of Millie's patience not to tell him to leave. Afterward, she caught him by the arm.

"Henry! What's going on?" She led him toward the window where they'd conferred before. She sat on the ledge and patted it. "Want to talk?"

He slumped down beside her. "Tirzah says we can't read together anymore." Rubbing the back of his neck with his hands, he spoke

120 Rebecca May Hope

dully to the floor. "Because Mr. Herrick is jealous. Mr. Hamilton says I need to focus on spiritual things. He says love will get in the way. He wants me to get the revival spirit."

Millie suppressed the urge to say *I told you so.*

Henry rested his elbow on his knee and his cheek on his fist. "So we've agreed we won't speak to each other for a whole week. She made me promise."

A flutter of hope rose in Millie's chest—he would be available now—but it quickly faded when Henry raised his head, revealing his sullen face. He needed encouragement and friendly advice. Putting aside her own feelings, she touched his arm. "They probably just want you to prove your self-control. And neither of you can be exclusive, you know."

"It drives me insane to not be with her." He shook himself. "And I don't dare imagine her in another man's arms."

"Henry!" Millie scolded. "That's exactly the attitude that will keep you separated forever." She raised her index finger. "Do you want to get sent to Wallingford? You know she's been chosen to have a child with Mr. Herrick. Would you rather share her, or not have her at all?"

He pressed his full lower lip into a pout. "I can't say."

She felt his agony. But for his sake, she'd play the schoolmarm. "One man has already seceded because of love for Tirzah. And there's a little boy in the Children's House who can never see his very own papa again."

A faraway look swept into Henry's eyes as he lifted them to the piano. "'All that a man hath.' She's my precious jewel, and I'd give up everything for her."

He was completely oblivious to the arrow his words sent into Millie's heart. He'd never pine for her that way. Not for her sake, but for his, she had to steer him from his reckless course. "Then give up your disobedience." She gripped his arm, and he turned toward her. "If you don't play by the rules, things will get a lot worse. Promise me you'll do what Mr. Hamilton says."

"I'll try."

His weak reply wasn't convincing.

That night when Meeting was over, Millie invited Henry to Hamilton Avenue. A game of squails might cheer him up. Descending

the north stairway, they met Tirzah on her way up. She glanced around quickly, then continued toward the balcony level. Henry followed her like a stray dog.

Millie hissed the loudest whisper she could manage. "Henry!"

Instead of turning around, he quickened his pace to catch up to Tirzah. Millie followed far enough to see first Tirzah, then Henry—a full minute later—enter the interview room in the North Tower. Her heart sank. Had anyone in authority seen them? If the people in the Upper Sitting Room had glanced toward the open corridor above them, they'd have easily witnessed the errant pair. But no one noticed. The lovers had renewed their tryst, this time in a different location—away from the prying eyes in Hamilton Avenue.

Shaking her head, Millie went downstairs.

What had come over Tirzah? She'd just been through a brutal Community-wide criticism. Why would she risk more censure? If she'd taken up with Henry to convince the Community that she'd fully forgotten Edward, this clandestine meeting didn't further that goal.

In some ways, Henry was what Germans would call Edward's doppelganger. He was a talented musician, had the same thick black hair, and had a fiery temperament. Perhaps Tirzah was using Henry to fulfill her fantasies of Edward—or to punish Edward somehow for his rumored engagement. If so, she was making Henry her puppet. But this wasn't a game.

Millie might not know much about love, but what Tirzah was showing Henry wasn't even close.

* * *

The next day Tirzah was in high spirits, constantly humming "Romance in G"—or was it F?—under her breath. But in the afternoon, someone placed a letter on her desk. Even from a distance, Millie recognized Father Noyes's familiar handwriting. Tirzah read the note, then stashed it in her drawer. After that her mood was subdued.

When Millie and Tirzah were the last ones left in the office, Tirzah pulled out the note. She held it in her fingers without unfolding it. "Father Noyes believes that associating with Henry will be a snare to me. He wishes I'd stop seeing him."

Millie assessed Tirzah with a penetrating stare. "Wasn't that what Mr. Hamilton already said?"

Tirzah stiffened. "I don't take orders from Mr. Hamilton." Then, in a meeker tone she added, "But Henry does."

"Or he should."

Tirzah seemed to have forgotten that Millie had seen the two of them together yesterday, in direct defiance of Mr. Hamilton.

"That was my fault." Tirzah's admission didn't sound very contrite—in fact, her lips were curling upward. "Father Noyes thinks that Henry's feelings for me are very like Edward's. He was amused to hear Mr. Herrick was jealous. He writes…well, let me read it."

Tirzah unfolded the letter. "God is using you to bring men to judgment. You are a great trap. It is pretty hard on you, but in one sense you ought to be glad that you are all used up in bringing the false love of men to judgment, for that is what you are doing, and I can see great benefit coming out of it all."

Tirzah's smug tone and arched eyebrows turned Millie's stomach. Tirzah was oddly proud of Father Noyes's appraisal.

Like Salome's mother when she watched her daughter dance for King Herod, Father Noyes had watched Tirzah perform her seduction. He may not have asked for a head on a charger, but he'd reveled in the pain Tirzah the Temptress had caused. This was a side of Father Noyes and Tirzah that Millie didn't care to see. Did Tirzah have any genuine feelings for Henry, or was he simply crass entertainment?

Tirzah read Millie's reaction, and her eyes softened. "My poor, dear Henry. He'll take this hard. But it's better coming from me than from Mr. Hamilton or Mrs. Skinner. Will you tell him to look for me after Meeting on the third floor?"

* * *

That night Millie tossed and turned, unable to fall asleep. She'd helped Henry meet Tirzah at the top of the stairs again, and she'd watched as they walked down the corridor together toward the interview room. How had he taken it when Tirzah broke off their romance?

She slid out of bed and shuffled to the window to read her clock by the moonlight: one-thirty already. A brilliant full moon shone above, and the velvet sky hung thick with stars. Gazing out her window, she looked west over the Tontine, north across the Quadrangle to where the new wing would extend from the library, and then east to the main part of the Mansion House, topped by the bell tower.

Under the bell tower was the garret. From here she could see its windowless side opposite the east windows. Tonight the full moon would be shining into the north windows, casting its silvery glow into the desolate space.

Her hands dropped to the window sill, and she steadied herself. Suddenly she knew why she couldn't sleep. Henry's troubled spirit was calling to her from the garret. Even now he could be pacing the shadowy room in the pale moonlight, perhaps in anger, perhaps crying, with no one to talk to and no one to comfort him. She had to help him. She quickly changed out of her nightdress and into her day clothes.

The hallway was very dark—the night watchman had locked the doors and put out the lamps hours ago. But she knew every inch of her home and could have navigated it all with her eyes closed. She tiptoed down the hall and glided down the stairway to the second floor. According to Henry, the watchman would have just finished his rounds for the hour and would be settling down for a doze on the main floor.

How eerie it was to pass the vacant Hamilton Avenue, usually a bustling social junction. When she reached Father Noyes's apartment, she stepped as softly as she could in case he was awake. She didn't want him, of all people, to discover her on an errand of mercy to Henry. She continued on her way, passing Virginia's room, where she mutely wished her pleasant dreams. She skirted between the pews in the Big Hall, ascended the north staircase to the balcony level, and rounded the corner to the closed door to the garret.

Without making a sound, she opened the door and felt for the lamp. It wasn't there, but the stairwell wasn't black. A yellow strip of light glowed above her where the lantern's rays leaked under the door at the top of the stairs. From there she heard a voice—Henry's. Perhaps in his anguish he was soliloquizing. She felt her way up the stairs, and as she neared the top, she heard another voice. She froze.

After dropping silently onto the top step, she pressed her ear to the door.

Henry spoke again, his voice agitated.

A feminine voice responded, in a calmer tone. Tirzah.

Stunned, Millie strained to hear the conversation. They'd started their meeting about four hours ago. Had it not been settled yet? Had they begun in the interview room first and then moved to this spot, or had they turned around after Millie left them, retreating to Henry's secret hideaway from the start? Millie pictured Lady Haas's bed. Meeting in the garret in no way assured that their communication had been strictly verbal. And judging from how long it was taking, more than conversation had certainly taken place.

She sat on the step, barely breathing. Curiosity anchored her to the floor, and she couldn't move—even if she wanted to.

Henry seemed to be standing very near the door, perhaps even leaning against it. "I can't let you go until I know there's *some* hope for me in the future. Do they mean to keep us apart our entire lives? I'm ready to fight the whole Community." His voice sounded fierce but plaintive at the same time. "You know I'm man enough to do so."

Tirzah's voice answered from farther away. Perhaps she was sitting on one of the damaged chairs. By straining, Millie could just make out her words. "Of course, you are. There's no doubt! But what does it gain us? I will submit to Father Noyes, even if you won't. I cannot oppose his clear instruction."

"So you're telling me there's no hope for us. I can never hold you in my arms again, kiss you—"

"No, Henry. We've been over this. You must give me up."

"If that's your final word, then I must go away. I can't live with you here, every day, knowing you can never be mine—even for a single night. It will drive me mad." His voice became muffled, as if he had buried his face in his hands. "I feel I'm going mad already."

"Henry, it's very late. You feel that way now, but things will look brighter with the sun. Let's go now. Will you let me pass?"

So Henry was standing in the doorway, preventing Tirzah from leaving. Yet Tirzah's voice seemed neither distressed nor annoyed. It sounded motherly, but sensuous as well.

"Pass? When you pass through this door, you pass out of my life forever. Just sit there as you are in the moonlight so I can memorize every atom of your beauty."

After a moment of silence, Tirzah said, "Shall we go now?"

"Yes!" Henry exclaimed.

Millie pulled away from the door, preparing to run. But it didn't open.

"We should both go!" His excited voice easily carried through the door. "You could leave with me. We could play for an orchestra and travel the country together. Don't you ever want to get away and live in freedom? Think of that whole wide world out there. Why should we be trapped here? We could take a train and travel west. To California. No one could ever tell us what to do again."

Millie pressed her ear to the door again to hear Tirzah's response.

"Henry, what nonsense!" Tirzah half scolded, half laughed the words, her voice a tinkling melody. Since she hadn't cut him off sooner, perhaps she was enjoying their imaginary escape. Or perhaps she was just letting him enjoy it. "You're forgetting I have two sons here. And I could never leave Father Noyes. I've promised him many times to stay by his side until the end, even if all others forsake him. I can't leave, and you mustn't, either. This is your home."

"A home of torture! A prison! A trap!"

"You'll come to see it differently."

"Oh, Tirzah!" Millie heard Henry walk across the space to where Tirzah's voice came from. A thud suggested he had dropped on his knees before her. "Give me one word of hope that we may be together again someday, and I'll let you go."

"I'm sorry, Henry. I can give you no hope."

The sound of a chair scraping across the floor meant Tirzah was standing now, and with Henry away from the door, in a few seconds Millie would be discovered. She slipped down the stairs and out the open door, closing it softly behind her, then passed quickly and silently down the north staircase to the second floor.

* * *

Neither Henry nor Tirzah was at breakfast that morning. But as Millie started across the Quadrangle toward the Little Court, Henry met her. Without saying a word, he touched the back of her arm and propelled her along the gravel path toward the north lawn.

"Henry! What is it?"

His eyes darted like a wild animal's. "Shh! Don't say anything until we get to the Summer House."

"The Summer House!" Millie shivered. "Henry, it's freezing out here!"

Tiny icy pellets whipped against their faces in the wintry wind.

Without answering, Henry hurried her along the path past Dunn Cottage until they reached the open gazebo. They ducked inside and sat on the rough benches, but the wind continued to whip through the window openings. Henry sat facing the Mansion House, and Millie looked into his troubled eyes.

His jaw was clenched. "You were right, Millie. They won't let Tirzah and me be together. She told me so last night."

Millie rubbed her upper arms vigorously against the cold. "That's what she wanted to see you about?" She tried to sound naive.

"Yes. We went to the garret. We wanted to be completely alone—with no chance of being overheard."

"Henry!" Millie wrinkled her brow. "Whose idea was that?"

"Mine. It was such a beautiful night, with the full moon. I wanted to see her there in the moonlight." Henry looked beyond Millie at the north windows of the garret. "She was so beautiful. It was glorious."

His voice trailed off, and his eyes grew dreamy. Despite the freezing temperature, Millie felt heat creep up her neck as she imagined what he meant by *it*.

He dropped his shoulders and his eyes. "But then she said we can't read together, we can't play music together—nothing." His anguished voice quavered. "I can never be with her again."

"I'm sorry, Henry. I'm so sorry."

"I don't see what the use of living is." His raised his eyes to the flat top of the North Tower. "In fact, I don't want to live."

Millie turned to confirm his line of sight. Ice filled her veins. He was envisioning flinging himself from the top of the tower to the ground below. There had never been a suicide at the Community, but as a symbol of despair, young people occasionally jested about throwing themselves from the Tower.

"Henry! I won't hear you talk like that!" She used the voice she used when a child did something dangerous. "Stop it this instant!"

Henry's eyes remained glued to the rooftop.

She put her hands on his cheeks and forced his eyes downward to look into hers. "Look at me!" The dullness she saw made her heart pound. She stood. "Where are you working today?"

"In the office with Mr. Hamilton. But I don't think I can stand to be near him."

Using every ounce of her strength, she pulled him to his feet. "Have you eaten?"

"No. I can't, Millie. I know I can't eat a bite."

"I'll go with you to the office and help you face Mr. Hamilton." Millie gripped the back of Henry's arm and guided him forward. "Then I'll get you a muffin. You can't go on not eating."

They climbed the steps under the front portico and entered the main doors. In the business office immediately to their left, Mr. Hamilton was already working at his desk. She led Henry to his station and guided him into his seat. Mr. Hamilton looked on, squinting.

Millie faced the older man. "Mr. Hamilton, may I speak to you in private, please?"

He rose and followed her into the hallway. "What is it?"

"I'm worried about Henry." She gulped, noting his irritated expression. "Last night Tirzah told him she couldn't see him anymore, and he's taking it very badly. Just now he told me he doesn't want to live. He was looking at the top of the North Tower as if he wanted to jump off."

Mr. Hamilton rolled his eyes. "Oh, now! That's rather dramatic."

She clenched her fists and pushed back her anger. She had to make him understand. "Perhaps. But when I look in his eyes, I see something dark, something not like Henry." She stepped over, creating sight line through the open door, and Mr. Hamilton followed her example. "Look at him."

Hunched over his work table, Henry seemed to have no bodily structure supporting him. His arms and legs were limp, and his head sagged.

Mr. Hamilton stepped away from the doorway looking less skeptical. "I see."

Millie took a deep breath. "He seems to blame you especially. He said he didn't want to be in your presence."

Mr. Hamilton nodded. "Don't worry. I'll go easy on the lad."

"I doubt he slept much, and he hasn't eaten anything. I'm going to the Tontine to get him a muffin, if you'll let him eat it here. That may lift his spirits."

Mr. Hamilton pointed his approval. "Bring some milk, too." He stroked his beard. "In the meantime, I'll write to Tirzah that she shouldn't speak to him at all. Any words from her, any contact whatsoever, would only make this worse."

Millie worried about Henry all day. When she finished at the *Circular*, they went to Hamilton Avenue and played backgammon. He told her he'd had a thorough criticism from Mr. Hamilton, and he was much better now. He fell asleep in the chair.

Millie let her muscles relax. She'd never been so afraid for anyone in her life, but the crisis had been averted. Though Henry's eyes didn't have their old sparkle back, they'd lost that glazed look of desperation they had when he looked at the Tower roof.

Watching him sleeping like a child, Millie's heart warmed with something like sisterly affection. But no romantic attraction. Yes, he was handsome. But someone who let his passions sweep him away as Henry had would always need to be coddled and watched over. If she ever lost her heart to a man, he would have more depth than Henry had.

After Meeting, Millie advised Henry to go straight to bed, but he complained of a headache, so she accompanied him to the Nursery Kitchen for headache powder and tea.

When they entered the room, Millie sucked in her breath and started to turn around. If only she were tall enough to block Henry's view. There sat Tirzah, in a rocking chair next to the stove, sipping tea and chatting with several other parents of young children. Mrs. Skinner and some other elderly people were there as well.

For the older members who associated a good talk with a good stove, this was the most comforting spot in the Mansion House since it was the only room with a stove. The tea kettle was always simmering, and the purr of the bubbling water was like a soothing lullaby playing behind the pleasant conversations. Here, too, grandparents could watch the bedtime rituals as their grandchildren came to bid their parents goodnight.

When he saw Tirzah, Henry kept his composure. They greeted each other formally. But while Millie busied herself making the tea, Tirzah kept talking to him. Millie gripped the handle of the tea kettle fiercely. Mr. Hamilton had ordered Tirzah to not talk to Henry, but here she was, chatting with him as if nothing had happened.

Henry, though, wasn't going to pretend nothing had happened. In a stilted voice, he said, "I'm feeling much better than when you left me this morning. I believe I can be very comfortable now with being just ordinary friends."

Henry's back was toward Mrs. Skinner, but the older woman's eyebrows arched. Her hearing was acute.

"I'm glad, Henry. I knew you'd come 'round," Tirzah said as calmly as if settling a dispute about strawberry leaf tea versus malt coffee.

Just then Judge Towner came in leading Haydn by the hand. Crouching, he brought his eye and eye patch level with the little boy's face. "Now it's time for us to go to bed. Say night-night to Mama like a good boy."

Haydn climbed up on Tirzah's lap, and she asked him a few questions about his day and what he'd played, which he answered intelligently. Millie longed to tousle his silky locks. What a darling.

Judge Towner cleared his throat. "Now say night-night, Paul."

The little boy's lower lip trembled, and he threw his stocky arms around Tirzah's neck and squeezed. Then he separated, all by himself, said, "Night-night, Mama," and, after one big-eyed backward glance, walked away hand in hand with Judge Towner.

Millie fought the urge to run after the little boy and scoop him up. The thought of his rooming with the fierce judge flipped her stomach. How could Tirzah stand not keeping him with her? Millie scanned the room. All the occupants, including Henry, had watched the tender scene.

When Haydn disappeared from view, Henry murmured to Tirzah, "He did well. If I could only do it as easily as that."

Tirzah's smile quivered, and her eyes glistened. Perhaps she wasn't so hard-hearted after all.

* * *

On her way to Meeting the next evening, Millie met Ellen coming out of her room, and they sat together in the balcony. After some entertaining music by the orchestra and some stirring recitations by the Rhetoric class, Father Noyes climbed the stairs, his posture and pace signaling his fiery mood. He pulled one of the chairs forward to the edge of the stage.

"Uh-oh," whispered Ellen. "Someone's in trouble!"

The prophet looked out upon the assembly. He cleared his throat repeatedly and attempted to speak several times. Each time his effort failed, his jaw shifted ominously and his eyebrows plunged deeper. Finally the words came, gruff but deep and distinct. "A matter has come to my attention that requires discussion. I call upon Mr. Henry Hunter to come forward."

Millie and Ellen gasped as one breath. Indeed, a general hiss spread throughout the room. Henry made his way down the center aisle, crossed the front of the room, and ascended the steps. As if connected to him via an invisible telegraph wire, Millie felt his mortification all the way from the stage to her seat in the rear balcony. He sat on the chair, knees together, hands folded in his lap.

"Two nights ago," boomed Father Noyes, his voice finally gaining strength, "Henry Hunter was alone with a woman of this Community for four hours in the garret. The woman expressed a desire to leave, but this man positioned himself at the door, blocking her way, keeping her detained against her will until after two o'clock in the morning."

Gasps rose around the auditorium. Millie's face burned, and her heart thumped.

Ellen leaned toward her. "I don't believe a word of it. Henry would never do such a thing."

Millie kept her face straight. Besides Henry and Tirzah, she alone knew firsthand about their tryst in the garret. Unless someone else had eavesdropped, too.

Father Noyes placed his hand on the back of Henry's chair. "Our social system rests on love—trust—and free will. In relations between the sexes, no person seeks to exert control over another."

People nodded vigorously as they glared at Henry.

"The woman in question reported being afraid. This is unacceptable." He wagged his finger. "There is no fear in love, for perfect love casts out fear. The love we practice is free from coercion. The moment fear enters in, it ceases to be love and becomes the most despicable act imaginable."

Henry sank lower in his seat as hundreds of eyes burned into him.

At each word from the prophet, he cringed as if a thousand scalding raindrops pelted him. Millie kept her gaze fixed on him, but her mind's eye saw Virginia, curled up and trembling on the library alcove floor. Her anger rose. Anger at this injustice toward Henry, anger at Father Noyes's hypocritical words. Afraid? When Millie was listening, Tirzah hadn't been afraid—she was calm and in control the whole time. What kind of lies had Tirzah told, to whom, and why?

Father Noyes droned on. "This is the type of so-called love practiced by the world. They oppress one another and harm one another in the name of love. Our calling is to show them the way of heavenly love. We cannot show them the way if the worst of their practices creeps in among us."

Again, murmurs of assent spread through the crowd.

"This … young … man—" Father Noyes split the air with his open palm at each word—"is a medium of a bad principality that we must war against." He drew his index finger across the crowd. "If anyone here ever thinks of treating another person in this Community, man or woman, in a way to cause fear, to usurp control in love, he will find himself similarly exposed."

Millie clenched her teeth. Perhaps she should rise to speak on Henry's behalf. Why was Tirzah not defending him?

Ellen squirmed. "Poor Henry! I wish there was something we could do!"

Turning to glower at Henry, Father Noyes took a deep breath. His posture relaxed when he saw Henry's devastated expression. "So as to not prolong Mr. Hunter's suffering here, I will entertain no discussion of this incident. Mr. Hunter, you may respond."

Henry's voice barely carried to the balcony, but Millie knew the rote response. "I confess Christ in me a spirit of subordination to Mr. Noyes and Mr. Hamilton."

Millie and Ellen each let out a long sigh.

"Thank God that's over!" Ellen said irreverently.

Millie slumped back in her seat. For once she and Ellen were in complete agreement. "Let's get to him right after Meeting. We'll show him and everyone else we're still his friends."

Ellen nodded, her lips pursed.

When Meeting was dismissed, the two young women descended the staircase as quickly as they could. At the landing, they encountered Tirzah on her way up.

Flushed, with red eyes, she looked directly at Millie. "Would you please come to my room?"

Tirzah seemed so agitated that Millie couldn't say no. She turned to Ellen, who squinted at her suspiciously. "Go on without me. Tell Henry I'm still his pal."

Tirzah hurried along the corridors with her eyes down, not greeting anyone. Inside her room, she threw herself onto her bed. Millie closed the door and watched her, not knowing what to expect.

Tirzah raised herself and motioned to Millie to sit beside her on the bed. "It was all wrong, Millie!" She pulled out a handkerchief and dabbed at her nose. "It's not like it sounds. Poor Henry. This is all my fault."

Not the slightest inkling of sympathy stirred Millie's heart. She crossed her arms and waited to hear the explanation.

Tirzah twisted the handkerchief. "You know that Henry and I met on Thursday night, and I told him we couldn't be together anymore. We *were* in the garret. And it *did* go too late. But Henry wasn't forcing me."

Millie answered with a skeptical gaze.

Tirzah rose and paced the room. "Last night in the Nursery Kitchen. You remember. Harriet Skinner was there. She knew George had forbidden Henry and me to speak to each other. But instead of talking to me about it," Tirzah said, flinging her arm angrily, "she dashed off a letter to Father Noyes. He told me to discuss it with her in person—that he wouldn't get caught in the middle." Tirzah sat on the bed again. "So I did. I explained how I met with Henry and broke it off, and I happened to mention how he stood against the door when I proposed to go."

Millie uncrossed her arms. Imagining how Mrs. Skinner might overreact, she felt a glimmer of warmth toward the distressed woman beside her.

Lowering her eyes, Tirzah wrung her hands. "I said that for one instant—I told her it was only an instant—I had such a sense of his great strength that a terror went through me of what he might be able to do to me if he wanted to. It was a foolish thing to say, but I realized it too late." She looked at Millie. "So I told her that as soon as I had the thought, I reproached myself for it, for he only treated me with

respect, and I truly had no fear of him."

Millie tilted her head. "Father Noyes seems to have heard a different story."

Tirzah began pacing again. "Aunt Harriet must have informed him of my *terror* and of Henry blocking the door without telling him the other things I said. She was angry at Henry for not using proper channels when we started seeing each other." She clutched her hands to her chest. "Oh, Millie, I shall die of self-condemnation for getting such a young man into such a dreadful scrape!"

"Father Noyes spared you. He didn't even mention your name."

"I know." Tirzah dramatically pulled a chair from the table and motioned to it. "I should have been on the stage with him—no, *instead* of him! I should have been accused. For I'm so much older." She collapsed into the chair. "I should be sent away in disgrace. Or if I'm allowed to stay, then I should be put in the lowest place here. The *Circular* may pass to you, or back to Harriet Worden. I'm not worthy to be the voice of our Community."

Millie suppressed an eye roll at the exaggeration. Tirzah, always the actress, was imagining the extreme. "What will you do?"

She straightened. "I'll request a committee to criticize me. I'll tell them everything I've told you." She clasped her hands in a pleading gesture. "I'll put myself at their mercy, and I'll ask Father Noyes to explain it all to the whole Community."

Even as the words tumbled from Tirzah's mouth, Millie discounted them. Father Noyes would never retract his statements. Whether Henry had committed the offense or not, Father Noyes would think he'd been righteous to rail against coercive actions in matters of love. He'd never subject Tirzah to scorn, nor would he admit he'd erred by judging too quickly.

Chapter 11: Postponed

Henry's public humiliation changed him—and not for the better. At play practice he could recite all his lines, but there was no punch, no conviction, no joy in his acting. His melancholy rubbed off on the rest of the cast and produced the most lackluster performance Millie had seen from them so far.

Afterward, she motioned for Henry to sit behind the piano for another heart-to-heart conversation. "We're supposed to perform our dress rehearsal in a week or two—though I still haven't announced it. Will you be able to see this through?"

"I hate to disappoint you." Henry studied his knuckles on his lap. "But I'm not sure I want to put myself on display—after what happened."

"Tirzah was going to set the record straight. Have you heard anything yet?"

"No, and I don't expect to." Henry hung his head. "Father Noyes told the truth about me, so there's nothing to correct."

"Now, Henry!" Millie placed her hand on his arm. "I've heard what happened from Tirzah's lips, and it wasn't the way he made it sound. He's just making an example of you."

"And a bad example shouldn't represent our Community to Outsiders. Not until I stop being a medium of a bad principality."

She shook her head. "You can't stop being one because you never were."

"Thanks, Millie. You're a pal." He patted her hand. "But to everyone else here, I'm somebody to keep an eye on. And not in a good way. Which is why they moved me to the Aquarium."

Outside the window in the gathering gloom the barren branches shivered in the chill north wind. Millie sighed. Winter always seemed endless this time of year. "Let's postpone the play. In a month or two, all this will have blown over, and things will be back to normal. Who knows?" She forced a cheery grin. "You might even get your old room back."

He managed a wry smile. "Maybe I'll get the revival spirit."

Walking to dinner with Tirzah the next day, Millie hoped to learn of her progress in restoring Henry's reputation. The March sun seemed brighter today, and the snow was melting, so spring was on its way after all. The ground was soggy as they crossed the road to the Mansion House driveway, and shimmering rivulets ran down the sloping rooftops of the edifice that loomed ahead.

"I'd like to postpone the play for a couple months."

Tirzah frowned with what looked like true sympathy. "It would be hard for Henry to appear in such a public manner."

Millie nodded. "Since we never announced it, no one will be the wiser."

"Whatever happened with that?" Tirzah tilted her head. "Is that another thing I've spoiled?"

Millie bit her lip at Tirzah's pitiful tone. She shouldn't have brought it up. "We were going to announce it the night of your criticism. Please, don't trouble yourself about it, Tirzah."

"But I should, because I didn't follow through for you, Millie." Tirzah stopped walking and stared into Millie's eyes. "Will you forgive me?"

Millie blinked back the tears that welled up as she viewed the beautiful, honest face before her. "Oh, Tirzah, there's nothing to forgive."

"You're kind, Millie." Tirzah touched her arm. "So much has happened in the last two weeks. I'm not proud of my behavior."

All Millie's harsh opinions of Tirzah melted and dropped away, shattering as decisively as the last icicle plunging from the Mansion House eaves. She grasped Tirzah's hands in hers and squeezed. "You're one of the strongest, most caring women I know."

Tirzah's face brightened at the compliment, and she began walking again, this time with more spring in her step. "You can't know what it means to hear you say that, especially today." She pulled Millie closer and spoke in her ear as they kept walking. "Tonight I'm meeting with my committee for criticism. I'll speak out on Henry's behalf. If you see him, tell him I'll do everything I can to clear his name."

At supper, Millie and Ellen arrived together and sat at the same table. Ellen scanned the dining room. "Have you seen Henry?"

"Not since play practice yesterday." Millie buttered her bread. "It was our last one for a while."

Ellen perked up. "Why is that?"

"We're postponing it for a while, until things get back to normal."

Ellen raised her eyebrows as if this were the juiciest tidbit she'd heard in some time. "He still feels the sting—while Tirzah remains the paragon of virtue."

Millie nearly choked on her coleslaw. "What do you mean?"

She didn't want to validate what Ellen had somehow ascertained.

"It was Tirzah who was in the garret with Henry."

Ellen didn't seem to care who heard her.

Millie shot a look at the others nearby. She spoke in a low voice. "Who's saying that?"

"It's common knowledge." Ellen jiggled her head. "Henry only had eyes for Tirzah. Everyone could see that."

Millie swallowed with difficulty. Ellen was right. Any observant person could have surmised that Tirzah was the unnamed woman.

"It's despicable that she didn't stand up for him." Ellen clenched her fists on the table top. "If they *were* in the garret, she wanted to be there. Henry would never hold her against her will. She lied about him."

Hot anger rose into Millie's cheeks. Ellen didn't know the story. Yet Millie couldn't defend Tirzah without giving away a confidence. "You weren't there, were you?"

"You're siding with Tirzah over Henry? Just because you work for her?" Ellen tossed her head and glared at Millie through narrow eyes. "You said you were Henry's friend."

"I am!" Millie said too loudly, causing people to look her way. She lowered her voice. "And I'm Tirzah's friend, too."

"I think you've made your loyalty very clear."

Ellen stood, jammed her chair against the table, and flounced away.

Millie dropped her eyes, ignoring the questioning faces that turned her way. She took another bite of coleslaw, trying to digest Ellen's words. Things weren't that simple. Ellen hadn't seen the true remorse on Tirzah's face. At this very moment Tirzah could be suffering disgrace before the central members as she tried to restore Henry's honor. What did Ellen know of it? Tirzah wasn't the enemy.

And neither was Henry. But who was? Father Noyes? Bible Communism? Or just some uncaring Fate?

Millie pushed her food away and went to her room.

* * *

Tirzah was in a bright mood the next morning. The criticism must have gone as well as or better than expected. Without saying anything, she made eye contact with Millie several times in a knowing way.

That afternoon when Millie, Tirzah, and their two co-workers were hard at work at their desks and several typesetters were busy at the counter, Father Noyes entered the room. Like the others, Millie straightened her posture and increased her attention to her task.

Nodding in the general direction of the workers, he strode directly toward Tirzah. "Good afternoon, my dear!"

She rose to greet him. "What can I do for you?"

"The exact question, the very question!" he boomed, his voice in fine form. He clearly wanted everyone to hear the conversation.

Not wanting to stare, Millie regarded him from the corner of her eye.

"I am still writing more than I want for the *Circular*—which distracts me from researching and writing about the American socialists."

He motioned to Tirzah to sit and pulled a chair next to her, but instead of sitting on it, he put one foot on the seat and leaned in toward his niece—close enough to invade the invisible border regions of her soul. Instinctively, Millie sat back in her chair, but Tirzah didn't flinch.

"So what *you* can do for me is this. Give up music! Become a writer!" He paused, letting his words sink in. "Devote yourself to your writer's craft as you do to your music, and you will be the best spokesman for Bible Communism that we will have—once I'm gone." Now he straddled the chair backwards as Theodore had done and glared at Tirzah. "So, what is your answer? Will you give up music for me, for the Community?"

Tirzah eyed him with disbelief laced with horror. She seemed unable to move, unable to speak.

Stunned, Millie gaped at the prophet. Surely he understood what he was asking. Everyone knew Tirzah's passion for music.

He locked eyes with her, ignoring the stares from the others in the room. "You know you can tell me what's in your heart, don't you?"

Tirzah drew a quavering breath. "If you want me to speak plainly, from my heart, then I must answer that nothing would hurt me so much as that."

Tirzah's voice caught as she spoke. Though the prophet had positioned himself so that Millie couldn't see Tirzah's face, she sounded on the verge of tears.

Millie felt her own throat constrict.

"That's because you're not thinking of this from the heavenly perspective." Leaning back, Father Noyes wagged his finger. "Music elevates and charms but for a moment. Your writing inspires and edifies. It can bring people to the knowledge of the truth, and unlike music, it remains, so that for generations your words will bear heavenly fruit."

Tirzah nodded her head slowly.

"You are our poetess, authoress, and editress. And when you are free from the piano, you can put your mind to it, so you will excel." The prophet stood, towering over Tirzah. "Now will you give me your answer?"

"You know I'll always obey you." A single tear trailed down Tirzah's cheek as she lifted her face toward Father Noyes. "If you require it, I'll give up music, though it will be turning my world upside down."

Millie eyed the prophet. Surely he'd relent now that she'd pledged her compliance.

"I can trust you to stick with me, Tirzah. You're too big a woman to be thumping the piano." Chin raised, he cast a disdainful gaze across the entire room and its people. "Leave that to the small fools!"

He strode to the door and let himself out.

A hush gripped the room as they all held their breath, waiting for Tirzah's response. She sat as if frozen, and nobody stirred, though Millie ached to rush to her.

Like a doomed prisoner being summoned to the gallows, Tirzah rose slowly. Looking around, she made eye contact with each woman, one at a time. She said flatly, "I shall not be playing the piano anymore."

Shoulders stooped, she walked to the coat hooks. She put on her cape and left.

The women exchanged sympathetic glances. This time, Millie refused to let her suffer alone. She strode to her cape, threw it over her shoulders, and ran after her. Tirzah had left via the back door and was heading toward the barren fruit trees of the Vineyard.

"Tirzah!"

Tirzah whirled around, and when she recognized Millie, she waited for her. Together they walked down the lane between rows of leafless trees that raised their dark, twisted arms to the leaden sky in bootless petition.

Eventually, Tirzah spoke. "Do you know what this means? Someone has told him about my committee last night. This is his way of reprimanding me. He knows he falsely accused Henry, and it's my fault."

"But—"

"No, it *is* my fault." Tirzah wrung her hands. "I said I deserved to be put out of the Community or relieved of all positions of responsibility here. That's what I told you, and that's what I told my committee. So this is my punishment. He's done it without humiliating me, except in front of the *Circular* staff, which I suppose I must be grateful for."

"But can he forbid you to play the piano?" Millie clenched her fists. "You're a grown woman, not a child!"

Tirzah eyed her feet. "He seeks to test my sincerity and love, even as God tested Abraham when He asked him to sacrifice Isaac." Her words fell dispassionately from her lips, as wooden as the lines Henry had spoken at rehearsal. "I must give up the thing that means the most to me—my music."

"Then it's just temporary." Millie gestured, palms up. "It's just postponing your music, like we're postponing the play. When he sees your obedience, he'll relent."

"Whatever the case, he has my loyalty." Tirzah stopped, turned around, and began retracing their steps. "He knows I'll do as he says."

As they walked, Millie contemplated God's test of Abraham, a story that had always bothered her. God, as God, had the prerogative to require something of Abraham that was extreme. But did Father Noyes, who wasn't God, have such a prerogative? He could only do it because Tirzah's loyalty was secure.

How would Millie respond if he commanded her to give up writing? She doubted she'd have Tirzah's faith.

* * *

The next ten days passed uneventfully. The first day of spring was dreary and rainy, perfectly matching Henry's and Tirzah's moods. Both seemed to adapt to the new rules—to a life less passionate, less joyful, and more acceptable to those who kept watch over them.

At Saturday's Meeting, Millie sat next to Ellen, who sat next to Henry. Ellen had swooped rather shamelessly into the gap left by Tirzah and spent every free moment with Henry, but that produced no pangs of jealousy in Millie's heart. She was glad Henry had a distraction, even if it came in the form of Ellen's blatant flirtations.

Before Mr. Woolworth dismissed the members, he called for everyone's attention. Millie lifted her eyes to the stage.

"I'm pleased to announce that Dr. Noyes will be returning within a few days. He'll be accompanied by architects from the New York firm that will draw up the plans for the new wing."

Millie froze in her seat.

A murmur of excitement spread through the auditorium mixed with some hisses of disapproval. The younger people were anxious to get the additional living space the wing would offer, which explained the smiles on Ellen's and Henry's faces. Others, mostly first generation members, thought bringing in New York City architects was another way Theodore Noyes was tainting their commune with his worldly ideas.

Millie brushed perspiration from her forehead. Such concerns were trifles compared to what Dr. Noyes's return meant for her. Soon she'd be going to bed with him; soon she'd become a Community wife. While the Outsiders were present, he wouldn't tend to his marital duties, but as soon as they left, Tirzah would schedule the interview.

If only Tirzah were not the go-between. Despite Tirzah's flaws, she was Millie's closest friend, after Jessie. Being in conflict with her again felt wretched. But Tirzah would brook no protests from Millie, not when she'd sacrificed her greatest love—music—for the Community and Father Noyes.

Millie pressed her nails into her palms. How could she prepare for the coming interview? If only she had a mother to talk to. Or who could talk to her. Every day she held the gray photograph in her hands asking for advice, but it couldn't respond. It was a mere two-dimensional representation of humanity.

As she looked around the Big Hall, her eyes came to rest on Aunt Sarah. Years ago her childhood teacher had gathered the girls and explained the transition to womanhood, but Millie hadn't paid much attention. At the time, when she was twelve, she'd had no interest.

Sunday dawned bright and clear, giving Millie the courage to seek out Aunt Sarah. She seemed surprised that Millie would want to talk alone, but she led her to her room on the third floor near the South Tower. Her window looked out over the veranda with a view to the lawn and fields to the south, including the two-story play house where the children could run about during cold or wet weather.

After some pleasantries, Millie began. "When Dr. Noyes returns, I'm to have an interview with him. My first."

"I see." Aunt Sarah's eyes widened, and she sat back in her chair. "Is that what you want to talk about?"

Millie nodded, averting her eyes from Aunt Sarah's steady gaze.

"Well, as I tell the girls when I prepare them for marriage, it's a wonderful thing. It means you're a woman now. Little Millie, all grown up!" Aunt Sarah's tone had become stilted and professional, full of feigned praise. Then she dropped her chin and knit her brows together. "But can it be you haven't begun yet? At your age?"

Millie squirmed. She shouldn't have come.

"Well, you *are* small." Aunt Sarah's eyes softened. "You're not looking forward to this meeting?"

"No, I'm not." Millie pictured the portly form of Dr. Noyes, his expansive bald forehead, and the fierce eyebrows that jutted out above dark, troubled eyes. There were few men toward whom she felt less physically attracted. "I've never even spoken to him in person. He doesn't know me from a factory hireling. It's only a duty for him and a duty for me. Why is it necessary?"

Aunt Sarah tilted her head as if considering a riddle she'd never heard. "You mustn't think of it that way, my dear."

She put her finger to her lip as if trying to concoct an explanation for a math problem a child couldn't grasp. Her eyes landed on a pencil. She picked it up, gripping it as if to write, but held it suspended between them.

"It's like anything new. Let's say writing in script. The first time you attempt it, it's bound to be awkward. Without a knowledgeable hand to guide yours, you would stray far above or below the invisible line." She waved the pencil in the air erratically. "But with an expert hand helping you form the letters, there's a beautiful outcome." She placed her left hand atop her right one and made the pencil dance smoothly in the air. "Soon you're ready to be released, and you continue the beauty on your own, without needing an expert to direct you."

She let her left hand drop slowly to the table while her right hand bobbed rhythmically along.

Millie's mouth went dry. It was one thing to have someone guiding your hand, but quite another to— Instinctively she rubbed the back of her hand against her lap to remove the taint of Aunt Sarah's disturbing comparison.

Aunt Sarah saw more persuasion was necessary. "Theodore may seem intimidating, and there are those here who doubt his commitment to our ideals, but the fact that he's pursuing his duty this way shows his love for us. I have no doubt you'll find him to be a kind and gentle lover."

Millie's flesh began to crawl. To kiss Dr. Noyes's passionless lips and feel his bristly beard on her face would be horror enough. To lie skin-to-skin with him would be an unfathomable nightmare.

She shifted uncomfortably on her chair and jiggled her leg. "I see. Thank you, Aunt Sarah. Thank you for talking."

There was no crossing over from Aunt Sarah's room to Millie's. Even though they were both on the third floor in the south wing, a section with only two floors stood between the South Tower and the mansard level of Ultima Thule. Millie descended the staircase to Hamilton Avenue, then walked down the hall to the end stairway.

Ahead of her, Constance was mounting the stairs. Millie quickened her pace to catch up. "Aunt Constance!"

Seeming to sense Millie's agitation, Constance invited her to her room, which was indeed the far reaches of the far reaches, lying in the southwest corner of the third story of the south wing.

With two windows, the room was bright and cheery. The quilt

was an elaborate pattern of fruits in brilliant reds, yellows, and greens, and a hand-woven oval rag rug lay beside the bed. The south window looked out over the same landscape that Aunt Sarah's did, but the room also offered a west view from its second window. That window opened to the common third-floor balcony and offered a vista of the gardens beside and beyond the Tontine. Although nothing was blooming now, in a few months the flower gardens would be bursting with color.

Constance motioned for Millie to take a seat, and she did so. She swallowed with difficulty and informed Constance of the upcoming interview.

Constance's face registered no surprise, no pride, no happiness—none of the awkward emotions Aunt Sarah had displayed. "You don't want to become a Community wife."

Her direct words were like balm to Millie's soul. "No! I don't! And I don't know why I have to. Aren't there enough wives here already?" Exhilarated by the freedom to voice her real opinions, Millie jumped up and crossed over to look out the west window. "Who should care if I don't participate?"

"Many will care, but you're right that there are plenty of wives to go around."

Millie turned toward Constance in surprise. "You're not going to tell me I'm selfish to withhold myself?"

Constance met her eyes. "I am not now and never have been a Community wife."

Millie gaped. "Is that possible? Isn't Shakerism forbidden?"

Hope struggled to spring up, just like the blades of grass below that would soon begin to turn green.

"More members practice it than you might know. But they must be discreet. Would you like to hear my story?"

Taking her seat again, Millie faced Constance eagerly.

"I came here about ten years ago with my husband." Constance's eyes bore a faraway look. "In those days, some people were joining just to participate in the free love they thought the Community allowed. Father Noyes made rules to screen out those types. So for three years, my husband and I were on probation and couldn't participate in complex marriage."

"But where's your husband now?"

Millie had never heard Constance or anyone else mention him.

Constance's body tensed and little vertical wrinkles formed around her lips. "He died in a sawmill accident."

Surprised, Millie brought her hand to her mouth. "I'm so sorry."

"Thank you." Constance licked her lips and continued. "They allowed me to mourn for a year. Then I was invited for an interview."

"And you said no?"

"For about six months, they let me keep declining." Constance clenched her fists. "Finally, they gave me a severe criticism, said my faith was small if I couldn't let Joseph go. They told me I was selfish and unloving."

"But you didn't give in?"

"No. I thought they might place me before the whole Community for criticism, but maybe because many still remembered the accident —and some felt guilty about it—they used other methods."

"Such as?"

Constance looked around her room and gestured with her arm. "They sent me here."

"To Ultima Thule!"

"Yes. But more than that." A cloud passed over her face. "For a month I wasn't allowed to eat with the Community. Someone brought me my breakfast, dinner, and supper here. When I worked, almost no one spoke to me."

Millie stared in disbelief. She'd never heard of such treatment at Oneida. "They shunned you?"

"They thought it would change my mind."

"But it didn't?"

"By then it was the height of canning season, and I'd been foreman of the canning operation for two years." Constance leaned back in her chair. "They couldn't do it without me—orders for preserves and jams were flooding in, and we couldn't keep the shelves stocked in the store. Much of the Community's income depended on me. Eventually, they told me I could eat in the Tontine, and no one ever approached me about interviews again."

Millie looked away. "I thought maybe you and my father—"

Constance gestured casually. "William and a couple other men invite me to their rooms after Meeting sometimes—for appearance' sake. That seems to keep everyone satisfied."

Did her father practice Shakerism? Millie wasn't sure she wanted to know. "But they kept you in Ultima Thule all these years."

Constance smiled smugly. "To my mind, I have the best room in the entire Mansion House."

"You do. It's lovely." Millie bit her lower lip. "But you were able to make your own choice because of your unique role here. What about me?"

"That's difficult. As a young person, you'll have more expectations on you than I did." Seeing Millie's countenance fall, she patted her hand. "But we can at least postpone things for a while."

Millie leaned forward. "How?"

Constance tilted her head and rested her chin on her fist. "We need to make you less visible here."

"I'm already in Ultima Thule," Millie smiled. "You can't get more out of the way than this."

The hint of a gleam rose in Constance's eyes. "But you can."

Millie squinted. "Like above the Tontine or above the store?"

Now Constance smiled broadly, her eyes twinkling. "Like The Villa at Willow Place."

"The Villa? But I'd be leaving the Mansion House and would be completely—"

"Off the beaten track," Constance finished.

"I wouldn't see Henry, or Father, or Virginia—or you! I'd have to stop working at the *Circular*." Millie slumped in her chair. "I'd have to work at the silk factory."

"That's all true." Constance acknowledged Millie's objections with an open-handed gesture. "It depends on how important this is to you."

They sat in silence for a minute. It was important. All important. Millie folded her hands on the table and leaned toward Constance. "How would I get transferred to Willow Place?"

"I think I can handle that." Constance tapped her fingers on the tabletop. "Ann Hobart can get you in at the silk works."

"But why would Ann want to do that?"

"Ann knows you're Tirzah's right hand on the *Circular* and Father Noyes's literary project. Ann's mother and Mrs. Bloom, who runs The Villa, are like this." Constance crossed her fingers. "So if Mrs. Bloom tells Mrs. Bailey she wants you as a kitchen helper..."

She pursed her lips as she thought through the plan. "And if Ann thinks it will bring more grief to Tirzah's life, she'll act on it."

Millie opened her mouth in protest. "No! What do you mean?"

"Ann feels Tirzah hasn't suffered enough in the affair of Henry Hunter. She was telling her mother as much the other day when we were ironing." Constance furrowed her brow. "Mrs. Bloom and I are old friends. I'll ask her to hint to Mrs. Bailey that you want to move to the silk works but don't want to leave Tirzah in a bind. Mrs. Bailey will pass that on to Ann, and she may bite."

Millie shook her head. "I could never do that to Tirzah." A sick feeling washed over her as she pictured Ann and Mrs. Bailey gossiping about Henry and Tirzah. Father Noyes had railed against *the Bailey spirit* more than once—the spirit of division that had caused Ann's brother to secede. Ann had changed her last name, but a leopard couldn't change its spots. "There has to be another way."

Constance looked down her nose. "There comes a time when the fruit has to be picked or it falls to the ground of its own accord—and then it's only good for the cider press."

The implications of that metaphor hung in the air. Millie shivered. "How did you decide what to do? After your husband died, I mean."

"I always just muddled along." Constance studied the pattern on her quilt. "But since God healed my arm, I believe He has a purpose for me." She met Millie's eyes. "And since we learned about the Spirit of Truth—I've been asking Him to guide me."

Millie started to nod politely, but stopped mid-nod. She didn't understand the way Constance spoke about God. "Thank you. You've given me some hope. But don't say anything to Mrs. Bloom yet. Let me think about this."

In her own room, Millie went over and over her options, none of them good. No matter how hard she tried, she couldn't reconcile herself to meeting with Theodore. She felt sicker and sicker every time she imagined herself in bed with him. To move to The Villa where she didn't know anyone would mean abandoning Tirzah, leaving a job she loved, giving up her literary studies with Tirzah and Mrs. Skinner, and working in a factory—which might drive her to insanity with boredom. How could she betray Tirzah to her rival, Ann Hobart, a woman known for her selfish and devious ways? Maybe complex marriage was glorious, as Aunt Sarah had said, and Theodore would gently teach her.

She needed advice from someone her own age. She wouldn't open herself up to Ellen's disdain for the world, and Dora Campbell's righteous admonitions would only parrot Aunt Sarah. She would write to Jessie.

To her surprise, she received a reply just two days later. Rather than sending it by post, Jessie had given her letter to someone returning to Oneida from Wallingford. The quick response was perfect —Dr. Noyes and the architects had just arrived. In the privacy of her room Millie opened the letter and read:

"My dearest Millie,

How fortuitous to get your letter today! I have been meaning to write. You must not show this letter to anyone, and I suggest you burn it after you read it. I have not told you, but George Ross and I are <u>in love</u>. He wants only me, and no other, and I desire only him. We do not agree with complex marriage, and George says we must secede and marry! Can you believe it? We are making plans about the proper time to make our departure. It will be in a fortnight —no longer! When I write you again, I will use an assumed name. How dastardly and mysterious! But they may intercept any correspondence from seceders. So look for a note from <u>Justine Wright</u>. That will be I—because my actions are <u>just and right</u>. A word puzzle for you!

Now with regard to your own dilemma, my advice is, do not submit! There is much talk here about doing away with complex marriage. Many here desire monogamy, and we hear that many at O.C. do, as well. (Dr. Noyes himself is in love with Ann Hobart and would marry her if he could!) Do whatever you can to postpone the ordeal, for I do not believe you will find Theodore to be the man of your dreams. But when you do find the right man for you, he will be everything you have hoped for, as my George is to me. It is just like one of your romantic novels, only so much better, for it is <u>real</u>.

All my love, Jessie (Justine Wright)

P.S. Mrs. Bloom at The Villa is a gem—George assures me you will love her! He came to Wallingford from there, you know!"

Millie read the letter four or five times. After committing it to memory, she brought it to the Nursery Kitchen. When no one was looking, she opened the door of the stove, tossed it in, and watched the flames lick it up, devouring it completely. Then she went to Constance's room and told her she was ready to move to Willow Place.

Chapter 12: Noah

Whether Millie worked next to a Community woman or an Outsider at the silk works, the minutes crawled by. The incessant droning of the machinery unraveled Millie's energy and spirit and prevented conversation. So despite working with a hundred women, she felt more isolated than she'd ever felt. How different from the jobs in the Mansion House, where pleasant chatter brightened even the dullest tasks. Millie often envied the elderly women in the Mansion House, parting and knotting the silken strands by hand.

Standing on one end of the line, feeding the reeled silk onto the spooler, was just as tedious as standing at the other end, watching the large spools fill up with thread and replacing them when they were full. Almost as maddening as the spinning threads were her spinning thoughts. Had she made the right decision, leaving her job at the *Circular* and her home at the Mansion House to work in this lonely, passionless factory? Was she wise to have trusted the word of Jessie, a woman she'd spent only two days of her life with, who was seceding from the Community to run off and marry a man she'd known for only a few months? Surely this was the maddest, rashest decision possible.

But if she'd taken that other course—going to bed with Dr. Noyes…. She'd come perilously close to losing something precious, something she still retained, despite losing other things she loved. Even so, how much time had she gained for herself? According to Jessie, things were changing, and she should postpone complex marriage as long as possible—and wait for the man of her dreams. Was that just a foolish fairy tale? Jessie had found the love of her life, but what were the chances of that happening to Millie? She was a child of the Community, destined soon to be a wife, whether she wanted to or not.

Happy are the hands that throw the silken strands.

A stab of violation had stopped her in her tracks when she first saw her own words, in print, staring back from placards posted around the factory. Now those words mocked her every day, reminding her that she belonged to the Community—mind and body—whatever feeble attempts she might make to retain her freedom.

Perhaps this exile to Willow Place would help bring her individualistic desires into harmony with Bible Communism. Where was the fervent idealism she'd felt on the trip to Wallingford? Constance's faith cure, being recruited to work for the *Circular* and write the play, assisting Tirzah with the literary project—had not all these fallen into place at just the right time? They should be proof enough that Bible Communism deserved her allegiance. Why couldn't she fully give herself to the Community the way other women did?

She was selfish and lacked faith.

But faith in what? In Father Noyes, whose imposing form she feared and whose ill-informed decisions had hurt people she cared about? In Theodore Noyes, who was an agnostic? She might have gained something from those Bible classes. Now they'd been broken up because people were having inspirations that conflicted with Father Noyes's inspiration. If they were both inspired by the same God, how could that be?

These doubts and questions spun around as dizzyingly as the thread on its spools. If only she could hear from the Spirit of Truth that Constance had spoken of. But, like little Haydn who didn't know how to pray because Judge Towner wouldn't teach him, she was ignorant of how to hear from that Spirit. She knew only how to confess Christ.

Sometimes she repeated over and over for an hour at a time the prayer she'd learned as a child. "I confess Christ a good spirit in me." Then she changed it to "I confess Christ the Spirit of Truth in me." But that seemed as mechanical as the rolling gears of the machinery. After that, she gave up and simply listened to the humming of the silken strands being drawn onto the spools, insisting, "The Spirit of Truth … will guide you into all truth." Once she became so mesmerized by the song that she missed taking off her full spool of thread. Scrambling to correct her mistake, she looked up, embarrassed to see Mrs. Jones, the supervisor, glaring at her.

One o'clock. She was free to go to dinner, and unlike the other workers, she wouldn't come back afterwards. With her four hours at the silk works completed, her only other duty today was to help Mrs. Bloom in the kitchen at The Villa. She threw on her cape and skipped

down the external stairs to the muddy lot around the factory.

She flipped up her hood against the steady drizzle. Keeping her eyes on her feet, she placed them in the least muddy spots of the road as she walked by the two boarding houses where the Outsider girls roomed. As she passed the squat, unattractive rental cottages that came next, she quickened her pace in case any of the rough hirelings who worked in the trap factory were loitering about.

She took a deep breath. The pungent smell of last year's decaying wet leaves tickled her nose, and the rushing of the waterworks on Sconondoa Creek calmed her worn-out ears with soothing music. After ten minutes she reached The Villa, the main building of the one-hundred-acre farm at Willow Place.

Inside the warm kitchen, she seated herself at the table, now vacant. The other Villa residents had earlier scheduled dinner times and had already returned to their afternoon labors.

Mrs. Bloom put a bowl of stew in front of her. "We need these April showers to bring the May flowers, don't we?"

Millie nodded, her mouth full of the warm concoction. Her whole body relaxed, and she let out a sigh. Imbued with Mrs. Bloom's positive vibrations, the entire farmhouse, but especially the kitchen, radiated comfort. Mrs. Bloom provided three hearty meals a day for the residents of The Villa who labored in the factories, sawmill, and machine shop. Meals with meat. Meat was seldom on the menu in the Tontine, but residents here feasted on chicken, turkey, and goose several times a week. Beef, and especially pork, were out of the question due to the Dansville Sanitorium diet that Dr. Noyes had introduced years ago.

Every morning Millie helped Mrs. Bloom prepare breakfast, and each afternoon she cleaned up the dinner dishes and helped with supper preparations. Most days she had plenty of time to sit in the parlor and read while Mrs. Bloom took her afternoon break.

Mrs. Bloom gripped a straw broom in both hands. "You know that one flirtatious guinea hen that keeps comin' up to the back step?"

"She saw me off this morning." Millie carried her empty bowl across the room and began pumping water into the sink. "What else has she been up to?"

"I was shakin' out some rugs, and she came up and wished me luck." Mrs. Bloom jammed the broom into a corner. "Good-luck!

Good-luck!"

"Is that what she was saying to me?"

Millie played along. The hen's clucking sounded just like that.

Mrs. Bloom leaned the broom against the wall and put her hands on her hips in mock offense. "I told her 'twasn't luck at all. 'Twas pure skill. I been shakin' out rugs for nigh on half a century."

Millie grinned. "Did she change her tune?"

"Well, she musta sensed I was affronted. When I turned 'round to go inside, she said as clear as day, 'Come-back! Come-back!'"

Mrs. Bloom's imitation sounded so much like the hen that Millie burst into laughter. Mrs. Bloom chuckled heartily.

Millie plunged the dinner plates into the wash water. "What about the one who's gone broody?"

"I've decided to let her hatch 'em. So we'll have us some keets in 'bout three to four weeks."

Cocking her head at the unfamiliar term, Millie squinted at the older woman. "Keets?"

"Mmmm. Guinea chicks." Mrs. Bloom's eyes sparkled. "Cute as can be. Just wait an' see."

Millie thrilled at the thought of the little chicks. The Mansion House was devoid of animals, but here there were cats, chickens, geese, turkeys, and guineas right out the back and dairy cows and horses across the field.

With the kitchen cleaned and some beans set to soak for the next day, Millie and Mrs. Bloom settled down in the large parlor. The Villa had been a farmhouse reconfigured as a tavern when the Community purchased it, so the first floor was one large common space. At the center of the room, a wide staircase led to the women's sleeping rooms above. Two rectangular dining tables and one round one stood near the kitchen. Chairs, sofas, and small tables cluttered the rest of room. The main floor boasted three separate fireplaces, one in the dining area and two against the west wall of the living area. How peaceful it was to sit almost anywhere and stare into the ever-changing flames.

Millie and Mrs. Bloom sat reading in silence, enjoying an hour's rest before the first workers came home. Before long, Mrs. Bloom's head, its bobbed gray hair scattered every which way, nodded forward onto her chest. Her book slid onto her lap, and a soft whistling snore escaped with each exhale. She still wore her blue-flowered apron, and her jolly full cheeks glowed from the heat of the fireplaces.

Rap! Rap! Rap!

Millie started at the light knock at the kitchen door, but it didn't break through Mrs. Bloom's slumber. Millie tiptoed past her into the kitchen and opened the door. She stepped back in surprise. There stood Noah Martinson, holding a low crate full of newborn kittens. The rain had stopped, and a gush of sodden air filled the room. With it a calico cat rushed in, circled the kitchen a few times, and meowed authoritatively as tiny squeaks issued from the crate.

Millie stifled a laugh. "Noah?"

She eyed the crate, which rocked in his arms like a barge at sea.

The cat pressed itself against Millie's legs so vigorously that her knees almost gave in, causing her to wobble toward Noah. She'd never before been petted by a cat. The calico wound around Noah's legs and returned to hers, completing a figure eight.

She laughed outright. "This must be the missing Patches. Unless you're selling kittens door to door."

Noah chuckled. "We meet again!" He looked around the kitchen. "I was told to deliver them to Mrs. Bloom."

Millie cranked her arm. "Please, come in."

As he stepped over the threshold, he stumbled. The crate brushed Millie, but he righted it before any kittens tumbled out.

He grinned. "I guess it's my turn to whack *you* with *my* basket."

Laughing, Millie pulled a chair away from the table, and Noah lowered the crate. As soon as it came to rest, the mother cat jumped into it and lay down. As eight fuzzy, blind balls nuzzled into her underside, a deep rumbling purr filled the room.

Mrs. Bloom bustled into the kitchen. "Patches? Where have you—?" She looked down into the crate. "Oh! I see how it is." She stroked the cat, and the rumbling intensified. A satisfied smile spread across the woman's face as she turned to Noah. "Where'd you find 'em, and how'd you know to bring 'em to me?"

While working at the trap factory, Noah had been tasked with cleaning out a storage shed in the yard. His supervisor, who lived at The Villa, recognized the mother as the cat that had recently disappeared.

Mrs. Bloom pulled a chair away from the table. "Well, you've brightened my day for certain." She motioned to Noah to sit. "Won't you stay for some strawberry leaf tea? And I'm sure I've got a biscuit an' some jam."

Millie sprang to action before Noah could nod his head. Soon they were all seated around the kitchen table.

Teacup in hand, Mrs. Bloom let out a long sigh. "Patches an' me go way back. It like to broke my heart when she went missin'. I thought sure a fox or coyote'd got 'er." She eyed the nursing mother affectionately. "And now she's got little ones again. Ain't they sweet?"

Millie and Noah looked from the animals to Mrs. Bloom's face, glowing with grandmotherly pride. Then their eyes met, sending a warm comfort down Millie's spine. How pleasant to be sitting next to him again—and here of all places. Life was full of surprises.

"So, you're a town boy, then?" Mrs. Bloom asked when she could take her eyes off Patches and her kittens. "What's your name?"

"Noah Martinson, ma'am. I'm staying in one of the cottages."

Something flashed in Mrs. Bloom's eyes. Perhaps, like Constance, she recognized the name. Millie scarcely allowed herself to inhale. Constance might have told Mrs. Bloom about meeting Noah on the way to Wallingford, but Millie couldn't be sure. She couldn't let on that she knew him without betraying a confidence. But Noah didn't know of her promise. He might let their secret slip.

"You're young for that. D' you like livin' there?"

Noah swallowed a bite of biscuit. "Can't say I do, ma'am. There's more tobacco and liquor and rough talk than I'm used to." He took another bite. "My father's a minister."

"You're Reverend Martinson's boy?" Mrs. Bloom squinted at him. "Shouldn't you be livin' at home, then?" She folded her hands on top of the table and leaned toward the young man, ready to give motherly advice. "The fact'ry provides transportation to town, y' know."

He brushed crumbs from his mouth with his hand. "I'm striking out on my own while I read law. Unless I decide to go into the ministry."

"Law versus grace, eh?" Mrs. Bloom glared at her visitor. "Should be an easy decision."

Noah laughed easily, as he had when Constance challenged him.

"I need some time to figure out what I want. And to find my faith."

"You've lost it, then?"

Mrs. Bloom tossed out the question like a cat toying with a mouse.

Noah hesitated. "Well, not exactly. I just need some breathing room."

Mrs. Bloom crossed her arms against her chest. "If you're seekin' the Lord, you're not likely to find Him in one o' them cottages."

Noah met her probing eyes as he sipped his tea. "No, ma'am."

With her elbow on the table, resting her chin on one hand, Mrs. Bloom drummed the fingers of her other hand on the table top. She moved her head from side to side as if conducting an internal debate. Finally she said, "I've got a space for you here."

Noah and Millie tilted their heads at the same time.

Noah's brow furrowed in confusion. "But I'm not joining your Community."

Leaning back in her seat, Mrs. Bloom crossed her arms on her chest again. "But you'd call yourself a seeker?"

Noah gave a slow, noncommittal nod.

"I've put up seekers before." She pushed her chair back and motioned to the rear of the house. "There's a vacancy in the men's dormitory. You could keep payin' rent for the cottage, but you could sleep an' eat here. I just need to clear it with Mr. Woolworth."

Millie's heart beat faster. She'd love to have Noah here, but surely he wouldn't defy his father by living among the communists.

"I'd be grateful, ma'am." His eyes brightened. "I can make myself useful around the house, too."

"Give me a day to work it out." Mrs. Bloom stood. "Come back tomorrow 'bout this time, an' I'll tell you if you're in."

Noah stood and gave a little bow. "Thank you for the biscuits, Mrs. Bloom."

He nodded to Millie, scratched Patches on the head, and let himself out.

Millie stared at Mrs. Bloom. "Why did you do that?"

Would making a convert of their biggest enemy's son be a feather in her cap? Or was she returning a favor to someone who'd helped her friend?

Mrs. Bloom pursed her lips. "Just didn't seem right—a nice boy like that livin' with those men from the World."

Her eyes rested on Patches, and she sighed contentedly.

The next day when Noah was due to come by, Millie planted herself, book in hand, in a chair with a clear view of the kitchen table. Mrs. Bloom had hinted that Mr. Woolworth had *somewhat* approved the plan for Noah to board at The Villa. If Noah accepted the terms.

Right on time he rapped on the door.

Mrs. Bloom led him to the table. "It's all settled." Her voice was cheery. "You can move in today."

"That's good news."

"There's just the matter of signin' th' agreement."

Mrs. Bloom produced a paper and pushed it across the table toward Noah. He stared at it in silence.

Mrs. Bloom sat. "Anythin' wrong?"

Millie could just make out Noah's low voice. "It says I'm investigating Oneida Community in good faith with intent to join."

"That a problem?"

"It doesn't quite describe my situation."

"I see." Mrs. Bloom sounded disappointed. "But you're examinin' *your* faith, an' while you're here, you might as well examine *ours*." She leaned across the table. "If you find our faith worthy, d' you think you could join the Community?"

"Well, if—but that's a large if."

"It is, it is. But—are you *willin'* to investigate us? To test the puddin', as it were?"

"I have been curious about communism," he said.

"There! Sounds to me like this agreement just describes you."

The pencil scratched as Noah signed the document.

Mrs. Bloom shouted, "Millie!"

She stepped into the kitchen just as Mrs. Bloom took the agreement from Noah's hand. "Good afternoon, Mr. Martinson."

His face brightened when he saw her. He nodded. "Miss Langston."

Mrs. Bloom placed her hand on Millie's shoulder. "Now, *Noah*, *Millie* here can show you the entrance to the dormitory." She emphasized their names as if to shoo away their formality. "An' she can answer all your questions 'bout Bible Communism. In fact, she's written a play to help Outsiders understand our life here, haven't you,

Millie?"

Millie's cheeks warmed. The play might never even happen now, and she was in no position to answer the inquiries of a seeker—especially one as well informed as Noah—with her own faith on such shaky ground. She felt like the miller's daughter again, but under Mrs. Bloom's prodding gaze, she nodded and smiled.

* * *

As usual, Millie spent Sunday at the Mansion House. At first she'd been reluctant to go back for fear of running into Tirzah and having to explain herself. But when they had passed each other, Tirzah greeted her pleasantly without any hint that she felt betrayed. Millie shouldn't have expected anything else—she'd flattered herself to think that she and Tirzah shared any kind of deep friendship. Tirzah was too powerful and popular to concern herself with someone like Millie, after all.

Today, after playing dominoes with her father and squails with Henry and Ellen, Millie headed to the cellar to the Turkish bath—a luxury The Villa didn't have. She descended the stairs from the Little Court, turned right, and stopped abruptly. Just to the side of the green wooden door that led into the bath, Victor Hawley stood with Mary Jones, who leaned against the block wall. With one hand Victor smoothed Mary's wet hair on her forehead. His other hand rested on her enormous belly. She grimaced in pain.

"It's all right, little one. Papa's here." Victor's voice was soothing as he caressed Mary's abdomen. "We'll see each other soon."

Mary's features relaxed as her pain subsided.

Millie nodded to them as she entered the bath, but they were too intent on each other to acknowledge her. Millie didn't mind. She was happy to see them together, even though they were flagrantly violating Community rules again. Victor seemed to have assisted Mary in the bath, even though men and women weren't supposed to enter together.

As Millie stripped down to her chemise and lay on the bench in the dry heat room, her heart warmed with her joints. Theodore had kept his word, allowing Victor to come back from Wallingford for the birth. Though Mary's pain could have been just a warning, judging by her size, her labor might well be starting. Very soon now Victor would be holding the baby as Mary had envisioned.

After dinner the following evening, Mrs. Bloom invited Millie to come with her to Meeting at the Mansion House.

Millie declined. She'd had the sniffles and a bit of a headache all day. So much for the health benefits of Turkish baths. "I'll go another time. Do you go often?"

"Several times a week." Mrs. Bloom removed her blue-flowered apron. "I keep up with the gossip that way—and my social life."

She raised her eyebrows to convey her meaning.

Since Mrs. Bloom was past childbearing age, she was in demand as a partner for the young men at the Mansion House who were not yet *teleoi*. She was probably hinting that Millie, too, might enjoy the broader selection of men there. Apparently Constance hadn't told Mrs. Bloom why Millie wanted to live at The Villa.

Millie's face grew warm, but Mrs. Bloom whisked away to the buggy.

Meeting at The Villa was simpler than at the Mansion House. With only about twenty-five people in attendance, the time passed quickly. Mrs. Jones and Mr. Conley gave statistics about the daily production at the silk and trap factories, and a few people read aloud articles of interest from the *Observer* or the *Standard*, the local newspapers. Sometimes someone read from the *Circular* or a published Home Talk of Father Noyes. Finally, a handful of people confessed Christ.

It lasted about thirty minutes, and then people formed little groups to play games or converse. The other women—Millie's three coworkers from the silk factory, and Grace, who operated the lathe in the wood shop—often worked on mending or their handiwork near the fire. Millie did so just to fit in, although her embroidery was abominable. Eventually she'd tuck it behind her and pull out her current novel.

Tonight she planned to retire to the room she shared with Grace early, but as she crossed through the parlor toward the stairs, she noticed Noah sitting alone at a small game table with a dejected look on his face. They hadn't spoken privately since he moved in, and Millie wasn't sure whether she should befriend him. Three months had passed since their dinner at the Astor House. Although she'd thought of him often, casting him as the hero of multiple imagined stories, he'd probably never thought of her again—except when they'd met by chance at the trap factory and now at The Villa.

Still, he looked like a lost puppy. She couldn't pass by him without some greeting. "Did you enjoy seeing your family yesterday?"

By the look on his face, that was the worst thing she could have said. "No, actually." His shoulders drooped. Then, as if remembering his manners, he straightened and motioned to a chair. "Won't you join me?"

She sat across from him, and he continued. "My father and I had a bit of a wrangle. He was upset that I signed the agreement to live here."

"Oh, I'm sorry." Millie folded her hands on the table. "Did you tell him there's no drinking or cursing here?"

Noah frowned. "He insists I lied by saying I'm thinking about joining. He wouldn't let it go. So I told him I *am* considering it."

Millie's heart leapt, but she squelched her excitement. "You left on poor terms, then?"

"You could say that."

She couldn't desert him now—he looked so forlorn. "Do you play dominoes?"

"It's my father's favorite game."

She winced. He'd think she was deliberately trying to give him the hypo. "Mine, too," she said, and added, "I mean, my father's."

They both laughed. Millie felt her headache lifting.

Noah shrugged. "Sure, let's play."

Millie got the game, and they played comfortably in silence for a time. Despite his conflict with his father, Noah's mannerisms were calm. His gentle hands caressed the ivory tiles and his lips parted ever so slightly as he considered his next move. A subtle arc creased the top of his strong chin, and perfectly shaped chestnut eyebrows topped the deepest brown eyes she'd ever seen. But it was his smile that was so utterly disarming. She'd seen it work first on Constance and then on Mrs. Bloom. And she'd experienced it herself. Every time he flashed those perfect teeth and his lips spread into his good-natured grin, she felt warm all over.

She searched for a safe and positive topic of conversation. "How do you like Mrs. Bloom?"

"She's wonderful." Noah lips curled upward. "Like a sunny flower. She's aptly named."

"I've often thought that, too." Millie stroked the cool, smooth surface of the domino in her hand. "She's so different from our head cook at the Mansion House." She hesitated for a moment. Then, leaning forward, she lowered her voice. "Her name is Mrs. Skinner. Whenever I made a mistake in her kitchen, I thought she'd *skin me alive*."

Noah chuckled. "Evidently names can be prophetic. What about this: A man named William Wordsworth became England's poet laureate. He had an unfair advantage."

"I believe he did." Millie grinned. "Do you like poetry?"

If so, he might become a new literary partner.

"I like some—mostly shorter poems." Noah played a tile. "Now it's your turn—to think of a name that matches the person, I mean."

Millie searched for names she'd contemplated before. "Oh— William Wilberforce. He had such force of will, hadn't he?"

"A great man." Noah rotated the ivory tile. "In fact, he inspired me to become a lawyer. So I can influence public sentiment for good as he did."

Millie arched her eyebrows. "Ministers don't promote the public good?"

Noah laughed. "Not the same way. Father still wants me to get a divinity degree at Hamilton College. But I've decided to read law at home for a year or two and then find an apprenticeship."

They discussed everything from Reconstruction of the South to the recent inauguration of President Hayes and the controversial compromise that installed him. Millie was fascinated. She'd never followed politics.

When they heard the horses and buggies returning from the Mansion House, Millie began boxing up the game. "I hope you're feeling better—about your father, I mean."

Noah's face clouded. "Thanks for the talk. It took my mind off him for a while. But I don't like being called a liar." He set his jaw. "*Do all you have agreed to do.* That's the basis of contract law. So I'll have to learn all I can about Bible Communism, like a real seeker." He touched Millie's hand as it rested on the table top. "But I'll need a teacher."

His gentle touch and kind eyes were impossible to refuse, even if she wanted to. Being his teacher meant more evening talks—a delightful prospect. When she worked at the newspaper, she'd grown used to being a halfhearted apologist, knowing she objected to complex marriage for herself. She could explain the Community, even when she disagreed with it.

She smiled. "Of course. But I'll warn you: It might be the blind leading the blind."

A few members who had returned from the Mansion House crossed the parlor, continuing a boisterous conversation. Millie said goodnight and began climbing the stairs. She heard Noah call out, "See you in the ditch, then!"

Just as she glanced back at him, she heard a loud sniff from the kitchen. Mrs. Bloom plopped down at the table, a handkerchief to her eyes. Millie rushed down the stairs and ran to the kitchen. She'd never she seen Mrs. Bloom cry. Noah joined them and sat next to the older woman.

"What is it?" Millie asked, leaning over her. "Are you all right?"

"Yes, child, I'll be fine in a minute." She blew her nose and dabbed her eyes. "We had some bad news tonight is all."

Dread washed over Millie. She glanced at Noah, who looked on with eyes full of compassion. "What was it?"

"It's Mary Jones. Her b-baby." Millie's heart sank even further as the tears flowed from Mrs. Bloom's eyes. "It was born dead."

Tears stung Millie's eyes, and heaviness gripped her chest. It couldn't be. She'd just seen Mary and Victor yesterday—and heard Victor's tender words to the unborn baby. She swallowed hard, fighting the tears, and dropped into the chair by Mrs. Bloom's side. She could think of nothing to say to make things better. She laid her palm on the older woman's hand.

Meanwhile, Noah had stepped to the stove and removed the simmering tea kettle. He prepared a cup of strawberry leaf tea and slipped it in front of Mrs. Bloom.

She lifted her tear-stained face. "Ah! There's a fine lad!"

By this time, several members were watching from across the foyer, but no one intruded.

Noah seated himself. "Do you mind if I pray?"

When both women shook their heads slightly, he folded his hands on the table top.

"Dear Father, we know the child is in Your loving arms, but we pray for the bereaved mother—that You will comfort her. Let Your mercy wash over her tonight and in the days ahead, and shelter her in Your great love. In the name of Jesus, Amen."

Millie and Mrs. Bloom stared at Noah. No one at Oneida Community prayed aloud. The last time Millie heard someone pray, she was a youngster in the Children's House sitting at the skirts of Lady Susan, who taught the little ones to confess Christ. She couldn't deny the peace that fell on her as Noah prayed those few sincere words for a woman he didn't even know.

Chapter 13: Choker

Standing at her station at the silk factory, Millie mulled over the tragic news about Mary's baby. As Mary's second stillbirth, it was all the more devastating. Was Theodore grieving for his child? Victor certainly was. Millie teetered on the verge of tears all morning, and she shuffled back to The Villa barely noticing the warm spring air or the chirping birds.

After a dinner of bread pudding, Millie talked about the tragedy with Mrs. Bloom, which seemed to help them both.

Suddenly the older woman backed away from the sink. "Dear me! I almost forgot. You got a letter today." Drying her hands on her apron, she scurried from the room and came back holding a thick brown envelope. She eyed it curiously, squeezing the lumpy package. "It's from Justine Wright in New Haven. Relative of yours?"

"N-no," Millie began in confusion, "I don't know—" She stopped herself and felt her face redden. That was the code name Jessie had warned her she'd use. "I mean, yes, that is, sort of a cousin."

Community members were all family, after all. Then again, if Jessie was writing under the secret name, she was no longer a member.

Mrs. Bloom stood staring as if she expected Millie to open the envelope right there. Resisting the older woman's prodding gaze, Millie felt the elongated shape of whatever was inside, then set the envelope on the table and continued washing dishes. "It's probably a bookmark or something. She likes to knit."

Her neck felt uncomfortably warm. She wasn't used to lying, and Mrs. Bloom was one of the last people she wanted to lie to. But she couldn't risk giving Jessie's secrets away or causing anyone to intercept future letters from *Justine Wright*.

When Mrs. Bloom sat down to read, Millie went upstairs to her sleeping room and opened the envelope. Along with the letter was something red and silky. She pulled it out and gasped. It was a crimson grosgrain choker necklace with a pink-and-ivory cameo—almost the exact choker she'd seen the woman at the Astor House wearing.

Remembering Noah's breath, she felt tingles spreading across her right cheek.

How like Jessie to recall the picture in *Godey's Lady's Book* and to find the very necklace. Millie spent several minutes feeling the texture of the band and running her fingers over the bas relief of the elegant female profile.

She'd never owned a piece of jewelry. Some women in the Community wore simple chains or rings. But when she was little, the jewelry spirit had become a much-dreaded scourge, and the women had all surrendered their gaudy possessions to a basket passed around during Meeting. She remembered a story—no doubt apocryphal—of a girl whom Father Noyes had invited to his apartment. She sat on his lap as he opened the center drawer of his desk and showed her rows of shiny bracelets and necklaces neatly laid out.

Millie wanted to put the necklace on, but she didn't dare—Grace could come in at any moment. And of course, she could never wear it in public. Silly Jessie. Still, she was touched at the beautiful gift. After stroking it once more, she hid it inside her pillow case and lay down on her bed to read Jessie's letter.

> "Dear Millie,
>
> 'Tis done! George and I are now husband and wife— only to each other! Mr. Denton gave us each our $100 parting funds—he was ever so kind and understanding— and we were off to New Haven. We found a judge to hear us say our vows, and now I am Mrs. Ross. George is so clever and has already found work. We are living in a hotel now, but when we are settled, you must come for a visit. I hope you like the necklace. I saw it in a shop in New Haven. I remembered your story about the woman's necklace and dog collars, though I couldn't quite recall the point. Still, I want you to accept it as a token of my sincerest <u>friendship</u> and my deepest desire to <u>see you again</u>. It <u>is</u> lonely here. But I have no regrets, and neither does George.
>
> All my love,

Jessie Ross"

Millie read the letter over several times. Of course Jessie wouldn't remember Constance's lesson about the choker. Millie could hardly recall it herself. Chokers and dog collars. The first were worn willingly, the second were not. But how ironic that, though she *wanted* to wear the choker, she couldn't. Could the absence of a necklace be a collar of sorts—used to choke her freedom, to keep her from expressing her true desires? She dropped her head on her pillow, her head swimming with the conundrum.

When Grace opened the door, Millie woke with a start. Sitting up quickly, she stashed the letter under her pillow. She'd slept for over an hour, and she needed to get down to the kitchen to help Mrs. Bloom. Grace, a woman of few words, gave her a curious look but made no comment.

Over the next two weeks, Millie sat with Noah in the evenings and tried to explain Bible Communism. She wouldn't broach the subject of complex marriage, of course. Noah could get all the details he wanted on that by reading Father Noyes's pamphlets, which were readily available around the town and commune. Nor would she discuss mutual criticism, the least Christian practice of the Community. But she stammered out what she remembered about Jesus' Second Coming in 70 A.D. and how the church on Earth was becoming the church in Heaven. To her embarrassment, the more she talked, the more confused she became.

Noah listened with a polite but amused expression when she faltered over doctrine. Eventually their conversations over dominoes or word puzzles veered toward stories about his family, his school days, or trips he'd taken to New York City and the ocean.

Noah and his younger brother had been inseparable, and he found it hard to be away from him. The two of them had teased their little sister incessantly but would gladly give their lives to keep her from harm. Even though love was the basis of Bible Communism, Millie had never experienced that kind of love—the unabashed love of a sibling.

On the first of May when her factory shift was done, Millie strolled toward The Villa, enjoying the gentle sun warming her face. Everything smelled fresh and clean. The bushes all had buds, and the busy robins and jays flitted about with straw in their mouths for building their nests in some well-chosen spot.

But the usually welcoming kitchen felt dull and lowering. While eating her dinner, Mrs. Bloom scowled and seemed brusque for no apparent reason.

Finally, Millie asked, "Is something bothering you?"

"Bothering? When you wanna strangle the woman who taught you everything you know, it's a bother."

She shook an imaginary neck in her bare hands, then plopped her palms onto the table top in exasperation.

"You mean—Harriet Skinner?"

Mrs. Bloom had told Millie stories of her early Community days when she'd learned to plan meals and cook for the commune at Mrs. Skinner's side.

"Yes, my dear Harriet, an' all the rest of 'em. Meddlers an' busybodies, that's what!" Furious contortions wracked Mrs. Bloom's face. She finished her last bite of potato and gruffly pushed her chair back with a "hummph!"

Millie pumped the water into the sink to wash up the dinner dishes. Mrs. Bloom planted herself next to her and started scouring a frying pan with vigor.

When she spoke, her voice was less fierce. "They've told Mary she can never have another child. Like it's for them to say. Don't they think if she's got the heart to try again, even after havin' two born dead, that she should have the chance? How can she ever get over losin' them babies if they won't let 'er try again? She did what they wanted, an' it didn't work out. Now they should let 'er do it her way."

Millie washed a plate and rinsed it, her chest heavy. "Is she *asking* to try again?"

"Two days later, bless 'er heart. Two days after she lost the baby, she tells Dr. Carpenter, 'I'm ready to try it over again.' That's spunk, right there!" Mrs. Bloom jabbed the air with the steel wool. "But Harriet an' Father Noyes an' Dr. Carpenter, in their wisdom, they decide she's not fit to have children."

Millie's shoulders sagged. "That must have been hard for her to accept."

"Ah, but she didn't accept it." Mrs. Bloom rinsed the frying pan triumphantly and plunked it down. "Not her."

She glared at Millie, her lips pursed.

"What do you mean?"

The older woman attacked a charred soup pot with gusto for a minute, then spoke without looking up. "Sarah Story tol' me everything. Mary stuck to it with astonishin' tenacity. *Astonishin'*, Sarah says. Mary looks 'em straight in the eye and says to 'em, 'If I tried again, I think I could bear a living child.'"

Millie's heart ached. "Maybe they just want her to wait?" She'd never seen a woman so excited about having a child—or so in love with a man who wasn't the child's father. "She wants to try with Victor, doesn't she?"

"You haven't heard the half of it."

Mrs. Bloom continued to scrub silently.

Millie carefully washed the teacups, keeping them from clinking. She suppressed the urge to roll her eyes. Mrs. Bloom told a story spoonful by spoonful, as if thickening a sauce.

At last she spoke. "They put it before the whole Meetin' last night. The one night I stayed here. First they read a letter from Dr. Carpenter sayin' she ought not to have a baby. Then they took a vote." Mrs. Bloom's chin began to quiver and her eyes became watery. She drew a handkerchief from her sleeve and wiped her nose. "Do you know, not one single person stood up for her?"

A dagger of guilt stabbed Millie's chest. She was no better. She'd never objected to the way Mary was being treated. Like a coward, she'd abandoned her in the sewing room. She was certainly no William Wilberforce.

"I'd 've stood up." Mrs. Bloom continued grinding the steel wool into the bottom of the pot. "I know what it's like for the chance to be a mother to pass you by."

Surprised, Millie ignored the teacups. "Do you?" she asked gently.

"I had a stillbirth," Mrs. Bloom said hoarsely. "'Twasn't a planned baby. They weren't allowin' children in them days. Everyone said since I was gettin' close to my turn o' life, it musta been a providence. But my little boy—he came out dead." Tears flowed silently down her cheeks. She gruffly brushed them away, leaving black streaks on her cheeks. "An' after that—well, I was too old then. So I never got to have a livin' child—just to carry one." She turned away and dabbed furiously at her eyes with her apron. "He'd be 'bout Noah's age by now."

"I'm so sorry." Millie's voice cracked, and she blinked back tears. "I didn't know."

Mrs. Bloom grabbed a saucepan and began to scour. "No one's got the right to tell 'er she's gotta give up. Not Harriet. Not Father Noyes. She's young enough to still have a child. An' if she doesn't, she'll have a hole in here that will never be filled." She tapped her fist to her chest twice. "Never."

Millie returned to the teacups, washing them silently as she pondered this new side of the woman who'd been so kind to her. Now she understood Mrs. Bloom's eagerness to take Noah in. He'd reminded her of her lost son.

Millie set the last cup to dry and drained the water. "I wonder how Victor feels."

"Devastated." Mrs. Bloom answered without hesitation. "There's a man who won't be here much longer, an' I can't blame him."

* * *

After supper that night, Millie went out on the back porch where Mrs. Bloom had rigged up a covered box in one corner for Patches and her kittens. Melancholy still clung to her like a wet dress. Her heart ached for Mary and for Mrs. Bloom—both denied the joy of motherhood. Which pain was greater: a mother's grief in losing her child or a child's grief in never knowing her mother?

Pulling a piece of silk thread from her pocket, she dropped down among the playful baby cats. She pulled the string along, and a little orange ball of fluff tumbled after it.

"They're growing up fast."

Millie turned to welcome Noah. "They sure are."

He plopped down next to her on the rug and picked up a gray tabby. "They're a lot cuter now than when I found them in the shed."

As he stroked the kitten, it relaxed on his leg.

Millie, too, relaxed in his calming presence. She could count on him to lift her mood.

The mother cat roused herself, marched over to Noah's kitten, and sniffed it. Then she returned, tail lifted high, and curled up on the

far end of the rug.

"Patches approves of you."

Noah shrugged. "She should—after what I did for her."

Soon the little tabby grew restless, and Noah set it down. It scooted over to Patches and began nursing. The large cat kneaded the air with her white paws, and the deep reverberations of her purr seemed to blanket the entire porch.

Millie wagged her finger at the mother. "Her philoprogenitiveness is showing."

Noah squinted. "Philo-what?"

"Philoprogenitiveness. You know—"

"That's a word I've never heard."

Millie flushed. She hadn't realized the word was unique to the Community. "It means…" She paused, searching for a way to explain the loaded term. "Loving your offspring too much."

"That's a bad thing?"

Millie checked for signs of mockery on Noah's face, but he seemed legitimately curious. "Of course. I mean, yes, the Community thinks so."

"How so?"

"Because it's selfish."

"She doesn't look very selfish to me." Four of the kittens had lined up along the mother cat's abdomen. "I'd call that more *selfless*."

Millie fingered her lower lip. She'd heard members discuss this topic all her life. It should be simple to explain. "But parents—human parents—can become too attached to their children. Can't they?"

Her question—amended so weakly after her explanation—hung thin and exposed in the air, like tattered garments on a clothesline. Her heart answered the question with a *No!* Her own father hadn't dared be possessive toward her because if he'd been sent away, she'd have been left without either parent. Mary and Mrs. Bloom had never had a chance to cling to their children—three little ones snatched away at birth. And her own mother had—she pictured the nervous mouth, the heavy-lidded eyes. Her chest tightened.

Noah rubbed his cheek. "Rarely, perhaps. But parents are supposed to lavish their children with love. That's how children learn about God's love. If a child grows up without loving parents, he might not understand God's love—or even believe God exists."

"Do you think so?"

Millie wound the silk thread around her finger and unwound it again. Unlike hers, Noah's words flowed smoothly, as if he knew the truth of them inside. They weren't helping her melancholy.

"Sure." Noah took up a little calico that strayed near his leg. It meowed delicately, and he cradled it in one arm and stroked it with his other hand until it calmed down. He nodded toward Patches. "God even compares Himself to a nursing mother."

The mother cat was trying to stand up, despite two kittens that were still latched on.

Millie absently fingered the rug in front of her. "Does He?"

"In Isaiah." He swayed slightly, rocking the kitten. "'Can a woman forget her sucking child, that she should not have compassion on the son of her womb? Yea, they may forget, yet will I not forget thee.'"

Forget. The word sank into a cavernous depth somewhere inside Millie that she didn't even know existed. It echoed sickeningly. And the only image in that dim, foreboding region was a blank, expressionless face between two little hands.

* * *

Two days later Millie was reading in the parlor after supper. Noah strode over and squatted beside her chair. "Would you like to come outside?"

Millie tilted her head at his conspiratorial tone.

He raised his eyebrows. "We've got keets."

The gloom of Mary's loss hadn't been easy to shake off. A walk with Noah on a pleasant day to see newly hatched fowl sounded perfect. They strolled north of the house toward Sconondoa Creek, toward the chicken and guinea coops at the back of the property. The grass was verdant from recent rains, and fragile little violets poked up in shady areas. The budding trees whispered a tantalizing hint of the lush green foliage to come.

"Look!"

Millie gasped the word as she spied a male and female guinea on parade with about twenty chicks stumbling over each other in little bunches, following their adult leaders.

The proud parents acknowledged the arrival of visitors with screeches of "Ker-pluck!" from the mother and rooster crows from the father.

Noah ducked into the chicken coop and returned with a handful of feed. As he tiptoed toward a bunch of seven or eight keets, they scurried away. He knelt on the ground, moving ever so slowly, and extended his hand, brimming with feed, palm up. He remained as motionless as a fence post.

Soon the little band of curious pecking chicks came closer and closer. One stepped onto his fingers and began pecking at the grain. Instantly a swarm of keets descended on his palm, pecking rhythmically.

Grinning with delight, Noah held himself perfectly still despite the wild activity at his palm. Soon the grain disappeared, and the keets scampered away, pecking the ground as they went. He stood up, brushing his hands together. Seeing Millie's awed expression, he dropped into a deep bow and laughed.

"You had them eating from the palm of your hand!"

With two bounds, he was at her side. "If you start to tame them young enough, they get used to you. Otherwise they're pretty skittish."

"You know about keets?"

"My uncle raises guinea fowl. I've seen several broods hatch."

Millie couldn't take her eyes off the scrambling chicks as they followed their dignified parents. "They look like two-legged gray tabby cats with orange beaks."

Noah nodded toward the elegant couple. "You know, those aren't necessarily the parents."

"Oh?"

"Any female guinea will sit on a nest that other hens have laid eggs in, and any rooster will help take care of the chicks."

She giggled, imagining the guinea hen in pantalettes and the rooster in a suit jacket. "Then they're communists and have a Children's House, just like we do."

Noah cocked his head. "It must have been different—growing up that way."

Millie shrugged. Different for him, but it was all she'd ever known. "Each week I'd stay in a different woman's room." She strolled with Noah about the yard, following the keets from a distance. "Some of them liked me, but sometimes I felt like a nuisance."

"Did you get to stay with your own mother?"

Millie felt a catch in her chest. Though she'd heard a lot about Noah's family, so far she'd deliberately avoided talking about her own. "My mother died before we came here."

"Oh, I'm so sorry!" Noah bit his lower lip in apology. "You never said."

"I don't remember her, so there's nothing to say."

She felt the stab of her father's silence anew. She didn't have even second-hand information about her mother.

"You must be close to your father then."

When her father had never shared anything about his life before Oneida, could they be considered close? Not by Noah's family's standards. "Yes." She nodded. "We're close."

An awkward silence hung in the air, punctuated by a discordant "Ker-pluck" as the mother guinea directed a straying group of keets.

Noah grinned at the chicks. "Playing with all the other kids must have been fun."

"There weren't very many my age. Nothing like that!" She pointed as several keets near them collided, jostling each other as they moved forward. "Only a handful were within a year of me. You've probably heard that we only started allowing members to have babies a few years after the war." Her cheeks grew warm, and she turned away. She certainly didn't want to discuss birth control with Noah. "So the children my age were either accidental—Providential—or joined with their parents, like me. And they came and went between here and Wallingford. Our teachers taught us to value ascending fellowship. Horizontal fellowship could get us into trouble."

Noah wrinkled his forehead at the terms.

They reached a fence. Noah offered Millie a hand, and they both sat on the top rail. As she explained horizontal and ascending fellowship, he jutted out his chin in thought.

He looked perplexed. "Did they let you play with toys?"

"Oh, yes, we had plenty of toys."

"My sister had so many dolls. But just one favorite that she treated like a real person." His face glowed with nostalgic brotherly mockery. "Every day she made us kiss Suzy good morning and good night."

"We weren't allowed to have dolls."

Noah's eyes widened in disbelief.

"Years before I was born, Mrs. Mary Cragin had a talk with the girls." Millie had heard the tale so often that she knew it by heart, like a familiar bedtime story. "She explained that playing with dolls was acting and speaking a lie—because they were treating them like human beings. Besides that, their dolls distracted them from being good helpers. So all the children took a vote, girls and boys. It was unanimous. They agreed to burn the dolls in the fire."

Noah gaped. "No!"

Enjoying his reaction, Millie held a pretend doll in her hands, positioning it before her chest. "They each carried their favorite doll and marched in time to a song, right to the wood stove. Mrs. Cragin opened the door, and one by one they pitched each doll into the flames." Millie reenacted the toss. "They watched those *abhorrent idols* perish before their very eyes. That was the end of the doll spirit, which had seduced them into frivolity and lying."

Noah's face looked as if he'd just heard an Edgar Allan Poe story. "Sadie would have called that murder."

"That was the point." Millie lifted her shoulders. "They had to murder the doll spirit once and for all."

Noah still gaped. "But dolls help prepare girls to be good mothers."

Millie waved her hand. "We did that by working in the Children's House with real babies, when we were older."

Noah kicked his heel gently against the lower fence rail. "I think Suzy gave Sadie a way to express her love—to practice loving. I think it was good for her."

Surprised at Noah's intense reaction, Millie stroked the pleats of her dress. She'd never loved a doll, so she couldn't comment.

He ran his fingers through his brown hair and studied her face. "What are some of your favorite possessions now?" He arched his eyebrows. "Or aren't you allowed to have any?"

Millie grew warm at the tease. He'd struck closer to the truth than he knew. "I-I have some," she stammered. "I have a beautiful mechanical pencil that Dr. Cragin gave me when I was at

174 Rebecca May Hope

Wallingford." It sounded so paltry that she quickly added, "And I have a necklace my friend Jessie sent me."

As soon as the words were out of her mouth, she wished she could take them back. How could she explain a necklace that stood for loyalty and defiance at the same time?

Noah eyed her with surprise. "I've never seen you wear it."

Millie looked toward the trees along the river. "It's more elaborate than the Community allows." She wouldn't tell him it was a duplicate of the one they'd seen at the Astor House and that it reminded her of his breath on her cheek. She felt his probing stare and turned toward him. "I keep it in my pillow case."

He seemed to sense the topic was sensitive. He placed his hand on the back of her arm. "I'd like to see it some time. If you're willing to show it to me."

Though she didn't say so, she dearly wanted to take him up on that offer. Would he recognize it? Did he feel any of the connection she'd felt with him that day—a connection that had grown deeper and stronger these last two weeks?

He felt inside his pocket and brought out a watch she'd seen him look at sometimes. "This belonged to my great-grandfather."

He held it toward her, and she opened her hand to take it. The silver case, engraved with a capital R on a shield, was smooth and cool in her palm. When he popped it open, his fingers brushed her palm, sending a little tingle up her arm. The ivory dial, fading with age, was rimmed with elegant Roman numerals.

"How lovely!"

He smiled at her reaction. "My mother's grandfather was a fighting parson in the War of 1812. But I don't think this watch saw battle."

Now it was her turn to cock her head at an unfamiliar term. "What's a *fighting parson?*"

"He was a chaplain in one of the militias. Most of the chaplains fought alongside the men, so they called them fighting parsons."

She viewed the treasure in her hand with respect. Her parents' wedding photograph was the oldest thing she owned, and she'd only recently obtained that. "It must be very special to you—part of your family history."

Picking up on her poignant tone, Noah eyed the horizon wistfully.

"I guess we all long for some connection to something bigger than ourselves. That's probably why I carry it."

He took the watch from her hand, sparking another charged tingle. He clicked it shut and returned it to his pocket. "Though it doesn't keep very good time."

Some obnoxious screeches from the guinea hens caught their attention. Noah hopped off the fence. As Millie moved to jump down, he placed both hands on either side of her waist and easily lifted her to the grass below. Once she was firmly on the ground, she thought he kept his hands in place a few seconds longer than was necessary. If she could, she would have soaked in the warmth of his touch much longer.

The next day, Friday, Noah left to visit his family. Millie missed him. She invited Grace on a walk to see the keets, but they found little to talk about. As the woman who held the most masculine job of any female Community member, Grace was something of an odd egg. Millie couldn't seem to connect with her.

* * *

The first half of the week was rainy, but Thursday dawned bright and clear. As Noah finished breakfast and left for the trap factory, he brushed Millie's arm and whispered in her ear, "Looks like it'll be a great night for a walk."

All day long and especially during supper, she could hardly restrain her anticipation. As soon as she finished eating, she slid up to her room and shut the door. She flew to her pillow and felt inside the case for the choker. Clasping the silky ribbon, she drew it out and stuffed it into her dress pocket just as Grace entered. She smoothed down her bed covers and, nodding at Grace, quickly exited the room.

Outside, the air was fragrant. Lilacs, crab apple blossoms, cherry blossoms—all the sweet odors tumbled together like a clump of riotous keets. The trees had fully leafed out after the rain. She and Noah followed the road beyond the chicken yard and veered to their right. The grass had dried well in the afternoon sunshine. Chirps, trills, and whistles sounded from tree to tree as every bird seemed to have some bit of gossip to share.

Millie's heart was light as she fingered the choker in her pocket.

Noah's gait was easy, and his handsome face wore a jaunty expression. He obviously loved the outdoors.

Soon they came to a well-trodden path—the common way of accessing Sconondoa Creek by fishermen, wild berry pickers, and people simply out to enjoy nature, like themselves. They walked in relative silence, sometimes mentioning a flowering bush or a flitting bird. As they neared the creek, the air grew thick with sounds, especially the rasping two-note barks of male mallard ducks. At an eddy of the creek bordered by the dry, gray stalks of last year's cattails, the mallards' chorus grew almost deafening.

Millie had to raise her voice to speak. "Now that's what I call diotrephiasis!"

Noah looked at her quizzically. "Say that again?"

"Diotrephiasis. You know. Loving pre-eminence." She spread her arm toward the creek. "Each duck is trying to push his case the hardest, and they're all talking over each other."

Noah chuckled. "I never thought of it that way. I just think of them all singing their hearts out for their Maker—although they can't carry a tune for the life of them. And God is their lenient choirmaster —enjoying their glorious cacophony."

Millie smiled. "Cacophony. Exactly."

Suddenly an image flashed into her mind, and she swallowed a laugh. John Humphrey Noyes stood on the bank of the swamp with a director's baton, his bushy gray eyebrows contorting furiously, adding his own raspy bark to the mix as he attempted to get the shiny-headed band to cooperate.

Noah's eyes queried her.

She pursed her lips and raised her eyebrows playfully. "Oh, I just had a funny thought. But not one I can share."

Noah assessed her face as if to see whether he might extract her secret, but she looked away. She could never utter such sacrilege against the prophet. But it couldn't hurt to create a bit of mystique for Noah.

As they walked along the creek nearer the woods, the sounds of the ducks faded and the forest birds' calls grew louder. Robins bobbed about on the path ahead of them looking for worms in the moist earth, and goldfinches, like beckoning will-o'-the-wisps, flitted between the branches of the lower bushes, their bright yellow feathers gleaming in the slanted rays of sunshine. Every so often they heard the haunting cry of a mourning dove.

"Ah-ooo-ooo-ooo-ooo," mimicked Noah.

"That's my favorite bird call."

"Mine, too." Noah grinned. "I always used to wonder what they were mourning about."

"I still wonder."

"But they're not mourning at all."

They reached the edge of a wooded area that bordered the stream. The large swampy eddy lay behind them, and a path through the woods wound away to their right. As the cooler air wafted toward them from the shady grove, Millie shivered.

Noah stopped. "Let's stay in the sunshine."

Millie eyed the grass with suspicion, and in response Noah produced a folded handkerchief from his jacket. He waved it with a flourish before spreading it out, then gallantly bowed and motioned with his arm for her to sit.

Millie laughed and sat on the handkerchief as primly as she could. It wouldn't protect her whole skirt, but it would help. "What were you saying about the mourning doves?"

Noah dropped beside her and leaned in, supporting himself with his right arm. "The males make that call when they're looking for a wife." He tilted his head and looked at her mischievously, widening his eyes. "It's a love song, not a lament."

Millie lowered her eyes. Was he flirting with her? Or was this just a brotherly tease? "Oh. I never knew."

"Then you probably didn't know that mourning doves mate for life. Unlike our guinea fowl, they're not communists."

Millie half-smiled at Noah's mischievous tone, then grew solemn, remembering Tirzah's tragic dream. Without giving names, she briefly related the tale of the star-crossed lovers.

Noah squinted, laying a finger across his chin. "So this woman practices complex marriage as you call it, but she longs to have just one husband." The teasing tone still laced his words. "I thought complex marriage was supposed to be the best part of communism."

She flushed and looked away. This was the conversation she hadn't wanted to have with Noah, and now she'd opened the door.

"It is." Too flustered to realize what she was saying, she let a rote reply escape her lips. "That is, it's one of our core beliefs. It's what makes communism possible."

She cringed inwardly at her words. Glancing back toward Noah, she tried to read the expression that flitted across his face. Disapproval? Disappointment? It wouldn't be proper to tell Noah she'd come to The Villa to avoid complex marriage—or that she was the only woman her age who wasn't a Community wife. How foolish she was to have fallen into this predicament.

"So you can't have communism without complex marriage?" Noah curled his fist under his chin playfully, as if ready to be enlightened. "Why not?"

She couldn't bear his taunting. She wished she could run back to her room and hide. Instead, she faced him, biting her lower lip. "I don't know. That's what Father Noyes says."

What must he think of her? His father had no doubt preached often against the Community's views on marriage.

Noah's expression softened. "I'm sorry." He touched her hand, causing waves of warmth to spread through her whole body. "I didn't mean to put you on the spot."

She laughed, trying to shake off her embarrassment. As she drew her hand away and across her lap, she felt the choker in her pocket— the perfect way to change the subject. "Oh, look!" She pulled it out. "My necklace."

Noah held out his hand, and she placed the crimson ribbon and cameo in his palm. His mouth dropped open, and he eyed her with surprise. "It's the same one the lady at the Astor House wore."

She grinned. He did remember.

He examined it, felt its texture, and ran his fingers over the woman's face, stroking it as gently as he'd held the fluffy keet and petted the calico kitten.

"I like it." He looked from the necklace to Millie's face. "It's a shame you can't wear it."

"I know. But—"

Breaking into his conspiratorial grin, he glanced around furtively. "No one here but us and the ducks. I'll tell you how you look in it."

Before she could respond, he scooted behind her. His warm fingers touched her throat as he drew the grosgrain silk across from left to right. His cupped left hand rested at the back of her neck for a moment. It sent a pleasant electric tingle all the way down her spine. Then his right hand tickled her neck under her hairline as he sought to fasten the clasp. When he withdrew his hand, he let his fingers slide across the surface of her skin.

Noah's delicious breath warmed her left cheek as he leaned around with his face ever so close to hers. She felt dizzy, as if she might faint. The air between their faces felt charged with the energy of an oncoming thunderstorm. Could he feel it, too? She turned her face toward him and saw his slightly parted lips and his chestnut eyes. If he moved toward her to embrace her, she'd throw herself into his arms.

But he didn't. He scooted away.

He held her gaze. "You look lovely." He dropped his eyes to her neck. "The necklace—it looks lovely on you."

Millie felt hot and cool at the same time. With her right hand she traced the outline of the ribbon along her neck, the path Noah's hand had just traveled. They sat for a while, enjoying the flowing water and the calling birds and ducks. She wished they could sit together forever, just the two of them. Finally, in spite of herself, she shivered as the air grew colder.

"Sun's going down." He stood, offering his hand. "We'd best get back."

As they reached the path, Millie began to unclasp the necklace.

Noah held up his hand. "Leave it on until we reach the barn at least. I like looking at it."

At the edge of the farm, she removed it and placed it in her pocket.

All night long she remembered the feel of it and the brush of Noah's gentle fingers on her neck. Songbirds and mourning doves and Noah's face next to hers filled her dreams.

Chapter 14: Preening

You look lovely.

The words sang over and over in Millie's mind. She savored them like vanilla ice cream on a sultry day. She didn't own a hand mirror, but strangely enough, Grace did. When Grace was out of the room, Millie picked up the glass to study her reflection. She glanced at herself in partial profile view, right and left, and practiced coy smiles.

Such vanity! Thank goodness no one could read her mind. What if Grace walked in while she was fluttering her eyelashes in the mirror? Such preening mocked the values of Bible Communism, and besides that, it was foolishness. She heard footsteps in the hall and quickly returned the mirror to Grace's bureau top, her heart beating furiously. She must give up her self-taught glamour lessons. But before that—the footsteps passed—what would Noah see if she tilted her head this way? Or shook her head with a reserved giggle?

She picked up the mirror again. She pulled a few strands of hair out in front of her ears. By dabbing a few drops of water on them and curling them around her finger, she created a hint of curly tendrils. She held the mirror at arm's length to examine her figure. She was becoming softer and rounder thanks to Mrs. Bloom's bountiful meals. Perhaps she was pretty after all.

If so, she must move differently. She stepped daintily now, and she swayed to music she alone could hear. She'd read of women pinching their cheeks to brighten their complexions, but she didn't have to do that. When she imagined Noah's gentle fingers gliding along her throat or resting on the back of her neck, her cheeks grew warm enough to give her plenty of color. The mirror confirmed it.

Mrs. Bloom called her perky. "Must be the warm weather we're havin'."

Several of the men at The Villa followed her with their eyes as she ascended or descended the stairs, but she barely noticed. There was only one pair of eyes she cared about—those kind brown eyes that had stared into hers at the creek. She could feel when Noah was watching

her. Sometimes she thought he was admiring her, but at other times she worried that he might be looking right through her, thinking of something else. Though she longed for his attention, she'd never let him know. She'd read too many romance novels to make that mistake. During their evening conversations, she acted outwardly as she always had despite the wild beating of her heart.

One night at the end of May a mystery appeared at Meeting. Like the other residents, Millie kept eyeing the item wrapped in a blanket that leaned against the wall between the two fireplaces. It was about three feet by three feet and not very thick.

Mr. Dole deflected the questions tossed his way. "It's a gift from the wood shop—that's all I'll say. You'll have to wait till Meeting's over to see it."

Grace sat there like the cat that swallowed the canary.

Rampant curiosity seemed to douse members' desire to confess Christ that night, so Meeting ended before 8:30. With exaggerated ceremony, Mr. Dole peeled back the blanket to reveal a large wooden circle and a little box of tokens. As members passed the box around, brows furrowed and noses wrinkled in confusion.

Millie clapped excitedly. "Squails! It's a squails game."

"Yep," Mr. Dole acknowledged. "All the rage at the Mansion House. They've been slow to break out the croquet sets this spring— they're so enamored of squails. I hear it's the same at Wallingford. So our wood shop created several games, and this one is The Villa's." He grinned at Grace. "It was Grace's idea. You'll notice her expert craftsmanship, especially on the discs."

Grace beamed as the group applauded her.

Mr. Dole scanned the room. "How many have played before?"

Millie raised her hand to the level of her face and waved it enthusiastically. "I have."

Everyone else looked at each other, shaking their heads.

Mr. Dole gestured toward Millie. "Looks like you'll be our teacher."

With more hubbub than Millie had ever seen at The Villa, members quickly dragged a small table to the center of the room, set the wooden circle on it, and drew chairs around it for better viewing.

While that was going on, Millie found Noah. She batted her eyelashes. "Would you like to play with me?"

"Sure!" Noah squinted at the board. "You need just one partner?"

She lifted her chin with a taunt. "Not partner—opponent."

"All right, then." He stood, clenching his fists. "A battle we shall have!"

Speaking loudly enough for everyone to hear, Millie explained the object of the game. She divided the smooth discs between her and Noah, choosing the red discs for herself. She presented Grace with pencil and paper for recording the scores. Then she set the jack—a lead disc the size of five stacked dimes—in its place in the middle of the circle.

"Now choose your position, and place your squail half off the edge of the board, like this." She demonstrated, making sure all the onlookers could see. "Then, give it a good tap like this." With her open palm she struck the squail where it overhung the side of the board. The disc skidded along the polished board and just barely entered the marked inner ring. "Your turn."

Noah positioned his black disc on his side of the table and gave it a slap. It zipped like lightning across the surface and dropped to the floor.

Millie giggled. "That's called a flute. Two points for me."

The onlookers laughed as Noah retrieved the overplayed disc.

Millie set up her next disc. She gave it a brisk slap, and it slid into the inner circle and stopped just an inch before hitting the jack. The crowd oohed with approval.

This time Noah judged his force better, and his squail landed inside the circle. Before long, Millie had five discs inside the circle and Noah had three. Millie placed her last disc, took aim, and sent it sliding. The red game piece skated across the board, entered the inner boundary, and bumped two of Noah's discs outside the circle before coming to rest just kissing the jack. A perfect shot.

Lifting her arms, she spun a dainty pirouette. "Wee-ooo!"

Everyone watched her, beaming at her success.

"Nice move!"

Noah raised his eyebrows and nodded his chin to show he referred not just to her play, but also to her jaunty twirl. The whole room caught the double meaning and burst out laughing.

Millie flushed. Without planning to, she'd duplicated Virginia's flamboyant whirl. Had she ever been the object of such admiration before? If so, it would have been when she was a very young child performing during Children's Hour. But this was different. Now she was a woman.

She smiled at Noah. "It's your turn now."

"I don't think I can match *that*."

Noah nodded his head on the final word to take in Millie's whole person.

Again the room erupted in laughter. Millie pictured Noah performing a graceful pirouette. She laughed, too. The pleasure in his eyes as he looked at her made her heart skip. He definitely wasn't looking through her now.

Noah made an adequate play, getting his disc inside the circle and jostling one of Millie's discs away from the jack. After measuring the distances of any questionable discs with the swoggle, they added up the scores.

Grace announced, "Three for Noah and twelve for Millie."

Millie checked Grace's scorekeeping. "Did you include my two points for Noah's flute?"

"Oh, fourteen then."

Noah bowed deeply. "Congratulations!"

Millie curtsied. "Thank you, sir!"

After that, everyone wanted a chance to play. Millie took some turns, but mostly she stood near Noah and cheered on the players. With so many people crowding around the table, Noah's arm pressed against Millie's. Occasionally he put his hand on the small of her back and guided her a few inches one way or the other so they could get a better view.

Millie pretended to be absorbed in the matches, but in reality the man standing next to her consumed every atom of her awareness. As the evening wore on, a conviction settled on her like a luxurious fur cape. His gentle touch and warm glances could mean only one thing: He was attracted to her, too.

* * *

At dinner the next day, Mrs. Bloom chuckled as she set a plate of fried potatoes and eggs in front of Millie. "You were a regular sensation last night."

184 Rebecca May Hope

Millie squirmed at the implication of her words. "Only because I've had more practice with squails than anyone else."

Mrs. Bloom winked. "That's not what I'm talkin' about." She smirked as she sat down at the table. "I'm thinkin' my friend Harriet's gonna be hearin' your name a lot."

"Mrs. Skinner? Why?"

Mrs. Bloom rolled her eyes. "The requests for the pleasure of your company are gonna be pourin' in."

Millie flinched. Her neck and face grew hot as she struggled to swallow the food in her mouth. "Do you think so?"

"I'm just sayin' there's a lotta men who never noticed you before who took good notice last night."

Mrs. Bloom pushed her chair back definitively and walked to the sink.

Millie's stomach churned even as her face cooled. Had she truly been so coquettish? She'd wanted to win Noah's approval, but she'd obviously taken it too far.

She washed the dishes without speaking—her dry mouth wouldn't have been able to release any words. But her brain was active, imagining the unintended consequences that awaited her. All her efforts to escape the interview with Dr. Noyes might be dashed because of one night of foolishness.

When they were about to retire to the parlor, the kitchen door opened, and Noah breezed in. Millie's heart leapt. Her fears fled at the sight of his face.

Mrs. Bloom brightened. "You're here early, now! We don't usually see you this time o' day—unless you're returnin' wayward cats!"

"One of the machines at the trap factory is down, so they let some of us leave early." Noah rubbed his hands together. "And it couldn't have happened on a nicer day. It's perfection out there."

Millie tilted her head to prompt an invitation. "Is it?"

"Absolutely! Let's see how the kittens are doing."

They were getting bigger every day. The calico bounded to Noah right away. She seemed to have a soft place in her heart for him—and vice versa. They sat down, making small talk, enjoying the warm breeze and the late May sunshine.

After a while Mrs. Bloom appeared with a basket. "I'm a few

eggs short for the tapioca pudding. How 'bout if you two pick me some?"

Noah jumped up. "You know me: always ready to oblige the cook. Especially when tapioca pudding's at stake."

Millie took the basket and followed him into the yard. The grass had grown thick, and wildflowers peeked up in random patches beside the path. Relishing another private walk with Noah, Millie inhaled the rich scent of grass and leaves and flowers. But when they got closer to the chicken coop, an unsettling ruckus jarred their ears.

Noah spotted the trouble first. "Quick, Millie! Run!"

Millie raced after him as he ran with all his strength toward a white, writhing, dusty mound. He waved his arms wildly. "Hey! Haw! Shoo! Go away! Stop!"

Millie reached his side as he dove into a furious clump of pecking chickens. They fluttered away in all directions, squawking angrily. Millie and Noah looked down at the remaining hen that lay in a bloody mass of feathers and flesh at their feet. It jerked a couple of times and then lay motionless.

"Oh! Oh!"

Millie dropped the egg basket and threw herself into Noah's chest, sobbing. The sight of the tortured bird tore at her very heart. Her own nerves jangled with the agony of those final twitches. She couldn't stop shaking and crying.

Noah held her tightly, his hands stroking her back and hair. "It's all right," he whispered. "There, there. Don't cry."

At last she could breathe. She pulled away, looking at Noah, not at the mutilated carcass. "Wh-what?"

"Cannibalism. Feather pecking." His tone was grave. "My uncle's talked about it, but I've never seen it."

"I-I'm sorry I acted that way." She still couldn't turn to look at the dead creature. "I shouldn't have—"

"No, I understand. It's horrific. Gruesome. You have a sensitive spirit. Don't look at it." He touched her arm and made direct eye contact. "Now, do you think you can do something for me?"

Millie nodded tentatively, forcing herself to breathe slowly.

"Go to the hen house and find a gunny sack. They're piled in the corner. Bring it back to me. I'll stay here so they don't come back."

Millie found the sack and returned. Noah stood between her and the carcass.

"Good girl." He kept his voice calm and steady. "Go on back without me. I'll bag this thing up and bring it to Mrs. Bloom."

Millie still felt lightheaded. She hated to be so useless. She squeezed her hands into fists. "I'll get the eggs."

Biting her lip to keep from thinking about Noah's task, she picked up the basket and returned to the coop. Once she found a dozen eggs, she made her way back to the house.

She set the eggs on the counter. "Mrs. Bloom!"

When the cook appeared, Millie told her what had happened and that Noah was bringing the hen. Just as she finished speaking, his step sounded on the porch.

Mrs. Bloom, her jaw set and her head shaking from side to side, opened the door. Millie slid into a chair as the older woman tossed out instructions to Noah.

"Bury it up beyond the fence line. Or down by the creek—that's even better. But before you do that, go back an' dig out the dirt where it happened. There's a bucket and shovel in the shed. Make sure you get every speck o' blood an' every feather. Take the bloody dirt down to the creek an' throw it in."

Mrs. Bloom was somber as Millie helped with the tapioca pudding. "Once they get the taste for it, sometimes they won't stop feather pecking. It can destroy a whole flock o' hens. Can't think o' what coulda got 'em started. Brainless brutes."

* * *

Millie's mind wandered as she sat with her father at Sunday night's Meeting at the Mansion House. Aimlessly she scanned the main floor, most of which was visible from her seat in the rear section of the balcony. Her indifferent gaze fell on the left balcony, where Henry sat with Ellen. She rested her eyes on his profile, but the man she saw was Noah.

Since the incident in the chicken yard, he'd become so much more solicitous. Her tears had had a powerful effect. Had she psychologized him? No—her sobs and her impulse to bury herself in his chest were genuine, and her spontaneous reaction had evidently stirred his heart. Still, the result couldn't have been better if she'd scripted the whole thing.

Suddenly her eyes focused and met Henry's across the expanse. He was smiling. So was she. How long had he noticed her staring at him and grinning? Embarrassed, she gave a little nod. When he started to mouth some words, Ellen tugged on his arm, and he bent toward her as she spoke in his ear.

Millie studied the painted muses on the ceiling and didn't look toward Henry again.

Near the end of Meeting a young man mounted the stairs to the stage, holding a piece of writing paper. He looked somewhat familiar, but Millie hadn't seen him for some time. She didn't remember his name. Murmurs and whispers arose from the crowd.

He positioned himself at the apron of the stage. After clearing his throat, he began to read. "My name is Peter Schenk. Most of you remember me. Today I returned home after being discharged from Utica Asylum. I want to express my great appreciation to everyone who wrote me letters while I was gone—and to Mrs. Skinner for sending me cookies."

His eyes found the woman sitting in the front row, and he beamed at her. A chuckle rippled across the audience.

His expression grew serious as he stared at the paper. "Most of all, I am grateful for the regular correspondence of Father Noyes and Erastus Hamilton. Without their kind and steady direction, my recovery would have taken much longer or may never have come at all."

His cadence grew more stilted as he continued to read. Sensing her father stiffen, Millie tried to read his reaction. His expression was nondescript, but his hands gripped his knees.

She returned her attention to the man on the stage.

"Their guidance allowed me to realize the deception that had seized me. To anyone who heard me espousing theories contrary to the precepts of Bible Communism and Father Noyes's teachings: I ask your forgiveness. Those were ramblings of an unsound mind and were symptoms of my insanity. I have humbled myself at Father Noyes's feet and have rejected all the notions I adopted during my insanity. I am ready to start anew here as a little child. Thank you."

Now Millie remembered him and the stir he'd caused when he left about a year ago. He'd been one of Father Noyes's protégés, being groomed for leadership. About twenty years old, he was popular and respected. She couldn't recall any of his "notions" that contradicted his mentor—which he now labeled as symptoms of insanity.

When Meeting ended, William made his way to the north exit before Millie could question him. She trailed behind. As he reached the staircase, Peter Schenk approached him, and they walked together to the end of the hall, just beyond the door to the garret.

Wondering what Peter had to say to her father, Millie was about to join them when Henry called out behind her. "Hall-oo!"

When he saw Peter and William conversing, he looked questioningly at Millie.

"Hi, Henry."

She barely looked at him. Standing in the opening of the balcony, they both stared at the secretive huddle for another minute. Keeping her voice low, she asked, "Did you know Peter well?"

"Fairly well. I'll never forget the day he left. So many whispers and wary looks. Nobody would say what was going on." Henry looked at her intently and flashed an odd sort of grin. "But never mind that. Tell me about *you*."

Before Millie could respond to Henry's unexpected interest, Ellen joined them from across the balcony. She stationed herself an inch from Henry's arm, as if Henry were a jack and she and Millie were competing squails discs. "Well, *Millie*," she said with exaggerated warmth. "Back from the farm?"

Millie ignored the sarcasm. "Spending Sunday with my father."

Again Millie glanced at her father and the young man, huddled together in solemn conversation. Her father's face wore an expression of discomfort—maybe fear?—and sadness.

Ellen picked up on it, too. "I wonder what they're speaking about so earnestly."

Millie wasn't about to let her father be fodder for a busybody. She moved around the doorway into the balcony where she couldn't see William, and the others followed her. "Nothing important, I'm sure."

Ellen stretched her neck toward the men at the end of the hall one more time, then turned her eyes on Henry and Millie. "Can you believe that ridiculous statement Peter was forced to read?"

Millie drew in her chin. "Forced?"

Ellen looked down her nose and crossed her arms over her chest. "You don't believe a healthy young man would say such things of his own volition, do you?" She tossed her head. "He had to do that to be accepted back. They wouldn't let him out of the asylum until he recanted his heresies."

Millie gasped. "What? Who wouldn't?"

"Why, Father Noyes and the powers that be, of course." Ellen waved her hand dismissively. "They sent him there because they didn't want him to lead a rebellion. I can tell you, he had several of us close to denying Christianity."

Millie couldn't believe Ellen's tone. Every time she saw her, Ellen became more outrageous. "I thought he had the hypo."

"Of course you did. That's what they told us all. But he was sent there to repent and reform. And it worked like a charm. No wonder! Living in a cage for five months makes this place seem like *liberté, égalité, fraternité*—despite all our rules."

Ellen made a show of her French pronunciation, making her R's breathy and guttural.

Millie looked from Ellen to Henry, her brows knit together. "Living in a cage?"

"That's what they do to the inmates there—at Utica. They put them in human cages."

Ellen delivered the explanation as if it were common knowledge.

Millie wasn't going to fall for it. She looked at Henry for support. "That's ridiculous."

Henry grimaced as if he'd tasted a rotten apple. "The Utica Crib. They invented it." He shuddered. "Horrific."

Millie searched his face for signs of teasing. Was he feeding her a line, the way he'd teased Virginia in the garret? Millie wouldn't be that gullible. But Henry's eyes betrayed no mischievous glint, and Ellen looked equally serious.

Henry apparently thought Millie needed more convincing. "My family came from Utica. I've seen pictures in the newspaper. It's like a crib for adults, but it has a lid on top that locks from the outside."

Millie shuddered as well.

Ellen raised her eyebrows. "You know, it's exactly what Father Noyes did to Victor, his second son."

Millie shook her head, confused.

"Victor Cragin—Mary Cragin's son," Henry clarified. "Ten years ago. I wasn't here, but I've heard about it."

Ellen leaned her face toward Henry and Millie playfully. "I guess you're only allowed to be an atheist around here if you're Father Noyes's *first-born* son!" She laughed heartily at her own joke, and Henry snickered, while Millie's jaw dropped. Ellen waved both hands. "Oh, Millie, loosen up! Theodore's not quite God, you know!"

Seeing Millie's horrified expression, Henry shrugged. "Don't mind her, Millie." He gave a sideways teasing glance at Ellen. "She's a devotee of politics. In future, we'll see her in the halls of the state house in Albany."

"Oh, no, no!" Ellen waved her hand briskly before her as if to erase the words Henry had spoken. "I'm never going to leave O.C. I'll always be here with you, Henry." She smiled into his face and batted her eyelashes. After a pause, she added with condescension, "And with you, Millie. This is our family, after all. Things will change, and they *are* changing quickly. But that's to be expected. Some people may get their feathers ruffled along the way, but nothing will ever destroy us."

Millie flinched at the mention of ruffled feathers, but her friends didn't notice. What changes was Ellen referring to, and how could she be so confident?

"Just remember you heard it from me first." Ellen seemed to have read Millie's mind. "My father sides with Judge Towner, and he has, shall we say, different plans for us than Father Noyes has. And then there's Virginia's father. He's working on changes as well."

Millie wanted to ask whether the changes that were brewing concerned complex marriage. She could share what Jessie had told her about Wallingford, but engaging in such gossip didn't feel right. She glanced away toward the main floor of the Big Hall. To her surprise, she saw Mrs. Skinner standing near the stage and looking up, studying her. Millie nodded, and Mrs. Skinner nodded back.

Millie's stomach sank. "I'd better catch my ride back to The Villa."

"But, Millie!" Henry stepped closer and put his face near hers. "I wanted to ask you about the play."

His voice was rich. As he slid his hand down the back of her arm, his touch and the fragrance of spearmint on his breath made her feel suddenly warm.

"Should I talk to Tirzah about starting rehearsals again and setting a performance date?"

Millie took a step away and raised her eyebrows. "*Can* you?"

"I think they're letting me talk to her again."

He opened his mouth as if to say more, but Ellen took his arm and started guiding him out of the balcony.

"Then please do!" Millie called as Ellen ushered Henry down the stairs.

At the end of the hallway, her father was still conversing with Peter. She waved goodbye, but he didn't acknowledge her, so she went down the stairs after Henry and Ellen. She still didn't like the look on her father's face.

* * *

After the simmering intrigues of the Mansion House, Millie's days at The Villa were a refreshing breeze. Here people seemed content to live and let live. Even working at the silk factory didn't bother her now—it gave her plenty of time to daydream.

She pictured herself with Noah on a train to California, snuggling close to him in the passenger car. Then she added a dose of reality to her dreams and imagined herself, poorly clad, sitting with him by the cooking stove in the Emigrant Coach. Both scenarios produced an equally unquenchable joy in her chest.

Of course, such musings were as fantastical as being visited by three spirits on Christmas Eve, but that didn't make her reveries any less pleasurable. Each daydream was like a priceless jewel. She smiled, remembering how she'd scolded Henry for calling Tirzah his precious jewel. She refused to chide herself for her harmless imaginings.

On Thursday, she walked, almost skipped, back to The Villa. In a few hours she'd see Noah again. When she neared the house, she saw a horse and buggy beside the kitchen door. Mrs. Bloom must be heading out on errands. The driver nodded, and Millie nodded back.

But as soon as she stepped into the kitchen, she sensed something was wrong—even before she saw a travel bag standing at the door.

Mrs. Bloom pulled her inside. "Millie, dear," she said thickly. "I don't know quite how to say this, so I've just got to come out with it. You're movin' back to the Mansion House."

Millie's jaw dropped. Mrs. Bloom wasn't one to prank. Her drawn lips and furrowed brow confirmed the pronouncement was all too real. "Why? What is it?"

"I got word from Harriet today." The older woman fidgeted with the edge of her apron. "You're to go back to work for the paper tomorrow."

"Did Tirzah want me back?"

Perhaps Tirzah was really pregnant this time and needed Millie's help again.

"I don't know 'bout that. She prob'ly does. But Harriet thinks your presence will enhance the social life of the Mansion House."

Mrs. Bloom turned down her lower lip as if to say *I told you so*.

Millie gripped the edge of the table to balance herself. "But you don't want me to go, do you?" Her lips quivered, and her throat ached. "Can't you say I'm needed here?"

"I'm sorry, Millie. I may rule our little roost around here, but I'm pretty low in the peckin' order over there." Millie's hope faded to despair as Mrs. Bloom's voice grew huskier. "There's nothin' I can do."

"Is that buggy for *me*? Do I have to go *now*?"

Mrs. Bloom nodded grimly.

Millie glanced around the room, trying to collect her thoughts. "I have to p—"

She stopped short. The bag was for her. A wave of panic gripped her as she thought of the choker.

"I packed your things myself." Mrs. Bloom nodded toward the bag. "And removed your bedding. It's all there. Even your personal items."

Millie exhaled. So Mrs. Bloom had seen the necklace. The look in her eyes said she'd keep the secret. Despite that momentary relief, Millie's chest squeezed as if gripped by a vise. She breathed shallowly and rapidly as her thoughts whirled. "I—I won't get to see the kittens grow up."

Mrs. Bloom looked away and patted her eyes with her apron.

"And—Noah." Millie didn't know what to say or ask that would lessen the twisting of her heart.

"I'll tell him what happened. That you had no warnin'."

No warning. Exactly. Why should she be treated this way? Like a dog on a chain. She batted away two tears that started down her cheeks.

"Goodness, child!" laughed Mrs. Bloom. "It's not like we'll never see you again. We're only a mile an' a half away. You can come back for visits any time." As more tears slipped from Millie's eyes, the older woman turned away again. "Patches will want to see you."

Visits wouldn't be the same. This had become her home, a place where she'd learned to be herself in a way she never had before. And Mrs. Bloom was a large part of that. She threw herself at the dear woman and hugged her tightly. Then she picked up the travel bag and stepped onto the porch where Patches, sitting on the rag rug preening herself, looked at her indifferently. She strode to the waiting buggy and got in.

"Bertram, isn't it?" she asked the driver.

He grinned. "Just call me Birdie."

He clucked twice and flicked the reins once. The horse plodded toward the Mansion House.

Chapter 15: Return

Millie shifted as she sat at the desk next to Tirzah, keeping her eyes on her work. It seemed as if a lifetime had passed since she'd first come to work for the *Circular*. In fact, the newspaper of Oneida Community was no longer even called the *Circular*. During the time she'd lived at The Villa, the paper had been recast as a review of American socialist experiments, and it was now called the *American Socialist*. Gone were the cheery articles about activities in the Children's House and new innovations members had come up with to make their work more pleasurable. There were no humorous little filler articles for Millie to write. There weren't even any reprints of Home Talks from Father Noyes.

Millie had no interest in other communes, particularly ones that were fully secular. Bible Communism was what had always set Oneida Community apart. Now the newspaper gave the impression that Father Noyes was more interested in communism than in the Bible.

Explaining the changes to Millie, Tirzah had lacked all her previous warmth. The whole time Millie sat proofreading articles, an awkward iciness emanated from her supervisor. Relieved when she finished the proofreading and could escape Tirzah's frigid presence, Millie moved to the compositor's counter. It felt ten degrees warmer across the room.

Yesterday Birdie hadn't simply dropped her off at the Mansion House portico. He had instructions to escort her to her room. Unsurprisingly, he led her to a room outside the Big Hall right next to Henry's and two doors down from Virginia's. At the end of the hall and beyond the stairway—just two doors to the south—was Father Noyes's apartment. She couldn't be more centrally located.

After supper Millie had dashed off a note to Noah to say goodbye personally. *Goodbye.* The word wrenched her heart. Would she never again sit with him in the evenings, pick eggs with him, or walk to the creek with him? Her eyes stung, and she squeezed back tears. The last two months had been the happiest she'd ever known. Why had that happiness been snatched away?

When the day's work was completed, Tirzah asked Millie to stay behind. Immediately her mouth went dry and her hands began to quiver. She clasped them together as she sat across from Tirzah.

Tirzah spoke sternly. "First, Millie, I want you to know I've taken some heat for you."

Millie didn't expect to hear that from this cold former friend. "Heat?"

"When Aunt Harriet found out you never had your interview with Theodore, she was irate." Tirzah folded her arms across her chest. "Of course, she blamed it all on me—although *I* wasn't the one to send you to The Villa. Ann Hobart did that."

She seemed to be waiting for a confession, but Millie only unclasped her hands and folded them again.

"It was a fine trick you played, and I'm still not sure how you accomplished it." She looked at Millie through narrow eyes. "But Aunt Harriet now believes I was part of some conspiracy on your behalf." She tossed her head. "I'm not above conspiracies, but I don't like being accused of one I know nothing about. As far as I knew, Ann had taken you under her wing and arranged your interview with Theodore. Of course, I was dismayed that she'd won you away from me, but I wasn't about to descend to her level and play her games. So I let you go."

Millie kept her expression blank as she realized for the first time how lucky she'd been. Constance's plan had worked like a charm. "I'm sorry I left the *Circular*. It wasn't that I didn't enjoy working with you."

"I thought we had a good relationship, even a friendship." Tirzah's tone softened at the apology. "But the matter at hand is your introduction to marriage. I'm charged with arranging the interview again, and this time I won't be thwarted. If I can't arrange it, Aunt Harriet will take the matter into her own hands."

Millie nodded.

Tirzah's erect posture and steady gaze signaled her unassailable determination. "It must be a week from Tuesday. Theodore will be gone next week, so that's the only day that will work for him. I trust you have no objections?"

She had a myriad of objections, but none that Tirzah or Mrs.

Skinner would accept. She shook her head.

"Good. Then Tuesday after next you'll call on Theodore in his room right after Meeting. I'll tell him to expect you." Tirzah stood and walked toward the door. She stopped and turned halfway back. "I hardly need say that your behavior has been highly inappropriate and must not be repeated."

Tirzah left without waiting for Millie to join her. Millie's face burned. More than anything, she wished she could run away. How could she endure working here if Tirzah was going to be so cold toward her? And now the dreaded interview loomed over her once again, but this time with Harriet Skinner behind it. The inevitable night in Dr. Noyes's room was only ten days away. It would be better if it were tonight. Having it hanging over her day after day would drive her mad.

She waited a few minutes to let Tirzah get far ahead, then left the office and climbed the stairs to the front door. As she plodded out into the sunshine, she squinted. Through watery eyes she saw a form standing at the bottom of the steps.

Tirzah took a step closer. "There's one more thing."

Millie's heart sank. What else could Tirzah have to burden her with?

Tirzah put on a smile. "Won't you walk to the Mansion House with me?" Millie walked at her side as Tirzah continued. "Henry wants to revive your play, and I agree. I told him, Leonora, and the others you'll resume practices this week. Do you know I'm in charge of the entertainment for our Independence Day celebration, July seventh? We expect attendance that Saturday to be the largest we've ever had from the Outside—bigger than last year's Centennial. Theodore has already had circulars posted in the surrounding towns."

Not grasping how all this affected her, Millie nodded politely.

Tirzah gently rested a hand on Millie's upper arm as they continued to walk. "I might be able to fit your play into the program. Wouldn't that be wonderful? Theodore and I will discuss it when he returns—after your interview. Once he's had a chance to get to know you, I'm sure he'll be even more supportive."

Tirzah expected her gratitude, but with the sick feeling washing over her, Millie could only manage a weak smile.

Alone in her room she tried to sort out what Tirzah had done.

She'd feigned more anger than she felt, knowing she'd turn around and entice her with including her play in the holiday celebration. It was like a reverse session in the Turkish bath, moving from a cold spray to a dry heat room. Evidently, if she didn't cooperate with Theodore at the interview, they wouldn't cooperate with her play. Was this how Christians showed their love? Wave after wave of heat and nausea passed over her as she lay on her bed contemplating her situation.

* * *

When Millie entered her room after work on Tuesday, she found an envelope pushed under the door. She tore it open. Seeing the signature, "Noah," her heart leapt into her throat and her pulse quickened. She read:

> Dear Millie,
>
> I must write to tell you how devastated I was to learn they had taken my Millie away from me. Patches and I have consoled each other in your absence. We all miss you here. Last evening found our squails matches to be severely lacking in <u>beauty</u> and <u>grace</u>. You know why.
>
> I hope to be able to see you this coming Saturday. My family intends to be among the visitors enjoying the first-of-the-season strawberry shortcake at Oneida Community. Sadie saw the circular posted at the mercantile and has spoken of nothing else since. Her incessant petitions have convinced my father that a family outing is in order. Would your schedule allow you to spend perhaps an hour with us that day? I am sure entertaining the visitors requires much effort on everyone's part, so if your work prevents you from socializing, we will understand. But my family would dearly love to at least meet the woman I have told them so much about. We should arrive at about 2 o'clock.
>
> Looking forward to hearing from you soon, I remain,

Your dear friend,
Noah

Millie hugged the letter to her bosom and contemplated what meaning lay behind the words. The first line was balm to her soul, yet it might be only hyperbole. The rest of the paragraph equated his feelings toward her with that of the cat and the other residents. She thrilled with pleasure to think Noah found her to be a person of beauty and grace, but when she re-read the sentence, she saw that "last evening," not Noah, found her to be so.

Sadie, not Noah, had recommended the visit to Oneida Community, and the reverend had agreed. Perhaps he was no longer the Community's biggest critic. Noah had told them *so much about* her. If only she could have been a bird at the window during those conversations. Had he told them that she was one of those peculiar Community women? Or that she was a *dear friend?* Or something else? Certainly not something else.

But never mind all that. She was going to see Noah and meet his family only four days from now. She dashed off a reply saying she'd love to join his family for shortcake on Saturday.

When the actors met on Wednesday afternoon to resume play practice, Millie's spirits were unquenchable. Her reunion with Noah was only three days away. After such a long hiatus, the actors were rusty and bungled every other line, but Millie's good cheer put them at ease. Soon they were all roaring with laughter at the slightest provocation.

When the other actors had left, Henry caught Millie by the arm. "You're in fine form today, my girl. Something has filled your balloon with hot air." He studied her face. "Can you let a fellow in on your secret?"

Millie laughed to think of herself floating away in a hot air balloon. She tossed her head with as much coquetry as she had in her, and at that moment—envisioning herself sailing into the beyond with Noah at her side—she had plenty.

Remembering how Henry had acted when he was in love with Tirzah, she winked at him. "You should know!"

Grinning, Henry nodded with raised eyebrows.

At exactly two o'clock on Saturday, Noah rounded the north wall of the Mansion House. With him were a slender woman dressed in a sky blue dress carrying a lacy parasol, a self-assured man in a white linen jacket, a boy in suspenders and rolled-up sleeves, and a curly-haired girl with a bright smile. So that was eleven-year-old Sadie. Noah's siblings were as good-looking as he.

Millie could hardly keep from skipping across the grass. She waved her arm. "Noah!" She faced his parents, whose expressions lit up with smiles, too. "I'm so glad you could come. Welcome to Oneida Community."

Sadie bounced at Noah's side, pulling on his sleeve.

He placed his hand over hers to keep it steady on his arm. "Millie, this is Sadie, my sister."

Sadie gave a small curtsy and bobbed back up, beaming. "I'm pleased to meet you."

After Noah introduced his brother, Andrew, and his parents, Millie ushered them to a vacant section at one of the long tables. Noah's father pulled out a seat for his wife at the end of the table, and she gracefully positioned herself there. Millie sat on her left, with Sadie and Andrew on her side of the table and the menfolk facing them. Soon the servers placed plates of strawberry shortcake in front of them.

As they ate, Mrs. Martinson studied Millie intently. Yet no judgment emanated from the pretty woman—just something like deep curiosity.

Smiling, the minister's wife reached into her day bag and pulled out a rectangular package bound with a pink bow. "I brought you a gift."

"I put the ribbon on!" announced Sadie proudly.

Millie untied the ribbon and opened the box, revealing a fountain pen. "Oh! How lovely!"

"Someone gave it to Mother," said Sadie. "I wanted it, but she won't let me use ink yet."

"I hope you don't mind an item that's already been used." Mrs. Martinson recovered smoothly from Sadie's naïve remark without so much as a disapproving glance toward her daughter. "I pass on my bounty when I can. Noah told us you're a writer."

Millie wasn't sure what warmed her heart more, the gift or Noah's acknowledgment of her talent.

Sadie chatted enthusiastically as they ate, recounting how she'd pressed her family to visit Oneida. She scanned the large building before her. "Where's your room, Millie?"

"It's on the other side from here—on the second floor. But for five years I had that room, right there." Millie pointed to her former room that looked out over the still-blossoming tulip tree. "It's in Ultima Thule."

"Ultima Thule!" Andrew perked up. "Do they send traitors there to banish them?"

They all laughed—only Millie knew the irony.

Andrew leaned forward around Sadie to catch Millie's attention. "What's your favorite part? Of this mansion?"

"Our library. We have thousands of books." Millie pointed to the peaked roof in front of them. "But the most interesting spot is under the bell tower there. The garret."

Mrs. Martinson lifted her eyes to the roof. "What makes the garret so interesting?"

"It's—just an old attic, so almost no one goes up there." Millie didn't want to mention anything personal. "You can look out the windows on the north and east sides."

Sadie picked up on Millie's hesitation. "Is it haunted?"

Andrew elbowed her. "Sadie!"

Seeing the pout forming on Sadie's face, Millie arched her eyebrows playfully. "Only when there are séances."

Andrew's eyes widened, but Reverend Martinson frowned. "Noyes allows séances?"

Millie gulped at his stern tone. "Not anymore. I haven't heard of one for a long time."

"I see." The reverend's face relaxed. "How long have you been here, Millie? Were you born here?"

"I came when I was four. With my father."

"And your mother?" Mrs. Martinson asked.

"She died before we came."

Mrs. Martinson's eyes softened. "I'm sorry for your loss. It's hard for a girl to grow up without a mother."

"That's why my father brought me here. So I'd have many mothers."

She must not have sounded convincing. Mrs. Martinson smiled, but her eyes were skeptical.

Sadie's wide-eyed gaze passed over the milling guests and members within the Quadrangle. "Do you like living with so many people? In a castle with towers?"

Millie glanced at Noah under her eyelashes. "It's nice, but I liked living at The Villa more."

He seemed about to agree when Sadie jumped in again. "Noah told us all about your adventures there. Kittens and keets—I wish I could have seen them! Noah says the calico loves him best. But how horrid for those chickens to have killed that hen!"

Millie shuddered.

"Noah said you cried. Did you?" Sadie pressed.

Noah glared at his sister reprovingly. "Sadie!"

Millie stiffened, her cheeks growing warm. Had he told them how she'd flung herself on him? If so, his parents would think she was brazen indeed.

"Of course, she cried," Mrs. Martinson said to Sadie. "Any sensitive woman would have." She covered Millie's hand with her own. "I've seen some gruesome things in my lifetime as well—in the barnyard and outside it. In this world we will have trouble."

Millie relaxed. Again, Mrs. Martinson emanated only kindness, not reproach.

With Sadie silenced temporarily, Andrew took up the interrogation. "Do you have any secret passages?"

"You children!" the reverend laughed. "You'll wear Millie out with all your questions."

Millie laughed as well. "Not that I know of. But there's a tunnel from this wing to that building over there—the Tontine." She pointed toward the route of the underground arched passageway. "So we don't have to go outside in the winter to get to our dining room."

Sadie looked at her father first, then her mother. "*We've* got a secret chamber."

Millie tilted her head. "Do you?"

"It's where the runaways hid when they were on the Moses Road."

Millie glanced at Noah for clarification. "The Underground Railroad?"

He opened his mouth, but Andrew snorted, rolling his eyes. "She keeps calling it the Moses Road because of Harriet Tubman—*that* Moses."

Noah jumped in. "Our home was a station for Negroes fleeing to Canada." His voice and eyes revealed unabashed pride. Reverend Martinson traced the rim of his lemonade glass with his index finger, and Mrs. Martinson feigned interest in some children running past on the lawn.

Noah looked from Millie to Mrs. Martinson. "One of my earliest memories is of a black man kneeling before my mother and saying, 'Bless you, ma'am, bless you.'"

Millie considered the woman next to her, who was still looking away. There was more to this kind lady than met the eye. "Helping runaways was dangerous, wasn't it?"

Mrs. Martinson smiled fondly at her husband. "We were young and brave in those days."

Millie turned toward the minister. "You could have been jailed for breaking the Fugitive Slave Law."

His eyes rested on his wife's face. "Matilda and I answered to a higher law." He propped his elbow on the table, set his chin on his fist, and met Millie's eyes. "Desperate times call for desperate measures, as they say. And the times were desperate."

With a sigh, Sadie tossed her head. "I wish *I* could have been in on it."

"You would have spilled the secret to everyone," Andrew said.

"No, I wouldn't have!"

"Yes, you would!"

A look from their father stopped the argument. Sadie turned up her nose at her brother and faced Millie. "Now we take in wanderers and vagabonds." She rolled her eyes. "Even *missionaries*."

Noah chuckled. "You make them sound like the worst of the lot."

Sadie and Andrew looked at each other and spoke in unison. "Sometimes they are."

Reverend Martinson attempted a scowl, but the sparkle in his eyes and his twitching chin suggested he agreed with his children's assessment.

Mrs. Martinson laughed. "The crusades James and I work on now are smaller ones. We open our doors to the needy, but we don't hide them under the floor anymore."

Andrew's eyes followed a boy his age who was pedaling the velocipede across the north lawn. "Look at that!"

"How extraordinary!" Sadie said with an air.

Smirking, Noah shook his head.

Millie gestured toward Andrew. "You can try it if you want. You'll have to wait your turn. Just go around to the front portico."

"May we, Mother?" Andrew and Sadie asked at the same time.

Mrs. Martinson looked toward her husband.

He gave a barely perceptible nod. "Remember to stay off the south lawn. That area is restricted."

After some discussion of the velocipede and other Community entertainments, Reverend Martinson quizzed Millie about the planned new wing, the Community's water source, and its industries. He was especially interested in how all the work assignments were made.

To Millie's surprise and relief, he didn't seem critical. In fact, he seemed to approve of how the commune was managed, so Millie grew more confident as the conversation went on. Nothing else drew his rancor like the reference to séances had. She couldn't blame him for disapproving of those. Perhaps he had warmed toward the commune despite disagreeing with Father Noyes over moral issues.

As Noah and his father began talking together quietly, Mrs. Martinson and Millie discussed their favorite books.

Mrs. Martinson had read and re-read *Middlemarch*. "I feel an affinity for Dorothea Brooke," she said. "Not to reflect on my husband, of course. He's nothing like Casaubon. James is a man of action. But I long to benefit my neighbors, just as Dorothea did."

"Such a kind and compassionate woman." Millie sighed. "I'd like to be like her."

Mrs. Martinson patted Millie's hand. "From what Noah says, I believe you already are."

Millie's heart fluttered at the compliment. Whatever Noah had told them about her, it must have been favorable.

As she continued talking to Mrs. Martinson, Millie caught a few snippets of Noah's conversation with his father. It was about college. Far from resisting the discussion, Noah seemed engaged—even excited. Foreboding washed over her. If the conflict between Noah and his father that brought Noah to Willow Place had disappeared, then Noah might, as well.

When the parents went to gather the children, Noah stayed behind. "What do you think?"

His smile showed he knew his family had left a good impression.

"Does Sadie know how lucky she is?"

"To have me for a brother?" Noah slapped his hand to his chest. "I tell her all the time."

"I meant that she's your mother's daughter." Millie wagged her head to drive home her tease. But she'd never spoken truer words—Sadie was the luckiest girl she knew. She squinted at Noah accusingly. "Why didn't you tell me about the Underground Railroad? You know I would have been interested."

"It's not good for a young man to speak too highly of his parents." Noah assessed Millie's face. "That's why I wanted you to meet them—so you could make your own judgment."

Millie's heart swelled, even as confusion nagged her mind. That he should ask her opinion was flattering, but why should he care at all about what she thought of his parents?

"I have an idea." He leaned forward. "What would you say to a little fishing expedition Monday afternoon?"

Millie tilted her head and pursed her lips, prompting him to clarify the invitation. "With you?"

Noah looked properly chagrined. "I could talk Mrs. Bloom into packing us a picnic supper. We could walk to the creek where it crosses under the bridge up there." He pointed north of the Mansion House. "I've heard people catch some good-sized crappies there."

They agreed to meet at five o'clock, and Noah would bring the worms. Millie waved as he bounded off to join his family.

What were his intentions? Did he have something to tell her, or did he just want a fishing partner?

"Penny for your thoughts."

Millie jumped at the words spoken behind her into her ear. Her father crooked his arm. She took it, and they walked toward the gardens.

When they were beyond earshot of anyone else, he spoke. "Who were your Outsider friends?"

She'd never found a way to tell him about Noah, so of course he was curious. "Noah Martinson lives at The Villa." Why did she always blush so easily? "We became friends, so he wanted me to meet his family."

Studying her face, William walked in silence a few paces. "I suppose that was about the time I said you'd changed." He eyed some flowers beside the path. "Makes sense now."

Millie's cheeks grew even hotter. "What does?"

William chuckled. "I'm not so old as all that, my dear." He assessed her again. "When you were sitting across from him, you had a look in your eyes that I've seen before. It made me happy and sad at the same time." He stopped walking, picked a daisy, and gently tucked it into her hair above her ear. "It was the way your mother used to look at me."

Tears sprang into Millie's eyes. The tenderness of his hand on her hair, the depth of his gaze, and the warmth of his voice made her heart ache. Her lower lip trembled, and a hot tear coursed down her cheek. "Did she?"

William drew her up in his arms and held her in an embrace, rocking her ever so slightly. Millie basked in their shared sorrow. How many times she'd longed to know about her parents' relationship, but her father had been unwilling to talk. Now his comforting hug proclaimed his deep love for his wife.

At length he let Millie go. "She would've been so proud of you—of the beautiful woman you've become."

Millie let out a trembling breath. "How did you meet?"

"In a garden." He motioned widely with his arm. "Not so different from this. She was pushing a baby carriage in a park—she was a nanny then." He offered his arm again, and they resumed their stroll. "I knew I had to speak to her, so I made up some sort of excuse. And things progressed from there."

"Until you married. How long did you court her?"

"Not more than four months. We were young and impetuous, of course. Things weren't going well with her position, and she was alone in the world. Neither of us saw a reason to wait."

"What happened to her family—" Millie hesitated to say the unfamiliar words. "My grandparents?"

William stiffened. He looked ready to retreat into the silent depths that had always surrounded her history. He licked his lips. "They perished in a fire. Her parents, a brother, and a sister. She was the only one who survived."

Millie's stomach flipped, and drops of perspiration sprang up on her forehead despite the light breeze. Any more questions along that line would be morbidly curious. "And what of your parents? You never spoke of them, either."

"My mother also passed on when I was young. I was an only child."

Millie risked one more question. She might never find him so talkative again. "And your father?"

"He lived to hold you—but not long after that."

The distant, sorrowful look in his eyes told Millie his memories were more painful than sweet. She couldn't make further inquiries. She squeezed her father's arm instead.

He patted her hand, then smiled down at her. "So? Noah—does he know?"

"Know what?"

"How you feel about him." William's eyes sparkled as his voice teased.

"I don't know how I feel about him," Millie lied. "I mean, he's not part of the Community."

"And that's important to you?"

"Of course. Shouldn't it be?" She'd never expected to have such a discussion. "Is it important to you?"

"That doesn't matter. What does your heart tell you?"

Millie watched her feet scuffling against the gravel and searched her heart. "That it's impossible." Now that she'd stated the situation verbally, she knew it was true. The words tumbled out of their own accord. "I have an interview with Theodore Noyes on Tuesday. My first."

To her relief, William didn't change his pace but continued strolling. Having left the garden, they followed the gravel path toward the Summer House.

"I didn't know whether you'd started complex marriage or not. But I assumed not from some hints that Constance gave. How do you feel about it?"

"I wish it wasn't Theodore." She kept her voice flat.

"I understand. But until recently, Father Noyes had that duty."

"So I should be *thankful*?" Now her voice betrayed a sneer.

"Not *should*. *Should* isn't for me to say."

She clenched her jaw. Why had she even brought the subject up? There was nothing he could do. He'd brought her here, after all, and fully knew what that meant for her.

William stared ahead. "Mr. Hinds is pushing for parents to be involved in how their daughters are introduced to marriage. If I were to ally myself to that group, perhaps—"

"Thank you, Father, but I'm seventeen. I don't think there's anything to be done."

"But if you think Noah …"

"He must think I'm already married."

Millie's chest ached with that truth. Noah wasn't naïve about the Community's radical social practices. And if he'd had any doubt about her, what she said at the creek would have convinced him that she was a Community wife. Surely he only considered her a friend.

William stroked his beard. "And yet he wanted you to meet his parents."

They reached the Summer House. No one was there. The Outsiders were heading back to the train station or to their conveyances, and members were cleaning the grounds and putting away the tables and chairs. After stepping inside the shaded gazebo, they sat side by side on one of the rude benches.

William took Millie's hands in his. "If this Noah is interested in you, if you want to leave the Community—you mustn't worry about me." He stared into her eyes. "Just follow your heart. For the last seventeen years, I've followed my heart—and that was to give you the best life I could give you."

She'd never seen him this passionate. She squeezed his hand.

"But I may have made a mistake. Now that you're a woman, the Community might not be the place for you. It's very womanly to want your own husband, your own home." He brushed her hair behind her ear. "Is that what you want?"

Birds chirped and bees buzzed around them. A warm breeze rustled the leaves above their heads. Here in their private little nest her father was baring his heart as he never had before. She felt snug and cozy next to him, with her small hands in his large, rough ones.

But he was pushing her out of the nest—urging her to leave the Community, something she'd never seriously considered. She lifted her eyes, pooling with tears, to his.

"Just say the word, and I'll talk to Mr. Hinds. Or Harriet Skinner, if necessary. Or Theodore himself." He ran his thumb across her chin as he used to when she was little. "Do you think he loves you?"

Millie bit her bottom lip. When he'd put the choker on her neck, an electric charge shot through her body—but she had no way of knowing whether he'd felt it, too. Though he seemed to admire her that first night of squails, it might have all been in good fun. In the chicken yard he'd stroked her hair and back as she clung to his chest —but that could have been brotherly protection. At times her daydreams had convinced her that he loved her as much as she loved him, but reality told her otherwise.

She couldn't answer the question—it would hurt too much to say it aloud. "He invited me to go fishing Monday night."

"And did you accept?"

"Of course!"

"Then that's your next step for now. What happens Monday may tell you what to do on Tuesday."

Millie leaned her head against her father's strong arm. She felt as if she were five or six again. But no. Even at that age, she hadn't felt this comforted and protected. Because she'd never felt threatened. She'd never needed a father as much as she needed one now. And here he was—right beside her.

* * *

As Millie entered the Big Hall for Meeting Sunday evening, Constance sidled close and asked for an update on her visit with the Martinsons. Millie's heart warmed as she recounted how lively and curious Andrew and Sadie had been and how special Mrs. Martinson had made her feel.

As they settled into their seats, Millie confided, "You know, I've never had a chance to see a normal family in person—I've only read about them. I can't quite describe the experience."

The look of pity that lined Constance's face was so disconcerting that Millie quickly changed the subject. "Oh! I found out Noah's parents were station masters on the Underground Railroad."

A playful smirk tugged at the corners of Constance's lips. "That's why I baited Noah a bit at the Astor House. To see if he shared his parents' passion."

Millie shook her head. How naïve she'd been—and in many ways still was. What other mysteries of common knowledge remained at large that her cloistered life had hidden from view? She spotted her father and waved for him to join them. As he did, she scooted closer to Constance so he could take the aisle seat. Positioned between the older, wiser adults, she suddenly felt years too young for her age.

Weighing the stirpicults took most of the evening. As cute as the babies were, she couldn't concentrate on how much they'd grown. *Tomorrow.* Tomorrow she'd meet Noah for their fishing trip, and at least one mystery might be revealed—why he'd invited her.

Abruptly she snapped back to reality. Murmurs spread through the room as Victor Hawley shuffled across the stage, taking a chair where Tirzah and Henry had sat before. Millie's heart sank. The same aura of fear mixed with morbid curiosity that had spread over the room at Tirzah's criticism was palpable now.

Erastus Hamilton, his eyes glowering under bushy gray brows, cleared his throat ominously. "Victor Hawley, the Community must be informed of your actions on Friday at the Dental Office."

Victor hung his head submissively.

"Judge Towner will relate the situation."

Dressed in a suit finer than those worn by the other men, Judge Towner mounted the stage. Dignified and stiff, with his slick black hair combed back from his face and his shiny black eye patch covering his left eye, he posed in partial profile.

"Mr. Hawley, in performance of your duties as dental assistant, you were in charge of assuring the comfort of Phoebe Allen, age eleven. Did you or did you not administer brandy to Miss Allen?"

"I did."

Confused whispers spread around the room. Millie glanced at her father, and he shrugged. Calming a patient's nerves with a sip of brandy before a dental procedure was common practice.

Judge Towner cleared his throat disapprovingly. "And the amount you administered?"

"About a third of a glass."

The ensuing buzz bore minor displeasure. That was a bit much, but did it deserve this level of censure?

"And do you know how it affected her?"

"She became ill and vomited."

A few gasps erupted from around the hall. Millie looked at Constance, who seemed to be trying not to roll her eyes. She, too, must feel this was being overblown. But why?

"Your action was a clear violation of the standards of the Dental Office with regard to the care of young patients. Putting our members at risk, particularly our young ones, cannot be tolerated." Judge Towner pulled on his vest indignantly. "The Committee has determined that you may no longer work in the Dental Office. Our dental and medical procedures follow the highest standards. Any assistant who violates those standards will be removed."

Millie cringed at the harsh words.

Slouching in his seat, Victor kept his eyes lowered.

Judge Towner glared at his prey. "You may now respond."

Victor straightened. "I offer my heartfelt apology to Phoebe and her parents." He scanned the crowed, then turned to Judge Towner. "Where am I to be assigned now?"

His personal question dangled awkwardly in the air. Judge Towner nodded to Erastus Hamilton, as if resting his case and leaving a decision in the hands of the court.

The white-haired elder intoned, "Mr. Hawley, the Community has shown you forbearance long enough. There is no other position for you here."

Millie sucked in her breath. What did that mean? All members had to work.

Murmurs of assent rose and mixed with murmurs of sympathy, but all whispers quickly subsided when the three eyes of Erastus Hamilton and Judge Towner stared into the crowd with matching resolute expressions. Mr. Hamilton turned toward Victor as if expecting him to declare his spirit of subordination to Mr. Noyes, but Victor remained silent. Clearly annoyed, the elder dismissed Meeting, and a subdued roar of muffled conversation filled the air.

Standing, Millie looked from Constance to William, who had also risen to their feet. Both were frowning. "Where's Mary? Did she hear this?"

Constance shook her head. "She's away on a trip with Victor's sister. They've been gone about a week."

"Victor's been so distracted since she's been away." William looked distraught. "I spoke with him while he was mounting insects a few days ago, and he was rambling on, not making much sense. I was worried for him then."

Millie shook her head. "But Phoebe recovered, surely. Wouldn't they simply suspend him for this? What will he do now?"

"They want to force him out," William said.

Constance nodded. "They're seizing the brandy incident as their opportunity. With Mary away, they think this can be handled quickly and without display."

Millie's anger boiled. "But this *was* a display!" She struggled to keep her voice low. "Why do it in front of everyone?"

"To prevent people from rallying to his side." William clenched and unclenched his fists. "This way they lose one member, at most two, without causing a schism."

That night Millie fell into a fitful slumber. She dreamt she was wandering barefoot in her nightdress at midday past Hamilton Avenue toward Father Noyes's suite. She entered the sewing room where Mary, her belly round with pregnancy, sat weaving a basket while Victor chatted playfully at her side. He held a glass of brandy. Leering, he staggered at Millie and pushed the goblet toward her lips. When she smelled the sweet alcohol, fear gripped her. Millie turned and ran.

She bolted past her room, Henry's, and Virginia's. She angled across the rear of the Big Hall and ran toward the wide stairway. At the museum case, she stopped, panting, and peered through the glass top. The mastodon tooth, three times its normal size, throbbed menacingly against the top of the case. She raced down the stairs, but instead of arriving in the main floor hallway, she found herself in the cellar outside the Turkish bath. Mary, great with child, leaned against the wall next to Victor, who held the same goblet he'd held in the sewing room. As Millie tried to back away, he drew her near and pressed the glass to her lips. She retched.

Instantly she was entering the library, still in her nightdress, holding *Lady Audley's Secret*. She'd meant to return it weeks—no, months—no, years ago. A man sat with his back to her, hunched over the nearest table. Victor. She inched toward him. *Don't approach!* screamed the part of her mind that knew she was dreaming. But curiosity compelled her forward. What was he reading? She peeked over his shoulder.

On a board in front of him lay the mangled corpse of the feather-pecked chicken, bloody feather after bloody feather pinned for display.

Chapter 16: Traps

Millie stood in the shade at the Summer House with her fishing pole in one hand and a basket in the other. She breathed in deeply. The potent aroma of rich earth and blooming things was powerless to calm her heart. It fluttered like a hummingbird's wings. This was just a friendly outing—she must remember that. Still, it could be something more.

The day was perfect. Cottony clouds dotted the azure sky, and a gentle breeze played in the flowers planted along the crisscrossing gravel pathways on the north lawn. The sun was just beginning to move toward the horizon, but plenty of daylight remained on this second day before the summer solstice. Birds chirped merrily everywhere, and butterflies, catching their tune, waltzed among the blossoms.

Weary of scanning the path to the north for Noah, she propped the fishing pole against the side of the Summer House and leaned against it herself, letting the rough timbers poke her back. She closed her eyes. High in the treetops she heard the confident two-note whistle of a cardinal, and a few seconds later the three-note reply. Though most members were inside eating supper, occasionally the crack of a baseball bat and manly cheers floated northward from the south lawn. Later, many would come to walk the paths, some as couples, some as groups. By the time they got here, she and Noah would have walked on another ten minutes to Oneida Creek.

She shifted her basket from one hand to the other. Constance had provided her with the biggest, most luscious strawberries for a special treat. Millie had protested that Noah was bringing supper, but Constance said the strawberries would add a special touch that would certainly win his heart. That wasn't what she was trying to do, Millie had insisted, but now that she was here, with only her anticipation for company, she could be honest. If Constance knew as much about love as she knew about fruit, this could go down in history as one of the most successful fishing trips of all time.

Muffled footsteps sounded on the other side of the Summer House, and Noah peered through the open walls of the gazebo, grinning. "Sorry I'm a bit late. Decided to wait for a ride from Birdie rather than hoof it." He rounded the structure and added her pole to his own, gripping them in one hand. "I've got it."

Sifted by leaves, a ray of sunlight dappled his handsome face. She searched his chestnut brown eyes for a clue. Had he come to court a young lady or to fish with a friend? He turned before she could glean an answer.

They started down the path toward the creek. As it meandered through a wooded area, chipmunks and squirrels scooted about ahead of them and in the underbrush.

"What's that?" Millie pointed. "A muskrat?"

They peered at the long dark form in the middle of the path ahead, closer to the river.

"No—maybe it's just a fallen branch. It's not moving."

After a few more steps, they both exclaimed at once, "It's a turtle!"

The creature's green-black shell was over a foot long. As they crouched for a closer look, it retracted its head, but they could still see its scowling mouth, hooked nose, and tightly drawn skin. It glared at them with angry eyes. The plates of armor on its front legs and its ridged, pointed tail were worthy of any dragon.

Millie laughed. "I believe I know this person."

Noah grinned skeptically.

"Noah Martinson, Mr. Dunn."

"Don't get too close," he warned. "It's a snapper."

"I've no doubt." Millie backed up. "So is our Mr. Dunn. Did you notice the little house next to the gazebo?"

Noah nodded.

"That's Dunn Cottage. In it lives a cranky old man who couldn't stand to be around people, so the Community built him his own little home. I've seen him poke his head out his door and scowl at the children just like our reptilian Mr. Dunn here." Millie puckered her face into a sour grimace in imitation.

Noah chuckled. "I guess communism isn't for everyone."

When they reached the place where the creek ran under the bridge, they chose a grassy spot where they could sit with their poles in the water. Millie pulled a blanket from her basket.

"Never thought of that!" Noah helped spread it out. "Good idea."

They settled onto the blanket, and Noah baited his hook. Millie wasn't especially squeamish around worms, but she held up her hook for Noah to do the honors. She gripped the pole and dropped the twisted silk line into the water.

They sat in silence for a while. Behind them the plaintive whistle of the Midland locomotive faded as it moved westward. Perhaps it was the same train they'd ridden to Middletown. Would Constance mind if she told Noah the story of giving their lunch to the family in the Emigrant Coach? Probably not, since he was an Outsider.

Millie recounted the tale. "That was the first time I fully grasped the reason for Bible Communism—that it's showing the world a better way."

Pursing his lips, Noah tilted his head. "I can see why that would leave an impression." He seemed to be selecting his words with care. "But the way Constance showed charity to those people—that's what impresses me. What she did—*that's* the radical solution. If I—if ministers— could convince just half their people to behave as Constance did, this world would be a different place."

Millie stared at Noah's profile as he watched his line. He had changed. He looked like the same Noah she'd lived with at The Villa, but his eyes had an even deeper glow and his voice a different timbre. Yet it reminded her of something—of when he'd prayed with Mrs. Bloom. His new-found confidence made him even more attractive, but it disturbed her as well. One of the things they had in common was their doubt for their own religions—wandering together as two blind gropers in the same ditch. But now that bond was fraying.

She couldn't voice those thoughts, but she needed to say something. "Is that what your father does? Teach his congregation to show charity to the less fortunate?"

Noah bit his lower lip in thought.

Sitting so close to him, Millie basked in the strength of his presence. His brown hair, tousled by the breeze, was already becoming blonder from recent days in the sun, and his arms under his rolled-up sleeves were tanned and muscular. A tremor passed down her spine. In his own way, he was even handsomer than Henry.

He shifted. "Not as much as I'd like. It's one thing to tell people to do something, but it's another to fan the flames of their own impulses—so they act from their hearts."

Millie nodded. Aunt Sarah had talked about having a fire inside. More than ever, Noah seemed to have one. From the first time she'd seen him on the train, she'd been attracted to that depth of purpose. No wonder she'd lost her heart to him.

"Not that I can fault my parents. They've always helped the needy. Over the years many folks like the ones in that Emigrant Coach have sat at our kitchen table. Mother would serve them corn meal mush with bread and jam and then scrounge in the pantry for some tidbit to send with them."

Millie's face warmed. What had been a life-changing revelation to her had been Noah's routine since childhood. The gap between them seemed wider than ever.

"The vagabonds Sadie talked about." She laughed off her unease. "At least they're not missionaries, right?"

The conversation lulled. Across the creek, on the opposite bank, a great blue heron stood motionless on a fallen tree trunk. Its beady eyes looked out sternly from under its gray-topped head. Flowing feathers hung down its long, straight neck and onto its chest like a grandfatherly beard.

"Look at him." Millie nodded at the spindly bird. "Like a disapproving professor—none too pleased with his students."

Noah squinted, frowning. "I'll have plenty of them in my life soon enough."

He stared at his bobber in the water and jiggled his pole.

"You will?" Her mouth went dry. "You've decided on Hamilton?"

He faced her, his eyes soft and his brow slightly furrowed. He placed a hand on her arm. "That's what I wanted to tell you."

An arrow pierced her heart. She couldn't hide her devastation. He could certainly read her reaction like a telegram.

"I'm heading to Hamilton in September, but I'm leaving the factory at the end of the week. Mother wants my help with some things before I go away. And Father's going to help me brush up on my Greek."

"That means you've decided against joining our Community." She managed a weak smile as she struggled to fend off the weight settling in her chest. "I haven't been a very convincing teacher."

Her attempt at lightheartedness sounded flat, but at least she'd kept her voice from quavering.

"You know that was always a long shot, right? Even if John Humphrey Noyes tried to recruit me himself."

She nodded.

Noah went on. "Having the time away has helped me see things more clearly. It's funny. Here I am, making traps every day. I thought my parents were trying to trap me, so I escaped. And I went to a *trap factory*. There's irony for you! But those Newhouse traps we make— animals can't get away. What my parents have been doing—"

He paused and played with his fishing line again. "I'd say it's more like a hook." He pulled his line out of the water, showing an empty hook. "Just as I thought. Some lucky fish got the worm and swam away unharmed."

With a laugh that threatened to turn into a sob, Millie pulled up her own line. She turned her face away to regain her composure. The worm was still attached, so she dropped the line back into the water.

Noah baited his hook a second time. "They only want me to become a minister if it's what I want, they say. Yet they keep dangling a fat, juicy worm in front of me."

He waved the newly baited hook in front of her face, and she drew back, scrunching her nose in disgust. She was glad for the tease —it helped ease the ache.

He dropped his line back into the creek. "Father's paved my way at Hamilton. He found someone to room with me, and he's persuaded a few professors to take me under their wings. I just hope they're not critical old birds like that one."

The heron was forming its neck into a tighter and looser S-shape, poking out its sharp orange beak in one scolding motion after another.

Millie sighed. Deep down, she had always known nothing could come of their relationship. She'd allowed herself to dream, but she'd known this day would come. All she could do now was make the most of their friendship by being his confidant.

"So is being a minister what *you* want—or are you just doing it to make them happy?" She must focus on his interests, not her aching heart. "Have they pestered you into a decision?"

"Father tends to push. But Mother's pressure is even worse, though she doesn't try to persuade me directly."

Millie tilted her head. She couldn't imagine Mrs. Martinson being more demanding than the reverend. "How so?"

"I know she prays two prayers every day." He waved two fingers. "She's prayed them every day since I was born. One, that God would protect my future wife. And two, that I'd be a minister of the gospel like her grandfather and father."

Millie pictured Mrs. Martinson on her knees. That kind of daily petitioning of God was not how Millie had learned to pray. Lady Susan had taught the children to say, "I confess Christ a good spirit in me," or "I confess Christ an obedient spirit in me"—not to ask God to do something for someone—especially for someone they didn't even know.

Did God care how people prayed? When they'd learned Mary's baby had died, Noah had asked God to comfort Mary, and as it turned out, she missed Victor's humiliation at Meeting—which would have heaped more grief on her anguished heart. Was that God's answer to Noah's prayer? Or just a coincidence?

It was within Noah's own power to grant his mother's prayers. He could become a minister and marry a good Presbyterian girl—the type of woman his mother was praying for. No wonder he could never be interested in Millie romantically. She couldn't blame him. If Mrs. Martinson were her mother, she'd do everything she could to please her.

"You feel it's your duty to make her prayers come true?"

"Not anymore." Noah languidly dragged his line through the water. "I moved to the cottages because I thought she was trying to manipulate me. That she didn't want me to be myself. But now I see it from her perspective. When I have a son, I'll probably do the same thing. Not to control him, but to bless him."

Millie swallowed against the lump in her throat and blinked rapidly. One day Noah would have a wife and a son—but she would never see them, never know them.

Suddenly she felt a tug on her line. She clenched her pole as her bobber sank. "I've got a bite!"

Noah dropped his rod and scooted to her side. He placed his left hand on the inside of her forearm and his right hand over hers. "We need to set the hook."

He jerked the rod sharply to the right.

With his hands still in place, they both stood, and he guided her movement so as not to lose the fish. Together they lifted the line from the water. Millie giggled as they brought the fish over the bank and dropped it onto the grass where it flopped a few times and then lay still, its silver scales shining in the slanted sunlight.

She abandoned her pole and hopped up and down in glee. "I caught one!"

Noah drew her into his arms and led her in two waltzing turns in the grass. When they stopped, she smiled up into his face. Suddenly, his lips were touching hers. The world kept spinning as the rich sensation spread down her neck and into her shoulders. His breath mingled with hers, and she drew it into her soul.

He released her from his arms and stepped back with a dazed look. "Forgive me! You just looked so beautiful. But I shouldn't have done that."

"It's fine!" Millie's lip trembled with embarrassment. She shrugged. "It was just the thrill of the catch."

Their eyes met. Each caught the pun at the same time, and they sputtered out a raucous duet of laughter. They dropped onto the blanket. Every time they looked at the other's face, they broke into more waves of laughter. The great blue heron, highly offended, spread its wings and lifted off its perch in a majestic huff, at which they each took a deep breath and exhaled.

Noah's face grew solemn, and Millie felt her smile crumble away.

She spoke first. "I'm the one who's in a trap, Noah." The bearded visage of Dr. Noyes flashed before her internal eye. The interview was tomorrow. She shuddered. "You have so many choices in life, and I have none."

Noah held her gaze. "You could leave the Community."

"What would I do?" Raising her shoulders, she bit her lip. "This is the only life I know. My father is here. I know no one on the outside. Except Jessie. But nobody near here."

"I don't know anyone at Hamilton."

"That's different. Your father knows people. My father doesn't." And yet, he knew Peter Schenk well enough to have a secretive conversation with him. She shook away the memory. There were so many things she didn't even know she didn't know. How could she survive in the real world? "How would I support myself?"

"In New York City there are women who work as typesetters."

"I could never live in New York." She shook her head rapidly. The editress block on the Best Quilt came to mind, symbolizing the vocation she'd set her heart on. "Oneida Community is the only place in the entire country where a woman can work as a full-time writer. It's hard to turn my back on a chance like that." She wrinkled her nose. "Even though it means writing about American socialisms—and nothing else."

"You could teach," Noah suggested. "The public schools are always needing more teachers these days."

"Hmm." She imagined herself in a one-room schoolhouse, and the thought felt surprisingly cozy. "I'd need to go to normal school in Oswego for that, wouldn't I?"

Noah brightened. "My parents know people in Oswego. That was the end of the Underground Railroad."

Turning her face away, Millie gazed at the horizon. Such dreams were as insubstantial and inaccessible as the puffy clouds assembling above. And dreams of a future that didn't include Noah held no charm. Why discuss things that were never going to happen?

She turned back toward Noah. "Your parents were so modest about their work with the 'Moses Road.' They're modern-day heroes."

"Don't I know it?" Noah's voice held a mixture of rue and pride. "My father leaves big shoes to fill—which is why I didn't want to follow in his footsteps. It's like Theodore Noyes and John Humphrey Noyes. People are bound to be disappointed with the son compared to the father."

Millie's stomach flipped at the mention of Theodore's name. Her very insides rebelled at comparing Father Noyes to Reverend Martinson and Theodore to Noah. Especially coming from Noah.

She stared at the opposite bank. At length she said, "Are you going to share your memories of helping the slaves escape?"

"I was so young. But I remember a few things." Noah pulled out the supper Mrs. Bloom had packed. While they ate, he entertained Millie with stories of hiding runaway slaves in the small cellar under a secret trap door in their home. "My mother taught me to pray the bubble prayer for them when they left."

"The bubble prayer?"

Perhaps it was some esoteric Presbyterian ritual.

Noah smiled at her confusion. "That's what I called it. As they left us, I prayed to Jesus to put a 'bubbul of imbizzibility' around our friends." He said the words as a child would say them. "I thought God put them inside shiny magic soap bubbles that the slave catchers couldn't see through."

Millie imagined a Haydn-sized Noah praying over his black friends. "Aw! You must have been such a dear."

"I was." Noah shook his head in mock arrogance. "According to my mother, I was *the most precious thing ever.*"

Millie laughed at his imitation of his doting mother, even as the image of her own mother's ever-mute countenance flashed across her mind.

"There was one runaway I'll never forget." A faraway look softened Noah's eyes. "Around his ankle he wore a metal cuff with a length of a chain still attached. I sat on my mother's lap in our parlor and watched my father try to get that manacle off with several different tools. He broke the first three things he tried. Eventually he sawed through it with a hacksaw. I was petrified. I thought he'd cut the poor man's leg off. That was the man who knelt down before my mother and blessed her."

As Noah spoke, Millie could see the man, the chain, and Noah's father and mother so clearly that she felt as if she'd been there with them. "What a picture to have seared in your mind from such a young age."

"I think what helped forge it in my memory—pardon the pun—is that Father let me keep the few links of chain that came off the manacle. He used to say that chain reminds us that God created all men with freedom. No man can fully take away another person's freedom—because every man has a free conscience. No man can control what another man thinks or believes."

Millie nodded.

"So on Saturday, I used his own words against him."

"Did you? How?"

"He started pushing me about Hamilton again. So I found the chain, and I laid it in front of him." Noah looked at Millie sternly, reenacting the confrontation with his father. "I told him he was trying to control what I believe."

"What did he say?"

Noah's expression softened, and he swallowed hard. "He wept," Noah said huskily, turning away. He swallowed again and looked back. "And then he apologized."

Her own throat tightened. Surely Father Noyes would never be capable of such humility. She straightened as the story's import struck. "Then you don't have to go to Hamilton!"

"No, I don't."

Millie's heart leapt.

"But I want to now."

Her own internal fire, which had flickered for a moment, went out. Her chin quivered, and she turned away. They sat in silence for a few minutes, Noah plucking at the grass, Millie studying the billowy clouds.

Finally she said, "Chains were part of my childhood, too."

"How's that?"

"When I was a little girl, I helped make chains for the traps. We all did. And the children still do. We spent an hour each day linking the chains together."

"Ah!" Understanding lit Noah's eyes. "They bring the chains in every day, but I never knew from where."

"I always found it rather eerie." Millie held his gaze. "Do you know why?"

Noah thought for a moment. "Because of Marley's ghost."

"Yes!"

Looking at each other, they moaned in unison, "I wear the chain I forged in life!" and burst into laughter.

Millie bit her lip. "There's something rather symbolic about it. Every link I've joined to another is a link in a chain that binds me to the Community."

And with Noah leaving, she had nothing—no one—to link her to anywhere else.

"I see."

Their paths, having run together for a short time, were diverging again. The realization glowered like a thundercloud.

Shaking off her sadness, Millie reached into her basket for the strawberries and offered them to Noah. He took a large red berry, and she chose one for herself. Too large to eat whole, glinting scarlet in

the waning sunshine, they were truly prize-worthy. Her mouth watered at the sight of them. As Noah brought his to his mouth and took a bite, she bit into hers at the same time. It was jarringly sweet.

But not as sweet as Noah's kiss.

After they'd eaten the strawberries, Noah sighed. "This has been wonderful, Millie. I mean it. I wish—"

She strained to hear what he wished, but his voice trailed off. She nodded. She believed—she hoped—she knew what he meant. At least they were parting in agreement with each other. Their dance, their kiss, their speaking the same words at the same time—each was a delicious morsel she would savor forever.

The sun was edging toward the horizon. He extended his hand to help her up, and they parted. Noah walked north toward The Villa with Millie's fish as Millie walked south toward the Mansion House with her fruitless basket. The wind picked up and blew her hair across her right cheek. In the treetops, the leaves gave a sympathetic rustle.

They'd made no plans to meet again.

* * *

Rumbling thunder woke Millie in the early hours of the morning. A storm had blown in. It was Tuesday.

Soon, much too soon, she found herself walking back from the newspaper office under a cheerless black umbrella as rain bore down unrelentingly. As she crossed the road to the Mansion House driveway, she stepped aside at the sound of an approaching carriage. Inside, staring out with the saddest expression she'd ever seen on a man, was Victor Hawley. She met his eyes from behind the rain-streaked window of the coach and raised her free hand. He raised his in return, and the carriage moved on.

Victor was leaving the Community. She'd probably never see him again. Thunder growled in the distance. She felt it deep in her chest, down her spine, and to the soles of her feet.

The interview was only hours away now. She shouldn't have bothered to go to supper; she couldn't eat a bite. Pacing her room before Meeting, she tried to develop a plan. Thoughts flitted about like fireflies that went out as soon as she was about to apprehend one. Every time a glimmering beacon tempted her to hope, it darkened when she tried to examine it.

Only one thought was lodged in her mind, unmovable. She'd said goodbye to Noah. That darkness kept dousing any other light.

* * *

At the appointed time Millie made her way to Dr. Noyes's room and tapped lightly on the door. Perhaps he'd been called away, or perhaps he'd forgotten their interview. But, no. Heavy footfalls sounded from inside the room, and the door opened.

Theodore motioned with his arm, inviting her in, and she stepped across the threshold. The room smelled sterile, like rubbing alcohol mingled with lye soap. It was dimly lit with one lamp, its wick trimmed low.

"Welcome, Millie. Good to see you."

He closed the door.

When it clicked shut, every nerve in her body fired. Standing in the middle of the room, she faced the portly figure. She'd never been this close to him before. He wasn't as tall as she'd perceived him at a distance, and he was heavier set. He wore a white shirt, unbuttoned at the neck, like Walt Whitman in the frontispiece of *Leaves of Grass*. But unlike the poet, he looked far from rakishly charming. He simply looked tired.

Inside her pantalettes, Millie's knees trembled. "Thank you," she mumbled, the words struggling to escape her dry throat.

"Won't you sit down?"

Theodore motioned to the bed, and she sat.

She cringed as the bed creaked. When he lowered himself to her side, the mattress gave way, and she anchored her feet to the floor to keep from sliding near him.

"I trust you had a pleasant day," he said.

"Yes, thank you. And you?"

If this small talk was meant to put her at ease, it was having the opposite effect. Every muscle felt like jelly. She clasped her hands together on her lap and rubbed one thumb across the opposite thumbnail to calm herself.

"Busy. Very busy. There's much to be done on the new wing." Theodore stood and turned his back to her, facing the table and chairs.

He began to unbutton his shirt. "You may undress now."

The words struck Millie. If his back hadn't been turned, he would have seen her flinch. She didn't move. She couldn't.

He took off his shirt and hung it over the back of the chair. His large back gleamed yellow in the lamplight. As he reached to unbuckle his belt, he turned to glance at her. Seeing her frozen in place, he returned to the bed and looked at her through narrow eyes.

Millie swallowed. Her tongue seemed twice its usual size. "Uh," she began unsuccessfully, cranking her neck to look up at him. She tried again. "Could I ask you a few questions first?"

Raising his eyebrows, he nodded and sat on the mattress. His round belly overhung his belt, and on his sagging chest grew a copious amount of curling black hair. It would feel nothing like the solid protection of Noah's chest when he'd comforted her in the chicken yard. Was her bare body to touch the flabby, hairy flesh of this older man? She stiffened to stop a shudder.

He looked down on her. Her face must be flaming red.

"I have a question about ascending fellowship."

The words came out as a whispered croak.

"Go on." His voice revealed more skepticism than curiosity.

"It's just that, well, I was wondering—"

She should have practiced her questions aloud, but she'd been too afraid someone would overhear. She was already appalled at the words she was about to say. For the leader of Oneida Community to hear them from a girl half his age would be outrageous.

She pushed past the sour, churning feeling in her stomach. "If I'm a believer and you're not, and yet this is ascending fellowship—does that mean that unbelief is superior to belief?"

It took a moment for her question to register. When it did, he drew back and glowered from under his bushy black eyebrows. He looked her over as if trying to diagnose a disease. "Who told you to ask that?"

Whatever she'd expected him to say, it wasn't that. "No one."

He continued to eye her with skepticism.

She swallowed. "I've been wondering about that for some time."

"It sounds like a question from Judge Towner. Did he put you up to this?"

"Judge Towner?" Her head throbbed. The blood rushed in her

ears, pulsing a sickening rhythm. "I've never spoken to Judge Towner about anything, as far as I know."

Theodore kept studying her as if trying to read a secret code. "Then you're part of some other effort to depose me?"

"Part of—an effort?" Millie shook her head. "No, no, not at all." She should have prepared for his anger. Now she was stumbling blindly down the path she'd begun. She forced the words from her dry throat. "I'm only asking for myself."

"That is your sincere question?"

"Yes."

Theodore brought his palms to his face and rubbed his hands over his eyes and down his cheeks. "Ascending fellowship. Yes, that's what we do here. My duty tonight is to introduce you to complex marriage. After that, if you believe any man who wants to be with you isn't your spiritual superior, you have every right to refuse him."

He looked past her while delivering this rote reply but now met her eyes to gain agreement.

"I see." Millie nodded slowly. Her knees quivered. She had to keep going. "May I ask another question?"

He didn't say yes, but he looked at her expectantly.

She squeezed her hands together, bearing down mercilessly on her knuckles. "When your body is united with mine, will your heart still be united with Ann Hobart?"

As soon as Ann's name left her mouth, a dark cloud of anger spread across his face. "What do you mean by that?" he growled.

Her knees shook so violently that he'd surely feel the vibrations. She dropped her eyes to her lap. His hot offense was palpable. "Only that, if your heart belongs to Ann, why would you unite your body to another?"

Her lack of defiance seemed to calm him. She sensed his body relax. "I do it because it's my duty to our Community. That is why. Did Sarah Johnson not teach you what to expect? Do you not understand Bible Communism?" It was the voice of a disappointed professor. "Have you not listened to Father's Home Talks?"

She relaxed as well. She knew how to be a student. "Yes, I understand the teaching. In my head. But not in my heart."

He let out a long, weary sigh. "This is why you should have been brought in when you were younger." He was lapsing into problem-solving mode. "It's our fault that we passed over you. I believe you came of age during Father's illness at Wallingford, when I was assisting him there. We should have delegated the task to someone here, but we were otherwise occupied."

Millie nodded politely. At the same time, a rush of disgust hit her. Her stomach burned as if it were disintegrating. She saw it now. For decades all the girls had been taken before they were old enough to think through what was happening to them or object to the process. None had ever had a real choice. Until now.

She looked at her hands, but her voice came out strong. "And if I don't want to become a wife now?"

"You know the answer. It's a requirement if you're going to belong to our Community."

She lifted her eyes to his. "Required by you?"

His anger was rising again, but he was keeping it in check.

Suddenly she knew completely, utterly, unassailably, that her bare flesh would never touch this man's skin. A bubble had formed around her to keep her separate. They were as far apart as if she were the inaccessible moon—hanging pristinely across a great gulf of time and space.

"Yes, by me." His voice reached her as if through a railroad tunnel, or over the humming of a silk machine, or under the rasping of a hundred mallard ducks. "I'm the leader here now."

Rage seethed inside her. What gave this man the right to enforce such a requirement? The muscles in her arms tensed as if covered by armored plates, and her spine stiffened as if tipped by a spiked tail ready to lash out.

"Then you'll have to take me by force," she snapped.

The words shocked her. They hung heavy in the air like a noxious fog at noon. They were an insult, cruel and undeserved, to this man who was merely trying to perform his duty.

Theodore jumped up from the bed and loomed over her, his eyes bulging under his gyrating eyebrows. The room was spinning, though her feet were still planted on the floor.

"That's a vile thing to say!" he bellowed. "Get out. Get out of here!"

Her heart thumped in her chest and her stomach somersaulted wildly. She bolted to the door, flung it open, and dashed out. A second later the door slammed behind her, and she fled down the hall like a rabbit escaping a trap.

Chapter 17: Exposed

Millie flew into her room and slammed the door. In the semi-darkness, she pulled off her dress, stepped out of her pantalettes, and threw the garment toward her chair. She burrowed under her quilt, pulling it over her head. Trembling, she tried to catch her breath. She listened for the sounds of heavy footsteps or voices outside her door. They never came. At length her body calmed, and shudders only shook her limbs at variable intervals.

What had she done? She would certainly face consequences. She'd escaped for now, but her rebellion was sure to be exposed. But how? Was Dr. Noyes on his way at this very moment to Tirzah's room to report what happened? Or to Harriet Skinner's? Or to Father Noyes's apartment, just down the hall? Perhaps Father Noyes himself would assume the task that his son had failed at. A fresh round of shivering enveloped her body, and she vigorously rubbed her upper arms to stop shaking.

Where could she run? She could try to make her way in the dark to The Villa, but rain was still drumming outside. And even if that were a possibility, she couldn't expect Mrs. Bloom to help her. If she went to Constance and asked for refuge, or to her father, or even to the dismal garret, she would find only temporary sanctuary. This escape was short-term, and the worst was yet to come.

When the sun rose, the clouds were dispersing, and the birds were in celebration mode. She skipped breakfast, afraid of whom she might see there. She braced herself as she entered the newspaper office, but Tirzah greeted her without looking up. After the first hour, Millie relaxed a little. Apparently Tirzah hadn't been charged with confronting her about the failed interview. But every time someone entered the room, Millie jumped, expecting the angry form of either Dr. Noyes or Father Noyes to appear.

At the compositor's counter, she relived the interview. Sitting on the uneven mattress. Being drawn toward Theodore's bulging abdomen. Saying things she couldn't believe she'd dared to say. Then his suspicion. How offensive her words must have been! Such impudence toward a man who'd devoted most of his life to the Community but still endured jealousies and disdain. Noah had pointed out how hard it was for a son to follow in the footsteps of a great father. Her face burned. How could she have spit out such unkind words at a man who was simply doing his duty?

But he didn't deserve her sympathy. She pressed her hand to her stomach to calm it as she heard again his cold command to undress and his starkly sinister remark. *You should have been brought in when you were younger.* She must fight against this way of treating girls. She could go to her father, and they could join with Mr. Hinds. Perhaps, if enough people objected, things could change.

But could any good ever come from rebellion? She pictured the disabled veteran at the Astor House whose empty sleeve was pinned to his side.

Eventually the worst moment flashed across her mind again. Never in her life had she been told she'd said a "vile thing." Shame spread through her once more. To suggest the leader of the Community would defile a woman by using force against her—how could she have sunk so low as to dare Dr. Noyes to act in that way? Henry had endured a harsh public criticism for merely keeping Tirzah in the garret against her will. The Community didn't tolerate even a hint of violence or oppression in social relationships between men and women. She knew that.

Suddenly the image of Virginia cowering in the corner of the library trembling like a frightened animal, came into full stereographic view. Had Virginia had a choice? Every girl in the Community for decades—every girl but herself evidently—had been married before she could understand the meaning and impact of the word. And once initiated, each girl would accede to the system— hook, line, and sinker—for if she didn't, she'd have to admit a reality too grave, too awful, to endure. That something personal and precious had been taken from her, without her consent or understanding; something that could never be returned. What young woman had the courage to attest to such a wrong having been done to her?

The Community reacted with righteous indignation when an eleven-year-old was given enough brandy to make her vomit, sending away the perpetrator of such a crime. But Virginia was twelve years old when something permanent and life-altering was done to her—by the leader of the Community, a man at the pinnacle of ascending fellowship. Millie glared at the reversed letters on her composing stick. Could no one else see the hypocrisy, the irrationality, the convolution of what was happening here? Was she mixed up? Or was she reading the truth that others couldn't decipher?

After Meeting she tried to read *Sir Rohan's Ghost,* a favorite Tirzah had recommended, but her eyes wouldn't focus. Waves of anger followed waves of shame. Periodically a deep sadness washed over her. Restlessly she set her book down, crossed to her window, and looked out over the front lawn. It was only dusk, the long day having dragged out interminably, it seemed. People were milling about here and there, enjoying the extended daylight and warm air. A group of men and women were pulling up the croquet arches from the lawn and gathering the mallets. A few children darted about playing a game of tag, their screams trailing away like the whistle of a locomotive. The contented, blissful life of Oneida Community played out before her, an idyllic scene that brought her no joy.

A light tap on her door made her jump. But the knock was so unassuming, it couldn't be Tirzah or Mrs. Skinner on a mission of correction. She walked to the door and opened it.

Constance stood before her. "May I come in?"

After she stepped through, Millie clicked the door shut behind her. No doubt the older woman had come at her father's behest. Millie fisted her hands at her sides, dreading the conversation to come.

"Your father suspects you're avoiding him."

Constance eyed the chairs.

Millie sighed. "Won't you sit down?" She positioned herself across the little table from her father's friend and met her direct gaze. "How much did he tell you?"

"Only that you had an interview with Theodore last night."

"And he wants to know what happened?"

Constance seemed about to say more, but then simply nodded.

Millie studied her hands in her lap. "He's right. I haven't wanted to tell him."

Constance started to rise. "Do you want me to leave?"

"No, please stay." Talking to someone would be better than remaining trapped by her ruminations and recriminations. She inhaled deeply. "I—it—did not happen. That is, I went to Dr. Noyes's room but—"

She eyed the open transom above her door. She couldn't risk someone overhearing. She got up and closed it, then returned to Constance, who sat on the edge of her seat.

"Oh, Aunt Constance! I said horrible things to him! He told me I was vile and shouted at me to get out!"

Millie hid her face behind her cupped hands and began to sob.

"Oh, Millie, dear!" Constance squatted next to Millie's chair and patted her back. "I'm so sorry. There, there, dear. It's all right. You go ahead and let it out."

After a few minutes, Millie drew her hands down from her eyes but kept them over her mouth. She stared at Constance, shaking her head, then dropped her hands into her lap. "What do you think they'll do to me?"

Constance returned to her chair. "It's a delicate matter." She pursed her lips in thought. "They certainly won't make it public. They'll make sure only a few know of it. I suspect Harriet will be informed, and she'll speak to you. Your father could go with you to Harriet. Or to Mr. Hinds. He's leading an effort—"

"An effort!" Millie interrupted. "That's what he accused me of— of being part of an effort to depose him. Father mustn't get involved!"

Constance's eyes widened. "Why shouldn't he—"

"Because I can't be part of a rebellion. I don't want our Community torn apart because of me."

"Oh, now," Constance soothed. "You're making this bigger than it is."

"But Dr. Noyes seems to think that Judge Towner wants to overthrow him. Is it true?"

Constance nodded slowly. "Some say that, yes."

"I get a bad feeling about him." Millie shivered. "I don't know why. What does he want?"

"Well, the eye patch can be disturbing." Constance seemed to consider her choice of words. "He's very commanding and tends to ... get what he wants. He was a captain in the Army, after all. Even though he's only been here a few years, he seems to be angling to head up the Community."

"He came with the group from Ohio?"

"Yes, Berlin Heights. The free love commune." Constance crossed her arms over her chest disapprovingly. "Father Noyes rejected him for many years, but Towner finally convinced him that they'd practice complex marriage—not free love. Father Noyes may live to regret the day he allowed them to join."

"Theodore seems like a good man." Millie bit her lip. "He's not self-serving, anyway. I'd rather have him in charge than Judge Towner. But I didn't—I do not—want to go to bed with him."

It felt good to say it aloud.

"You've put him in an embarrassing situation."

"Why am I so different?" Millie rose and paced to the end of the small room and back. "What's wrong with me? No other girls here have had this problem. Why don't I fit in? I don't have any friends here. The only friends I've ever had are Jessie from Wallingford and Noah—an Outsider." She dropped onto her bed and sat with her head in her hands, looking at the floor.

"Oh, Millie. There's nothing whatever wrong with you. You're exactly who you're supposed to be—exactly who God made you to be. You just have more courage and more insight than others your age."

Millie didn't look up. Those words described someone else.

Constance sat next to her on the bed and rubbed her back. "Speaking of Noah—how was your fishing excursion?"

Millie lifted her head slowly. "It was lovely." She tried to smile, but her chin quivered uncontrollably. "But I'll never see him again. He's going to Hamilton College in the fall—and he's moving back home in two days."

What was the point of trying to be brave about it? She draped her arms around Constance's neck and cried on her shoulder. Constance soothed her again. Finally Millie drew away and wiped her eyes with the handkerchief Constance offered. Her sobs had uncovered a gnawing emptiness in her chest.

Constance's eyes were glistening. "Life is full of sorrow."

Millie sat up straight. "How I'm carrying on! In front of you! You lost your husband in an accident. My sadness is nothing compared to yours."

"Not so. Your sorrow is very real. Do not deny it."

Millie nodded, but couldn't speak. Tears started again, though she fought them back.

Constance squeezed her hand.

Millie let out a long breath. "What do you think I should do?"

"If you're not ready to be a wife, you're not ready. You're not wrong to stand for your beliefs."

"I don't know what I believe."

"You know more than you think you do." Smiling, Constance wagged her finger. "And remember: You're not alone. I'm here, and your father is here. And God is with you."

Millie stared at the floor, unseeing. If only she had Constance's faith. She would confess Christ more starting tonight. It couldn't hurt.

* * *

On Friday when Millie entered the *American Socialist* office, Tirzah stood to greet her. In the hearing of the others in the office, Tirzah said breezily, "Millie, I have some news for you. Theodore says all went as expected Tuesday evening, and he's quite behind your play. He agrees we should include it in our Independence Day program. Now, see here," she waved a paper before Millie's eyes, "here is the order of our program. I've put the play right between the recitations from Mr. Underwood's oratory students and the final musical number."

Millie struggled to pay attention. Tirzah continued gushing about the order of events at the upcoming celebration, now only two weeks away. What did it mean—*Theodore says all went as expected?* Had Theodore said those exact words, leading Tirzah to believe the interview had been completed? Or had she interpreted that from something else he said?

At any rate, Theodore had approved her play, despite his anger three nights ago. Was he protecting Millie, or himself, from embarrassment? Himself, certainly. This way he didn't have to admit what others could say was as a failure of leadership on his part. After all, if he couldn't control a seventeen-year-old girl and assure she followed the rules, how could he fend off festering rebellions?

Where did this leave her? In an instant she knew. In the coming days she'd be deluged with requests for interviews from the older men in the Community. Men her father's age and older would be inviting

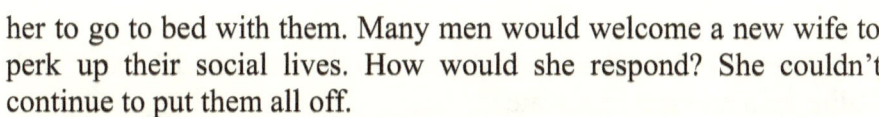

her to go to bed with them. Many men would welcome a new wife to perk up their social lives. How would she respond? She couldn't continue to put them all off.

Theodore's response was nothing short of brilliant. It would drive her back to him, with an apology, or she'd find herself, completely inexperienced, in bed with an older man who took for granted she knew what to do.

She felt unbearably warm and drew in an uneven breath.

"Millie? Millie?"

Tirzah was breaking through.

"Yes?"

"Will your actors be ready? For the dress rehearsal?"

"Dress rehearsal?"

"My, but you're distracted today!" Tirzah's laugh was friendly, not condemning. "On July 4th, for our own Community celebration, at Meeting. That would be the perfect time for the dress rehearsal, wouldn't it? For your play, and for our entire program. Isn't it a splendid idea?"

"Yes, splendid."

She couldn't match Tirzah's mood. Apprehension chilled her veins.

Saturday and Sunday were again devoted to entertaining Outsiders with strawberry shortcake. To help herself deliver the famous Oneida hospitality, Millie imagined the visitors as the Martinson family. When she noticed older men from the Community paying more attention to her than previously, she quelled the bounce in her step. Still, what would come, would come. Based on the pairings that occurred after Meeting, even the least attractive women at Oneida Community were not without regular partners.

Thank goodness she hadn't yet received a message from Mrs. Skinner. She watched the ambitious, hardworking woman managing the serving of the guests. Setting up interviews was probably the last thing on her mind.

* * *

When Millie came out of the Tontine after supper Monday night, chatting with Leonora about her recent trip to Cozicot, she almost collided with Harriet Skinner, who had planted herself in Millie's path.

"Excuse me, Leonora," said Harriet primly. "Could I speak with Millie for a moment in private?"

Leonora winked at Millie. "Oh, by all means."

She'd easily guessed the topic of Harriet's conversation. Millie's mouth went dry. There was only one thing Mrs. Skinner would want to talk about.

"Lovely evening, isn't it?" she began.

Millie's stomach cramped. She said nothing.

"I'm here to pass along an invitation."

The usually severe woman smiled as if she were about to bestow a Christmas gift. Millie tried to appear pleased, but her lips quivered and refused to turn upward.

"Judge Towner requests an interview with you. Would Wednesday evening be acceptable?"

Millie's stomach dropped to the ground. Of course Judge Towner would be the first man after Theodore to seek her out. Meeting the stiff lawyer in person and looking into his one eye would terrify her under any circumstances. But to go to bed with him....

"Would Wednesday be acceptable?" Mrs. Skinner repeated.

Suddenly Millie relaxed. She had an excuse. A real one. "I'm sorry, but I won't be able to. My time started today."

Mrs. Skinner didn't miss a beat. "Then would a week from today be acceptable?" Her baked-on smile didn't waver. Behind her wire glasses her piercing eyes—so used to commanding obedience—fixed on her target.

If Millie had meant to object to Judge Towner as a partner, she should have said that at once rather than claim her time of month. But how could she turn down such a prominent and highly respected member of the Community? Under Mrs. Skinner's insistent gaze, Millie gulped and felt her head nod even as she willed it to remain still.

Mrs. Skinner bade her goodnight and walked away with a determined step.

Millie plodded across the Quadrangle. Out of a searing frying pan and into a raging fire. Going to bed with Theodore would have been bad enough. For him the intimate act would be a duty only, and he would perform it obediently, just as he'd done when he started Mary

Jones's baby. But what did Judge Towner have in mind? By inviting her for an interview right after Theodore, he was staking his claim, declaring himself the next most powerful man at Oneida. Was she nothing more than an animal in a bizarre mating ritual?

No, it was worse than that. She stopped in her tracks, causing someone to step on her heels, but she barely noticed. She left the path and dropped onto the grass under the tulip tree.

She imagined the interview with the judge. When he discerned she'd never been initiated, he'd have ammunition against Theodore. And as a former Army Captain, he'd use that ammunition to his advantage to seize the Community from its current leaders. The scenario that Constance pooh-poohed might indeed come to pass, and Millie would be responsible for ripping the Community apart.

* * *

Friday afternoon Tirzah received word of a crisis related to the Independence Day program that would take her away from the office for the rest of the day. "Millie," she pleaded, "I need your help. There's an article from Father Noyes that must be proofed today so it can be typeset tomorrow. I meant to get it from his apartment this morning, but it slipped my mind. Would you be a dear and run over there for me?"

Millie gulped. "To Father Noyes's apartment?"

Tirzah waved a delicate hand. "Oh, he's not at home. He had an important meeting in town."

That made it less intimidating.

"He said he'd leave it on his desk. After you've proofed it, drop it in the typesetter's box." She was already rushing out the door. "I'm off!"

After making her way to the Mansion House, Millie knocked on the door of Father Noyes's suite just in case. Hearing no response, she cautiously turned the knob, tiptoed into the room, and silently closed the door behind her. Even though she lived just down the hall, this spacious apartment seemed like a foreign land. Six of her sleeping rooms could fit comfortably within the suite. An overpoweringly masculine atmosphere greeted her: musky scent, heavy furniture, dark colors.

She spotted her destination, the large mahogany desk against the far wall, but she let her eyes roam the room. Along the door wall stood the bed; after a quick glance, she turned away. On the left wall was a recessed book shelf; she approached it and scanned the titles of dry volumes by Voltaire, Darwin, Lyell, Marx, and Engels.

She crossed to the south wall, where light streamed in from four large windows. Looking out the last one, she viewed the southeast formal garden, now gloriously in bloom. To the right grew the towering black walnut tree, beyond which little children dashed about on the lawn beside their two-story playhouse.

When she turned away from the windows, a large upholstered chair beckoned her. She sank in so far that it was difficult to get up again. She tried the other chair and the sofa, imagining herself as Goldilocks. She must hurry. What if Father Noyes should come back from his meeting early?

She walked toward the east wall. Resting upon a white painted pillar to the left of the desk was a bust sculpted of white marble. Instantly she recognized Mary Cragin's features from her portrait in the Big Hall. She and Father Noyes's legal wife, Harriet Noyes, were revered above all women as the mothers of Oneida Community. After Mrs. Cragin drowned in Brooklyn over twenty-five years ago, her body had been returned to Oneida for burial. A few years ago, when the Oneida Community cemetery was relocated for the railroad, her body had been exhumed, and Father Noyes ordered its head removed for phrenological study. Had he commissioned the bust at that time?

Millie stood before the graven image, which seemed somehow familiar. An irresistible attraction pulled her closer, and before she realized it, she was resting her hands on the cool white cheeks and staring into the stony, expressionless eyes. Drawn forward by that unseen force, she aimed her lips at the closed mouth. Just as she'd kissed her mother's unmoving mouth in her recurring dream.

Her flesh crawled. Sickening tingles moved up her back and down her legs and arms. She dropped her hands and shook them out vigorously. Whatever made her do that? She harbored no reverence for Mary Cragin. Shivering, she backed away, rubbing her upper arms.

Moving to the heavy desk, Millie looked out the window it abutted. From here the father of the Community could clearly see all the comings and goings from the road. How easily she could be watched as she walked to and from the newspaper office each day—if Father Noyes cared to do so. But he had more important things on his mind. He probably didn't even remember her name.

The handwritten article lay on the desk. She should grab it and be off. Instead, she stroked the smooth mahogany in a sidewise figure eight. Beneath her very fingertips might be resting the bracelets and necklaces the women sacrificed so many years ago. Here was her chance to confirm the possibly apocryphal story of the jewelry collection.

She pulled the drawer out by about three inches. A row of wooden toy tops of different sizes wobbled and came to rest. Some were painted in bright lacquered stripes, others were varnished wood. Some were large and pear-shaped with metal tips while one was small with a long handle and wooden point. Was the jewelry farther back? She pulled out the drawer to its full length, revealing two more rows of tops.

A piece of paper covered the last row, and as she picked it up to look at the toys beneath, two words caught her eye: *William Langston*. She shook her head. Things had gone from unnerving to unexpected to uncanny.

On official stationery, the letter displayed the tiny, flawless script of a professional copyist. Beneath a sketch of an imposing building she read the typeset words "New York State Lunatic Asylum at Utica." The addressee: William Langston, Oneida Community.

Her face and hands grew warm. A sour taste sprang to her tongue. Propriety urged her to stash the letter back in its place, but her eyes began reading before she could do so.

Dear Mr. Langston,

We understand that you are the husband and next of kin to Carrie Langston, a patient admitted to our care on March 3, 1864. We regret to inform you that Mrs. Langston passed away from pneumonia on January 15th of this year. We apologize for such late notice of this fact. Until recently your whereabouts were unknown to us. Please accept our sincere condolences.

The matter of the outstanding account related to Mrs. Langston's care requires your attention. Since you are gainfully employed at Oneida Community, your wife was not eligible to have her treatment, room, and board paid by the State of New York. By statute, that benefit is extended to the indigent. Your wife accrued a balance of $3,340. Please remit payment at your earliest convenience.

Again, we extend our deepest sympathies.

The letter shook in Millie's hands, making the words dance crazily before her eyes. It was some grave error. Her mother had died thirteen years ago. She read it twice more to identify the mistake. Her legs felt flimsy. She dropped into the chair.

Her mother's name *was* Carrie. In 1864, when Millie was four, her mother had died. Supposedly. It was impossible for her father to have not known she was there all these years. He had abandoned her in an insane asylum and had lied to Millie about it. And not just any asylum. Utica Asylum. Where they kept people in cages.

Millie's stomach churned so violently she feared she might vomit, but she continued to examine the missive. In pencil, scrawled in the upper right corner in Father Noyes's hand, were the words *Wednesday Meeting.* She returned the paper to its place. Her head spun as if one of the tops had been set in motion. She slammed the drawer shut and snatched up the article she'd come to retrieve.

Her vision swimming, she cast her eyes on the uncaring, unknowing, unseeing marble bust of Mary Cragin. The urge to strike it down, topple it off of its column, and shatter it to pieces whelmed her. But she wheeled around, turning her back to the passionless icon, and stumbled toward the door. She rushed down the stairs, hurried through the Nursery Kitchen past several pairs of inquiring eyes, and made it down the hall to the lavatory in the Children's House, where she heaved up the contents of her stomach.

Barely able to see the road before her, Millie staggered back to the newspaper office. Proofreading the article felt like translating a foreign tongue. Father Noyes's sentences didn't register in her brain. In their place she saw *lunatic asylum* and *pneumonia* and *condolences* and *indigent* written in cold, institutional script. Finally she completed

marking up the article and placed it in the typesetter's box.

Millie flopped onto her bed, barely remembering the walk across the street and up the driveway or the climb up the wide front staircase. Under her quilt she squeezed herself tight, trying to stop shaking. At last her body grew still and numbness descended.

She had to think. It was possible her father hadn't seen the letter. Father Noyes may have intercepted it. When Jessie warned about having her letters intercepted, Millie had smiled at her friend's overactive imagination. But by now she'd seen enough here to know Jessie was probably right. On the other hand, her father may have presented the letter to Father Noyes to ask him to pay the account. How would Father Noyes react to a bill for thousands of dollars? Surely the Community didn't have excess funds to pay such expenses. Unless Father Noyes had authorized the plan to cover up her father's past.

But none of that mattered as much as one indisputable fact. Her father had lied to her. Her mother had been alive up until a few months ago, but Millie had lived most of her life believing her mother was dead. There was no satisfactory explanation. Her father had lied about the most important thing in her life. She could never forgive him. Never.

How close she had felt to him during their recent conversation in the Summer House. But it had all been a charade. Now that his wife had died, he felt free to talk about his wife after so many years of silence. If he'd spoken of her before, he might have used the present tense and revealed that she lived.

Lived. For thirteen years her mother had lived in an asylum. What horrors and agony had been her lot? Millie pictured her mother, clinging to the bars of a cage. Wondering year after year why her husband and daughter didn't come to visit. Hoping to be released, but never being set free, and dying—coughing and breathless—among strangers. She saw her mother's lifeless body sprawled on the floor of a wretched cage. She sobbed into her pillow until it was soaked with tears and exhaustion swallowed her up.

She awoke with a crisp image in her mind—her father talking to Peter Schenk after he'd been released from Utica Asylum. The grim look on her father's face. Perhaps Peter had just told him of her mother's death. The fear in her father's eyes. Peter may have been the one to divulge to the asylum the whereabouts of Carrie Langston's husband. Thus her father's despicable secret had been exposed.

Millie pictured the scrawled words *Wednesday Meeting* on the letter. The word *Meeting* was capitalized, so it could refer to the upcoming evening Meeting next week. That seemed unlikely. There would be no reason for the issue to be discussed in front of the Community at Meeting, especially on Independence Day—unless Father Noyes wanted to expose her father's lie to the entire Community to make an example of him.

The doleful face of Victor Hawley as he left the Mansion House forever flashed in Millie's mind, and a heavy weight settled in her chest.

Chapter 18: Misunderstood

That night when Millie saw her father in the Tontine and at Meeting, she turned away without acknowledging him. Once she perceived the pain in his eyes, and satisfaction welled up. It felt good to return some of the agony that gnawed at her heart.

Avoiding him on Saturday was easy since she spent her time serving Outsiders. As she placed two dishes of shortcake on the table in front of an elderly couple, she glanced across the lawn to the Summer House. A thought flitted by. She must have misunderstood the entire situation—there was a perfectly reasonable explanation for it all. Her father would never lie to her. Trying to examine the idea was like glimpsing a hummingbird from the corner of her eye. It vanished like a figment of the imagination.

After work on Sunday, Millie ensconced herself in a group of young people so her father couldn't approach her. Henry delighted in making her giggle, and she returned his attentions by flouncing and batting her eyelashes, all to show her father she didn't need him.

When Monday dawned, she had a fluttery feeling in her stomach —different from the seething rage she'd been nursing for the last two days. It was dread. Tonight was her scheduled interview with Judge Towner. After Meeting, she'd pair up with the former free love adherent who had taught Haydn Miller that his papa was a "bad, naughty man," who refused to help the abandoned child pray for his papa's return, who'd been the first to criticize the absent Edward Inslee, and who'd eagerly prosecuted Victor Hawley for endangering a minor with brandy. She'd be both a feather in his cap and ammunition against Theodore. Dismay and fear weighted her every movement as she washed and dressed.

She ran her hands over her face, chest, and abdomen. She was becoming gaunt. Having had no appetite for the last two weeks, she was wasting away. If she didn't force down at least a breakfast cake or muffin, she'd put her health at risk.

The morning inched by as if she were slogging through mire.

Despite her resolve to keep her body under control, she could only eat a few bites at noon. Every organ, every tissue strained to escape the interview with the judge. But she could discern no way out. After she dragged herself back from the Tontine, the proofreading blurred before her eyes as she hunched over her desk.

Tirzah kept glancing her way with a concerned expression, and Millie smiled less and less convincingly until Tirzah finally said, "Millie, you don't look well. Is something wrong?"

Millie let the pencil slide from her fingers. "I have a fearful headache. I hoped it would go away when I ate, but I'm feeling worse."

"Oh, my dear!" exclaimed Tirzah sympathetically. "I know just how that feels. Sometimes there's nothing for it but to go to your room and lie down in the dark. That's exactly what you must do. Try to put a blanket over your window and make it as dark as you can. And get some headache powder from the Nursery Kitchen."

It sounded blissful. If only her problems could be solved by rest and medicine. She attempted a polite smile. "Thank you. I'll try that tonight."

"No, no! I mean right now." Tirzah was earnest in her role as nurse. "You must take the rest of the day off and do just as I said. I'll have Aunt Harriet send supper to your room. Don't go to Meeting. Just take care of yourself."

Millie tried to stand, but wobbled. She crumpled into her seat. "I can't. I have an interview with Judge Towner tonight."

Tirzah shook her head emphatically, setting her auburn curls in motion. "Oh, no, you do not! You're in no shape for that. Do not consider it. I'll send him a note explaining you're ill."

Relief flooded Millie, but her headache stabbed. She flinched, and her hand flew to her temple.

Tirzah rushed to Millie's side. "Do you need help getting back to your room?"

"I'm fine. I can make it."

Tirzah escorted her to the door.

As Millie shuffled across the road and up the drive, her muscles relaxed. Thank Heaven for Tirzah. What immense good fortune. As she approached the rustic bench under the butternut tree, she almost started skipping, but her eyes fell on the east façade of the Children's

House and Father Noyes's window. He might be observing her. She slowed her pace and hung her head. Yes, the headache was still there —she hadn't made it up to avoid the interview. A flash of euphoria had simply masked the pain temporarily.

Inside the Mansion House she started up the stairs but stopped on the third step. The headache powder. She slipped back down and turned right toward the Nursery Kitchen. Once there, she found the powder, mixed it into water, and swallowed the bitter remedy. She returned to the stairs and started up again but stopped on the fourth step. She had nothing to read—she'd finished *Sir Rohan's Ghost* last night. If the headache subsided, she'd want a book for company. She trudged down the stairs and, turning left, entered the library. The room was empty, but she knew where to find *Northanger Abbey.*

As she headed toward the door after securing the little book, a newspaper headline leapt out at her. Picking up the copy of the *Observer*, the local daily, from where it lay on the newspaper table, she read, *LOCAL MINISTERS LAUNCH CRUSADE AGAINST ONEIDA COMMUNITY.*

Curious, she scanned the first paragraph. Reverend James Martinson, pastor of First Presbyterian Church, had formed a league with several local ministers. Their goal: to convince city and state governments to investigate the commune for "an environment of rampant adultery and gross indecency toward the commune's girls and women."

Millie's knees trembled as she read. Seeing her home reviled struck at her very core. She slumped into the nearest chair and finished the article, which was studded with quotes from Reverend Martinson. Oneida Community's young girls, he insisted, were treated like slaves of the Old South's most despicable plantation owners. "Girls as young as twelve years old are used as concubines by men four and five times their age," Millie read.

She wiped perspiration from her brow with shaking fingers. Why was he interfering? This was a Community matter. It didn't concern Outsiders. He had declared war against them.

She began to sweat, and her stomach, rebelling against the recently swallowed headache powder, clamored to give up its contents. She hurried down the hall to the lavatory and honored her stomach's wishes. She wiped her mouth and shuddered. If she never saw or tasted headache powder again, it would be too soon.

After leaving the lavatory, she dragged herself to her room and managed to rig up a blanket over her window as Tirzah had suggested. Lying down on top of her quilt without undressing, she drew what comfort she could from the warm darkness. She inventoried her pain: eyes, eyebrows, temples, scalp, neck, shoulders—even her very earlobes ached. But there was pain elsewhere, too. Her chest was heavy, and her heart felt broken and lifeless.

She unbuttoned two buttons of her dress and slipped her hand over her heart to check. Feeling no beat, she spat out a rueful laugh. "Nothing there," she whispered, buttoning her dress again.

Not surprising, considering that first her father and now Noah had betrayed her, piercing her heart with their dissimulations. She cringed, remembering Noah's touch on her hand when he persuaded her to be his teacher. He'd used her to spy for his father. Even his friendship on their railroad journey was an artful ruse designed to ingratiate himself into the Community through two trusting women. The Martinson family's friendly visit for strawberry shortcake was nothing but pretense. Noah's decision to leave The Villa was transparent now. Conveniently, he left just as his father launched this crusade—a crusade against a Community that had welcomed Noah with open arms, bending the rules to accommodate him and treating him as one of their own for months.

Millie's face burned at the vile things Reverend Martinson had said. He made Oneida Community sound like a debauched society of free lovers. If Noah believed that about them, why had he kissed her? Did he mean to prove how easy it was to become intimate with a Community girl? She was surprised their kiss wasn't recorded in the newspaper.

She pounded her pillow with her fists. *False, false, false!* Her headache stabbed her back blow for blow, and she dropped her head onto the abused pillow. What about God, whom Constance had promised would be with her? Hadn't He betrayed her as well? Allowing her to grow up without a mother, trapping her in a web of duplicity from which there seemed to be no escape? Millie let out a quivering sigh.

She must have dozed off, for she started awake when she heard a knock at her door. Disoriented in the dark room, she rubbed her eyes,

not sure what day or time it was. She stumbled to the door and cracked it open. There stood Dora Campbell.

"Mrs. Skinner asked me to bring you this." She held out a basket and looked at Millie with concern. "Would you like some company?"

Millie blinked dumbly. Her brain still felt muddled. Was Dora offering her horizontal fellowship? The gentle brown eyes and delicately furrowed brow signaled empathy and kindness. She could invite Dora in, pour out her story. But, no. She couldn't share her rebellion and doubts with the Community's paragon of virtue. Dora would reject her, just as Millie had distanced herself from Mary Jones in the sewing room.

"Thank you. I'll be all right."

Still in a fog, Millie lit her lamp and sat at the table. She took a cautious bite of the buttered bread. It tasted sweet and satisfying. She quickly finished it off and devoured the potatoes and string beans. Her head began to feel almost normal.

She pulled out *Northanger Abbey* and rejoined the familiar journey of Catherine Morland, developing heroine. But the men in her life kept crowding into the story. Her shoulders and neck tightened, and the headache crept back, almost as bad as before. Her father, Noah, Judge Towner—was there not an honorable man on the face of the earth? Where was her very own Henry Tilney? Must she go to Bath to find him, as Catherine had?

How odd it felt to stay in her room during Meeting. From the Big Hall she heard music, applause, and at one point even raucous laughter. She forced herself to keep reading, imagining herself in the Pump Room with Catherine. Finally, she heard Meeting end. Had Tirzah remembered to send a note to Judge Towner? The hubbub outside meant people were dispersing, some to Hamilton Avenue, others to sleeping rooms, alone or with this evening's partner.

She'd seen it all her life, but now she saw it through the eyes of Reverend Martinson and the other ministers. Who was right? When it came to morality, their commune was the aberration. But they'd always claimed theirs was the more advanced view. To the ministers, evidently, life at Oneida Community was uncivilized and heathenish.

The muscles between her shoulders tensed tighter, and her head began to pound. She set her book down and lay flat on her back once more. As soon as she settled, two brisk taps sounded. She didn't recognize that knock. Who would be calling? She rose, smoothed her dress, and went to the door.

When she opened it, Henry peeked in. "We missed you at Meeting." He assessed her face. "Dora said she brought you your supper."

The hallway was empty now, but laughter and loud conversation wafted over from Hamilton Avenue.

"I have a monstrous headache."

"Would you like a massage? Proven to cure the most recalcitrant pain." He smiled at his own advertisement.

Millie tried to return the smile but could only grimace. She opened the door wider, and he stepped in.

After shutting the door noiselessly, he dimmed the lamp until only a soft glow suffused the room. "Now, lie on your back."

She obeyed.

He rubbed his hands together to create heat and stationed himself at the head of the bed. Stooping over and placing his hands between her head and the mattress, he began to massage the base of her skull.

Millie groaned softly as he kneaded the knots in her muscles.

From there he worked down between her shoulder blades, then outward to her shoulders and down her upper arms, following the tension and chasing it away.

Millie sighed deeply. Relaxation began washing over her.

Henry's hands kneaded her scalp, and the pain fled before his expert touch. He knelt and ran his strong thumbs down either side of the back of her neck, occasionally performing a circular motion to smooth out a stubborn knot.

Millie grew increasingly limp. She sank deeper into the mattress as if her weight had quadrupled. Closing her eyes, she welcomed a blanket of glorious numbness as her muscles released their longstanding vigilance. She let everything go.

Still kneeling, Henry moved to the side of the bed. With his warm fingers he traced her eyebrows symmetrically, starting at the bridge of her nose and working outward in soothing strokes. The tension in her closed eyes vanished.

Henry's steady exhale warmed her cheeks, and she breathed in a pleasant scent of spearmint. He moved his fingers to her temples and with a circular motion continued rubbing until the bones of her skull felt loose. His soft hands followed the edges of her jaw and then gently pinched her earlobes, rotating them slowly.

Millie felt mesmerized and sleepy. When Henry's lips touched hers, she kissed back, naturally, easily. He was on the bed next to her, continuing to massage her neck and shoulders as he gently kissed her mouth and cheeks. He unbuttoned her top two buttons with silky fingers. His warm lips moved along her collar bone, first one side, then the other.

She was floating on a sultry sea. Waves of warmth and excitement washed over her in turn, and she returned his caresses. *This is how it feels to belong. To be fully accepted at last.* Henry's body next to hers was blissful, perfect. He unbuttoned the next two buttons, and his kisses moved lower. She longed to be close—closer —to Henry forever. To bask always in the luxury of his touch.

Licentious! Libertines!

The words flashed into her mind. Words printed in the newspaper.

A different kind of heat flushed her cheeks, and she wriggled out of Henry's embrace. She sat up on the farthest side of the narrow mattress, leaning against the wall, her legs folded under her. Still lying on his side, Henry eyed her quizzically, his full lips slightly parted. This must have been the same routine he'd performed on Tirzah that led to their romance. No wonder Tirzah had succumbed.

"Henry! What are you doing?"

He propped himself up on his left elbow and smiled confidently. "Loving you. Isn't it grand?"

Millie shook her head. "I—I don't know."

How had their friendship progressed to this point?

"*I* know." He laughed pleasantly. "And I know something else." His eyes sparkled under his mound of black hair. He'd never looked more dashing. "You're in love with me."

Millie's mouth dropped open. She closed it quickly. Tilting her head, she looked at him through narrow eyes. "What do you mean?"

"Oh, Millie, we needn't pretend." He continued to smile jovially. "You as much as told me so, remember?"

"I did? When?"

"The day we started play practice again. And you can't deny you've been flirting with me terribly the last couple of days. Ellen's beside herself with jealousy."

The hot air balloon day. She'd hinted to Henry that she was in love with Noah. He'd clearly misunderstood her. Of course, he couldn't know that her recent coquetry was meant not to draw him closer but to keep her father at bay. He'd be disappointed that he wasn't the object of her affections, but she had to be honest.

"Oh, Henry! I've misled you. I feel terrible."

He raised himself up and sat facing her, one leg under him and the other resting on the floor. "Oh! There's someone else, then?"

His cheery voice displayed no distress.

Millie smirked and rolled her eyes. That was the world's fastest recovery from being jilted. He was waiting for her to name a name. "It's someone you don't know. But it doesn't matter. I'm not in love with him anymore."

The twinge in her heart scolded her for lying.

"An Outsider?" Henry cocked his head playfully. "You *are* full of surprises!" He reached for her hand. "But if it's over, there's no reason we can't—"

Millie ignored his proffered hand and shook her head. "We haven't arranged things properly…"

"Oh, that!" Henry tossed his head. "Nobody follows *those* rules anymore."

"But Dr. Noyes announced it. We have to fill out weekly reports now."

He laughed at Millie's wide eyes. "That's simple. If neither person reports it, there's no problem."

Millie considered Henry's offer. If he brought her into marriage, Judge Towner wouldn't be her first husband. Hadn't she a mere hour ago been dreaming of her own Henry Tilney? Here he was, right on her bed. He wouldn't be hers exclusively, of course. Sometimes he would be Ellen's Henry, and perhaps Virginia's, perhaps even Dora's —and many older women's. But sometimes he would be her Henry, and that blissful feeling of belonging would be hers as well.

Her father's words, spoken in the warm security of the Summer House, came back to her. *It's very womanly to want your own husband, your own home. Is that what you want?* Catherine Morland settled down with her very own Henry at the Woodston parsonage, their very own home. What could be more satisfying? Certainly that was every woman's dream. Except Oneida Community women.

Millie's brows knit together as she pictured her father again.

"Headache coming back?"

"You could say I have a headache—not a physical one now. Henry, can I tell you something in confidence? You can't tell a soul. Not Ellen or anyone."

He snorted. "Ellen would be the last one I'd tell anything to. Unless I wanted the whole Community to know it by noon tomorrow."

Pursing her lips, Millie looked down her nose. "This is serious, Henry. It may help me to talk about it."

"You can trust me." He slapped his palm to his chest. "Go ahead and let your cat out of the bag."

She took a breath. She'd have to begin at the beginning. "On Friday, I had to go into Father Noyes's apartment to get an article from his desk. But when I was there—he wasn't at home—I started nosing around. I opened the middle drawer of his desk—"

"Where the tops are!"

"Yes."

"He still has them, then." Henry grinned. "I saw them the year I came here. I was tending some young boys, and Father Noyes invited us up to his room to play with the tops. He let each boy pick one out of the drawer, and we set them all spinning at once on the floor." Henry's gaze was soft and distant. "What a sight!"

Millie cocked her head. The young boys, but not the young girls, had been invited to Father Noyes's room. Suddenly a wave of nausea swept over her. If she'd experienced the normal course of events, she, too, would have been invited to Father Noyes's suite as a girl of twelve or thirteen, not with a group, and not to play with tops, but to have a very different experience of the Noyes apartment.

"Go on." Henry jarred her from her thoughts.

She poured out the saga of the letter, her father's deception about her mother's death, the great sum of money being demanded, and Father Noyes's cryptic scribble.

"Wow, old pal. That's a heavy load. No wonder you've been tense."

"But what can I do? I only saw the letter because I let my curiosity run away with me. And now I can't bear to look at my father. He might not know about the letter. Maybe he doesn't even know my mother is dead—though I think Peter Schenk informed him."

"Their mysterious conversation." Henry nodded slowly and his eyes lit with understanding. "There's nothing to do but wait. It'll all come out soon enough. But whatever happens, I'll be here. I'm right next door, and I'll stick by your side come what may."

He reached for her hand again, and this time she gave it without hesitation. His was a hand that would be what she chose it to be—the hand of a lover, or the hand of a friend.

Millie walked Henry to the door and let him out. Coming toward them from Hamilton Avenue, Ellen looked at them with surprise. Her eyes dropped to Millie's unbuttoned dress. Millie stepped back, said good-night through the half-closed door, and clicked it shut.

Chapter 19: Sentence

At breakfast the next morning the Tontine buzzed with talk of the article in the *Observer* and Father Noyes's plan to counter the ministers' crusade. Far from being concerned, the members seemed buoyant in the gathering storm. The old-timers remembered previous campaigns that had tried to interfere with the Community's way of life, and those had only resulted in stronger public sentiment in favor of Oneida Community. This time, some friends in town had warned Father Noyes of the coming attack. Prominent business and political leaders pledged their support, and newspaper articles defending the decency and integrity of the Bible Communists would soon appear.

Impressing the visitors at the Independence Day celebration that Saturday would help their cause. With the extra publicity, the celebration would likely top all previous attendance records. Curiosity would draw many people to see the controversial commune for themselves while many supporters would turn out to show their solidarity with the communists.

Because it portrayed them as devoutly religious, Millie's play was central to appeasing their critics. Several people told her they were looking forward to the dress rehearsal the next evening.

A white-haired gentleman Millie often saw in the library approached her table. "How providential, my dear, that your play has come at such a time as this." He patted her shoulder. "You're our very own Esther."

Millie's head swirled in confusion. Only days ago, though only three people knew it, she had defied the Community's core tenet. Her spirit continued to chafe by the hour at the onerous requirements their social system had placed on girls for decades. Yet her play spotlighted the Community's godliness. The irony was too much.

Yet in many ways the commune was commendable—which was why so many Outsiders sided with them. Its business dealings were honorable, and it employed hundreds of people. Their factory offered better conditions and wages than any factory anywhere. And their legendary hospitality caused Outsiders to flock to the Mansion House each summer to enjoy the lovely grounds, free entertainment, and delicious food. These qualities merited her allegiance. Yet she rejected their sacred tenet—complex marriage.

Scanning the dining room, Millie felt more isolated than ever. She shivered at the sight of Judge Towner—he would surely renew his invitation soon. Across from her, Henry's handsome face broke into a smile. Should she accept his advances?

"That Reverend Martinson needs to keep his nose out of our business." Leonora wagged her pretty nose. "What an old troglodyte!"

The others at the table laughed and nodded.

Clenching her jaw, Millie stopped herself from arguing that the reverend had helped the poor and downtrodden more than anyone in the Community had. Still, she understood their anger. He'd vilified the only home she'd ever known—a place that had welcomed his own son. Mrs. Bloom had treated Noah like a member—no, like the son of her womb. Reverend Martinson's vicious attack could not go unanswered.

Millie felt like a weak sapling blowing about in a thunderstorm.

As she stood at the compositor's counter that afternoon, her father's tangled web continued to strangle her heart with every sort she placed. She called up every fond memory of him and stamped it with the truth: betrayal. She rummaged the depths of her past for the slightest memory of her mother. It was useless. The only memory she could muster was the one from her dream when she knelt on her mother's lap and put her hands on each cheek, but her mother's face remained stony and still.

At the final practice before the dress rehearsal, the show ran perfectly. But as Millie tried to focus on the content of the play, evaluating it as an Outsider would, it rang hollow and meaningless. How naïve she'd been to believe that Constance's faith had healed her. And yet, Constance's arm had been restored—that was undeniable. Every day Millie saw her bustling about as if her pain and disability had never occurred.

But her mother hadn't been healed. Millie had never even had a chance to see her during the last thirteen years of her life. Séances had been performed here in the past; perhaps there was still a way to speak with her mother after all. Ann Hobart was a powerful medium.

Maybe Ann could—Millie shook her head. She obviously no longer knew what she believed, and the childish simplicity of her own script mocked her.

At last Wednesday arrived—July 4th. Independence Day. Although it was a working day for the Community, a festive air pervaded the Mansion House. Harriet Skinner provided a special breakfast, and the children performed patriotic skits, which parents took time off from their duties to observe. Millie's day at the *American Socialist* was like any other day, except that Tirzah was distracted and flitted in and out of the office, tending to little details for the night's program that only she could handle.

As Meeting approached, those involved in the evening's entertainment took their seats near the front of the Big Hall. Millie sat by Henry. He squeezed her hand but seemed excited rather than worried. Did he remember Father Noyes's words scrawled at the top of the letter? Perhaps he thought she only had director's jitters.

The musicians and orators performed their pieces flawlessly for the boisterous, easy-to-please audience. When the play began, the audience hushed. Millie thrilled at the sense of anticipation in the hall. Almost everyone remembered Constance's personal drama in detail, and her play would draw them all together within its magic circle.

During the third act of the play, Millie sat up straighter as a chill passed down her limbs. There was a character in the play that she hadn't written into the script—one she'd never noticed before. God. Her eyes widened as enlightenment washed over her. She'd done to God what Father Noyes had done to her from this very stage six months ago. Father Noyes had credited her writing to Tirzah, which was bad enough, but she'd credited God's work—the way He healed Constance—to Father Noyes and Bible Communism.

Communism hadn't healed Constance. Father Noyes had been impotent in the face of her injury. It was God. The God who compared Himself to a nursing mother had looked down on Constance in her distress. *He* had shown His special love toward His daughter by healing her.

Surprisingly, Millie felt no chiding from that God for her blunder. Instead, she felt a gentle, almost playful commendation that she'd figured it out at last. As if He was saying, *Now you know how I feel… and I know how you feel.* Comfort sprinkled gently over her, like the refreshing surprise of a sun shower. She and the Creator of the Universe shared an intimate bond—what the Community called special love—but this love, no one could forbid.

Before she could fully explore the feeling, the play reached its denouement. The audience hung on the edge of their seats as Leonora, in her role as Eunice, delivered her final sentences: "Amazing things can happen when you have faith. There's no doubt about it."

A chuckle spread through the audience as people caught the play on words. The cast waited for the height of the response, and then, dropping their personas, turned to face the audience, bowing in perfect time. Thunderous applause erupted from all corners of the Big Hall.

As the actors took a second bow, the audience rose to their feet. Millie stood, too, grinning at the members clapping around her. A few calls of "Author! Author!" rose from the rear of the room. The first voice sounded like her father's. As more people picked up the chant, Tirzah left her seat in the front row, approached Millie, and gestured for her to follow.

Keeping her eyes on Tirzah's back, Millie mounted the stairs and walked to center stage. Tirzah motioned to Millie with both arms, and the applause crescendoed. She scanned the approving faces before her and curtsied. Her father, standing and vigorously clapping near the back of the room, had never looked prouder. Sans false beard, Henry appeared from behind her with a bouquet of long-stemmed flowers and placed them in her arms. The applause diminished. Henry ushered Millie back to her seat, and after flashing her a triumphant grin, hurried to join the orchestra.

One last instrumental performance from last year's Centennial, *That Banner a Hundred Years Old*, capped off the evening. The swelling music matched the satisfaction and gratitude in Millie's heart.

But her thrill of success instantly faded when, during the final applause for the orchestra, Father Noyes and Theodore climbed the stairs to the stage. They stood as close as they could get to the audience, their toes at the edge of the apron. Henry slipped into his seat next to Millie again and cheerfully patted her arm, oblivious to the dour expression on the prophet's face.

Picturing *Wednesday Meeting* in his handwriting next to the picture of Utica Asylum, Millie couldn't take her eyes off Father Noyes. She tucked her hair behind her ears, brushing away perspiration. With trembling hands she stowed her flowers under her seat and folded her hands in her lap. She rubbed her thumb over the opposite thumbnail. Her jubilation had made a quick exit and dread had taken center stage in her stomach and chest.

The crowd quieted, and Father Noyes spoke out in his loudest hoarse voice. That he was attempting to speak from the stage with his voice this raspy gave his message great import, and the room became completely silent.

"I have a matter of great importance to discuss tonight."

Sitting so close to the stage, Millie could hear every word he spoke. Her blood froze even as her heart thumped in her chest.

"As much as it pains me to end this triumphant evening on a sober note, it is vital to deal with this immediately."

Theodore repeated his father's words so those sitting farther away could hear.

Millie's thumb came to a full stop. This couldn't be about her father. The letter had been in Father Noyes's desk for over a week, so this couldn't be *immediately.* When she looked at Henry, he shifted in his seat, but his expression was blank.

"Theodore will read a statement regarding the situation that reflects both our views. We will then ask for your confirmation of our decision."

Theodore rephrased the statement, then read from a paper in his hands: "A disturbing matter has recently been brought to our attention concerning one of our members that has repercussions for the entire Community. We have learned that William Langston, who joined our Community in April 1864 by signing the same agreement you all signed, deceived us and united with us under false pretenses."

A collective gasp rose from the floor of the Big Hall, and Millie slumped in her seat. Even if she turned around, she wouldn't be able to discern her father's expression since he was seated so many rows back. Was this coming at him sight unseen? The memory of Victor Hawley cowering in his seat on the stage told her all she needed to know. No matter how angry she was at her father, she should have alerted him. Her face burned, and her knees trembled.

Henry put his hand on her forearm, calming her enough to

concentrate on Theodore's next words.

"Although Mr. Langston represented to us that he was a widower and was admitted with his daughter, Millie, under that status, we now understand he had a wife at that time. We are in receipt of documentation that Mr. Langston's wife was a patient at the New York State Lunatic Asylum at Utica until January of this year, when she passed away."

Murmurs of sympathy spread through the audience.

"Along with this notification came a bill in the amount of $3,340, which the hospital expects this Community to pay."

The spreading whispers grew indignant. Millie's face burned.

"Not only has Mr. Langston deceived the Community and brought a staggering debt upon us, but he has done so at a time that puts us in an untenable position with the outside world."

Dreading the next words, Millie sank farther into her seat as Theodore's voice droned on.

"At the very time the world is looking to find a chink in our armor to prove that the crusade against us is valid, this deception and fraud arise, presenting them the perfect opportunity. We cannot be responsible for a bill that was incurred without our knowledge and approval, yet we cannot have it spread abroad that we do not pay our debts.

"Therefore, as much as it grieves us to do so, we find that we must expel William Langston from our midst. The good name of our Community is critical to our survival, and we must act swiftly to stamp out any blots that sully our reputation at this critical time. Rest assured, if we fail to act decisively, our enemies will use this situation against us."

The words echoed in Millie's ears. *Expel William Langston from our midst.* No mercy. No second chance. No place for him now.

Theodore let the hand holding the paper drop to his side and looked out at the crowd. Father Noyes had surveyed the audience during Theodore's reading, glaring out severely from under his bushy gray eyebrows. Now he nodded authoritatively, punctuating what Theodore had read.

Theodore continued. "Our decision is that Mr. William Langston be expelled from among us without delay—tonight."

"All in favor, say aye," croaked Father Noyes.

"All in favor?" repeated Theodore.

A chorus of "ayes" resounded throughout the room.

"Opposed?" Theodore asked.

A handful of "nays" popped up from the floor and the balcony, but Theodore said, "The ayes have it and the decision is confirmed. This Meeting is now adjourned."

Millie quickly stood and scanned the rear of the room for her father. With everyone milling about, she couldn't spot him. She felt the room sway.

"Millie? Are you all right?" Henry helped her back into her seat.

She buried her head in her hands. They were sending her father away. Immediately. Why? Surely there were other ways to handle it. Looking up at Henry, she saw Ellen at his side. She braced herself for Ellen's condemning words.

"Oh, Millie! It's outrageous! Such a harsh sentence. They didn't need to do this. What a shock for you!" Ellen's eyes brimmed with sympathy. "I'm so sorry about your mother."

This was a new Ellen. A kind Ellen. Millie stood and faced her. "Thank you. Not a complete shock, though. I had a hint. But I had no idea they'd expel him."

"My father voted *nay*, just so you know. I think most people were too surprised to vote the way they felt. They rammed this through."

"Why?" Millie asked.

Ellen spoke close to Millie's ear. "Father says it's a bone to the Outside. So they can prove their integrity—that they don't tolerate financial mischief."

"But why do it tonight and ruin our celebration?"

Henry shook his head, sharing her perplexity.

Gears were turning in Ellen's brain—almost visibly. "No doubt they waited as long as they did so you could have your moment of glory. Now we claim you as our own—apart from your father."

"Like setting the hook." Henry made an abrupt motion with an invisible rod. "We keep you on the line that way. So we don't lose you, too."

Millie was now a beloved personage in her own right. The audience had embraced her as she curtsied from the stage. Perhaps the Community leaders had shown her kindness in their own way. "I need to find my father before he goes."

"You have time." Henry rested a gentle hand on her shoulder. "He has to be checked out in the business office. Erastus Hamilton and Judge Towner will have him sign a release and then give him his separation funds."

"Release?"

"Sure," Henry said. "Anyone who separates has to sign a release declaring the Community doesn't owe him wages for the time worked here."

Ellen nodded knowingly. "But in your father's case, they've probably drawn up something more elaborate to say they won't pay the bill from the asylum."

Millie tugged on her hair and bit her lower lip, trying to make sense of it all. "Why would they make him leave tonight?"

"Less chance to stir up sympathy for him," Ellen said. "They don't want this to cause any kind of schism."

Millie held her palms upwards. "But they gave Victor two days."

Henry stroked Millie's shoulder to calm her agitation. "They're on edge because of the ministers' crusade."

Ellen pursed her lips. "That means they're more worried than they've let on."

Millie scanned the crowd again. "I need to talk to him."

Could she face him without lashing out? She didn't want to deepen his wound, but her own pain was tearing her apart. Still, she couldn't let him leave without saying goodbye.

Henry cast his eyes over the sea of people. "Come, Ellen, let's get her through this crowd."

They each took one of Millie's arms and escorted her down the center aisle toward the rear exit. They managed to move about five rows back when a group of members thronged them.

Aunt Sarah moved in first and grabbed Millie's hand. "I'm so sorry about your father. It must be so hard. But I'm so proud of your play! What a delight to see it performed! And to think I had a little hand in it. You're an asset to our Community, dear, an asset. I always knew your talents would take you far."

Barely able to interpret her words, Millie stared at her childhood mentor. The play was of no consequence compared to her father's disgrace. She nodded politely.

After that several others pushed toward her.

"Congratulations on the play, Millie!"

"A shame about your father dear, a real shame."

"Our condolences, Millie. You did well with the play."

"You must focus on all the good you're doing here. Don't let this disappointment spoil your success."

Members had never taken so much interest in her. She took two steps forward, before several more people pushed in, expressing similar sentiments. They were kind, but they couldn't know her agony. After living in obscurity for all these years, she was suddenly recognized for her talents. But it didn't bring the joy she'd imagined —it didn't touch her. She seemed to hear everyone from inside a bubble.

As she approached the rear of the Big Hall, the people nearby looked beyond her, and she heard deliberate steps behind her back. Henry and Ellen dropped her arms, and the three of them turned around at the same time. They faced Theodore and Father Noyes, walking side by side with their eyes fastened on Millie. They stopped in front of her.

She met Theodore's eyes first. Was there a glint of satisfaction that he'd caused her pain? No, only professional detachment.

Smiling, he said, "Wonderful play, Millie. Fine performance."

She nodded politely. Father Noyes took her upper arm in both hands and drew her close. He stooped so his face was very near hers. She strained to hear his voice. It was hardly more than a whisper, difficult to discern with the hubbub around her.

Their faces were so close that the prophet's gray whiskers brushed her cheek. His breath was hot and stale. "I apologize for what I had to do tonight, Millie."

She froze. The founder of the Perfectionist commune was apologizing to her. He had called her by name.

"You must not take it personally." His whiskers scratched her face as he talked, and his raspy voice sounded vaguely nefarious. "You displayed great talent with tonight's play. Our Community needs young women like you—writers to carry on our work. Now that Theodore has had a chance to get to know you, I look forward to meeting with you myself. Mrs. Skinner will let you know when."

As he loosened his grip on her arm and backed away, his eyes passed up and down her body. He bent his head close again. "You will be a mother to the Community one day, my child."

She stiffened to suppress a shudder. "Thank you, Father," she mouthed.

Prophet and son strode past.

Millie, Henry, and Ellen stared after them.

Ellen gaped. "What did he say?"

Henry's eyes were wide.

"He said—" she swallowed, repressing the urge to retch. She batted at her cheek, chasing away the itch of his whiskers. "He said he liked the play."

She allowed the shiver to pass through her, down to her very toes.

Chapter 20: Fireworks

"We'll meet you by the South Tower to watch the fireworks."

Henry brushed Millie's arm as he and Ellen left her at her father's door. She watched them walk away. Bless Ellen. She wasn't so bad. With friends like Henry and Ellen, life without her father would go on in much the same way. And under Bible Communism, she had many fathers.

She blinked back the thought. How easily the years of training surfaced in her mind, even when she knew better. Those fathers would now be her husbands. How many of them besides Father Noyes would invite her to go to bed with them over the next year? Men whom she once considered her fathers and grandfathers were now to be her lovers, repeatedly playing out an inverted and warped Oedipus tragedy.

She shook her head and shoulders. She would face that problem later.

She knocked. Hearing muffled steps within, she clenched her fists and tightened her jaw. What could she say to this man who had deceived her for thirteen years? Who had allowed her mother to waste away in an asylum? Every moment they'd spent together—from his visits in the Children's House, to their many games of dominoes, to their recent conversation in the Summer House—all were now tainted by his duplicity.

When William opened the door, he looked tired and frayed—as if he'd instantly aged several years. Yet his eyes brightened at the sight of her. "I was hoping you'd come."

Millie entered. After removing a travel bag half filled with clothing from a chair, he motioned for her to sit. At least they were letting him take his clothes. She tried to telegraph anger through her eyes, but her lower lip betrayed her with a quiver.

Rather than taking the other chair, he dropped to his knees before her and took her hands in his.

She didn't withdraw them.

Tears stood in his eyes. "Millie, I'm so sorry." He cleared his throat and brushed his hand across his eyes, then returned it to hers. "There were so many times I almost told you. But I wanted to protect you. I wanted to protect you from the pain."

Millie pushed back her sympathy and summoned her anger. "You lied to me all these years."

"Not exactly. I never lied to you."

She glowered. "How can you say that? You told me Mother died when I was four."

"I never said that. I told you we lost your mother when you were four, and that's true." His gentle voice seemed sincere. "Do you want to hear the story? The story I could never bring myself to tell you?"

Millie's stomach gnawed. She pulled her hands away and crossed her arms against her abdomen.

Remaining on his knees, William drew in a breath. "You know your mother's family perished in a fire. Your mother was kind and sensitive, like you. It haunted her that she survived and they didn't. When we married and you were born, those torments disappeared, I thought. But when you were four—we were living in Syracuse—there was a tragic house fire in our neighborhood. Our home wasn't in danger, but we could smell the smoke and hear the fire wagons. People were gathering to watch. I begged your mother not to go, but she was frantic to see how the neighbors were. It was just the wife and her young children. Her husband—he was Irish—got drafted and was too poor to buy himself out."

William brushed away tears with his calloused hands. He took out his handkerchief and blew his nose. "The woman and her children all died, and your mother—she saw them carrying out the bodies. I tried to pull her away, but she was rooted in place. She kept saying that if he—the husband—survived the war, he'd be left with nothing and no one—just as she'd been. I finally led her into our living room, and she sat by the window. She pulled you onto her lap. She wanted *you!* She loved you so much."

Millie struggled to catch her breath. A feeling of dread was rising, rising. She could feel her mother's lap, the folds of the crinoline skirt.

Again, fumbling with his handkerchief, William blew his nose. "And then, then—she froze. She was staring, and she didn't move. You were squeezing her cheeks, kissing her mouth, and she didn't

respond."

Tears streamed from Millie's eyes. She could see it all. She could feel it all. The expressionless eyes. The straight mouth. The stony silence. Her own panic, wondering where her mother was. Trying to draw out the person from the immovable body with kisses.

"They called it stupor at first, but later a specialist told me it was something called *catatonia*."

Millie shook her head in denial. She wiped the tears away angrily. "But she must have gotten over it! You let her live thirteen years in a cage!"

William drew back in confusion. "In a cage?"

Millie scowled. "I know what they do to people at Utica Asylum. They keep them in cages."

Slowly, understanding spread across her father's face. "You mean the protection beds."

Millie cocked her head.

"Those were only used for the most violent patients—never for your mother. She was always well cared for."

Relief flooded through Millie. She drew in a quavering breath. "When was the last time you saw her?"

"About five years ago."

Millie hardened her gaze.

William's eyes pleaded with hers. "Millie, you have to understand. She never got over it. When I committed her, Utica Asylum was one of the most advanced hospitals in the world. The specialist there told me her best chance for recovery was to remove all reminders of her life outside the hospital. He thought that might draw her out."

He brushed Millie's hair behind her ear tenderly. "They wouldn't allow her to see you—and I didn't think it was good for you to see her that way. You were so upset. You kept asking why your mama wasn't in her body—where she'd gone."

The panicked craving she'd felt in her dream rose in Millie's throat. Her mother was there but not there. *Why don't her eyes move? Why doesn't she kiss me back? Is she dead?* She grabbed her father's hand.

He wrapped her hand in both of his. "It almost killed me when she didn't recognize me. All she could do was repeat what someone said. She was like—an empty shell."

He began to sob, and Millie threw her arms around his neck. Her own tears flowed down his already wet face. They held each other, sobbing low moans from their very depths.

At last they dried their tears, and William sat in the chair facing Millie. "So, you see, I told you the truth. We did lose your mother when you were four."

Millie nodded reluctantly. "And that's when we came here?"

"I was beside myself." William placed his elbow on the table and rested his cheek against his fist. "I didn't know what to do. Neither your mother nor I had any family. I wandered into a church service— a Perfectionist congregation. Everyone was talking about Oneida Community. No one was being drafted here, and the year I'd bought myself was just about up. I wasn't afraid to fight, but I couldn't leave you without a parent. Here I could have you nearby while I worked, and there were many mothers for you, and children for you to play with—to take your mind off..."

He buried his head in his arm on the tabletop, sobbing.

Millie ached for the pain he'd been through. To endure all that alone. To hold that pain inside all these years, never sharing it with anyone. She watched his shoulders heaving. No wonder he'd been unable to speak of it. But she needed to know everything.

When he regained his composure and looked up, she asked, "Did you lie to Father Noyes?"

William shifted and looked away. "I honestly don't remember whether I did. I don't think I called myself a widower—but I certainly said I'd lost my wife. And I never told anyone about her."

"And you didn't tell the hospital you were here?"

He shook his head. "We were broke. If I'd applied, the State would have accepted her as indigent. By the time she went to the asylum, I'd used all our savings and sold everything we owned to pay all the doctors who saw her."

He studied the rag rug at his feet. "The people who worked at Utica were top notch—truly loved the patients. There was a nurse there—Lucy—who took pity on me. She told me—maybe it was bad advice she had no right to give—that I should move away without leaving my address. So the State would pay the bills. But she gave me her home address to correspond with her."

"But you went to visit Mother."

He dropped his eyes. "Not exactly." He gulped. "Lucy wrote that your mother never improved. She never recognized anyone. She told me it would be useless. But a couple of times I managed to leave here and go to Utica. Lucy had her in the yard, so I saw her from the drive."

He broke down again. He wiped his eyes and continued. "They led her around by the arm, and she'd walk wherever they brought her or sit wherever they told her to sit. But she never acted on her own accord."

He looked at Millie, biting his lip. "I could never have let you see her that way. It almost killed me the two times I saw her. I did deceive you, but only to protect you. Will you forgive me? Can you find it in your heart?"

Millie went to her father and wrapped her arms around his neck again. With her cheek touching his, she nodded. "Yes, I can. I forgive you."

As she pulled away, Millie saw this man in a whole new light—as a good man who'd survived a wretched ordeal. Without anyone to help him through a life-shattering horror, he'd made a courageous decision. Perhaps not a flawless one, and perhaps without realizing the long-term consequences. But he sought out a better way. What he did was for her benefit, not from selfish motives.

Her heart beat with love for him. All their times together, his patient words of advice and encouragement, meant so much more now that she knew his story. A conviction burst upon her like fireworks lighting up a dark sky. She had to support him now. She couldn't let him face another calamity by himself.

"I'm coming with you."

"To the business office?"

She grasped his hands in hers and shook them excitedly. "I'm leaving Oneida Community with you. Tonight. Forever."

William stood, raising his hands in protest. "I can't let you do that." He held her shoulders tenderly. "This isn't your doing—it's mine. You have a place here. This is your home. I saw how everyone honored you tonight, and I'm so glad. It helps me feel better about leaving." He wrapped her in a hug. "You're surrounded by people who love you and value your talents. And we can still visit. But you belong here."

She backed away. "But I don't." She'd never spoken a truer word. "That's what these last six months have shown me—how different I am from the communists. And tonight didn't change that."

William looked unconvinced. She'd have to broach a delicate subject. "I don't know if Aunt Constance told you about my interview with Dr. Noyes."

Her father remained expressionless, perhaps not wanting to give away a trust.

"Well, I refused him. And I've refused Judge Towner twice. But I can't keep refusing the men here—and I can't go live in the garret like crazy Lady Haas or in my own private cottage like Mr. Dunn."

William smiled and squeezed her hand.

"I just don't think complex marriage is for me. Maybe I've read too many romance novels."

"I thought as much. But you seem to be much taken with Henry."

A pang shot through her chest. "Not in that way. I only value his friendship."

"You still have feelings for Noah."

She dropped her eyes. Before she could form an answer, a quick knock called him away. He ushered Constance into the room.

She carried a package wrapped in brown paper and tied with string. "A little something to remember me by." She tucked it inside the open travel bag under the clothing, then looked from William's face to Millie's. "Am I interrupting?"

"Aunt Constance, I've decided to leave the Community as well."

Millie held her breath, awaiting her response.

Constance's lips parted in surprise, and she took a seat. "I didn't expect that, but now that I think of it, it seems right."

Millie exhaled slowly.

William motioned to the older woman. "What about you, Constance? The more the merrier."

They exchanged a look that suggested it wasn't a new question.

Her eyes softened, and she shook her head. "Not yet. I believe God has more for me to do here." She rose quickly and turned toward Millie. "Have you packed? Have you notified anyone you intend to leave?"

"No to both."

She was truly leaving. Tonight.

"Then we don't have much time. I'll help you. William," she said brusquely, assuming her foreman role, "when you get to the business office, tell them Millie will be right down to sign her papers and receive her settlement. It won't take us long."

As Constance and Millie rushed along the hallway and down the stairs to the second floor, Constance whispered, "This may cause a bit of extra fireworks. Don't let them sway you—if you're sure this is what you want."

"I'm sure—but what do you mean about fireworks?"

As if in response, a string of firecrackers sputtered outside where people were gathering on the south lawn for the yearly fireworks display. Startled, Millie grabbed Constance's arm—too firmly—and they both laughed.

"The central members will be sorry to lose you. They don't like it when people secede."

Secede. That's what I'm doing.

Everything had happened so quickly. "*Am* I doing the right thing?"

They entered Millie's room, and Constance retrieved the travel bag from the closet. "Only you can know that. There's still time to change your mind."

Millie shook her head. She wouldn't turn back. Hastily she removed her chemises and drawers from her bureau and pushed them into the bag. In her closet, she reached toward one of the dresses with its attached pantalettes, then laughed. "I won't be needing these anymore!"

She packed her nightdress, some stockings, a sweater, a shawl, and a cape. From her small personal bureau she removed her writing instruments and paper. She looked around the room. She gasped as her eyes landed on the wedding portrait sitting atop the bureau by a stack of books. "I nearly forgot!"

She handed it to Constance, who packed it carefully inside the sweater. Millie ran her fingers along the spines of the books and across the marbled cover of *Northanger Abbey,* the pinnacle of the little pyramid. Unfortunately, they belonged to the library.

She latched the travel bag, and after one more look around, followed Constance out the door. As they came to the stairway, she stopped abruptly and set the bag down. "Wait! I'll be right back!"

She ran to her room and reached her hand inside her pillowcase. Feeling around to the far corner, she found the silk grosgrain ribbon with its cameo. She slipped it into her right pocket and ran back to Constance.

As they passed through the vestibule, Millie fondly scanned the museum display case. She might never see the mastodon tooth or the relics from Pompeii again. At the bottom of the wide stairway, they proceeded to the end of the hall. The door of the business office was open, and men's voices echoed within.

Constance motioned with her head for Millie to enter the room. "I'll wait here and walk you out."

In the office where she'd once brought a suicidal Henry an emergency muffin, the austere forms of Judge Towner, Dr. Noyes, and Erastus Hamilton stood around a desk facing her father. The men looked up as she walked in.

Dr. Noyes addressed her first. "Your father tells us you want to leave the Community with him." His voice sounded skeptical.

Judge Towner glared at her from his right eye. "It is our duty to confirm that you are under no duress in having made this decision." He spoke precisely, as if launching an interrogation. "Are you acting of your own free will, under no coercion from your father?"

"Yes, I am." Millie's voice sounded frail in contrast to the gruff voices of the men. She found a friendlier face in Erastus Hamilton and kept her eyes on him. "I want to leave."

"We all wish you would reconsider." The elderly man's tone was kind. "It grieves us to lose a young person as talented as yourself. Especially when you've just come into your own here."

Constance was right. They were trying to talk her out of it, each in his own way. She squared her shoulders. "All the same, I would like to leave." The men stared at her mutely, as if by coordinated effort they could mesmerize her will. She looked at each one in turn. "Is there something I need to sign?"

Judge Towner grudgingly produced a sheet of paper. "Read it thoroughly, and then sign at the bottom."

It was short and to the point, stating that she hereby dissolved all association with the commune and gave up all rights to any past and future earnings due her based upon the work she had performed while

living there.

As she raised the pen, Theodore spoke. "If you'd like to leave open the possibility of returning, you have the option of taking only half the settlement now. In that case, you'd be welcomed back to full membership if you bring such a petition within two years of leaving."

Judge Towner, perhaps realizing he'd omitted that detail, glanced at Theodore with irritation, but Erastus Hamilton nodded his head.

There was no temptation in Theodore's offer. Now that she'd decided, she couldn't wait to shake the dust of Oneida Community off her feet. She would never return. "I'll take the full amount, please."

Theodore produced two envelopes, one for Millie and one for William, and Judge Towner counted their settlement funds into them.

"The carriage is waiting." Theodore motioned stiffly toward the door. "It will take you into town. You'll find several hotels on the main street."

"Thank you." William seemed to be expecting some kind word regarding the thirteen years he'd invested in the Community, but none came. He turned away.

Erastus Hamilton shifted awkwardly. "You are, of course, welcome to return for visits at any time. You have many friends here."

Millie could see her father's face, though the men on the other side of the desk could not. His jaw slackened as he blinked hard several times.

Bless you, Erastus Hamilton.

Following her father, Millie passed through the door into the hall. With her back to the main entrance, she looked toward the Children's House where she'd spent first her childhood and then much of her youth, teaching the little ones. Her gaze lingered over the entrance to the library, a room that had, perhaps more than any other, formed her into the woman she was now. She wanted to say goodbye to so many places—the Chain Room, the garret, her old room in Ultima Thule, Hamilton Avenue, the Nursery Kitchen, and the Tontine. She wanted to put her arms around the dear old tulip tree and hug it. She wanted to run her fingers through the boxes of sorts at the newspaper office. She wanted to sit with Mrs. Bloom one more time at her friendly kitchen table. But there was no time for any of that. The carriage was waiting.

Constance pulled her close and hugged her. "We'll see each other again—and often." She pressed a note into Millie's hand. "I promise."

Millie stashed the note into her left pocket and, after wiping her eyes, picked up her bag and followed her father out the door. Descending the front steps, she met Henry and Ellen. They took in her face and the travel bag.

Ellen's jaw dropped. "Millie! Don't go!"

Henry looked like an abandoned puppy. "You're—you're coming back to us, aren't you?"

Millie couldn't speak. Her lips quivered, and hot tears strayed down both cheeks. She shook her head.

"This isn't right!" Ellen stomped her foot. "Let me get my father. He'll tell Theodore what's what!"

Millie grabbed her hand. "I think it's for the best." She looked from Ellen to Henry and back, implying he'd be Ellen's now, and she calmed down.

Henry shook his head mournfully and placed his hand over his heart. "The Aquarium is losing its prettiest fish." He bent his head close to hers and ran his hand down the back of her arm. Exuding a faint scent of spearmint, he whispered in her ear, "Goodbye, Millie. I'll miss you. Good luck, old pal."

As she approached the carriage, Millie heard voices four stories above and behind her where people had gathered on the roof of the North Tower to watch the fireworks. Tirzah's laugh tinkled brightly into the starry night.

Holding the reins at the front of the carriage sat the ever-agreeable Birdie. He hopped down and opened the door for them as elegantly as any footman. William entered first, then extended his hand to help Millie inside.

As the carriage rolled down the driveway, the first stunning flower of fireworks lit up the sky to the south. Birdie turned the carriage to the left, and the happy festivities receded.

William blew his nose on his handkerchief and wiped his eyes. "I don't even know where I'm going."

Glad that she couldn't see his face in the dark, Millie patted his arm. "I do."

When they entered the town of Oneida, Birdie pulled the carriage over and got down to speak with them, shining a lantern toward their faces.

Millie leaned forward. "Do you know where First Presbyterian Church is?"

"I know where pretty much everything is in town." He tucked in his chin. "Is *that* where you want me to take you?"

She raised her shoulders. "Do you know if it has a parsonage next door?"

"The Underground Railroad Station house." Birdie nodded. "Used to hear stories about that place." Laughing, he wagged his index finger. "But I think those days are over—and you aren't slaves!"

William and Millie chuckled, dispelling some tension.

"Please take us there," William said.

When they arrived at the house behind the imposing brick church, Birdie jumped down, holding the lantern, and offered Millie his other hand.

Once on the ground, she touched his arm. "Will you say good-bye to Mrs. Bloom for me?"

Birdie blinked hard a few times, swallowed, and nodded.

Soon they were standing before the door of the parsonage. William raised the knocker and clanked it down with three solid knocks. Despite the warm air, Millie shivered. Footsteps came running toward the door.

It swung open, and Andrew stared at them. "Oh! It's Millie!" He turned and yelled back into the house. "Mother, come quick!"

After hearing their preliminary explanations in the hallway, Mrs. Martinson showed them into the parlor. Soon the reverend, Sadie, and Noah joined them.

Mrs. Martinson served tea while William explained the situation, including the story of Millie's mother's illness and death. Millie squirmed as her father shared the personal details, but their story didn't make sense otherwise. Noah sat in a chair opposite Millie and kept watching her during the long tale. She fixed her eyes elsewhere, taking in either the handsome décor of the room or Sadie's ever-changing expressions.

Pursing his lips, Reverend Martinson pressed his fingers together in front of his chest. "I'm afraid I've played a role in the turning of your fortunes."

"Not at all." William shook his head. "It was just a coincidence that this all came up at the same time as your crusade."

"Or we might call it—Providence."

Reverend Martinson spoke directly to William, then turned to smile warmly, eyes twinkling, at Millie.

She returned the smile weakly. Was she missing some secret meaning?

"At any rate, I'll help you in any way I can," the minister continued, addressing her father. "I didn't intend for our Ministers' Crusade to bring hardship to any individual at the commune."

How odd to see her father sipping tea and discussing employment and housing possibilities with Reverend Martinson—who had so recently been vilified by her closest friends and companions. She'd been wrong to suspect that he'd used her to help him gather information on the Community. She sensed only kindness from him now. He owed them nothing, but he was offering to introduce her father to people around town.

Leaning toward his mother, Noah whispered something Millie couldn't hear. Mrs. Martinson nodded, and Noah approached Millie, holding out his hand.

"Would you like to see the trap door that leads to the secret chamber?"

Millie grinned. Of course she would. Placing her hand in his, she stood to her feet.

Sadie jumped up. "Can I show her, Mother?"

"No, dear," Mrs. Martinson said calmly, "but you may refill the teapot."

Noah led Millie into a room which, though not as beautifully appointed as the parlor, was still charming. At one end a large gilded mirror hung above a squat fireplace. Noah lifted the rag rug in front of the hearth, revealing a square outline.

"Here's the trap door." He opened it to reveal a dark, cramped space. "The freedom seekers hid down there." He closed the door and replaced the rug. "And this was where Father sawed the manacle off the runaway slave's ankle."

He faced Millie, his features softening. "I'm so happy to see you again. I've missed you."

Millie tingled with pleasure. "I hope it wasn't too forward of us to come, but I remembered how your parents take in vagabonds. I guess that's what we are now."

"I'm so sorry they treated you that way."

"You know, I'm not."

Noah raised his eyebrows.

"It's been quite unpleasant at the Mansion House since I returned."

She stared at her feet, biting her lower lip. How could she speak to him about her dilemma there? Though she had no right to believe it could make a difference, she wanted him to know the truth. "The things your father said about the Community—the things in the newspaper—everything he said is true."

Noah nodded solemnly.

She lifted her eyes to meet his, looking out from under her lashes. "Except for me. You may find this hard to believe—and I do myself— but I wasn't a Community wife yet. But I was supposed to be. And while I was trying to figure out how to avoid it, this happened."

Noah looked at her as if he didn't grasp her meaning. She felt her face burning. Perhaps he thought she was making it up.

"You weren't—"

His expression changed as her words sank in.

She lifted her shoulders. "I can't quite explain how it happened— or didn't happen."

Noah studied her face. Then he grinned. "It's as if you were in a bubble."

Millie tilted her head. "Bubble?"

Noah laughed. "Yes, a bubble. Remember what I told you about Mother's prayers?"

Millie knitted her eyebrows. She remembered every conversation she'd ever had with Noah—even some imaginary ones—but what did bubbles have to do with her?

He touched her arm. "Maybe you're the girl she's been praying for all these years."

That girl. Noah's future wife. Millie grew warm and cozy all over. She studied the rug at her feet. How had she come to be standing here, on the very place where others, escaping slavery, had obtained their freedom? Providence, Reverend Martinson had said. Perhaps the Spirit of Truth had been guiding her after all.

Tears stung her eyes. Her mother, in her insanity, may have

forgotten her daughter, but God had not forgotten His. This is what it felt like to belong, to be part of something—no Someone—bigger than herself.

A flood of emotions kept her from raising her eyes to Noah's. Could he ever consider marrying a Community girl? Fingering the left pocket of her skirt, she felt Constance's note inside. She drew out the folded slip of paper.

Noah eyed it curiously. "What's that?"

"A note Aunt Constance gave me when I left." After unfolding the paper, she read it silently. *Happy are the hands that throw off the silken strands.* She chuckled and gave the paper to Noah, who read it and looked perplexed.

"It's a long story." She smiled. "But it's a pun, don't you see? In the factory, they throw the silk, and I once created a little rhyme that said, *Happy are the hands that throw the silken strands.* But Aunt Constance says *my* hands are happy because I've thrown *off* the bonds of the Community."

Noah nodded slowly. "Silken strands. They make it hard for you to leave—because life is so pleasant there."

"In some ways, yes." As pleasant as a dream and as horrid as a nightmare, all at the same time. And now it was part of her past. She put the note into her right pocket and felt the choker necklace. She pulled it out and held it up. "Remember this?"

Noah nodded, eyes wide. "Of course!"

"Now I can wear it anytime I want to." She held the crimson grosgrain ribbon in both hands and rubbed her thumbs across the grain, taking in the calm, confident profile of the cameo.

"May I?"

Millie placed the necklace in Noah's hand. Gently touching her shoulders, he centered her before the mirror over the fireplace, turning her so she could see her reflection.

He stood behind her and drew the ribbon from the left side of her neck around to the right, letting his fingers brush across her throat.

She must be in heaven. She had re-lived the experience in her imagination a hundred times, knowing she'd never feel his warm fingers against her neck again. He clasped the necklace at the back of her neck and then let his fingers glide along her skin. As she shivered with delight, smiling into the mirror, her eyes locked with those of the

man behind her.

He rested his hand on her shoulder. "There. Perfect." He grinned back at her reflection. "You look lovely."

She agreed. But more importantly—life was lovely. No more chains, no more traps, no more hooks. From now on, only freely accepted bonds would link her to the people and ideas she cared about. As she stared at their reflection, the wall behind them became a black sky bursting with glorious fireworks in celebration of her personal independence day.

The End

Author Notes

In this novel, I've attempted to faithfully recreate the historic Oneida Community in the first half of 1877. However, I've used some writer's license, converging the timelines of some historical people. I've peppered the narratives with many historical names without attempting to accurately reflect their true personalities, especially with minor characters. Where certain facts are disputed or controversial, I've chosen a stance, realizing some historians would disagree. I've correlated scores of details from diaries and memoirs while weaving this fictional narrative. In addition to providing historical background for those who are interested, the entries below clarify which people, events, and details are documented and which are imagined or adjusted.

Abbreviations:

O.C. = Oneida Community

JHN = John Humphrey Noyes

Arnotte, Constance **Spoiler Alert	Mostly fictional. The faith cure Constance experiences was reported in the *Circular* dated Feb. 9, 1874, as having been experienced by "Mrs. M." who was living at Wallingford. By 1877, spinners rather than wringers were used at O.C. and hirelings worked in the laundry. The rest of Constance's experiences are fictional, although the fruit preserving business really was supervised by a woman, as was the travel bag industry. It seems likely that some members practiced "Shakerism" (celibacy) at O.C., although it was strongly discouraged. For the likelihood of a woman being banished to the far reaches for failing to participate in the social system, see "Ultima Thule."
Ascending	The principle of seeking out more spiritually

fellowship	mature Community members for companionship and sexual relations. This idea discouraged cliques of young people and "best friends." The paradox that two people cannot both be practicing ascending fellowship with each other was evidently ignored.
Bible classes	Started November 1876 after George Miller came from Wallingford to lecture on the Bible. They led to a "revival spirit" that resulted in some O.C. members criticizing Wallingford members for being too "worldly." The classes stopped in April 1877 because they conflicted with JHN's role as prophet.
Birth control	JHN "invented," practiced, and promulgated a form of birth control known as male continence. I won't go into detail here. It was generally effective; only 1- 2 accidental pregnancies per year occurred among 250 – 300 members during the years it was practiced. Young men were initiated into complex marriage at puberty by post-menopausal women and were paired only with them until they mastered the birth control technique and were considered *teleoi* (see).
Bloom, Mrs. **Spoiler Alert	Completely fictional. At least five stillbirths occurred at O.C. The historical woman who ran The Villa made it a pleasant, homey environment, but her name was not Mrs. Bloom.
Campbell, Theodora (Dora)	Historical. 1861 – 1904. As a Community child, she was known for her "good behavior." After the breakup, she went to New York City for missionary training with the Christian Alliance. She returned to Kenwood, the village near the Mansion House, and started a Sunday School that eventually became the Alliance church. She became a missionary to China, where she died during the Boxer Rebellion.

Chain Room	Children spent an hour a day linking chains for the Newhouse animal traps that supported the commune for decades.
Charles, Mrs.	Historical. In 1875 the meal preparation at O.C. was hired out to eight black outsiders with Mrs. Charles in charge.
Circular	The weekly newspaper of Oneida Community that contained articles by JHN and newsy items about communal life. It was recast as the *American Socialist* before 1877. Tirzah was editor for a time, but not during 1877. It was printed at Wallingford for several years and then moved to Oneida, where the print shop was located in the Tontine. I've placed the office of the *Circular* in the Post Office across the road just to add variety in setting. The two blurbs Millie writes are actual snippets from the *Circular* from before 1875.
Communism	The practice of living in a communal environment. In nineteenth-century America, thousands of communes—most tiny and short-lived—sprang up around the country. A person who believed that such cooperative societies represented the new cultural ideal was called a *communist* (not capitalized). After the Russian Revolution of 1917, *Communism* and *Communist* (capitalized) acquired new meanings.
Complex marriage	The sexual system practiced at O.C. in which every adult male was married to every adult female. Distinguished from free love in that it was controlled by male continence (see "birth control"), ascending fellowship (see), and committees. Young women were initiated into marriage at puberty, primarily by JHN. For a seventeen-year-old to have remained a virgin is highly unlikely; it is a "miracle" in this book and would have been miraculous if it had actually

occurred. Some unconfirmed reports suggest some girls were initiated even before menarche, at 9 or 10 years old. In the late 1870s the younger generation revolted against complex marriage; many youth failed to fall under JHN's spell, and the desire for monogamy was widespread.

Cragin, Dr. George	Historical. 1840 – 1915. Mary Cragin's son. Educated at Yale Medical School. His words spoken to Constance are taken from the *Circular*, Feb. 9, 1874. He was at O.C. when the patient with the injured hand came to him from Wallingford.
Cragin, Mary	Historical. 1810 – 1851. Highly revered founder of the Perfectionist commune with JHN and his siblings. JHN had an idolatrous love relationship with her and began complex marriage, it seems, to satisfy that desire. She died in a boating accident in 1851 but was held up as almost a saint by JHN and others. The story of Mary Cragin overseeing the murder of the "doll spirit" is historical. When the Community cemetery was moved to allow the railroad to be built on that land, her body was exhumed and the skull was taken for phrenological study. No one seems to know what became of it. The bust is fictional.
Desk, John Humphrey Noyes's **Spoiler Alert	Both accounts of what JHN kept in his desk—jewelry and tops—are supported. The psychoanalysis writes itself.
Dunn, Mr.	Historical. A cottage was constructed for him because he couldn't tolerate the noise inside the Mansion House. Whether he was "cranky" or looked like a snapping turtle is unconfirmed.
Guinea fowl	Raise their young communally. The female call sounds like "good luck" or "come back." Whether they were raised at The Villa is unconfirmed.

Haas, Lady	The name is fictional, but the story as Millie relates it is one of the legends of the Mansion House.
Hall, Mrs.	Historical. Her story of being healed from consumption overnight by JHN and Mary Cragin was recorded in a "Free-Church Tract" dated "Oneida Reserve, 1850."
Hawley, Victor **Spoiler Alert	Historical, b. ca 1846. His passionate devotion for Mary Jones is documented in his diary. In January and February 1877 he spent a lot of time with Mary, with whom he had wanted to have a baby. She got "started" by Theodore Noyes at Wallingford and came back to O.C. in November 1876. In April 1877 the Community separated them for exclusive love; in late May they were allowed to associate with each other again. Mary had a stillbirth June 22, 1877, and two days later asked for permission to try again. On July 30 he was removed from his dental assistant job and given no other work because of the brandy incident. On August 2 he left O.C. while Mary was away on a trip with his sister. Mary seceded in October. They married and had five children together. Their first children born after leaving O.C. were twins, born Feb. 21, 1879.
Hinds, Virginia **Spoiler Alert	Historical. Was introduced to complex marriage at the age of twelve on Dec. 19, 1876, by Theodore Noyes, according to Tirzah Miller's diary. Virginia's reaction isn't recorded, but Tirzah thought Theodore had behaved "very wisely and discreetly," whatever that means.
Hinds, William **Spoiler Alert	Historical. Father of Virginia; attempted to change the way young girls were introduced to marriage after what happened to his daughter. Whether it was to protect the girls or to gain more access to them for himself and men his age is unclear.
Hunter, Henry	Historical. 1859 - ? Joined O.C. at the age of 14.

His affair with Tirzah Miller is documented in her diary as having taken place in February and March 1877. The massage, the garret incident, and the criticisms and punishments he received are from the diary, although the criticism wasn't in front of the whole Community. I've given Henry dark hair like Edward Inslee; in reality, he had brown hair, but he did remind Tirzah of Edward, especially in his passion. At the breakup of the Community, he left the area.

Jessie Hayes Ross	Completely fictional, as is George Ross.
Jones, Mary	Historical. See "Hawley, Victor."
Langston, Millie	Completely fictional.
Langston, William	Completely fictional.
Mansion House	The first brick Mansion House was constructed in 1862. In 1870 an L-shaped "Children's House" wing was added to the south. The "New House" wing was constructed in 1878 but was not completed until after the breakup. Later, during the company years, it was finished and used as apartments. Eventually another addition was built joining the Tontine to the New House, completing the four sides of the rectangle. Today the house contains a public museum, bed and breakfast, and private apartments as well as meeting rooms that can be rented for events. I had the pleasure of staying there in May 2016 and was able to view many of the places described in the book.
Martinson, Matilda	Completely fictional, but inspired by Matilda Joslyn Gage, a minister's wife who operated an Underground Railroad Station in nearby Fayetteville, NY. The story of the runaway slave

	bowing to and blessing Mrs. Martinson is based on a story told by Matilda Gage's son about his mother.
Martinson, Noah	Completely fictional, as are his siblings.
Martinson, Reverend James	Completely fictional, but inspired by Reverend John Mears of Hamilton College who spent years trying to galvanize public opinion against O.C. and to get legislation passed against their practices. In 1879 his crusade succeeded in forcing JHN into exile to Canada for the remainder of his life—and in achieving the ensuing discontinuation of complex marriage (see "Noyes, John Humphrey").
Miller, Tirzah **Spoiler Alert	Historical. 1843 – 1902. Niece of JHN. Her first child was fathered by her other uncle, George, without approval from the other central members. Her second child was with Edward Inslee as part of the stirpiculture experiment. Tirzah's interactions with Henry and JHN are from her diary, as are the descriptions of her relationship with Edward Inslee and her pairing for stirpiculture with Homer Barron and James Herrick. She arranged the interview between Virginia Hinds and Theodore Noyes and congratulated him when he had done it. She was an excellent musician; JHN asked her to give up her music for writing in May 1877. She married James Herrick in 1879 and remained loyal to JHN until his death in 1886, living with him for a time in Canada after his exile. She was editress of the *Circular* prior to 1877. Interactions with Millie, of course, are fictional.
Mourning doves	Mate for life. Tirzah's dream about mourning doves and Edward Inslee is recorded in her diary.
Mutual criticism	JHN began this form of spiritual improvement while he was still in college; at O.C. it was used to keep members in line. Most criticisms were

conducted by committee; some were requested by members and some were meted out as discipline. The historical criticisms I have presented as Community-wide criticisms (Henry Hunter, Victor Hawley) were actually done in small committees. However, Tirzah did present herself for Community-wide criticism related to Edward Inslee.

Noyes, John Humphrey

Historical. 1811 – 1886. Founder and prophet of the Oneida Perfectionists. Anyone who joined O.C. had to pledge allegiance to him and his religious principles. Although he liked sharing his power with the multiple committees that administered life at the commune, when necessary he would pull the "prophet card" to get his way. As he aged, he became more deaf, suffered from a throat ailment that diminished his voice, and became less sexually appealing. Consequently, his hold on O.C. began to slip in the late 1870s. His insistence on passing the reins to his son, Theodore, despite Theodore's secular and agnostic/atheistic approach made many members question his leadership. He fathered 13 children at O.C., all with different women. His principles of selective propagation revolved around "breeding in and in," which meant, to him, getting the highest concentration of Noyes blood possible in the offspring. That's why he suggested having a child with Tirzah, his niece. That never happened, but he did father a child with Tirzah's sister, Helen. Although he stopped short of openly advocating parent/offspring or sibling incest within O.C., his writings show he believed such incest taboos should be struck down. In the summer of 1879 he was warned of impending prosecution for statutory rape, so he slipped out of the Mansion House in his stocking feet in the middle of the night and fled to Canada, from whence he never returned. Whether

286 Rebecca May Hope

	the threat of prosecution was real is disputed; both internal discontent and outside pressure led to JHN's departure. O.C. voted a year later to become a joint stock company, Oneida Community Ltd., which would become famous for manufacturing silverware. Many of the words that pass between Tirzah and JHN in the novel are from her diary.
Noyes, Theodore	Historical, b. 1841. First surviving son of JHN. Educated at Yale Medical School in 1857. Became an agnostic there. Left and returned to O.C. at least twice, once after a stay at Dansville Sanitarium. Investigated spiritualism (see "Seances"). Instituted health practices at O.C. such as diet and the Turkish bath; for constructing the new wing, he found architects who followed state-of-the-art ventilation design. Although he acknowledged the cohesion and control of the Community depended on complex marriage and the initiation of young women into it as early as possible, he didn't relish that role for himself. He had a special love relationship with Ann Hobart, a woman who caused dissension because of her desire for control. He foresaw the breakup of the Community years before it happened and determined to be an advocate for the women and children, who would potentially suffer the most from it. After the breakup, he helped manage the Oneida company. He did not marry Ann Hobart; she seceded prior to the breakup and married the father of her child, who had previously seceded.
Nursery Kitchen	This popular gathering place was a hub not just socially but also architecturally since it was the only way from the east end of the Children's House to the west end. The interaction described between Tirzah, Henry, Haydn, and Judge Towner is recorded in Tirzah's diary. In addition to being a favorite place for "hanging out," its pantry housed

	O.C.'s medicines.
Oneida Community	A commune founded by John Humphrey Noyes in Oneida, New York, in 1841 based on the principles of "Bible Communism." It was ostensibly Christian, but in the sense of Perfectionism as understood by JHN. Members held all things in common, including spouses and children, and submitted to JHN as God's representative on earth. Although it was one of the longest-running and perhaps the most successful American utopian experiment, in the late 1870s it began to crumble from within as the younger generation, who didn't have their parents' zeal, began to chafe under the restrictions of complex marriage and mutual criticism. In 1879, things became so contentious that it seemed a full-on war could break out within the commune at any time. On January 1, 1880, by vote of the members, it disbanded as a commune and became a joint stock company. This novel takes place at the height of the Community's success but as rumblings of discontent are increasing.
Philopro-genitiveness	Excessive love for one's offspring. This was selfishness, just like exclusive love between a man and a woman, and led to criticisms and separations.
Sarah Johnson, Aunt	Historical. A teacher of the older children.
Schenk, Peter	Completely fictional. However, his case duplicates the case ten years earlier of Victor Cragin, JHN's second surviving son. The language in Peter's letter reflects what JHN told Victor he must say in order to be released from Utica Asylum.
Séances	JHN originally ridiculed spiritualism, but in order to help his agnostic son, Theodore, regain his belief in the unseen world, JHN authorized him to study spiritualism during 1874 - 1876. Theodore

identified a handful of women at O.C. who were the best "mediums"; the most talented was found to be Ann Hobart. When Theodore traveled the country attending séances, he found many to be hokum, but he saw enough unexplainable phenomena to convince him of the existence of the spirit world. Thereafter he acknowledged spirits, although he never embraced orthodox Christianity. Theodore held séances in the north end of the garret, although a few were held in the Big Hall for the entire Community to observe. Later, in the last two years of the Community, JHN is said to have conducted daily séances in his suite. After JHN's death, some of the managers of Oneida Community Ltd. tried to discern their former leader's wishes for the company by holding séances.

Silk Manufacture

I've reflected the state of silk manufacture at O.C. and Wallingford in 1877 according to my understanding. It's difficult to determine exactly what operations were performed where during any given window of time. Although sources say silk manufacturing was moved from Wallingford to O.C. in 1875, a picture of the hirelings in front of the Wallingford factory constructed in November 1876 shows many women and girls—who, presumably, could only have been hired for the silk works. Since things were moved back and forth a lot, the silk works may have started up again at Wallingford after having been moved in 1875. Therefore, I write about the "throwing" of silk as occurring at Wallingford while the Oneida factory at Willow Place also did throwing, with the dyeing and finishing processes taking place at the main complex of O.C. in the Tontine. The hand skeining described continued well beyond the breakup of O.C.; elderly women working in their rooms in the

	Mansion House performed the task for the joint stock company.
Skinner, Harriet	Historical. JHN's sister. A central member who was in charge of the kitchen for many years and oversaw social interactions, acting as a mediator for interviews. I imagined her as an intimidating woman because of her photograph.
Stirpiculture, stirpiculs	The word JHN coined for eugenics. O.C. started pairing women and men for childbearing for the Community in 1869, and the experiment continued 10 years, producing about 50 children, known as "stirpiculs." An unintended consequence of stirpiculture was an increase in exclusive love relationships, perhaps in part because the strictures of complex marriage had been removed. Which parent the children would go with after the breakup was an especially difficult and traumatic decision.
Stoner, Ellen	Completely fictional. However, she was inspired by the girl Jessie Baker Kinsley's memoir mentions as a younger girl who "only hovered on the edge" of Jessie's "class" of girls.
Teleoi	The term used to describe a young man who had mastered the required birth control method and was free to pursue relationships with women of his own age and choice. From the Greek word meaning *mature*.
Tontine	Originally a free-standing three-story building to the west of the Mansion House that housed the communal kitchen and dining hall. O.C. loved creating names for things, and this is a good example. After the breakup, the new wing was joined to the Tontine by an addition, making the entire complex a rectangle.
Towner, Judge	Historical. He lost an eye at Pea Ridge fighting as a captain in the Union Army. He was a member of

the free love commune at Berlin Heights, OH, and petitioned JHN for five years to join O.C. He was a lawyer and a judge. In 1879 he led the Townerites group, a faction that opposed the leadership of JHN. He performed father duties for Tirzah's son, Haydn/Paul. After the breakup of O.C., he went west and became the first superior court judge of Orange County, CA.

Ultima Thule — "The far reaches." The nickname O.C. gave to the sleeping rooms on the third floor of the Children's House beyond the two-story mansard section. The practice of banishing members there, especially for "Shakerism," is documented, but some dispute it. In general, O.C. changed members' living arrangements frequently at the central members' discretion.

Villa, The — The home where about 30 Community members who worked at the Willow Place factories lived, set on a 100-acre farm located about a mile and a half northeast of the Mansion House and one-quarter mile east of the factories. It was part of O.C. I decided to put meat on the menu there, but their menu was probably similar to the Tontine's. The house, now converted to a duplex, still stands.

Wallingford Community — A branch of Oneida Community located in Connecticut. Constant comings and goings occurred between the two branches. Wallingford was frequently used to separate people who had become too close to a friend, child, or lover. Edward Inslee was sent there to separate him from Tirzah, and after he seceded, she was sent there to help her get over him, leaving her infant son, Haydn, in the care of Judge Towner. Wallingford was plagued by malaria; several deaths from malaria and cholera are recorded. In the summer of 1877, Theodore Noyes decided to bring almost everyone from Wallingford back to O.C. to improve unity. About 40 came to Oneida, leaving a small number at Wallingford. Wallingford started manufacturing spoons in 1879, and that eventually morphed into the silverware manufacturing operation that Oneida is most famous for. The operation was moved to Niagara Falls, Canada, and then to Sherrill, NY. Today none of the Wallingford Community buildings remain.

Willow Place	The name given the factories (animal traps manufacture and silk works) and the associated buildings located about a mile and a half north of the Mansion House, now the city of Sherrill, NY. Besides the factory, Willow Place included a foundry, two boarding houses for women who worked in the silk factory, multiple small rental cottages for male hirelings, and The Villa (residence and 100-acre farm—see "Villa, The"). Its power source was a waterworks on Sconondoa Creek. The Mansion House and Willow Place kept in constant contact; in 1877 Willow Place even had a telegraph connection to the Mansion House. The factory complex still stands and is being used by Sherrill Manufacturing to produce flatware—currently the only domestic flatware manufacturer in the U.S. The boarding house buildings also remain; one is the current American Legion.

About the Author

Rebecca May Hope delights in reading and writing the well-crafted phrase. While wordsmithing is its own reward, her weekly writers' group provides the impetus to keep writing and polishing—so she has something to share with her fellow authors. Rebecca couldn't imagine a life without teaching. Her middle school, high school, and college classes give her a chance to share her passion for words with a new crop of young people each year. When she feels the need to follow Wordsworth's advice ("Up, up, my friend, and quit your books!"), you'll find her playing with or rocking her grandbabies; walking her rambunctious ninety-pound Labradoodle on the nature trails near her home in Champlin, Minnesota; or pampering her softer-than-air Ragdoll cat.

Learn more about Rebecca and her writing at
www.RebeccaMayHope.com.

Coming Soon from Gabriel's Horn Press

Shattered Faith

by Rebecca May Hope

Faith, a successful author of suspense thrillers, has a personal mystery to solve. Isme, her ten-year-old daughter, is seeing things. Weird things that come true in bizarre ways. On her quest to find out what could be going on with Isme, several friends hint that her husband, Lance, needs watching. She ignores their suggestions until a second vision from Isme—a black cat on her parents' bed—directs Faith to physical evidence that Lance is having an affair.

Faith springs into action, putting her fictional sleuthing skills to work in real life. She has a weekend to gather clues before Lance returns from his annual convention. Surprises keep popping up, including the revelation that her grief over her stillborn son has been poisoning both her marriage and her relationship with God. Can she trust the God who broke her heart to fashion something good from the horror every married woman dreads?

Look for more at www.gabrielshornpress.com. Learn about new releases and new authors. Join our mailing list there.

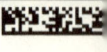

www.ingramcontent.com/pod-product-compliance
Lightning Source LLC
Chambersburg PA
CBHW031102260626
47172CB00001B/178